LAST SUMMER IN ARCADIA

LAST SUMMER IN ARCADIA

Deirdre Purcell

headline

First published in 2003
by HEADLINE BOOK PUBLISHING

Excerpt from the play *Da* by Hugh Leonard is reproduced by
kind permission of the author. Copyright 1973 by Hugh Leonard.
First presented in the summer of 1973 in Olney, Maryland, and
in the Olympia Theatre, Dublin, in October 1973.

10 9 8 7 6 5 4 3 2 1

Cataloguing in Publication Data
is available from the British Library.

ISBN 0 7472 6859 2 (hardback)
ISBN 0 7553 0149 8 (trade paperback)

Typeset in Bembo by
Letterpart Limited, Reigate, Surrey

Printed and bound in Great Britain by
Mackays of Chatham Ltd, Chatham, Kent

HEADLINE BOOK PUBLISHING
A division of Hodder Headline
338 Euston Road
LONDON NW1 3BH

www.headline.co.uk
www.hodderheadline.com

For Declan, my brother

ACKNOWLEDGEMENTS

Sincere thanks to playwright Hugh Leonard, who kindly and without hesitation agreed to allow me to quote a great line from *Da*.

Thank you to Laly Calderon, who, with alacrity and zeal, double-checked facts from an eclectic list.

Thanks to Bernard and Gloria Farrell for helping find the title.

Thank you to the bemused citizens who found themselves unexpectedly at the end of a telephone call from myself: Cormac Callanan of Aconite Internet Solutions, who put me straight on so many mysteries of the Internet and associated topics; Phil Hines of St Laurence O'Toole's parish; Caroline Preston; Frank and Marie Kennedy.

Huge gratitude to my agent, Clare Alexander of Gillon Aitken Associates, my indefatigable editor at Headline, Marion Donaldson, her sunny assistant, Sherise Hobbs, and my bosses there, Martin Neild and Kerr MacRae. Also to Edwin Higel and Joe Hoban of New Island.

Heartfelt thanks to Patricia Scanlan, great pal and the rock to which so many of us cling.

What would I do without the loyalty and generosity of friends who, during all these years, have supported me through a multitude of alarums and excursions? So thanks again to Patricia and Frank Byrne, Carol Cronin, Pat Brennan, Eithne Healy, Karen Erwin, Emer O'Kelly, Audrey Conlon, Suzannah Allen, Mona McGarry, Catherine Hogan, Marian Finucane, Jacqueline Duffy, Bríd Dukes, sister (in-law) Mary and cousin Barbara. And of course to Declan, to whom this book is dedicated.

Thanks, in the end and with deep love, to Adrian and Simon, two great sons, and to Kevin, a great husband. It is all for them.

CHAPTER ONE

Last night I dreamt that everything was as it had been in Arkady. The curtain had not gone up on the theatre of the past two months, and life was routine, even dull. The dream held one gleaming detail: I was happy.

In it, I was preparing a large lasagne, Tom and Jack were playing a complicated two-handed computer game on Jack's laptop, and Jerry's key was turning in the lock of the front door as he rejoined us from work. This dream, therefore, was set on a Friday, because on every other weekday, and on some weekends, my husband was not able to get home for dinner, or supper as we call it now. To give him his due he normally tried to hold Fridays sacrosanct, unless he was abroad.

I slipped the lasagne into the oven and turned to greet him. But his hair was long and ringleted, and he had grown a beard and whiskers. He was the Beast from *Beauty and the Beast*.

I woke up, pulse hammering in my throat, but could hear no echo of a scream in the bedroom, or even in my head: my screaming, too, must have been part of the dream.

I also knew instantly that the monster reference had come from seeing the stage show earlier this year at the Point. This was irrelevant because as my pulse slowed, reality, like a veil thick with soot, floated slowly downwards from the corona over our bed to cover me with dread. I looked at the bedside clock: it was just after half past five. Jerry's side of the bed was vacant – and cold.

What I did hear, seeping through the house, was the unmistakable blare of horns and trumpets from the family room downstairs. He always listens to *The Ring* when he is distressed and I could picture him, hunched miserably in his leather 'listening' chair, pulling on a cigarette. He gave up smoking almost six years ago but, because of what has happened, has reverted to consuming twenty, maybe thirty a day.

We all smoked, years ago, everyone in our close circle, Fergus and Maddy, Rita and Ricky, Michael and I. We smoked unthinkingly – lighting up as we reached to answer the telephone, took the first sip of tea or coffee, before we went to bed to top up the nicotine for the night. Earlier still, Maddy, Rita and I had smoked our heads off over yellowing towers of civil-service files long before the non-smoking ethos hit the institution; and years later, while the new health-consciousness was sweeping into Ireland from America, I was furtively glad when Jerry replaced Michael that he smoked too: I did not have to give up just yet.

From our bed, I listened for a while as Wagner's narrative, ethereally dimmed by distance and expensive wool carpeting, rose and fell.

Appreciation for music is one aspect of my youth that still stands to me – not that you would know it, these days: I have not touched the Steinway in the drawing room for years, and as for my cello, the object I used to choose without hesitation as the one item I would save from my burning home, I have not seen it since it was put away for safekeeping when Jack was born nearly eighteen years ago. (Having left everything to the professional movers, I did not even notice it during the transfer to Arkady.)

Over the years, Maddy, Rita and I have operated a sort of musical barter system: they would agree to come to the National Concert Hall with me, if I would go with Maddy to stage musicals or with Rita to 'icon' performances – Frank Sinatra, Neil Diamond, Sandie Shaw, Garth Brooks.

The Diamond concert at Lansdowne Road football stadium is particularly memorable for Rita's delight. Actually, 'delight' does not quite cover the hopping, dancing, waving bundle of ecstasy she was on that occasion. I can still see her, red woolly hat bobbing above the collar of her sheepskin jacket; I can still feel her sturdy biceps gripping mine as she hauled me to my feet.

By far the most zest-filled of us three, she excelled herself that night, succeeding in cajoling four out of five of the spectators in our area of the cold, windy stand – young, old, middle-aged – to join her in yelling along to 'Sweet Caroline', 'I Write The Songs' and 'Love On The Rocks' at the top of their voices.

And I remember looking across at Maddy, so healthy then, catching an expression on her face that I can describe only as surprised joy as she, too, belted along at top volume. I ached for her. Maddy is a performer and she should have been enabled to do her thing. Rita and I should have pushed her harder – and to blazes with Fergus and his needs.

I am not sure why that vivid little episode at Lansdowne Road has floated to the surface of my mind after . . . what is it? Four years? Five? And at this point of crisis. Or why I am describing it to you at such length.

Perhaps it is because uncomplicated pleasure like it has been absent this summer. Or perhaps, at the risk of sounding defensive, I need to illustrate from the outset that I can and do enjoy myself.

At that concert, for instance, once I overcame a reluctance to look silly by waving my arms in the air, I forgot my embarrassment and joined in with a full heart. And when the micro-dot below us that was the singer himself had left his piano for the last time, I led our section in turning to Rita, including her in a standing, cheering ovation. (Being Rita, she acknowledged our homage as graciously as if she were the Queen Mum.)

Secretly, I long to be swept away like that every day, to be an extrovert like she is, instinctively sociable and 'uncomplicated', but my upbringing and early training has served to embed in me an innate reticence. My two best friends would describe me accurately – and with some understatement – as the quietest of us. Within my house, I am confident, Arkady's chatelaine. Outside it, while I hope I give a good impression of being briskly in charge, I feel far from it.

I read somewhere that shyness is a supreme form of selfishness. There is some truth in this: reserved people like me operate within a circle of self-assessment – *do they like me?* – and can detect barometrically the chilliness or warmth of response to a fraction of a degree. In my case, certainly, a 'third eye' operates whenever I am with more than one or two people – *You idiot! Why did you say that? Now they'll think you're stupid!* – and sometimes, as you will see, it operates to take me out of my body altogether.

I am aware that even by offering an apologia at such an early stage – *Make allowances for me, please. Like me. Look beneath* – I am hanging myself.

Enough. You will judge me for yourself.

Maddy certainly seems to take me as I am but Rita has not given up on trying to break me down. At every opportunity she tries to draw me out, as she would call it, and while she is respectful of it, insists that my passion for listening to what she calls mourning music, has coloured my personality too darkly. Consequently I have been dragged not only to her concerts but to circuses, Funderland, even Torville and Dean. Thank God for gusty, gutsy Rita. Thank God for Maddy, too. Thank God for the two of them and their support. Without them I might have been a sad sack altogether, even a social recluse – Jerry has always been too busy to attend any event where he is not entertaining corporately.

I did not go down to comfort him this morning in the family room because I have run out of things to say and, in any case, I find I am still ambivalent. My heart has burned to ashes, if that is not too melodramatic but that is how it feels. There is a bitter, cold, gritty feeling in the centre of my chest.

As I relate this now, it is five hours after that horrible waking. And as we, my husband and I, sit here in the drawing room of Arkady, staring at the sea-fog trailing its ragged coat on the calm, drab water far below, I feel nothing much.

The thoughts running through my head are at half, even idling speed and, strangely enough, have little to do with the immediate traumas of the past couple of months and weeks. At present I am at the mercy of others so no panicked thoughts or worries on my part will shift what seems to be inevitable.

I have therefore reverted to the mundane. Assuming that I can find someone to take care of Tom (who is at that awkward age where he does not want a baby-sitter but still needs one), I might play tennis this afternoon, but only if this fog lifts. Or perhaps even if it does not.

I might telephone Rita or Maddy, or both, and we could meet for coffee in town. Or we could sweep through one of the shopping malls we can all get to, these days, on the M50 – we haven't been together on an outing like that in Dublin for ages.

I might go to the cinema – I have not seen a film for a very long time.

Or then again, I might just make a start on clearing out my wardrobe. Those charity-shop sacks glare accusingly at me from the hall table every time I pass.

Jerry, who is sitting across from me, seems shrunken. He is more than six feet two inches tall, but today he seems as little as an old man although he is barely fifty. On a normal day at this time he would be at work, running the universe.

I must not be glib.

How did this whole thing start?

Where do I start?

I was an old child. When I look back on early snapshots I see a grave, unsmiling little girl with an ugly pudding-bowl haircut and a worry line between eyes that observed too much. Internal time has not moved much for me and in middle age I feel exactly the same – and just as worried – as I did when I was seven.

I do not mean to imply that I had an unhappy childhood or that I have always walked under a permanent cloud. It is not so. Our lifestyle is privileged now and I would be thoroughly ungrateful if I did not thank God for it.

And I love Jerry. I definitely do. I have made that decision and just as I hold fast to Arkady, as a beautiful, consoling constant in this floorless world, I will try to hold on to that, too, whatever happens.

I will not begin this narrative, as a child does, on the day I was born. This is not my life story: it is an attempt to put order on the chaos around me. Maddy and Rita, no doubt, will tell you from their points of view how they have coped with this past summer – and with me. Thank God none of us could see into the future before it bore in on us all to such nuclear effect.

For my part, I will be trying to re-create events, conversations and feelings as they occurred on the day, eschewing hindsight. Or is it foresight in this instance? We do not live our lives chronologically, I think: more and more, as the years go on, I might seem to be living mine in a continuum, so that events of twenty or thirty years ago are re-imagined alongside what actually happened yesterday or, even, what is happening now. I am not unique in this, of course: our minds all work this way, whether we recognise it or not.

In any event, I will relate my story as much for myself as for the record, mostly in an effort to understand how my husband and I came to this point, too drained to speak to each other while we wait for the police to arrive.

Knowing where to begin is difficult but I think the best way to set about it is to go back to the month of May and the day we departed for Collioure.

CHAPTER TWO

From the moment I first heard it, the smooth young voice of my husband's PA reminded me of a clarinet, the plaintive, virginal notes of which I had loved since first hearing the instrument.

Although Susan had been working for Jerry for more than nine months, I had never asked him to describe her, not wanting to give the impression that I was insecure. Naturally, she and I had introduced ourselves over the telephone and we spoke to each other a lot, sometimes daily, to co-ordinate the domestic and work diaries.

At some stage he volunteered that she was smart and dressed well, and if I were asked at that time to guess what type of woman went with that dulcet, slightly husky voice, I would have plumped for a tall, slim brunette. That busy mid-May day of departure, though, I was far from visualising her as we spoke.

Rita insists that a woman's brain can cope with up to seven tasks simultaneously and I was certainly multi-tasking during that call, ticking items on a fistful of last-minute lists and interrupting myself to shout instructions at the boys, who were still rummaging around upstairs. 'I was just about to call you, Mrs Brennan,' she said, immediately after answering. 'The car is outside. It will be leaving here in about five minutes.'

'Great.' I ticked 'garlic crusher'. I never travel anywhere without my own: I find that, no matter how plush the rental accommodation, they never include a decent one in the inventory.

'And Jerry asked me to tell you he'll meet you at Check-in with the others. He had a few things he wanted to finish up here.'

I placed a red mark against 'Jerry's Lens Fluid'. He had only recently converted to contacts and was very fussy about them. 'That's fine. Thanks, Susan.'

'I hope you have a wonderful holiday, Mrs Brennan.' She never called me Tess.

'We will, if we ever get out of here!' 'Gold Sandals.' Tick. 'Jungle Formula. Mobile phone charger.' Tick. Tick. ''Bye now!' I hung up.

We, our gang of three couples and assorted offspring, had been holidaying together for ten years. We hired two minibuses – 'people-carriers' now – choosing a different destination each time. The stipulations were that the house had to have a pool and enough bedrooms – at least six – with three *en-suites*, for the adults, a cleaning and cooking service, and that it was less than an hour from a golf course. For the youngsters it had to have satellite TV and computer connections in case it rained, and also to be within walking reach of a beach so we wouldn't have to drive them all the time. And, very importantly, it had to be within striking distance of a large town or city so we girls had somewhere decent to shop.

There was one other rule, introduced by the three women three years ago: no one could take more than one suitcase. This was designed to cut out competition between us and, more particularly, between Rita's girls as to who looked most glamorous in the evenings.

Or so Rita and I insisted. The subtext was that she and I did not wish to show up Maddy, whose wardrobe is not as extensive as ours. She has enough on her plate without having to worry about feeling inferior to us in the clothes department. Although it makes no intellectual sense, this does matter among friends.

I reread the last-minute instructions for Mrs Byrne, our treasure who, during the month we were gone, would come to the house for two days each week instead of her usual three. I wanted her to clear out the hot press and bag up any towels, face flannels or sheets that had passed their sell-by dates. She could drop them off at one of the charity shops on her way home. She was also to take down the family-room curtains for collection by the dry-cleaner . . .

I tore a fresh sheet from my pad:

And if you have time, Mrs B, it would be great if you could take up the rugs in the den and the drawing room – and the study of course – and, weather permitting, ha-ha!, give them all a bit of a beating out in the fresh air.

Mrs Byrne and I had been together since we moved to Arkady. I chewed at the end of the ball-point. Then:

That's it, I think. All the routine stuff, too, of course. Don't forget to water the ficus and check the sell-by dates of the stuff in the freezer, and there's quite a bit of ironing in the laundry room. And I'm leaving the machines running so you'll have to empty them. Thanks. Hope everything's OK at home. See you on 17 June! I'll bring you back a parrot!!!!!!

I added the fresh sheets to the sheaf of instructions already bulging under Mrs Byrne's magnet on the fridge and looked round my pretty pastel kitchen, with its free-standing, fretworked cupboards under their festoons of dried herbs and lavender. From behind the doors to the utility and laundry rooms came the low, satisfying hum that told me all the machines were doing their cleaning thing.

Then the familiar clench under my breastbone: if Mammy could only see how well I'd done! She would be in awe of Arkady, that's for sure. There isn't a day I don't think about her and I still really miss her, even though she's been dead for nearly forty years. At this stage of my life, I find it difficult to separate my real images of her from those I had created. I wondered for the thousandth time what she would have made of Jerry.

I cast a last look round my lovely kitchen, then hurried into the hall. 'Come on, fellas,' I yelled, from the foot of the stairs. 'The car'll be here in five minutes. Get your act together!'

'Mummy, I can't find my Wranglers.' Tom, wearing only underpants, shoved his head through the balustrade across the landing from his bedroom.

'No time to look for them now, sweetheart, we'll buy you a new pair in Duty Free – OK?'

'Pathetic!' Jack came out of his room, beside his brother's, and barrelled down the stairs.

'Don't you read anything, Mum? We're not going outside the EU. We can't buy Duty Free.'

The doorbell rang and I opened the door to Mick, Jerry's driver, then raced up the stairs to Tom's bedroom where I could hear him flinging open drawers. 'Come on, chop-chop! The plane will go without us!'

'I'm going as fast as I can, *Mummy!*' Spoken with as much sarcasm as can be mustered by an aggrieved eleven-year-old.

He was snuggled in beside me and sucking his thumb when at last we scrunched off down the driveway. I forbore to comment on his outfit of Liverpool T-shirt over khaki bermudas, and glared at Jack to silence him when he raised an eyebrow.

'Bye-bye, House!' I whispered, as the gates closed behind us and we headed down the hill towards the village. I say this every time I leave; it's a superstition I have. I feel, somehow, that Arkady, with its mullioned windows, graceful portico and beautiful gardens, could be a mirage. That if I don't give it its proper due it won't be here when I return and I'll be bounced back to Ballina.

When the estate agent drove me round Howth while I was house-hunting on Jerry's behalf, she was so garrulously complimentary about every damp-ridden bungalow she showed me that I was beginning to despair. Some were in fine locations with wonderful sea views but would have needed knocking down and rebuilding. Those that were in good repair and attractive in themselves were either hidden in swampy hollows or came with such small plots that a decent garden was out of the question.

At the end of our 'tour' we parked in the woman's Starlet at the summit of Howth Head. Far below us, a car ferry rocked in the wake of a giant container ship as both vessels made their way into Dublin port; overhead, an Aer Lingus plane banked on its approach to the airport. I had sold Jerry on the notion that of all the places available in Dublin, this was where he *had* to buy, and on that sunny day in winter, Howth, showing its bones in style, confirmed the sale. So much so that I was depressed at the paucity of what was on offer both from this agency and others I had contacted. 'Is there nothing else?' I asked the woman.

'No.' She peered at her list. 'Not at the moment, I'm afraid, unless . . .' She thought a little, then: 'We're expecting a house to come in on our books some time this week,' she said thoughtfully, 'but we haven't actually signed it yet and I can't show it.'

She looked across at me, as though assessing my psychological health. 'I won't lie to you, Mrs Butler, it will need a lot of work, and although I don't have a precise figure yet, of course, it may be a little beyond your budget. But to judge by the way you've reacted to what I've already shown you, it just might suit you.'

At this point, I thought, I had nothing to lose. 'Does it have a sea view?'

'This view. On a clear day as far as Wexford!' she fired up, and nodded for emphasis, her blonded, lacquered hair retaining the shape ordained for it.

'Could we just drive by it? So I could get an idea?'

'Sure, although we won't exactly be driving by. It's at the end of a cul-de-sac.'

The gates of Arkady were locked tight with a rusting chain and the enormous sloping garden to the front and sides was seriously overgrown, but on the instant the woman stopped the car, every molecule of my body jumped to attention, and my skin grew tight in an effort to contain the lust to possess this house.

The estate agent did not notice my reaction because she had launched into her spiel and was gazing across me up at the house. 'It's an executor's sale. I haven't seen it myself, as I said, but I understand, as I'm sure you can see for yourself, Mrs Butler, that it will need work. On the positive side, while the interior is old fashioned and could do with updating, you will find that the roof is sound and that the . . . yakkity-yakkity.'

I didn't hear anything else. I had stopped listening.

Standing well back above the road, the plain grey façade of Arkady's three storeys was set with a multiplicity of windows, a few obviously broken, and hung, as far as I could see from this distance, with old-fashioned nets. Its double front door, with an ancient, bleached sun-awning hanging off it in tatters, was set into a wide porch, on each side of which was a specimen-sized box ball, so badly neglected that the clipped shapes had been almost obscured by new shoots. The lawn had reverted, with tall grasses, thistles, nettles, buddleia and two-foot-high scraggly wild flowers fighting for space and winning it from the roses and lupins in what had once been flower-beds.

I loved it. Irrevocably. I cannot explain why, but this decrepit structure, far too large for Jerry's needs, called to me like a forlorn siren. It took just a nano-second to answer that call, for my brain to calculate how much my own house in Sallynoggin would fetch. I would want to have something to bring to the table when Jerry Brennan and I came to live together in Arkady.

CHAPTER THREE

To say I was shocked by the unexpected thought that Jerry Brennan and I would live together is an understatement: up to that moment, I had not realised I had been thinking of a permanent arrangement between us.

In the three months that had elapsed since the concert where we met, we had begun cautiously to date, a concert one week, a play the next, a corporate outing to a race meeting, one or two intimate dinners where the chat was general. We had not slept together although when we said goodnight to each other, despite a tacit understanding that neither of us was looking for a second serious relationship, he had taken to kissing me.

But as I gazed at Arkady, I grasped in this moment of intense, fused life that I, for one, had been wondering where we were headed. During the day, I had found myself looking forward to our outings, thinking about his deep blue eyes and lean frame, and how, when he wasn't under pressure, he could make me laugh with his dry wit. I had considered the fit: religion (important but not crucial. Church of England folk are generally easy-going and he seemed to have no objections to my Catholicism), money (we were both conservative, he more than I), music. The last was an important bellwether for me, and I was glad to find we had broadly similar tastes: Schoenberg would have been the outer limits of what either of us could tolerate in a symphony. Similarly, our operatic tastes lay broadly within the band called 'lollipops' – Verdi, Puccini, Rossini, Handel – with the addition of Richard Strauss and Britten. Jerry ventured as far as Wagner, but while I adore the chorus work, the orchestration and some of the lusher scenes in the operas, I find most of the arias and recitatives too dense – and too long.

Actually, the word 'glad', used about the discovery of our musical sympathies, is not sufficiently resonant, considering the context. It was more like placing a tick in the positive column of a mental list I now saw I had been compiling. For instance, the 'respect' box was ticked positively because I admired his mind: Jerry Brennan was widely read and quick to grasp the most abstruse points of the Irish political system, a labyrinth that defeated many natives. I also admired the way he was driven to achievement by energy and ambition, so unlike the dreamy meandering of my beloved Michael.

Michael's mind had been so constantly engaged with the past that it frequently excluded the nuts and bolts of the present. He had compulsory mortgage-protection insurance, of course, but it took constant nagging by Daddy for him to make a will. It had turned out to be a three-line affair, hand-written on a piece of lined A4 notepaper, naming me as his executor and stating that his estate was to go to me.

It took a further sustained onslaught from my father to engage Michael sufficiently in the dreariness of taking out life insurance, a task he completed only two months before he died. (Which, of course, led to much questioning by the insurance company while I was still lost in a grief-stricken haze: *Had your husband been depressed recently? Was he showing signs of stress? Had he many financial worries?*)

All of this flashed through my mind that day, while the estate agent continued to talk about this house I wanted so desperately that I could taste its dust in my mouth. I broke into the sales patter: 'How much?'

'I can't honestly tell you, Mrs Butler, without seeing the interior. One of my colleagues knew the owner and was at a party in that house years ago. It was he told me we would be getting it from the executors for listing. Six bedrooms and apparently it has a very fine bifurcated staircase. That means—'

'I know what it means. Give me your best estimate.'

Belatedly, she recognised my fierce interest: her expression changed and she became businesslike. 'You must understand that whatever figure I give you I can't be held to it, but I would think – just give me a minute here.'

She turned off the engine of the Starlet and reached into the back seat to retrieve her clipboard. I found the tension almost unbearable as, paging through other properties, she rattled on: 'You see, I didn't think you were in the market for such a big house.' Then, delicately: 'Will this sale be contingent on your selling a property, Mrs Butler?'

'I'm not sure yet.'

I rolled down my window and watched the bright sea. I had lied. I *was* sure. I would sell everything I owned to possess this run-down money-trap.

Ostensibly my eyes were fixed on an elongated flock of seagulls wheeling above the wake of a trawler but I wasn't focused on the aerial ballet. I was busy constructing my own sales pitch to Jerry. *Just come out to Howth and have a look, Jerry. I think you'll be impressed. There are one or two others you should consider as well, of course . . .*

That would be a blatant misrepresentation. There were not one or two others to be considered. Arkady was it.

'About two forty,' the woman said eventually, bringing me round to look at her again. 'Now, as I said, I could be wildly off.' She met my gaze. 'Of course, you could always make an offer and we could present it to our clients.'

'Leave it with me,' I said shortly, disappointment so acute it felt like a fresh wound. My house would fetch only seventy-five or eighty thousand pounds, I knew that. When stamp duty and fees were added, how could I convince Jerry to pay more than two hundred thousands pounds for what, on first sight, I was sure he would think was a dump? (At today's grossly inflated prices in Dublin, these figures sound ludicrously low, I know, but this was the early nineties, remember.)

The woman was watching me closely as I struggled to prevent this setback showing. 'Will I telephone you to arrange a viewing?'

'Yes, please.'

'Fine.' She scribbled something in her notebook. 'I have your number. Will your husband be with you?'

She had assumed I was married and I did not disabuse her of the notion. 'I – I'm not sure.' The hesitation was minor. I had already recovered my determination and, whatever it cost, I was going to get this house.

'Fine. No problem.' She threw the clipboard over her shoulder into the back seat and restarted her engine, smiling at me. 'It's women who make these decisions anyway, isn't it, Mrs Butler? We all know that.'

'Mmmm . . .' I smiled back at her and as we drove down the hill towards the village, I looked back over my shoulder. The roof of Arkady stood proudly above its confrères at the height of the road, a galleon in full sail attended by vassal tenders and tugs. 'Bye-bye, house,' I whispered. 'I'll be back.'

That's how the leave-taking tradition, or superstition, had begun.

'Great day for it, Mrs Brennan.' Jerry's driver, Mick, was as sunny as always as we bowled down the hill. Good old Mick, seventy if he's a day but still trying to pretend he's fifty-nine. The firm should have pensioned him off when he was sixty-five but Jerry saved him. I was glad because it is relaxing to be in his company, perhaps because he never speaks, for good or ill, about anyone in the firm and so, you think, he won't be talking about you.

In this instance he was right, it was a great day for it, and as the Merc swept along the sea-front, I lowered my window to breathe in the fishy, salt-laden breezes clinking cheerfully through the forest of sunlit yacht riggings in the harbour marina. I had fallen in love with Howth when I was a girl and newly arrived in Dublin and have never for one moment fallen out. I am also well aware of how lucky I am that Arkady is perched on the airy heights of the summit, above the new townhouses and apartments, day-trippers, weekend overcrowding and litter of which all the natives complain.

Thank God. I mean that. I do not take a single aspect of my good fortune for granted.

Even our relationship with the neighbours in the four other houses in our cul-de-sac is civilised but not overly friendly, which suits my nature. We exchange cards and bottles of wine at Christmas and are available in emergencies, but otherwise the alliance between us runs little further than a greetings exchange of the 'Good morning, isn't it a lovely day?' variety.

Traffic was moving freely along the Black Banks Road but we got caught in roadworks on the motorway, so all the others were there when the boys and I got ourselves and our trolleys inside the airport. Queues without number, of course, even at the Premier Gold Circle desk, which is supposed to be exclusive and fast-tracked.

'Here she is at last. Hello, Tess.' Maddy, in raffia sandals, was shivering in a yellow sundress over which she had draped a thin cotton cardigan. She looked across my shoulder, searching the crowd: 'Jerry not with you?'

At that time, Jerry was the unchallenged leader of us all. I am not quite sure why: it might have been by virtue of his job where he was used to being in command, but it might also have been sheer force of personality. 'He'll be along – hi, Fergus!'

Maddy's husband, standing beside their son, acknowledged the greeting with a gesture from his place in the queue in front of her. 'Something last minute came up as usual,' I continued. 'Hi, Rita, Ricky – girls!' I waved at them and at their four daughters, each of whom was wired into her personal CD-player. Rita was wearing a white silk tent. Adored by her husband and four girls, Rita, as you have gathered, no doubt, is the archetypal earth mother in *The Darling Buds of May*, warm expansive and (sorry, Rita!) well upholstered – to the extent that she cannot bear the constriction of tights, never wears them, and does not care a fig for anyone's opinion of her varicosed legs.

I took out my mobile and squinted at its little green face. No messages. He probably hadn't even left the office yet. Being CEO of a big company has its perks, but it has drawbacks too. Like never making it on time for any family affair, even missing some, such as Tom's confirmation last month.

My husband's work life was one long crisis; I had stopped listening to the individual dramas. I could have taken out a patent on the art of looking interested and asking relevant questions, while mentally running over any lists I needed to compile for the following day.

He could not even spend an entire holiday with us – 'A month is too long to be away, Tess, and last year was a disaster. How many times do I have to tell you?' – so he would grace us with his presence for only the first three weeks. I suppose I should have counted myself lucky that he had granted us that much.

When my turn came, the girl refused to check Jerry in, even though I had his passport and ticket. Her attitude was understandable, I suppose, in light of the 11 September tragedy in New York the previous year. But you would think, would you not, that they would be well acquainted with Jerry Brennan, who flies to London or Europe or Russia at least three or four times a month, sometimes even more frequently? I did not have the nerve to argue: the Germans behind me were clearing their throats and looking over my shoulder.

I took his ticket off the counter but checked in his suiter with the rest of our luggage. In most circumstances, where my relationship with Jerry is concerned, I think I could be described as 'accommodating', even sometimes 'meek'. Right then, however, I had what Daddy would describe as a rush of blood to the head and, on the pretext that my flight was on last call, insinuated my way past the queue at the ticket desk, leaving Jerry's ticket and passport with one of the clerks. Then I stabbed out a text message to him, telling him what I had done. It was going to be his own lookout if he missed the flight.

That felt good, I thought, as I went back to rejoin the others. But before I reached them, the headiness evaporated and it happened again: one of those weird, unsettling riffs of third-eye objectivity that arose on the oddest occasions. This time I saw myself as if I was in a film, the camera zeroing in from a distance. The shot isolated a waxed, middle-aged, middle-class woman, ladies' singles champion of her tennis club, with toned thighs, perfectly oval nails and cream-coloured hair, her poise underpinned by the knowledge that her house was a showplace, her personal bathroom a sanctuary, and the walk-in wardrobes in her dressing room rich with silk and linen.

Tom came into the laundry room one time when I was recovering from one of these eerie little departures, and before I knew what I was doing, I had told him what was happening. 'That happens to me all the time, Mum,' he said, in his detached way. 'Do you feel far away and you're looking at yourself?'

'That's right.'

'It's nothing. You just deal with it, OK? It's easy. Are my tennis socks dry?'

I 'dealt with it,' naturally, since I had no choice but to do so. But as an aside, the sleek 'Tess' Butler Brennan I saw during these episodes was a triumphant evolution of Teresa Cahill, the fat, frumpy girl with mousy hair brought up over her father's news-agent's in Ballina.

But surrounded as she was, that day in the airport concourse, by busy, swirling crowds, Teresa could see quite clearly through her camera's pitiless lens that Tess's glossy skin and perfectly draped pashmina hid the fact that she often felt as dry and empty as a coconut husk.

CHAPTER FOUR

Collioure is in Catalonian France, just north of the Spanish border: 'a delightful and historical fishing village', according to the bumf that came from the rental agent, who had found us a big old villa in the hills above the town. What's more, the place has street cred: it is where Patrick O'Brian lived to write his series of maritime novels and where Matisse did a lot of his painting. Names to drop when holiday yarns were to be swapped at dinner parties during the long nights of winter.

Jerry and I were arguing on the wide, red-tiled terrace from which, dressed in shorts and tank top, I had been keeping vigil to meet him on his arrival.

When Meek Tess saw him climb out of the taxi, almost a day late, Heady Tess remembered how aggrieved she was and made her displeasure fully known. He tried to gloss it over, work, paperwork, blah blah – 'You wouldn't understand, Tess, it'd bore you' – but for once she was having none of it. 'Please don't treat me like an imbecile,' she said stiffly, her voice low but deadly so none of the others, not awake yet – or, at least, not up – would hear. 'I have been living with you and the Sentinel Group for ten years. I can understand the finer workings of your hierarchy and its problems. You were never staying for the full holiday and now you've shortened it even further. Explain it to me again. What was so urgent?'

'Drop it, Tess, will you? The sky didn't fall in, did it? You had Jack and Tom to help you, if you could have been persuaded to give that pair of dainty violets of yours a gee-up. It's a long, complicated story and if I embarked on it you'd get the glassy look in your eye you think I don't notice. So give it a rest. I got here as quick as I could. I could have waited for the direct flight from Dublin to Barcelona later today but I stayed at bloody Heathrow last night to catch a flight to Perpignan before bloody dawn.'

He saw me drawing breath to have another go and put a hand on my arm. 'I'm here now, lass,' his voice was soft, 'don't make me wish I weren't.' Jerry's Yorkshire accent has virtually extinguished itself in the corporate-speak of big business, yet sometimes, particularly when he is exasperated or angry, it surfaces and his vowels broaden. There is a hint of Scotland too. He had begun his working life as an insurance salesman for a large company out of a sub-office in Glasgow.

He watched me carefully as we teetered on the edge of an all-out knockdown row. The air resonated with it. But behind us rose the formidable peaks of the Pyrenees, striped on their lower reaches with vineyards and dotted with ochre-roofed farms; a windscreen sparked in the sunshine flooding the corniche below us and below that again, the blue, blue Mediterranean quietly filled the harbour of Collioure, curving between bell-tower and breakwater. It should have been wonderful. It *was* wonderful, so I bit hard. I had had my say, I had made it clear how upset I was, no point in banging away and sending him into one of his extended icy sulks, especially given that we were going to be in close company with our friends. 'All right, we'll leave it there.'

'Good. Now, what's on the agenda for today?' Item settled. On to next item.

'What do you want to do?' I was still annoyed of course, but told myself that the last thing any husband needed after a stressful journey was a resentful wife. 'Why don't we stroll down into the town and get the baguettes?'

'Shit, Tess – I thought we were paying for that kind of thing. Are you telling me that we've paid a fortune for this place and they don't even deliver the goddamned bread in the morning?'

'*Relax*, will you? They do. It's here already, in the kitchen. But wouldn't it be nice to do the French thing for ourselves? I bet it's wonderful in those patisseries down there. Come on, be adventurous.' It was my turn to put out the hand of conciliation. 'Don't be such an old curmudgeon.'

'Whatever you say.' He picked up his travel bag. 'I'm going in to have a shower. Which is our bedroom?'

'First on the left after you go through the kitchen.' As he moved to go in, the dregs of my anger were dissipated by the sight of his tired gait and travel-weary suit. 'C'mere, you!' I ran after him, grabbed his sleeve and planted a kiss on his stubbly cheek. 'I've laid out your shorts and a T-shirt. And don't you even think of wearing socks! I'll meet you back here in fifteen minutes. Now, give me that mobile, we're going for a walk, just the two of us. Your office can do without you for one hour—'

'Tess! Stop it!' He marched away. I could see it would take more than a kiss on the cheek to prise him away from business.

In case I have not made this clear so far, I might explain here that I am not Jerry's original wife nor is he my first husband; I met him at a Carreras recital almost a year after being widowed.

I found myself seated next to this tall, quite impatient person, who seemed to be hosting a corporate group and was obviously not happy about it: one of his knees jigged continuously like a little piston. I must have sighed or shown some sort of irritation at this because the jigging stopped and he smiled apologetically at me. I smiled back.

We bumped into each other again at the wine table during the interval and got chatting. I discovered he was in the process of moving to Ireland to take up a new post as CEO of the Sentinel newspaper group. 'I'm having difficulty finding a house. I'm not good at it – my wife always did that kind of thing.'

'Is she not with you?'

'We're divorced,' he said tersely.

'Oh! I'm sorry!'

'Don't be.' He clammed up.

Hastily, I reintroduced the subject of houses, because if there is one subject on which I am an expert – and was even then – it is the Dublin house market. I have always been an avid reader of the property supplements in the newspapers. 'If you'd like, I could help you to find one. The estate agents in Dublin are good but you'll find that, understandably, they're all anxious to sell off what they have on their own books rather than match you to a particular property. You can't beat a bit of independent advice and local knowledge.'

He was taken aback that a total stranger would make an offer like this. 'That's very kind of you, but I couldn't dream of imposing.'

'You wouldn't be. Not at all. Since my husband died last year, I'm underemployed, especially during term-time when my sons are at school. And I love looking at houses. It would be great to have a legitimate excuse.'

He hesitated again. 'I'm sorry to hear about your husband. Was it sudden?'

'Yes.' It was my turn to clam up. Even at that stage, a little more than ten months after Michael's death, I could not speak of it without becoming upset. And I had been serious about having time on my hands. I could have taken on a job, but I felt it was too soon, that the children needed me at home. We were always strapped for cash, but we were managing. 'So is it a deal, then?'

The interval bell went. 'Well, if you insist.' He drained his glass. 'It would be a great relief. Of course, you must allow me to do something for you in return. Could I hire you as a paid consultant?'

The idea of a few extra shillings was tempting but I rejected it. The house-search would be far less enjoyable if I was under pressure or obligation to show results. 'Absolutely not necessary,' I said, as we joined the crowd moving towards the auditorium. 'I'd be taking pleasure in it. Honestly!'

'Can't understand why. It would be my idea of Hades. Thank you very much. But only if you allow me to buy you the best dinner Dublin can provide.' He smiled broadly at me and I noticed how white his teeth were. It was the first detail I had seriously registered about any man since Michael died. I suppressed it. 'Again, dinner not necessary. I'll accept a bottle of champagne if I find you a house you like. And I'll bill you for my petrol. I can't say fairer than that.'

After we had taken our seats again and he had put on his glasses to read the programme notes, I noticed for the first time how much he resembled my late husband. It is, no doubt, deeply psychological but not the kind of insight into which one would like to probe too deeply. Tall, rangy men with myopia are evidently my 'type'.

So this was how I found Arkady and, a year afterwards, ended up living in it with my two surprised sons – although Tom was still too young to pay much attention – and a new husband.

I was a little defensive about marrying so soon after my abrupt widowing, although no one could have accused us of flaunting or being flashy: we got married with no guests, no reception and just two of Jerry's work colleagues as witnesses. Our honeymoon was one night in Hunter's Hotel in Wicklow because at the time he was engaged in a complex acquisition for Sentinel and could not afford to take any time off. I didn't mind: I loved Arkady so much, and had such plans for it, that it was no hardship to fly back to its embrace.

Now on this terrace above Collioure, I scuffed one of my sandals in the sandy infill between two tiles. Here we were, Jerry and I, all these years later, our corners well rubbed off, our compromises all in place.

The group vacations had started for me during the first year of my widowhood, when the other two couples, who had holidayed together before, insisted that the boys and I went with them to Crete. Then, after I married Jerry, he was simply tagged on. We brought nannies and au pairs during the early years and every year we say it will probably be the last, that it is a miracle the older ones still want to come, that we should take advantage of their company while we can. Our Jack is the eldest and I was astonished that he showed an interest this year. The attraction, I'd say, was the watersports school, or it might even have been Kitty, Rita's eldest, who is turning into an attractive little thing.

I hope I'm not telling you too much too quickly.

With a little time to put in before Jerry came back from his shower, I decided to go into the chapel. Although I would no longer consider myself pious, I have never lost the habit of morning prayers, ingrained during boarding-school and reinforced over the two years I spent in the novitiate immediately afterwards.

I had been delighted to discover that, although it had not been mentioned in the brochure, this beautiful old house boasted a little oratory, with stained-glass windows, the tomb of a former owner, and a small, ornately gilded altar.

Entering it was like floating into another century, calm and far less complicated. It was also deliciously cool. I knelt at an age-blackened prie-dieu, one of six, and basked in the rainbows showering the air and tiles through the deep colours of the glass. Then I closed my eyes. 'Please, God,' I prayed, 'please let us all relax, especially Jerry. Don't let me put my foot in it to provoke him. Don't let Tom fray too many nerves and don't let Jack be too bolshy or drink too much or do something stupid with some girl. Please let our family get on together and with the rest of the gang and let all of us have a good time and go home refreshed. Amen.' Not much of a prayer, but who ever said God demanded polished prose?

I had articulated my dearest wish for the coming month. There is a tendency, when so many people are around and so much entertainment is on offer with so many traditions that have grown up over the years – the first drink (champagne), the last drink (Cognac), the penultimate meal, the card games, the after-dinner charades and so on – to forget that one of the purposes of a family holiday is to renew your own family.

My reference to Tom was heartfelt. He is an odd little creature, a puzzle, not only to everyone close but to his teachers. Although he causes no trouble in the classroom, when he is asked to do something he does not want to do, he simply says a polite 'No' and nothing will move him. Now the school has more or less given up on him and leaves him to his own devices. This may be no bad strategy because his academic grades remain within the average range.

Another kid exhibiting such eccentricity might be bullied, but not Tom. It does not faze him that his classmates give him a wide berth – or so it appears; he does not want birthday parties, never invites anyone home and has never complained that he has no friends, or that he is unhappy.

One of the more sympathetic teachers explained to me once that he seems to inhabit a sort of exclusion zone and, in school at least, to keep others deliberately at bay. I knew exactly what she meant because he does it at home, too, most of the time.

One of his more trying quirks is that he obsesses about particular objects, food and clothing. For certain periods, perhaps, he will eat only green food. Then, overnight, this might be replaced by a diet consisting solely of Ambrosia Creamed Rice.

For years I wore myself out defending his strange, isolationist behaviour to friends and family, to my father. Daddy, in his words, would be inclined to give poor Tom a good old-fashioned root up the arse. Thank God he still lives in Ballina so he and Tom don't meet that often. Jerry, too, of course, is not without his own, forceful, opinions.

As for me, I am silent these days, letting them all hold on to their view that he is a spoiled brat. I really do not believe that – all God's creatures may sing in the choir and so forth – but sometimes even I find his behaviour so provocative that I feel like strangling him. Then I see the wayward little V of hair, inherited from my dear, dead Michael, in the hollow of his neck at the back.

I went back to the terrace. Far out to sea, a long flat container ship trailed a finger of smoke against the horizon, and down by the harbour I could see a man setting up an easel. I leaned on the parapet and, stretching the back of my neck to invite the sun's blessed warmth, took deep breaths to oust the remnants of the fight, still rumbling like an old steam engine inside my chest. As everything quieted, I tried to identify and separate the sounds and odours particular to this part of France. Along with the warm smell of old stone rising from under my elbows, I could distinguish a clayey tang from the vineyards, also a hint of lavender and some other floral sweetness I did not recognise but might have emanated from a yellow-flowering weed at the base of the parapet.

I fancied I could even get the scent of wild garlic – although the latter might have come from the open kitchen casement, just ten yards behind me, where the cook was already at work.

As for sounds, we were so far above the road and the village that nature was dominant outside the house. Because it was still May and the lull of full summer had not yet descended, the birds were vocal against the faint background boom of the sea. I am no ornithologist but during my years of human silence in the novitiate, I learned to separate the calls of the various species we could hear from the fields and the lake lapping at them.

Here, in the stunted trees surrounding the villa, I could identify the territorial calls of sparrows, robins, the warning clack of magpies – and, from somewhere hidden in the roof, of pigeons or doves. But, of course, there were some calls I did not know. Strangely, there was neither sight nor sound of seagulls, which were such a feature of the skies above our own harbour of Howth.

How would Michael have enjoyed this? Not a lot, probably. Too pretty, too *nice*.

CHAPTER FIVE

I find I retreat to the memory of my first husband when Jerry and I fight; this is not fair, of course, especially when you consider that I would be seriously put out to think that he might compare me to his first wife.

I was Teresa then; I did not become Tess until I entered Jerry's corporate world.

Although physically alike, as I've said, Jerry Brennan and Michael Butler could not have been more different in personality. Michael was an academic archaeologist who liked nothing better than to spend our summer holidays scratching away at the sand in some rocky remoteness. I loved him dearly and could count on one hand the number of serious altercations we had over the fourteen years of our marriage, but those endless months of dust and (for me) boredom tried my patience, especially when Jack was small.

While Jerry is as quick as mercury and surprised by little, Michael, as might be expected from his profession, had the patience of a tortoise and, to him, every minute he spent on this planet was a revelation.

If my first husband was, well, *restful*, my second is anything but, and instead of mellowing as he gets older, Jerry seems to be getting crabbier. I noticed this especially in the months leading up to this holiday when I could say and do nothing right. I put his bad humour down to the stress of work: he was intent on modernising Sentinel's plant and machinery and apparently money was haemorrhaging into it. As well as that, diversification into local radio and allied music venues, Jerry's personal pet project, was proving even more threatening to the core business.

See? I do listen, sometimes.

I had humoured him and his irritability in the belief that this trip would improve matters. By the end of three weeks of sunshine, a Mediterranean diet and good company, I hoped, we would be back on an even plateau of affection.

I had come to believe that the measure of a good relationship is not how the partners get along in day-to-day life, but how they cope when thrown together twenty-four hours a day on holiday, in illness or retirement. In the history of *Homo sapiens*, nine-to-five – or, in my husband's case, 06.30 to 19.30 – is a recent encumbrance. Jerry and I are not passionate people but as a rule we are kind to each other and good companions when he leaves the office behind.

I was lost in these domestic musings when a yawning Ricky, still in his pyjamas and with ludicrous Mickey Mouse slippers on his feet, came out to join me. 'Howya, Teresa. Jerry here yet?' Alone among our friends, Ricky had never made the transition to Tess.

'Having a shower.' I smiled at him. 'Sleep well?'

'No. You know me. I like me own bed.' He yawned again and looked around at the landscape. 'But this is nice, wha'?' He scratched his paunch, as round as a little pig.

'It certainly is. It's gorgeous. I think we're going to enjoy it here.' I offered this tentatively, with good cause: he was with us this year on sufferance and, like Jerry, would not be staying the whole course. Ireland had qualified for the World Cup, a matter for wild national celebration. Ricky, an avid supporter of the Irish soccer team during all the lean, no-hoper years, had booked himself a flight to Japan from Barcelona a full week and a half before the rest of us flew back to Dublin. The last week of our holiday was going to be strange with two of the men missing.

With Ricky's World Cup in June, Jerry having serious doings at work throughout July and Fergus's series filming again in August, it had been tricky to organise the holiday this year. Providentially, none of the kids was sitting state exams so we had taken them all out of school and come early in the season.

Ricky and Rita Sleator are by far the wealthiest of our group and – probably because they have so much – the least concerned with money. Although Rita flashes the credit cards, Ricky uses them only as a last resort and always carries rolls of notes in large denominations. His phlegmatic demeanour and rotund stature mask phenomenal personal drive and shrewd business sense.

He left school early and was apprenticed to a butcher in Raheny where he watched and learned so thoroughly that eventually he convinced a bank manager to take a punt on him and lend him enough to open his first shop. Within twelve years, Sleator's Victuallers had become a successful city-wide chain.

He did not stop there. The Sleators also co-own many other businesses: bookies' shops, a hardware emporium in Blanchards-town, a panel-beating garage, a hackney firm, even a combined veterinary-supply and pet store somewhere in the Midlands. They live at San Lorenzo, named by Rita to honour St Laurence O'Toole, patron saint of Dublin, but translated into Italian to give it more oomph. This rambling, crenellated pile is in North County Dublin, surrounded by hundreds of acres of grassland to fatten the stock for the butchers' shops and graze the girls' horses.

I heard scratching behind me and turned to look. One of the resident cats was playing with a dry leaf on the tiles. Ricky hadn't moved. 'Penny for them, Ricky?'

'Ah, nothin',' he said. 'I'm just tired, that's all. I'll be grand after the first day or two. *No problemo.*'

'Better rest up! It's a long way to Japan.'

'Tell me about it.' His expression, naturally lugubrious, clouded further. 'I hate them long flights. I can't understand why they don't build more Concordes. And I'm not looking forward to eating that sushi stuff.'

'You won't have to if you don't want to. It's Japan, not Siberia! They'll have a McDonald's on every corner.'

Jerry arrived then so he and I left Ricky to his contemplation of the landscape and set off for Collioure, not far on crow's wings but about two kilometres distant along the snaking, unpaved roadway leading downhill from the villa.

At home I am not an enthusiastic walker: despite the undeniable physical and mental benefits I find it boring to 'go for a walk', however lovely the day or magical the surroundings. Perhaps this has something to do with the forced marches we endured as boarding-school inmates: every Sunday afternoon, we had to

squelch over miles and miles of rainswept bogland in our whop-
ping 'outdoor shoes', then limp back with blistered toes and
skinned heels.

Nowadays, eschewing the windswept heights of my own neigh-
bourhood around Howth Head, I keep fit with tennis in the
summer and swimming in the local pool in winter. In addition, I
use the equipment in our home gym at least twice a week. One of
my ambitions is to install a covered pool in the grounds of Arkady.
I will, too, when I get round Jerry's outrage at the estimates of
how much it would cost to run it.

The muscles around my shins protested as I tried to keep up
with him on our march. He is a squash player and possessed of
much longer legs than I, so no matter how I pushed my poor
tortured calves, he stayed a few feet ahead, almost as though he
was towing me along.

Just when I thought I could take no more, we reached the town
and the blessed flat. Although it was still early and the temperature
was a pleasant twenty-four degrees celsius, I was sweating. 'You all
right?' He turned round.

'Could we stop for a coffee or an orange juice or something?
I'm parched.'

'Sure. I'll see if I can get a paper.'

That is another thing. We could be in the wilds of Borneo or
Papua New Guinea and my Jerry's first priority would be to locate
an English-language newspaper. No matter that he might have
read them the day before at home. It is the ritual that counts, and
anyway, he says, these could be different editions.

We stopped at one of the open-air restaurants beside a wide,
stone-walled culvert below what seemed to be a ruined fort. I sat
under an umbrella and looked around while he shot off on his
errand.

The culvert led to a charming little harbour where, under the
buzzing heat, a few colourfully painted fishing-boats were being
loaded with nets and lobster-pots. The artists were already out in
force, easels lined up on the promenade opposite, lunch baskets at
their feet. Saturday was obviously market day, and on the far side
of the main bridge over the culvert, a jumble of food stalls was
doing brisk trade under striped awnings. I could see vegetables,

olives, oil, wine, cheeses, meat, fish and enticing-looking displays of preserves and condiments. I was itching to get closer.

But first things first. When Jerry came back with his thick bundle of newsprint, I picked up the plasticised menu on the table. It offered *Le Grand Breakfast Anglais*, and *Le Petit Déjeuner du Pain et Café au Lait*. 'Something to eat?'

'I thought you wanted just coffee. I thought we were getting bread we don't need and going back up to the house with it. Won't the kids be wondering where we've got to?' So much for my romantic notions of browsing together in a charming patisserie.

'Ricky knows where we are, and the kids aren't up yet.' When Jerry is being picky, I deal with it by pretending not to notice and always adopt a particularly jolly tone. 'So, what would you like?'

'Coffee will be fine. I ate on the plane.' He shook open the previous day's *Daily Telegraph*, which, along with the *Daily Mirror* and *USA Today*, seemed to be the newspapers of choice for the English-speaking population of Collioure. 'Well, I haven't eaten since last night,' I chirped. 'I'm going to have something.'

I called over the waitress and ordered apple juice, crêpes 'avec sucre et citron, s'il vous plaît, et café au lait pour deux.'

'Merci, Madame!' The waitress bustled back into the café. It was lovely to use my school French, but I am always chagrined when they automatically use 'Madame', rather than the younger and far more flattering 'Mademoiselle'. All that grooming and exercising and torture from electrolysis needles and hot wax brought to naught – like so much grease-spotted burger wrapping – by one pert little girl with her effortless French *chic*. I could see nothing of my husband except two pairs of knuckles clutching the raised newspaper. No point in fighting it. I sat back in my seat, tightened my tummy and concentrated on getting to know my surroundings.

Disappointingly, although the tourist season was not really under way yet, I found that while the food stalls across the bridge were besieged by locals, we were surrounded in the restaurant by English and Germans. Rather than watch them, I concentrated on the pavement parade: a woman with a poodle under one arm and a pair of baguettes under the other treble-cheek-kissing another carrying a basket filled with onions, potatoes and brown-paper packages tied with complicated twine bows; a barefoot young man wearing a hat from which swung a fringe of corks. As I watched, two girls, dressed almost identically in navy business suits and white blouses, stood aside to let a thin, elderly man, stooped and brown as old smoke, manipulate his wife's wheelchair around the pair. Maybe, I thought, she isn't his wife. Maybe she was his lover? Maybe, French fashion, he is faithful both to her and to his wife unto death.

'France. We're in France!'

I had not realised I had spoken aloud until Jerry looked round the side of his *Telegraph*. 'What did you say?'

'Sorry. Listen, after we get the baguettes, could we take a stroll around the market? I bet they have wonderful craft stalls.'

'Tess, I thought—'

His mobile rang. He pulled it out of the breast pocket of his T-shirt and looked at its face: 'It's the office, I'm afraid. Look, I know you hate mobiles in restaurants so I'll take it out here on the street.' He discarded the newspaper, flipped open the mobile and stood up. 'Good morning, Susan.'

Before I could protest that it would be OK, that I didn't mind him using his mobile here in France, out in the open where no one knew us, he was walking away out of earshot.

I turned to my crêpe, recently arrived. It was light, crisp around the edges, utterly delicious. When I had finished it, and there was still no sign of Jerry, I contemplated ordering a croissant with that apricot jam you get in Spain and France, then decided against it. After forty (and I am a good way after!) you have to watch what you eat, but don't let anyone tell you that your stomach shrinks over time if you keep your calorie intake down. It may well shrink but no one informs the hunger-receptors in your brain.

It was not unusual that Jerry was nowhere in sight: he tends to pace when he is talking on the telephone or trying to tease out a work problem.

The little harbour at the end of the culvert was only about seventy yards away and I became fascinated by a young family – mother, father, three kids, all five white-blond – who were rigging a pair of dinghies and preparing to put out. It tugged at my heart to see the way the two boys, around seven and nine, were gravely helping their little sister belt herself into her lifejacket. Where and when do boys lose this gentleness? More importantly, why?

I would have loved to have a daughter . . . Maybe if we'd had a daughter together, or even if I had had a daughter from Michael, Jerry might have been a little more tolerant of Jack and Tom. It is never easy, I know, for spouses to cope with children of previous relationships but I find it difficult to hear the way my husband's voice mellows and lightens by at least two keys on the rare occasions he talks to his daughter, who is reading English at Edinburgh University. I think he still has what the Americans would call 'issues' with his first wife, and contact with either his daughter or his son, who works 'in computers', is sporadic. He rarely speaks about them and as I know the subject distresses him I don't bring it up.

I turned away from the dinghies. I would not go down that cul-de-sac today. Not with the sun shining, the taste of *café-au-lait* in my mouth and a holiday ahead during which there was every chance I could narrow, even close, the three-branched rift that had opened between Jerry, me and my sons.

Resolutely, I turned my thoughts to the day ahead. The rest of the gang were sure to be up and about by now and the plan, formulated the previous night, was that after a lazy breakfast we would go to the beach to play together until we broke up into the various age and interest groups for the remainder of the holiday. This idea had been resisted by Jack and, perhaps surprisingly, by Colm, Maddy and Fergus's wan sixteen-year-old who had never previously had either the gumption or the energy to object to anything. But we grown-ups had stood firm: the deal was that if they were to be subsidised for their own activities, all the young people had to come with us on this first day.

We could play Happy Families for one day at least.

CHAPTER SIX

As with most groups of married friends, the nucleus of ours is the long-standing interrelationship of the women. Jerry, Fergus and Ricky, friends by association, have little in common and would never have gravitated towards each other by choice. We three, however, had bonded indissolubly during the years we spent together in the quiet brown recesses of the civil service, in the days when that institution was as safe and joyless as an old banknote in a Swiss vault.

As clerk-typists, a junior grade that at the time did not necessarily require any typing, we scratched away with our government-issue Biros and pencils in Seomra a Seacht – Room Seven – of our department.

Maddy, whom no one called 'Madeleine' except her mother and Fergus, was born in Ballineen, a village in West Cork. She was the ambitious one when we three first became friends. Her life was going to be dedicated to her art.

And when I first knew her, almost all of her spare time was spent in the services of a thriving amateur dramatic society. Because Rita and I were loyal camp followers and got to know the other members of the group, we knew how much she was valued. This was not only for her acting skills – she received honourable mention at the All Ireland Drama Festival in Athlone for her grey-wigged and heavily aged Miss Prism – but for her willingness to turn her hand to anything, scene-painting, nudging props from reluctant friends and neighbours, even prompting during the shows in which she was not cast.

In those days our Mad was a little dynamo. At every opportunity she auditioned for semi-professional theatre companies around town, and although she was never successful, remained undaunted. She was convinced that her breakthrough was only a matter of watching, working and waiting. The Abbey Theatre was the Holy Grail.

I will never forget the day she got a walk-on part there in O'Casey's *The Plough and the Stars*; she had registered with a drama school and had been chosen from it. 'Lads, lads!' She rushed into Seomra a Seacht after lunch, waving a bit of paper. 'I can't *believe* it! I'm going into the *Abbey*! The *Abbey Theatre*! This is the best day of my *life*!' She grabbed the hat-stand inside the door, hugged it, would have waltzed it across the floor if it had not been laden with wet coats.

When she calmed down we learned that she had no lines. She was to be 'a woman in the pub' during a fight scene, 'a looter' and 'a young girl in the crowd' during a rabble-rousing speech. 'All I have to do, lads, is to look as if I'm paying attention and react at the right moment! But listen, they won't know what hit 'em.' She hugged herself. 'This could be the start of something big!' She could not have been more excited if Cecil B. de Mille had called her to Hollywood to play the lead in one of his epics. Our supervisor came in then and we had to go to our desks.

Rita and I bought tickets for the opening night. Maddy would not allow her parents or other relatives to come until she had 'settled into the parts', and we felt privileged that she trusted us. We discussed with her what we should wear but, like us, she had never been to an opening night at the Abbey and said she would feel stupid asking the actors in the company. We decided that, given the august reputation of the place – after all, it is Ireland's national theatre – we had better pull out all the stops.

So, about a month later, wearing our best dance dresses and almost as excited as Maddy herself, we joined the first-night crowd, most of whom seemed to know each other, in the foyer of the theatre. The chatter and laughter were deafening and there was a lot of kissing.

And we were seriously overdressed.

The vast majority of the audience wore what would nowadays be called 'smart casual', although there was a fair smattering of scruff: tatty sports jackets or worn black jumpers with dragged necks. (I assumed that those in the latter were poets and writers, although I did not recognise any of them.) 'What do you think?' I whispered, in Rita's ear. We had found a vacant bit of wall just beside the stairs and jammed ourselves in against it.

'I think nothing,' she said.

'We're dressed all wrong, Rita.'

'Feck it! It's a theatre, not a fashion parade,' she hissed, although I could see she was as ill at ease as I was. 'We can't go home and change. It's too late. Anyway, no one's looking at us.'

We forgot all about ourselves, of course, when the play went up (by this time we had been indoctrinated in theatrical jargon) because the actors were magnificent and *The Plough and the Stars* is a masterpiece. I even forgot to be nervous for Maddy.

We had been worried that we would not be able to spot her among the others in the crowd scenes but we had no problems on that score: there were only three 'extras' altogether and Maddy was the only girl. In fact, I felt a bit let down. I would have thought the Abbey could have risen to a few more: red-haired Maddy was almost too visible in her scenes, despite her varying costumes. They should at least have given her different wigs.

One of the great thrills in prospect was that she had invited us to come backstage after the show to the dressing room she shared with the girl who played Mollser. We felt really important going round to the stage door, as she had instructed, and being seen by the homegoing *hoi-polloi* to announce ourselves there, to be let in by the stage doorman and directed up the stairs.

The door of the dressing room – brightly lit, grey and utilitarian – was open. Mollser, the 'real' actress, already had her makeup off, was in her street clothes and packing her bag to go home when we approached. Beyond her, we could see Maddy, still in full regalia, waiting for us.

We all fell on each other, Rita and I congratulating her wildly, Mad seeking assurances: 'Was I really all right? You really thought it went OK? You're not just saying that now?'

'Of course not!' we chorused, continuing to extol Maddy's virtue as, in Rita's words, 'by far the best reactor. Honestly, Mad! We couldn't take our eyes off you. You were great!' Mollser, who left quietly as Rita was reaching new heights of encomium, must have been highly amused.

Unfortunately, this triumph never led to anything better for Mad. And then she met Fergus.

As for me, up to the time I met Michael, and even for a considerable time afterwards, I was a prim ex-novice who didn't know what she wanted to do with her life and who was afraid of any shadow, particularly if it was young and male.

In retrospect, I was supremely lucky to be sent to Room Seven where the other two, so much more socially advanced and streetwise than I, were already ensconced. Because of my aborted religious vocation, they had had a two years' head start and might have ridiculed and ignored me. Instead, they took me under their wing, enabling me to look back later with affection and amusement on my four years in the service of my country even though the job was soul-destroying.

Miss Santini was the staff officer in charge of us. Her romantic Italian name could not have clashed more incongruously with her appearance and personality. A tiny, hunched woman with a bronchial wheeze engendered by a rampant cigarette habit, she crept nervously around the office and hid her coughs behind the personal coat-rack her status warranted. As the most junior member of staff, one of my duties every day was to trot across to the chemist to buy Zubes for her. As a result, Room Seven reeked of Zube-scented smoke, as did our coats and jackets. I hated that smell.

In fact, I hated every aspect of my job. It was during those years, I think, that my passion for vivid colours and light first surfaced because everything in Room Seven sported a variation of buff or brown: walls, lino, desks, even the paint on the sashes of our little barred window. There were not even any street sounds to liven up the place: Seomra a Seacht was at the back of the department and looked out only on the equally small dull windows of the office block behind ours.

In my case, the work entailed nothing more than the transcription of addresses on to manila envelopes under the claustrophobic supervision of Miss O'Connor, our clerical officer. She insisted on checking every address I had written, ticking it off on the envelope with one of the red pencils she kept sharp as sewing-needles.

But I was in Dublin and I had my friends. I was free, funds permitting, to go to the cinema, the chipper, the ice-cream parlour or the occasional dance, if Maddy could be spared from her latest play.

Money, lack of, was the abiding problem for all three of us, but few office workers were flush in the Dublin of the middle and late sixties and everyone was fairly good humoured about it; the streets were full of bicycles and buses, unimpeded as yet by private cars, and it was easy and cheap to get around.

So, except for the irritations of my job, which I put up with because everyone did in the days before the word 'career' became permissible in girls' mouths, I was happy. My friends' kindness and jollying along also meant that I grew in confidence. So much so that by the time I met Michael – at a bus stop, would you believe? – I was bold enough at least to answer when he spoke to me.

It happened so easily. Juggling handbag, umbrella and the bag of buns I had just bought for my tea, I dropped the lot into a puddle in the gutter and he helped me pick them up. 'Cold evening.' He handed me the ruined buns.

'Thank you very much, yes,' I agreed, looking up at his long, lean face and managing to smile at him without blushing. 'And it looks like it's going to rain.'

'Good job you have the umbrella.'

'Yes, it is.'

'Are you waiting for the number ten?'

'I am.'

'Great. So am I.' He grinned.

On such banalities are everlasting memories forged.

Michael. As ever when I thought of him, I found myself smiling. With his forehead perpetually wrinkled as he pored over his journals and blurry photocopied articles, he would be so lost in concentration that I would have to go right up to his ear to call him to his tea, or his supper.

At least he was there for tea – unlike Jerry, whose meetings and evening functions spread their tentacles over our life to squeeze me out. On cue, I spotted my husband's distinctive stride as he cleaved through the ambling pedestrians. He had two baguettes under his arm.

So that was the end of the foolish little daydream in which I had pictured the two of us wandering hand in hand into a lovely little patisserie, perhaps to engage the buxom *patronne* in advising us as to our purchases. 'I spotted a bakery,' he folded himself on to the plastic chair, 'so I thought I'd save you the trouble.'

It always takes Jerry three full days, sometimes a week, to relax when he comes on holiday. True to form, his body now was as curved and tense as a bow and while waiting for me to finish my coffee, he was short only of drumming his fingers on the table. I pointed to the untouched cup in front of him, scummed with the cooled milk. 'Are you going to drink that? Will we get you another?'

He glanced at it. 'It looks disgusting. I'll have a cup when we get back. Ready?'

'I'll just finish this.' Doggedly, I sipped at my own cup. 'How much were the baguettes?'

'A few euros, who knows?'

I had merely been trying to make trivial conversation but gave up and put down my cup. It was plain that we had reached the end of our first marital outing to Collioure. 'I can't face the walk back up that hill,' I said matter-of-factly. 'We'll get a taxi. OK?'

'Fine.' He stood up immediately. 'The rank is over there on the other side of the bridge.'

As he paid the waitress, I took one last, longing look at the market stalls, then trooped obediently behind him towards the taxi stand.

When we pulled up in front of the villa, Jack was the first person I saw. He was sprawled on the grass by the pool, one hand stuck into the pocket of his jeans, the other supporting his mobile jammed against his ear. Beside me in the back of the taxi, I felt Jerry's tense body grow tighter: 'What's that fella doing?'

'Relax, Jerry, we can afford it. Anyway, someone might have called him.'

'Yes, we can afford it, but he can't. What has he ever contributed to this family besides lip? And even if someone has called him, have you never heard of roaming charges?' Before I could remonstrate further, he had flung a few notes at the taxi-driver and jumped out. As I waited for the change, I watched him approach Jack. He was too far away for me to hear what he was saying but it was not hard to guess. Nor was it difficult to understand Jack's body language as he snapped shut his mobile, stood up and stalked off.

I knew the episode had had little to do with the cost of mobile calls. Sometimes just the sight of Jack, or more usually Tom, sets Jerry off when he is preoccupied or in a tense mood. *Look away, Tess. Leave them to it, don't get in the middle.* So I took my own advice and turned my back on the house while I waited for the driver of the taxi, one of those big, saggy Citroëns, to sort out the change.

A great start to the day. And the walk down to the village had been a waste of energy, as far as I was concerned.

CHAPTER SEVEN

When I got into the kitchen, Ricky looked up from the crumb-covered table where he, Rita and two of their girls were gossiping over coffee and *pain au chocolat*. 'What's eating him? He marched through here like Napoleon's army!'

'First day.' I shrugged. 'You know how he is. He still hasn't left the office. He'll come round. Did Jack come through too?'

'Didn't see him. Want a cuppa? I'll get fresh.'

Rita lumbered to her feet.

There are some people who should never wear shorts and Rita is one of them, but Ricky never seems to mind how fat she gets. He slapped her heartily on the bottom as she passed him. 'Go on, ya fine thing. I'm a lucky man, eh, girls?'

'Puh-lease, Dad, spare me!' Alice, fourteen and their second youngest, curled her lip, but Patricia, younger again by two years and still at an age where she didn't feel she had to show public derision of her parents, laughed. The two of them were playing some form of complicated card game involving only the picture cards on the deck. Ricky was unabashed. 'Bring us in a hottener too, eh, Reet!' he called through to the kitchen.

I settled into my chair. 'Going to be a warm one, Ricky.'

'Yeah. Spare me!' Ricky suffered in the heat but was good natured enough never to object to the group's choice of holiday spots. Not for the first time I envied Rita's selection of partner.

When we were in Seomra a Seacht, Rita was the one whose all-consuming – indeed, only – temporal desire was to meet a nice man and get married. Her campaign would have done any army proud as she trawled the Dublin ballrooms, the National, the Olympic, the Crystal, even the Ierne Hall.

After one or two outings, I was not all that keen on accompanying her: she always set out with a sincere intention to look after me but her systematic manhunt meant I was frequently left to wilt on the margins of the dance-floor while she worked her way through the available talent.

Looks were not at the top of her agenda, as Ricky so ably demonstrates, but she did have a checklist, short but requiring strict compliance from any candidate: he had to be clean, he had to have good manners, he had to have a job with prospects. And, most importantly of all, he had to have no mother. Rita was from a poor background in the inner city and knew from experience that she would have been regarded with suspicion by any mother of a son for whom there were 'hopes'.

Her campaign proved successful and she carried off Ricky long before either Maddy or I had even come off the romantic starting blocks.

I remember the evening she met him. She and I had arrived at the so-called nurses' dance in Barry's Hotel just as the support band were winding up before the interval. We went immediately to the cloakroom to titivate, having to fight our way through the crush to get near the mirror. At least, Rita fought. I lurked behind the back row, waiting for her and trying not to inhale too much lacquer, perfume spray, cigarette smoke or the strong communal odour of underarm perspiration.

'Right, are you ready?' At last Rita pushed her way back towards me. Under her towering beehive, she was wearing a strapless, knee-length sheath in peach and cream-coloured striped taffeta. As was fashionable then, she was heavily made up with tan foundation, bright blue eye-shadow and pale lipstick. In retrospect, she looked like a big, multi-coloured ice-pop, or, more unkindly, a moving deck-chair. But she was no better or worse than most of the girls there that night. 'What's the matter, Teresa? You look like your granny just died! At least put on a bit of mascara – you're as white as a ghost.' She began to root in her handbag.

'No, thanks,' I said miserably. My own rig-out was a white top over a blue, wasp-waisted circular skirt patterned with white daisies. My hair was short and incapable of making a beehive and

I had always hated the feel of makeup. I was regretting, once again, having yielded to Rita's admonishments that I 'had to get out more'.

'What are we going to do with you?' She looked critically at me, as though she was my mother. 'Buck up, kiddo. You'll never get asked up looking like that. You've a lovely smile, Teresa girl,' her voice softened, 'now use it. Come on. The dance'll be half over and all the best fellas'll be spoken for – excuse *me*!' She glared indignantly at an interloper trying to squeeze between us, then grabbed my hand. 'Come on, up at 'em!'

As we came out into the heaving ballroom, Eileen Reid and her band, the Cadets, were gearing up on stage. She was, still is, a great belter, with a breezy, humorous presentation and a person-ality bursting through the buttons of the quasi-naval uniform she wore. As they swung into the first number, I slunk off to take up my usual position as a wallflower but, surprisingly, Rita came with me. 'Look, over there,' she hissed into my ear, taking such a tight grip on my upper arm that I helped.

'Where? What?'

'Over there,' she let me go, 'beside that gang standing at the pillar.'

I looked. All I could see was an ordinary crowd of sweating, red-faced young men pushing, shoving and egging each other on, pretending not to notice that there were any girls in the room but all the while sizing us up and preparing to make a move.

'That fella in the brown jacket. Him!' She grabbed my arm again. 'But be careful. Look, look, he's getting up with that young one with the glasses. Don't let him see us watching.'

Obediently, I peered from under my eyebrows. The group in question was fanning out towards the press of girls. The boy in the brown jacket was smaller than the rest, and as young as we were, but he carried himself a little differently from the others as he took his chosen partner into the centre of the floor to be swallowed out of sight. 'I saw him,' I said, having to shout now to be heard above Eileen Reid's exuberance, 'what about him?'

'Let's watch him,' she yelled. 'I think I could have a go, there.'

And that was how Rita chose Ricky.

The high-ceilinged French kitchen where he and I sat with

their daughters waiting for her reappearance with the coffee was cavernous, with a flagged floor, rush mats and enormous storage cupboards. Although it had a sink, electric cooker and a big American fridge, all the food preparation was done in a second kitchen just off it. In this, through the open doorway, we could see and hear our cook chopping salad vegetables and chatting with the general housekeeper in a language that I realised was not French. Yet both women looked French and had been introduced to us as Yvette and Marcelle, names as French as they come.

'It's Catalan, apparently.' Rita saw my interest in the chatter as she came back in with an enamelled coffee pot and a mug. Before pouring mine, she deftly topped up Ricky's: 'Get that down yiz, the two of yiz now.' She laughed. 'It'll put hair on your chest. Want a croissant, Tess? This chocolate bread is fantastic.'

'No, thanks.'

She was right about the coffee, so strong it invited chewing. 'Are Kitty and Carol up too?' To hell with diets, I thought, and broke off a chunk of *pain au chocolat*.

'Still asleep.' Rita took another piece for herself. 'Don't worry, I'll roust them out of it in a minute. They won't know what hit them! Want me to give Tom a shout?'

'Ah, leave them. Sure what's the rush?' As Ricky stretched his little arms luxuriously above his head, his wife leaned over to tickle him, to his obvious delight.

Suddenly I was jealous of this family's togetherness, of their easy manner with each other, so different from the polite, spiky quadrilles we had been conducting lately at Arkady. 'I think I'll take this out to the terrace,' I said, picking up the coffee. 'It's such a gorgeous day.'

'Do that.' Rita plonked herself down again beside Ricky.

I was punished for my mean-mindedness because, by contrast to the relaxation in the kitchen, the atmosphere on the terrace, despite the sunshine, was dour and I was immediately sorry I had come out.

Fergus and Maddy were seated at one of the white, cast-iron tables, a bottle of Evian water between them. He was frowning over a script, using a pink highlighter to mark up his lines; Maddy, whose thin face was drawn and pale, was sipping daintily at her water. In the clear Mediterranean light, I noticed that her skin had become translucent and quite wrinkled where the supporting flesh had dissolved beneath it.

And since when had her shoulders resembled coat-hangers? Although she had been wearing the same sundress the previous day, I had been too harassed during check-in to notice that she had become almost skeletal. We all knew Maddy was on a perpetual diet, as I was, but compared to her I sported the frame of a hippopotamus.

She smiled immediately on seeing me. 'Nice walk?'

'Would have been if I hadn't been with the Road Runner.'

'Ah, he'll get over it. Fergus will sort him out on the golf course tomorrow, won't you, darling?' Fergus is by far the best of the husbands at golf, probably because he has a lot of free time to practise.

'Hmm?' He looked up from his script.

'Apparently Jerry needs to wind down, surprise, surprise. I said you'd give him what-for at the golf tomorrow?'

'Sure. Whatever.' He returned to his script and she threw another smile in my direction. 'This is a film script Fergus has been sent. It's being directed by a real Hollywood director. Fingers crossed!'

It pained me to see and hear this brightness. Where Fergus Griggs was concerned, the novelty of having a celebrity in our midst had worn off the rest of us long ago and after years of making allowances, Rita and I have agreed that we cannot stand him. Of course, we would never betray this to poor Maddy who, in the service of his ego, has gradually worn herself into a shadow of the wild, enthusiastic whirlwind we used to know.

Tactfully, we have also gone along with her assertion that she has not been frustrated by giving up her own acting ambitions to support his. 'You can't really have two actors in the same family,' she said to us one evening, when we were being particularly honest about our marriages. 'It's hard enough for poor Fergus without having me preoccupied with the same career, and what would happen if I got better parts than him? You can imagine! A man needs support. I'll be fine. I was never going to make it anyway.'

Maddy's husband earns their money through his portrayal of a warm-hearted, quizzical hotel-keeper, lodestone of a long-running and popular soap opera on RTE. As such he is famous and much loved among the general public. He maintains his affable on-screen image when he is out and about, but in reality he is insecure and hugely disappointed that starring in the small fishbowl of Irish television, with the addition of a few parts in straight-to-video movies, has been the height of his achievement. His need for reassurance is insatiable.

There is something else. While Jerry could be termed thrifty, his diatribes about our profligacy are formulaic. He is not mean. Fergus, on the other hand, is a downright Scrooge. We don't know what he earns, I doubt that even Maddy knows, but given his pivotal part in the show, he has to be well paid – otherwise they could not have afforded to live in their fairly upmarket estate of detached, five-bedroomed houses in the southside suburbs of Dublin. But he questions every penny his wife spends, scrutinises every utility bill and calls her to account for any wastefulness he detects. During these holidays, all three husbands groan showily about the extravagance of us wives. With Ricky and, to a lesser extent, Jerry, this is simply a blokeish mantra but Fergus means it: if Maddy splashes out on so much as a headscarf she never hears the end of it.

Rita and I conspire with the fiction that our friend works part-time in a ritzy swap shop simply to occupy her time but we know she does it to keep herself in clothes.

I had no choice but to sit down with them. 'Hi, Colm!' I called across to their son, sprawled on the deck-chair and staring glumly over the balustrade. 'Seen Jack?'

'No,' he mumbled.

'Why don't you have a swim, darling?' Maddy beamed at him. 'It's such a lovely pool?'

'I will,' he did not turn to face her, 'later.'

'He's a bit down,' she whispered to me. 'We wouldn't let him bring his laptop – we're hoping that without it he'll be forced to get a bit of fresh air and exercise. Especially because he says the computer here is crap. Not enough gigs or rams or something to run whatever it is he wants to run on it.'

Colm is a technology geek. I have always felt sorry for him without knowing why. He is an intelligent kid, probably sensitive, but since he makes no effort to be sociable it is hard to tell. Jack has no time for him, and Rita's girls, who used to try to include him in their activities, were repelled so often that they gave up. His pale, pimply complexion doesn't help, and on him, his mother's petite frame looks merely underfed. Privately, I believe poor Colm suffers from his father's dislike and his mother's disappointment that she could never produce a brother or sister for him.

'So, what time are we all going down to the beach?' Maddy clapped her hands with overstated delight. 'What a treat! I promised myself I'd drink only wine this holiday, but wine's very heavy at this hour of the morning so I think I'll have a little G and T. How about you, Tess?'

When I declined, she turned to her husband, still immersed in his film script. 'You, Fergus? Would you like a beer or something?'

Fergus glanced pointedly at his watch, his mouth pursed like a ferret's. Madeleine pretended not to notice his disapproval. 'Come on, we're on holiday!' she cried gaily. 'And I for one am going to enjoy myself! I'll get you a Coke, Colm.'

As she left the terrace to fetch the drinks, I watched her go, then glared, ineffectually, at the poll of Fergus Griggs's head, lowered again over his papers.

CHAPTER EIGHT

While Maddy, the girls, Jack and even Colm played a noisy game of beach volleyball against the three husbands, Rita and I sat under our parasols sporadically watching Tom build a small, tottering sandcastle, knock it down, then build it again. Over and over. He had refused to don a swimsuit and was dressed in shorts and the T-shirt currently in favour, a threadbare item from which the logo had long since faded. Rita made no comment, thank God. I don't have to be defensive about Tom's eccentricities with her; almost alone among my friends and relatives, she accepts him as he is. Everyone should have a friend like her.

We three had met when the marriage bar still existed in the civil service, and after her wedding anyone but Rita would have become just a memory, briefly sustained for the first few years at Christmas with an exchange of cards. But she stayed in touch, inviting us often to her new home in a corporation house in Finglas, outside the city and regarded by culchies like Maddy and myself as Wild West territory, little better than where we had come from. She made even that little place so cushy and welcoming, however, so unlike the dingy digs we inhabited, that Maddy and I trekked out to it at every opportunity for tea and a bit of mollycoddling.

'I could get used to this!' She stretched her legs now, wiggling her toes. Then, smoothing the polka-dotted expanse of her strapless two-piece, constructed, it seemed, over some sort of wire cage: 'I'd hate to tell you how much this cost.'

'Then don't.' I smiled affectionately at her. My own suit, one-piece, modest and black, had cost a bomb too, but didn't look it. I suppose that is the essence of cool, as Rita's Kitty would say.

'All right, I won't.' She shifted and wriggled a little in the sand to create a trench for herself. 'But what I paid for this would probably have fed an African village for a year.' She lay back and closed her eyes.

The beach was glorious, a vast blue-flag expanse of coarse white sand stretching for miles. We had brought all the gear supplied by the villa, parasols, windbreaks, folding chairs, beach-mats, and had pitched camp near the water's edge to take advantage of the considerable breeze which ameliorated the heat, now twenty-nine degrees according to Colm, who had a temperature gauge incorporated in his wristwatch. For this first afternoon, we had chosen to come to Argelès-sur-mer just a few kilometres from Collioure because, according to the leaflets left for us in the villa, there would be lots of water sports for the youngsters and a wide choice of restaurants in all categories.

There was one advantage of being here in May: we had acres of beach space to ourselves. However, our early arrival was also to our disadvantage: Argelès, a sprawling town with a multitude of car parks and a vast promenade, was seasonal and now only partially operational. Behind the prom, set well back among the restaurants, there was a mall of sports, clothing and souvenir shops and outdoor stalls. Those that were open displayed a variety of cheap clothes, pareos, ceramics, candles, shoes, local and Oriental art and second-hand books. Most, frustratingly, were locked.

Secretly, I have always liked the mournful atmosphere of a seaside resort out of season. An expanse of deserted sand brings back childhood memories of outings to the rainswept if magnificent beach at Enniscrone, a short journey from Ballina, where, despite goosebumps and sodden feet, Daddy, Mammy and I ate ice-cream with stoic determination. We were here, and because we'd made the effort, *we were going to enjoy ourselves*.

Rita, who would opine that my fondness for sad, empty spaces fits perfectly with my fetish for mourning music, now raised herself up a little and looked over her shoulder towards the volleyball match: 'Speaking of African villages, what are we going to do with her, Tess? She looks dreadful.'

'I agree. I got a fright when I saw her. You don't see it in the winter under all those jumpers.'

We watched as Maddy ran to retrieve a ball. As she leaned over to pick it up, I saw that the cups of her bikini top were redundant, riding on nothing, as on a pre-pubescent child. 'Should we say something?' Rita lowered her voice: 'Is she anorexic, do you think? I've no experience with this. Would we make things worse?'

'Better not. I saw a documentary on TV a few weeks ago and apparently one of the things anorexics do is cover themselves up completely in huge clothes to avoid attention. She's certainly not doing that so it's possible she's just dieting too much. Anorexia is very complex. Most times apparently, it has little to do with food. It's about trying to hold something within your own control, like your body. Let's not rush to judgement just yet, let's wait for a few days. Anyway, this holiday might do her the world of good. A few gins will loosen her up. We'll watch her. OK?'

'That's another thing.' She leaned closer. 'I feel awful bringing this up, but now that you've mentioned it, have you twigged she's first up to the bar, these days? First, second, third and fourth?'

'No, I hadn't actually.' I looked at my nails. This was not fully true: because I had noticed over the past year that, during any outing, Maddy was indeed always the first to suggest a drink – and the first to have a refill.

Rita took the hint that it would be disloyal to continue on this tack. 'Would you look at him.' Her tone had changed. 'He can't resist showing off, the little gutty!'

I followed her line of sight and saw Maddy's husband diving showily for the ball and missing. He keeps himself in shape, though, and, probably because of his very public profession, sports a perma-tan, which in the sunlight had taken on an orange hue. Beside him, Jerry's beanpole figure, although healthy and fit, resembled a tall, waving daisy. 'Isn't my fella a great trier, all the same?' Rita chuckled as Ricky, paunch wobbling, punched the next return into the net. 'I'll have to put him on a diet when we get home. Don't want him dying on me with a heart-attack.'

She turned back to face me. 'Do you miss Michael?' she asked, as quietly as the sea and the general happy uproar would allow. 'His anniversary is this month, isn't it?'

'I do miss him sometimes, and yes – it's been eleven years. On the twenty-second. Wednesday of next week.' I didn't feel like talking about Michael, or any relationships, just now. She looked sharply at me before lying back on her towel and raising her face to the sun. 'Sorry, I hope I didn't upset you.' She closed her eyes. 'Isn't this blissful, Tess? Isn't the breeze wonderful? Will you ever forget bloody Marrakech that time?' We had spent most of that Moroccan month languishing in the air-conditioning of the hotel. 'Let's hope this holiday will be one of the ones to remember.'

'It will.'

Tom was still engaged with his sandcastles so I picked up my paperback and attempted to read. But the typeface was small and it became a chore to follow the closely packed lines in the white flare of the sun.

I let it rest on my lap and, head propped on my inflated pillow, stared out to where an instructor in a small dinghy with an outboard motor was patiently instructing a class of windsurfers, obviously beginners to judge by the number struggling in the water. Beyond them the water was empty, except for a banana inflatable bouncing along the wavelets and a motorboat idling along, towing a paraglider who hung from the blue sky on a rope that seemed to be as fine as spider silk. Rita had hit a nerve. I do miss Michael, sometimes more than others, but always coming up to his anniversary.

That Tuesday eleven years ago was the nadir of my life then, even worse than Mammy's death. You kiss your husband goodbye at the doorway of your house with your feeding baby in your arms; you say something jokily insulting to him about his daffy appearance, something you have tried and tried to remember but never can; two hours later you answer that same door to a Gárda and a Ban-Ghárda: 'May we come in, Mrs Butler?'

I knew immediately. My life had unreeled to that moment and the odd thing was that, although I was shattered, I was not surprised. It was my own fault if I was upset. For a little while, as my marriage bedded in, I had forgotten to stay alert.

Tom was resting from his labours with the sand. 'Don't suck your thumb, darling.' The admonition was automatic but I had little hope of being obeyed; his front teeth arch like a little Bridge of Sighs and will soon need attention from an orthodontist. In many ways I have only myself to blame: I had suffered from the bitter aloes spread on all my fingers to little effect by my own mother and had refused to countenance all the traditional deterrents, believing them too cruel. He glanced at me curiously while keeping his thumb firmly jammed between his lips, looking for an instant so like his pipe-smoking father that I was jolted.

Poor Michael. Knocked down by a bus while crossing a street. Such a prosaic accident to extinguish such a gleeful, searching spirit.

I sat up and checked Tom's shoulders to make sure they were not burning. 'Try, Tom, at least try to give that thumb a break for a few minutes. Are you hot? Would you like a drink, a Coke or something?'

'No, thank you.'

'I'm going for a swim, would you like to come in with me?'

'OK.' I had not been expecting acquiescence but, to my astonishment, he stood up immediately and set off towards the water, just a few yards away. 'Hold on, Tom, wait for me.' I threw down the paperback, struggled to my feet and caught him just as he was entering the sea, which shelved steeply. 'Don't run away on me like that, darling, we don't know how dangerous this sea is.'

'There's a lifeguard up there,' he said, absorbed in watching the way the swelling water was painting dark crescents on his shorts.

'Where?'

'On top of the tower.'

I looked round. Sure enough, about a hundred yards to my left, I could see the wooden structure. My eyesight is not as good as my son's, of course, and although I could not see any figure seated on the lookout chair, I had to take his word for it. In any event, he was already fifty feet away, swimming strongly out to sea. One of his more unusual talents is that, with very little teaching from us or anyone else, he swims like a seal, powering up and down the lanes of the pool until he, and he alone, feels he has swum enough. Many were the times I had given myself a full manicure while waiting for him to be finished. I plunged in.

I was out of my depth after just a few strokes. The water did not feel cold but it was choppy and slapped against my face as I breasted directly into an onshore wind. After the tenth mouthful of salty wavelet I decided I had had enough. I could still see Tom, treading water now, beside where the windsurfers' instructor was patrolling up and down alongside his charges. I yelled that I was going back, getting another mouthful of brine in the process, but the breeze whipped away my words and he did not react.

I swam back until my feet touched the sand and turned round to check again. The back of his small head bobbed easily over the chop as he continued to watch the windsurfing school.

'That didn't take long. How was it?' Rita protected her expensive two-piece against an onslaught of sand and sea-water while I towelled myself. 'It's lovely, but I've a confession to make. I'd prefer a pool.' Gazing out to sea again, I pulled a comb through my hair. It was hard to pick him out now, but I did. He still had not moved. I should probably organise a few windsurfing lessons for him if he was that interested, I thought, but I would leave it up to him to ask.

The volleyball game was still in progress, although I could see that Patricia and Alice were taking time out for a rest. Surprisingly, Colm was giving it real welly. So was Jack. Could there be a testosterone contest going on between the two in front of the fair Kitty?

I flopped down beside Rita. 'Can I ask you a personal question, Rita? What do you really want out of your life?'

'I beg your pardon?'

'You heard me. I really want to know.'

'Having a mid-life crisis, are we?' She laughed and inserted both hands inside the wiring of her swimsuit to ease it out a little. 'I got fitted but this is bloody killing me, dammit. Vanity, vanity . . .' She sighed. 'Listen, this is supposed to be a holiday, Tess, not a self-help seminar. Anyway, it's a bit late to be asking that now, isn't it?'

'Is it?'

She raised herself on one elbow. 'You're in a funny mood. Is something the matter?'

'Oh, I don't know. Nothing I can put my finger on. But it's everything too.' The thought flashed through my mind that if I could confide in anyone about those brief, weird out-of-body experiences, it was Rita. But I discarded it. She was right: now was not the time. 'These days, I'm fed up for no reason that I can describe, Rita. Or that I could describe without being thought of as an ungrateful bitch.'

'*Tess!*' Shocked, she sat up. My 'thing' about bad or profane language, except for the relatively milder epithets, is a hangover from my convent days and is the target of gentle teasing within our group. 'There's no one here except us two,' I said rebelliously, 'and I mean it. It would be ungrateful to complain. How many people would love to be in my shoes, your shoes, our shoes? Look at Arkady, look at your place, look at this lovely villa we're in at the moment. We don't have to slum it with the plebs in holiday apartments with walls like paper. Our kids are healthy, our husbands support us and don't beat us. And without it costing us a thought, you and I have each paid the equivalent of some people's monthly mortgages for a *swimsuit*, for God's sake. We're the lucky ones in this world, Rita.

'Did it ever occur to you that since we left the civil service, neither of us has had to do a tap of paid work? Maddy as well.'

'I work – you work. Working in the home is beginning to be seen as a career option.' Rita was becoming offended. 'And thank God for it!'

'Yes, but do you never feel guilty?'

'No! I don't! Are you going leftie on me?'

I realised how pompous I'd sounded and had to laugh. 'Of course not.'

'So what are you on about, then?' She lay back again. 'Has something happened between you and Jerry?'

'Nothing more than usual,' I threw myself on to my stomach and picked up my book. 'Sorry I brought it up. I'm just being stupid.'

'You're not.' She was watching me closely. 'But I have to say it's not the kind of question I ask myself any more. What more can I want? What more can you want, Tess? You listed it all off yourself.'

'I know. Just tell me to shut up.'

'What are pals for?'

We lay quietly for a few minutes. Again, I tried to concentrate on the thriller, but my attention drifted away so that I had to go back to the top of the page a second time. When I found myself rereading its first sentence for the third time I gave up and closed it.

What was the source of this dissatisfaction? Why, when I truly had no right to complain about my life, did I visualise myself as a body with no core? Rita had been flippant about a mid-life crisis but might well have hit on the truth. Was it as simple – and as complicated – as that? A few handfuls of HRT and I could go back to being Sunny Tess, the People's Friend?

CHAPTER NINE

The volleyball game seemed to be winding down as first Kitty, then Maddy crashed on to the sand beside us. 'That's that done for this year, thank God.' Maddy's thin ribcage was heaving. 'I'm getting too old for this.'

'Serves you right for volunteering.' Rita wriggled deeper into the comfy hollow she had made for herself in the sand. 'Listen,' she asked dreamily, 'want to baz off, just us three? We could get our hair done, or have an ice-cream?'

'But today is Family Day.' This was Maddy, still breathless.

'Ah, bugger that.' Rita snorted. 'At home, every day is Family Day for us. Anyway, girls, we're getting settled into a rut with these holidays, such-and-such a day for this, such-and-such a day for that,' she pulled a disparaging face, 'because that's the way we've always done it. It's getting like Butlins. Holidays are supposed to be so we can have new experiences. Have we forgotten?'

I pointed out that getting our hair done was hardly a new experience. 'Anyone feel like a game of tennis?'

Neither of them did, of course. 'Certainly not with you, Billie-Jean!' Rita was appalled at the idea of such violent activity.

'I know what Rita means, Tess,' Maddy piped up. 'Maybe it's time we took stock of this whole group-holiday thing.'

I was surprised, to say the least. Whatever about some of the routines, it had never occurred to me to question the edifice that housed them, but I could see from Rita's face that it had occurred to her too.

'Well, I like them. I don't want to change!' Kitty, whose long, nut-brown hair was caught up behind her head in a scrunchie, stood up and wound it tighter still. She was turning into a beauty, I thought, petite and totally in proportion, with pale, lightly freckled skin and violet eyes. It was not surprising that Jack and Colm had been strutting their stuff in front of her. 'I'm going in for a dip,' she said, 'and while I'm gone don't make any decisions about future holidays. We should have a say too, you know, and much as I love you and Dad and the girls, Mam, it would be too, too boring to spend a month on our own.' She glanced quickly, almost furtively, towards the volleyball net.

Aha! I thought. So there is something going on between her and Jack. Or her and Colm, although that would have astonished me.

'Don't stay in too long,' Rita warned, 'you don't feel it with this breeze but you know how you burn.'

'Oh, Mam.' Kitty threw a handful of sand on to her mother's belly. 'Put on your glasses. I'm wearing a goddamned T-shirt.'

'Language, Kitty! There's a nun present.'

'Don't mind her, Kit,' I said lazily. 'I've just been in, you'll enjoy it, the water's lovely. Keep an eye on Tom, will you? He's out there gawping at the windsurfers.'

'Where?' She turned to gaze out at the sea. 'I don't see him.'

I sat up. 'He's probably too far out to see him from here, honey. It's hard to distinguish one head from another.'

I stood up. I was not worried. Like I said, Tom swims like a seal. It is one of the triumphs I always mention when other mothers are boasting about their offspring's achievements.

I walked down to the water's edge and scanned the surface of the sea. The windsurfers' guide boat was motoring back towards the shore, mother duck being followed in a bedraggled line by her ducklings; the paraglider was descending slowly. Only the banana boat was still beavering away at full throttle. No sign of Tom.

Kitty came to stand beside me. 'See him, Auntie Tess?'

'Not yet. But he swims like a seal, you know that.'

'Yeah. Remember in Crete when he wore out that guy in the pool and won a hundred drachmas?'

I smiled. 'Yeah.'

I was not worried in the slightest. Yet those sea-diamonds winking at the sun were no longer merely irritants to the leisure swimmer like me but snares to trap small boys and suck them under. 'You keep an eye, Kitty, will you?' I spoke as calmly as a guru. 'It's time he came in. I'm afraid he'll burn. I'm going up to get Jerry. He's a much better swimmer than I am. In the meantime, if you spot him, yell!'

'Sure, Aunt Tess. Don't worry.'

'Oh, I'm not worried.' I smiled at her again, then walked unhurriedly past our camp and Rita towards my husband. 'Listen, Jerry,' I said, when I reached him, 'Tom's in swimming, but I can't see him. I'm not worried, of course, because he swims like a seal, but he's been in for a while and I'm afraid he'll get sunburned. Would you mind going in to get him? You're a much better swimmer than I am.'

Jerry was covered in sweat and his fine, floppy hair was plastered to his head. 'Sure,' he said genially. He is always in better form after punishing physical exercise. 'We've just about finished here anyway. I'm afraid we men whipped the women and children as usual.'

'So, what else is new?' I smiled. My lips began to feel as though they were glued to my teeth. 'Thanks, Jerry.'

I walked beside him to the sea's edge. Kitty was in the shallows now. Jerry kicked off his beach sandals and joined her. 'Any sign of him?'

'Not so far.'

'Where did you see him last?' He turned to me as I too reached Kitty. 'Straight ahead, maybe sixty, seventy yards out. He was watching the windsurfers, by the rope there, but they're finished. There they are,' I pointed, 'they're all on the way in now.'

'Right. Not to worry, lass.' He patted my arm. 'He's probably out already, digging a hole to China.' He plunged head first into the water, surfaced, then swam out strongly.

Kitty and I watched him for a few moments. 'Uncle Jerry's right,' she said. 'Why don't I go one way and you the other?'

'Fine. We'll do that.'

I walked along the beach, watching Jerry over my shoulder but also searching through the sparse groups of holidaymakers and locals on the beach.

Nothing could have happened to Tom. He swims like a seal –

there is that, of course – but he was surrounded by people at all times and there was a lifeguard on duty. I peered towards the lifeguard's tower. Now that I was closer, I could see there was no one in the chair.

It did not matter, really. If anything had happened, if he had swallowed too much water and got sick, for instance, or if he had been badly stung by a jellyfish, or got a cramp, or if that damned banana boat had hit him on the head so that he had lost consciousness, if anything like that had happened there were people around. Someone would have spotted his difficulty.

And he was no longer a baby. An eleven-year-old is quite sensible, really. Certainly able to draw attention to any trouble he might be in.

Jerry was a good distance out, almost as far as the rope.

On the map, this part of the Mediterranean is called the Gulf of the Lion, and today you could certainly see why. Was it my imagination or was the wind strengthening? Some of those chops out there had developed little white horses . . .

Jerry had stopped swimming. I could see him hanging on to one of the barrels supporting the swimmers' rope. He was looking right and left.

I stopped too. There were hardly any swimmers as far out as he was. Those little white horses were definitely jumping higher now . . .

But the sun was still shining. And this was the Med, for God's sake.

Then I saw Jerry waving at me, trying to catch my attention. Dear God, he looked as though he was signalling urgently—

Like a bull elephant charging through a picket fence, panic burst through my defences and I could see Tom's greenish little face drifting below the surface of the water. I could see huge crabs nipping at his eyes, big, spiny things getting caught in his hair. Just in time, I stopped the scream that bubbled up into my mouth but it hung around just below my throat as I ran into the shallows and, heedless this time of the slapping, choking water, swam frantically towards my husband who was already returning to the shore. 'What's happened?' I could barely get the words out when I reached him.

He was calm. 'Look behind you, woman!'

'Where? Why?' I turned so quickly I went under, then, spluttering, resurfaced. 'I can't see anything.'

'Who's that with Kitty, coming along the edge of the sand?'

Treading water, I peered in the direction he indicated. Sure enough, it was Tom, trailing casually behind Rita's daughter. The breath I had been holding expelled itself from my chest and I almost sank again.

'Sorry, Jerry, I'm really sorry. I just overreacted.'

'He is eleven years of age, Tess. He's not a baby.' Because Tom was my son and not Jerry's, because I knew this relatively mild criticism concealed a much denser forest of impatience with Tom's behaviour, or maybe because it echoed the thought I had voiced to myself, I went immediately on the defensive. I was in no position, however, to remonstrate and a row would have been ridiculous in these circumstances, both of us immersed to our chins, Beckett-like, in choppy water. 'Thanks for swimming out to look for him, anyway. I freaked when I couldn't see him.'

'No problem. I'm going in.' He swam away from me, leaving me slowly to follow.

I was seriously rattled, and not only because of what Tom had done and my reaction. I spend a great deal of psychic energy anticipating how Jerry will react to Tom. Events had knocked out my customary caution.

By the time I reached our spot on the beach, I had myself well under control. Kitty and Tom were already seated beside Rita and Ricky and she was helping him with his resumed interest in sandcastles, Jerry was towelling himself, Colm, Jack, Alice and Carol were listening to their headphones, Patricia was reading and Maddy was oiling her legs. Although there was no sign of Fergus, everyone else was on the radar.

Kitty relinquished her interest in the sandcastles and I sat in front of my son. 'How come you got out of the water, Tom? You gave me a fright. I couldn't see you.' I said it loudly enough for Jerry to hear.

Tom did not look up. 'I saw Daddy,' he said. 'He called me out of the water through his loudspeaker. He said I'd been in there long enough and that it was going to get more waves and that I might be in danger.'

'But you couldn't have seen Daddy, darling,' I said, taken aback. 'Daddy's in heaven. Where did you think you saw him?'

'Up on the tower.' He patted the little heap of sand in front of him. 'He's a lifeguard.'

'Did you speak to him after you got out?'

'I went over to the tower but he was gone when I got there.' Pat. Pat.

'How did you know it was him?'

He shot me one of the considering looks (*Do I have to explain everything?*) in which he specialised. 'He's my daddy. It was him.'

I glanced around but Kitty, who was nearest to us, had now donned her headphones. No one else was listening.

'What did he look like?'

'The same as always. He was wearing goggles.'

'Swimming goggles?'

'Don't know. They were big.'

No matter what I said, Tom was unshakeable in his conviction that he had seen Michael; he was uninterested in discussing it or expanding on the experience. Finally, he shut me out.

It was the first time I had come up against this in practice but I was reminded forcefully of something the headmistress of his school, a wise old nun, had said to me once during a parent-teacher meeting. I had approached her to ask what I should do next to sort out Tom's 'problem'. (At one stage I was bending ears and asking opinions of practically everyone I met. I was certainly a bore on the subject.)

The nun, a huge woman with a farmer's hands, gazed at me. Then she pulled me aside into a corner of the room, out of the general hubbub. 'He's a strange little boy,' she said. 'Different. And although I believe you shouldn't, I can see how you'd worry. Parents worry so much, these days, don't they?'

'With good cause, Sister.' Paranoid as always on the subject of my parenting skills, I was trying to winkle out what rebuke had been implied.

'Mmm, maybe.' She smiled. 'We don't encourage difference in our society any more, do we? But Jesus was different, when you think about it, and although I don't know too much about Mozart's life, I'm sure he caused his parents a few headaches.'

I seized on this. 'Mozart? Are you telling me Tom might be gifted?' The nun chuckled. 'Now, now, Mrs Brennan!' she chided gently. 'I think if young Tom is a genius, this is as yet undiscovered.' She thought a bit. Then: 'You should probably encourage his drawing. He seems to love that.'

'Yes, maybe.' Privately, I was doubtful. Tom's artwork had never seemed to me to be anything special. He tended to copy objects over and over again until he was satisfied.

'There is one thing I would be a little concerned about.' The nun fingered the silver cross hanging neatly against her blouse. 'I'm sure you know that he makes up stories about his dead father, as if he's still alive.'

This was serious news, which raised more questions than offered explanations. If he did, why did Tom 'make up stories' about Michael at school and not at home? 'But he couldn't remember his father.' I flew to defend myself, blushing with guilt as though I had personally murdered the father of my baby. 'He was so young when Michael was killed. I've hawked him around counsellors and consultants, Sister, an army of them, and not one has reckoned my husband's death as being a factor. They've ruled it out. They've all said that Tom is confident, even well adjusted, if you can believe that . . .' I laughed uneasily, watching for her reaction.

The nun smiled gently. 'Yes. But we have no idea, really, do we? Only God knows how much even the youngest mind can absorb and what it can be affected by. If a baby in the womb can be calmed by hearing music in its mother's bedroom, who knows what that baby can hear and understand once its born. Science has not caught up with God yet, has it, Mrs Brennan?'

I had not been exaggerating when I referred to an army of experts. An MIR scan had shown no abnormalities or brain injuries. Psychologists and psychiatrists I had consulted had discounted syndromes like ADD and Asperger's.

Tom is able to communicate brilliantly when he wants to, but only when he wants to. It appears he ran rings round the professionals. Less than six months before that conversation with the nun, the last man, an eminent counsellor recommended by one of Jerry's work colleagues, even admitted as much to me: 'He's way ahead of me, Mrs Brennan.' We were talking at the man's gate.

'But why is he so odd?' I glanced round to where Tom waited for me in the car. He wasn't trying to eavesdrop on our conversation, although he knew it had to be about him. He was playing with his Gameboy.

'We're all odd in our own way,' said the counsellor. 'Tom is just one of those rare people who doesn't try to hide his oddness. That's my impression anyhow. I'm afraid it isn't very helpful. And I think, well, I *hope*, you'll find he'll grow out of it, whatever "it" is. My advice is to try to find some way of stimulating that imagination of his, art, perhaps, or music, or acting. In the meantime, he's not disruptive, he's not unhappy and I think you're wasting your money bringing him to me. But don't take my word for it. I'll give you the name of someone who has had very good results with kids of all sorts when the rest of us are stumped.' He took a notepad out of his breast pocket and scribbled a name on it.

I had not yet used that telephone number. And on that beach in Argelès-sur-mer, as I watched my son's earnest engineering with his plastic spade, I decided to drop the search for answers. In prospecting for a flawless little boy, I had been guilty of hubris and, from now on, I would leave Tom's timetable and Tom's childhood to Tom. I would be his mother, not his shrink, and he and I together would build ramparts against all-comers.

I looked around for Jerry. Stretched on the sand a small distance from the parasols, eyes closed, belly to the sun, he seemed soft and vulnerable and I knew how fundamentally I loved him. Yet I also knew that Jerry's continuing disapproval of Tom would be difficult to withstand.

Fergus rejoined us. He was flushed, not just from exertion or heat. He told us he had to fly home immediately. He had just been on to his agent in response to a text message: his television series had been axed.

CHAPTER TEN

'It's difficult to believe there was no hint. You must have seen it coming.' We were in council in the drawing room, with Jerry, our leader, piloting the discussion. The youngsters were watching satellite TV somewhere about the house and Tom's episode – my episode – no longer rated.

As for the holiday, it was disintegrating: it looked now as if we would have no males, at least no adult males, in the villa for the last week.

'I had no idea, none of us had, bastards, shites! Apparatchiks!' Fergus, whose flight home was already booked for the following day, pounded a fist on the arm of his chair. 'It's typical, isn't it? The cast is always the last to know.'

The evening sun mellowed the parquet and the muted colours in the room, everything except the mood. Maddy's eyes were enormous in her pale face as she continued to debate with herself about going home with him, a debate that became more repetitive – and more agonising – with each gin and tonic. 'Of course,' she refilled her glass and downed a healthy mouthful, 'as I think I've said already, we'll have to ask Colm, it has to be his decision.'

'Shower of bean-counters!' Her husband paced the room, a traditional parlour with faded but exquisite wallpaper, heavy furniture and lace on every chair and sofa arm – in fact, on every horizontal surface, except the ceiling and the floor.

Although I had sympathy for Fergus's predicament, I could not suppress the thought, as he became increasingly angry, of what his loving public would think of their jolly hotel proprietor if they could see him now. What was more, his pacing struck me somehow as too theatrical: it seemed to me that he was seizing his moment in the limelight rather too fervently and had jumped the gun in insisting on going home immediately. But, then, it was all very well for me: I was not the one whose livelihood was at stake.

Nevertheless, I could not get away from the sense that he had seized on this as an opportunity rather than a necessity. 'Do you have to go, Fergus?' I offered. 'After all, if you don't have to rehearse, if there's going to be no series, what's the point? Your going home is not going to make them change their minds, is it? And this holiday is paid for, why not enjoy it?'

'Don't be stupid, Tess! I have to be there, I have to show them that we're not going to take this lying down. And I have to see my agent. I'm not going to let them cast me on the scrap heap just like that. I've been in that series for nine years, I *am* Chester Malone – I've handed over my bloody life to that character. I'm his bloody face and identity, for God's sake. Taxi drivers call me Chester, the shawlies in Moore Street call me Chester, the dogs in the street piss on Chester's shoes! Who's going to cast me as anything else now? Bastards!'

I felt so sorry for Maddy, whose distress, like grey dust, curdled the air. I turned to her, reiterating the suggestion that she should stay, and was immediately echoed by Ricky and Rita.

'But I should be with Fergus. I should be – he'll need—'

'They're right, no need for you to traipse home, Madeleine,' Fergus interrupted. 'No point in us all being miserable.'

'But, Fergus—'

'No arguments!' A small gob of spittle flew from his mouth and landed on her cheek. 'You'll stay and there's an end to it.'

Maddy glanced at Rita and me, but made no attempt to wipe off the saliva, which elongated as it ran down towards her chin. She got up to go over to the drinks cabinet and, with shaking hands, again refreshed her drink. Although I was bursting to yell at Fergus to leave her alone, I controlled myself. Any intervention would have made things worse between them.

Rita had no such qualms or suspicions. She winked quickly at me, then turned to him. 'It's a good plan, Fergus,' she said. 'No need for everyone to suffer. And I'm sure you'll get something else very soon. You'll be snapped up. We'll look after Maddy and Colm, won't we, pet?' She winked again, at Ricky this time.

'*No problemo.*' Her husband cracked open his second beer and settled it on his little-pig tummy.

'It's settled, then.' Jerry's tone told us that he had facilitated the discussion long enough and this was a wrap. He stood up from where he had been sprawled in an armchair and moved to the sideboard where the drink was stored. 'Since this is to be our last night together, we should have the official last-night Cognac. Agreed?'

But even the Cognac, good as it was, could not lift our spirits. On top of all the gin Maddy had previously consumed, it served only to make her tearful. So it was a gloomy parcel of friends that dispersed to the various bedrooms less than an hour later.

In our bed, I slid across the cool sheets to wrap my arms around my unyielding husband. 'Still thinking about the office?'

'I asked you to lay off, Tess, I can't stand this constant interrogation.' Although he did not move away from my embrace, his long, thin body, warm to the touch, felt like the trunk of a tree.

Recklessly, I carried on, although caution – and Jerry's body language – indicated that this might be a big mistake. 'I'm your wife, Jerry, please confide in me.' Gently, I massaged the muscle, as taut as a bowstring, between the curve of his neck and the knob of his shoulder. I wasn't looking to make love that night, only to break through to him, although we usually relaxed sufficiently on holiday to have more sex than usual.

Oh dear, I'm representing myself as a colourless, passionless individual. I don't think this is true: Michael and I had a very passionate relationship. It is simply that the bedroom routine into which Jerry and I have settled has become just that. Routine. Even before we became carelessly busy with other things, sex between us has always been polite rather than urgent. A state of affairs I rather like, even though I feel guilty about it. Especially when I hear people like Rita, who loves it, talking about sex. When Michael died, he took my lust with him.

'Tess, lass, leave it.' Jerry disentangled my arms, gently enough. 'I'll be better tomorrow but I've had a helluva a long day and I'm tired. Go to sleep now.' He kissed me briefly, then turned over and pulled the sheet up round his ears.

Next day, leaving Jack and the girls to lounge by the pool at the villa, with Jerry and Ricky deputised to keep an eye on Tom, we three women and Colm went to see Fergus off at Perpignan. The airport proved to be one of those perfect miniatures into which it must be a pleasure to fly. There was no physical barrier to peering into the arrivals and Customs area; it seemed that your aircraft landed right beside the terminal, you walked into the little Immigration and Customs hall, where your luggage was on the single belt before you. Then it was a short stroll across a forty-foot concourse into the sunshine where your hired car or your taxi was waiting. I was fascinated. This was what travelling should be like, must have been like in the early days, rather than the exhausting and time-gobbling process it had become in the vastness of 'hub' airports.

Check-in for the Ryanair flight was a doddle too: the girl simply crossed Fergus's name off a list, took his luggage and he was through. So much for the privileges of paying through the nose all these years for 'special' treatment.

We were all heading towards the little coffee counter when the unexpected occurred. Maddy, who was walking between Rita and me, stopped dead. 'I'm going. I don't care what anyone says, I'm going with him.' Before I could intervene, she had rushed over to the Ryanair ticket desk.

'What about your stuff?' I was first to catch up with her.

'You can take it home for me?' Her eyes were laced with an emotion I did not understand. Fear? Of course she was entitled to go if she wished, but I was puzzled at the depths of her desperation: it seemed out of all proportion. What was so dreadful about being left with us? I had thought she might even welcome a respite from her husband.

Colm, who had been walking ahead of us with Fergus, had now come over to the desk too. 'I'm going with you, Mam.'

If Maddy heard this she didn't react. 'There's nothing in that villa I can't do without, Tess, I certainly won't need the sun gear.' She turned to the clerk and ascertained that a seat was available on the flight.

Fergus, clad in his public plumage of affability in case there were any Irish people about, had joined us at the desk and divined what was going on. 'Excuse us, girls, I'd like to have a word.' Smiling wryly at Rita and me, Mr Avuncular personified, he took his wife's arm and drew her away from the desk, turning his back on us. We could still see Maddy's face, her downcast eyes, her quivering lips.

Colm was sweating a little, although it was not hot in the little terminal, whose doors were open to the breeze. I felt so sorry for him I could have hugged him. 'Don't worry,' I said quietly, 'it'll all work out.'

'I'm not worried.' His gaze was fixed on his parents.

The upshot of the exchange between Maddy and her husband was that our friend, usually so pliable where Fergus was concerned, proved in this instance to be unbending. She was going home with him and that was that. 'Sorry, Tess, Rita,' she said, looking from one to the other of us. 'I hope this doesn't ruin the holiday for you. And I know it's a bit rich of me to ask you to pack up my stuff—'

'And mine!' chimed in Colm, who, like a piece of slack string, was still hanging about.

'Of course not, Mad!' I could not bear to see her panic. 'There'll still be plenty of us left!'

'Sorry.'

'Stop saying sorry, for God's sake.' Rita threw her arms round her and crushed her tightly. As well as being more ample in every sphere, as it were, Rita's personality, too, is more generous than Maddy's or mine. Hugging is always her first reaction to any calamity and, in her view, there is no badness that cannot be ameliorated with affection or, failing that, food.

'Thanks, girls.' Maddy extricated herself and blew her nose. 'Give us a call now and then, let us know how things are going.'

'What about me?' Colm's voice cracked. Maddy turned to her son, as though she had only now become aware of him. 'Oh – yes. Of course. What do you think, Fergus?'

Fergus was annoyed. 'In my day,' he puffed, 'if my parents had brought me on a luxurious holiday to the South of France, do you think I'd have gone running home, tied to my mother's apron strings?'

Colm flushed and Maddy sprang to defend him. 'Leave him alone, Fergus. You should count yourself lucky. We both should. He's not on drugs, is he? He's not a layabout.' Like a defiant bantam, she raised her chin. 'You should thank your stars that he's still talking to us. What were you like at sixteen?'

Fergus, whose neck was growing a good red mottle, was astonished. He opened his mouth to engage with her but, conscious that to continue with this little scene might attract adverse attention, thought better of it and closed it again. While Maddy continued to glare and his unfortunate son shifted from foot to foot, he pulled his wallet out of his inside jacket pocket and moved to the ticket desk. 'What do I owe you for two tickets to Dublin from here?'

Half an hour later, after goodbyes at the security gate, Rita, who was wearing an unwisely chosen top in black Lycra, was easing our big Chrysler Voyager from the airport slip-road on to a highway and into the speeding traffic. 'What did you make of all that? It's a real pity. I would have enjoyed force-feeding her with ice-cream. She might even have enjoyed herself without Mr Toad blocking her every move.'

'Ah, Rita, come on, he's not that bad.'

'Oh, really?' She raised an eyebrow cynically.

'All right. He's hard to take.'

'Hmph! Miss Congeniality. That's you.'

'Stop it, Rita!' I did not enjoy defending Maddy's husband; nevertheless my on-the-one-hand-on-the-other streak insists on seeing both sides of every story. 'The guy's not here to defend himself,' I added unconvincingly, earning myself another withering look.

CHAPTER ELEVEN

Within a few minutes of leaving the airport I was stricken with remorse about Maddy: I had not been as attentive to her recently as I might have been. Should have been.

I had made all sorts of excuses to myself: I was being run ragged in my day-to-day life because, with Jerry's work schedule and the disparate personalities involved, it was difficult to keep everyone happy and my first duty was to my family.

Arkady is a big house to keep in order.

I had not picked up the phone because I would not have been of much help: I had run out of cheering things to say.

Now, however, I was haunted by the memory of that wan little face above the perky little sundress and, in the clear light of southern France, had to acknowledge that all of this had been bunkum. I had been pure selfish, as they say in Ballina, I had been protecting myself. In the last year or so, talking to Maddy had become a chore and I had got tired of listening to someone whose life was always in crisis, who asked constantly for advice, then took none of it. This was no excuse, I saw now. What a friend I am.

Not! As Kitty would say.

'Should we ring her, Rita? Like tonight?'

'What do you think?' She glanced across at me.

'I don't know. Maybe we should let them work things out between them.'

'Next week, then, when things settle down a bit.'

'Good idea.' Off the hook in the short term.

'It's a real turn-up,' I said now to Rita, as the Voyager picked up speed. 'I'm as mystified as you are, but have you noticed that she has been very nervy for a good while now? More than usual, I mean. Did she say anything significant to you?'

She shook her head. 'Not a dicky bird. But I could tell there was something really, really wrong. Like that weight thing – I know, I know. Before you say it, I should have her problems!' She pulled ruefully at the black top, which had ridden up, exposing a roly-poly wodge of flesh above her skirt.

'Oh, stop that! What does it matter at our age?'

'It doesn't, I suppose. At least, I wish it didn't! It's all right for you – I'd give anything for a body like yours.'

'No, you wouldn't. Would you give up chips? Swiss roll? Chocolate?' I had spoken more vehemently than I had intended. 'Sorry, Reet,' I touched her arm, 'I didn't mean that to come out as though I was the food police. No offence, I hope?'

'No offence. But that doesn't mean it didn't hit home.' She pulled again at the recalcitrant top and, following the road sign into Perpignan *ville*, indicated that she intended to change lanes – to the sublime indifference of every other car and truck driver on the road. 'Jesus! I'd better concentrate on this. Hold on to your knickers!' She tightened her grip on the steering-wheel and edged the car into the stream on our left.

I adjusted the air-conditioning a little. 'Between ourselves, I'm sick of watching what I eat all the time. And watching what other people eat too. It's not natural. Anyway, I was right earlier, what does it matter? Your husband loves you the way you are, and he is a butcher, after all. You'd hardly be a wholesome advertisement for Sleator's Victuallers if you went around like a stick insect.'

'Yeah,' she said gloomily. 'I'm wholesome, all right. Oh, I wish I lived in the sixteenth century when flesh was fashionable!'

'Be honest now. You wouldn't really like to be as thin as poor Maddy, would you?'

'Give us a break, Tess! I tell you, looking at her . . .' She tightened her lips. 'When we get back home, Tess, as God is my judge I'm going to drag her to a doctor. I don't care what she says.'

'I'll come too. We'll all go. Have lunch afterwards. Make a day of it.'

'It's a date. And,' her tone became careful, 'should we say anything about the booze?'

'I'm not sure about that. Or even if it's our business. Maybe one of us should get in touch with the sister.' Maddy's twin sister had settled with her husband and twin daughters in Los Angeles and had been home on a visit only twice in thirty years. Neither Rita nor I had ever met her. 'Her parents are getting on but this – well, it's sort of a private family thing, isn't it?'

We both considered this. 'Let's think about it.' Rita pursed her lips. 'It might be making a crisis out of something that's not a crisis at all. She might never forgive us. We're not experts, are we? I mean it's not as if she's falling around or out of control.'

'That we know of.'

'Mmmm,' she said thoughtfully. Then, 'Mind if I turn on the radio? We'll talk about it again, OK? Meantime, I'll ask Ricky's advice.' She twiddled for a little before hitting on the French equivalent of Lite FM and, as the anodyne strains of a Gallic pop song filled the car, I settled back to watch the countryside unrolling. We had come off a dual carriageway and were travelling along one of those straight avenues bordered on one side by a row of tall, dusty old trees you might think were planted solely to exist as illustrations on postcards or in arty coffee-table books with names like *Long Walks In France*; behind them, the landscape, hazy with heat, stretched like bleached and parched old skin towards the shimmering Pyrenees; on the opposite, naked side, it led the eye towards a smudged pencil-line of sea-light.

So, what we look like or what we weigh does not matter at our stage of life? Big talk from me, with my Weight Watcher's instruction sheets, my manic exercycling in our basement, my personal hairdresser, my weekly facials, massages and my acres of bathroom shelves groaning under their shoploads of creams, lotions and serums all trumpeting that they could postpone the dreaded sag. Well, the wife of a CEO has to look good.

For 'look good', read 'competitive'. These good friends of ours apart, a feature of Jerry's and my so-called social circle is the lightning fast up-and-down surveys we wives and girlfriends conduct on each other in the instant before our warm, delighted hellos and kisses. We all struggle with the advance of time, but if one of us is showing too much root, or if a jowl is developing or a little strain showing around a buttonhole on a blouse, it engenders a slight but undeniable thrill. It is almost as though one's own state cannot be affirmed unless that of others has slipped.

Have I become that superficial?

And why are we competing? For what prize? For the prize of one's husband being envied – even teased – by his peers and colleagues? Are we vying with the battalions of younger models lining up behind us?

And what would Michael, who had adored his Teresa from the sticks, his fresh-faced 'little nun', make of this sleek, air-brushed Tess?

Rita accelerated hard off one of the roundabouts so beloved of French road-builders, throwing me back against the seat. 'Sorry!' Then, when we had resumed a more sedate pace, 'You know, I think Fergus had forgotten he's a freelance actor. For the past few years he has sat in that part as though it's pensionable. Even the newspapers have been saying that the series has run out of ideas.'

'Listen, Rita, did anything strike you about the way he's reacting to the whole thing? I know he's upset, and he has a right to be, but I couldn't shake the feeling that he was just a little bit too theatrical about it, even for him.'

'Me too.' She drifted to a stop at yet another roundabout to let an articulated lorry pass in front of us. 'I wouldn't have guessed you'd seen that.'

Then she dropped her bombshell. 'I'll tell you what I think. I think Fergus is having an affair. And I think Maddy knows it. That's what's wrong with her.'

'Ah, Reet! *Fergus?*' I laughed out loud at the absurdity of it. 'Are we talking about the same Fergus?'

'We see him one way. Don't forget he's very good at the public-face thing. And he's an actor, Tess, he doesn't bother trying to impress us, has his guard down, but he can put it on when he wants to.'

'Ah, yes, but . . .' I still could not believe that someone as self-absorbed, as *mean* as Fergus Griggs would attract someone other than his long-suffering wife. 'What proof do you have?'

'Not an iota! I just feel it here.' She tapped her chest. 'And I think Colm either suspects or knows too. Look at the way he watches the two of them. That poor kid.'

'You've been watching too many soaps, Rita.' Rita's devotion to *EastEnders* and *Fair City* was legendary.

'At least they have plots I can understand!' Then, lightly, 'So how would you react if Jerry had an affair?'

'I don't know.'

She glanced across at me, her expression sceptical.

'Come on, Rita. Jerry? Are you serious? Where would he get the time?'

'They always find the time if they want to. Time is not the problem. He's an attractive man, your Jerry.'

'Rita! Are you trying to tell me something?'

'Nah – of course not! I'm just hopping the ball. But for some reason – must be our age, Tessie – I have been asking myself recently how I would react if my own head-banger went for a walk on the wild side. They do it, you know, around this age especially. They like to be flattered, young ones telling them they're great and that we don't value them enough and that they're only here for the one go-round and this isn't a rehearsal, blah-di-bloody-blah!' She chuckled affectionately. 'But in all honesty, I can't see any girl, God love her, going for Ricky Sleator with his Ireland jerseys and his bald patch and his beer belly.'

'How about for money?'

She stopped laughing. 'There is that,' she said thoughtfully. Then her expression cleared. 'Nah,' she said decisively. 'Not Ricky. He's too comfortable. And he adores the girls.'

'That's certainly true. What brought all this up?'

'Mad and Fergus and A.N. Other.'

'Oh, yes.' We drove on.

Unsettled, I watched the brief, fatal struggle of an insect caught in the blade of the windscreen wiper in front of me. In my case, I had perhaps revealed something very private. From time to time, I had secretly and ashamedly wondered if I had married Jerry for money. More specifically, for Arkady.

It was not as though the possibility of my husband's infidelity had not crossed my mind, as it does every woman's, I suppose, but

I believed that Jerry and I had settled amicably into each other. 'Now that we're talking about it,' I said to Rita, 'it's not something that keeps me awake. I'm too busy making sure Jerry's life runs smoothly. Me and Susan both.'

'I thought the subject was closed?' She was quizzical now. 'Have I stirred up something?'

'Of course not.' Even to myself I sounded unconvincing. 'But you can't just drop something like that into a conversation, Rita, and let it lie there.'

'You're right.'

'Seriously, let's drop it. This is really depressing.'

'I've dropped it. You're the one that's picking it up.'

'Well, let's talk about something else, then.'

'Lookit, don't mind me. I'm just in a funny mood, that's all. And I'm seriously pissed off – sorry, Sister! – that I won't get the chance to fatten Maddy up. Wipe that frightened look off her face. Ah, well, we'll see her in a month.'

We drove into yet another roundabout.

It had never occurred to me that the source of Maddy's distress might be what Rita had just suggested, but now that the topic had been aired, I could see its logic. And actors are probably more susceptible than most. They do spend a lot of intimate time together.

Maddy knew that score. Although he did not encourage it, she occasionally visited Fergus on the set and had described to us how intimate and clannish things were in the bosky groves of RTE. 'No spouses need apply, girls!' She had made us laugh with her mimicry of the over-emoting on set and told us how kisses sometimes went on a bit longer than allowed for in the script, and how, when everyone in cast and crew was insulated in the knowing tolerance of that liberal, arty community, it was easy to spot who was involved with whom. If Fergus was having an affair, it was most likely with a colleague and, with hindsight, maybe Maddy's light-hearted gossip had not been that light-hearted.

That evening after dinner when, under normal circumstances, the six of us would have sat down together and drawn lots to see what we would do for the night, Jerry, Ricky and Rita decided to play poker. 'You in, Teresa?' Ricky squinted at me through his wreath of cigarette smoke.

I hesitated. I could hear the pounding of techno-rock as the older ones upstairs, Jack, Kitty, Carol and Alice, were getting ready to go into Collioure to see what entertainment they could find. Outside, Rita's youngest, the twelve-year-old Patricia, was glumly keeping Tom company as, through clouds of midges, he swam relentlessly up and down the floodlit pool.

'Well?' Jerry raised an impatient eyebrow. 'Make up your mind, Child Bride, are you joining us?'

I hate it when he calls me that and he knows it. I am two years older than he is. 'No, thank you,' I said calmly. 'I think I'll just step outside for a bit.'

'Don't forget the insect repellent!' Rita was breaking the seal of a new pack of cards.

Outside on the dusky terrace, it was so still I fancied I could hear the shush of the sea. The compound scent of oncoming night, piny resin, cats and warmth released from stone seeped from the cool air. A crescent moon towing a star from its lower tip had already climbed high above the horizon.

Below, the lights of Collioure gleamed and winked like necklaces of yellow topaz against dark velvet, and I remembered my mother explaining that twinkling effect; sadly, it has little to do with magic but is caused by pollution and atmospherics. Mammy was one of those people with a rag-bag memory: she could barely remember the name of the parish priest, yet some small scientific detail from *Reader's Digest* or *Ireland's Own* would stick in her mind for years.

I shivered ('Someone just walked over your grave,' she would have said) and pulled my silk shawl round my shoulders. What was it that had had me looking backwards all day? Maddy's distress? Jerry's off-handedness? Simply this dissipating holiday?

I closed my eyes and discovered that the absence of noise was a sound in itself, a muted roar: that even the very faint, muffled thump of the stereo through the thick walls of the villa served only to emphasise the absence of other sound. Then, barely audible, I heard a tiny splash from the front of the house. Tom was still in the pool. I opened my eyes again.

Tom. I suppose we're lucky that he's so well tolerated by this group. Correction: I suppose I'm lucky – Jerry is not all that involved.

I turned my back on the perfect vista and gazed at our temporary home. The villa, too, was perfect, giving off its distinctive, sweetish scent as it cooled.

But it was not Arkady. I missed my house so much that to appreciate another house seemed like a betrayal. The missing was physical, a sucking at the blood.

I hate admitting this, but I must be truthful, however shallow, even bizarre it will seem: I love my children, my husband, my Dad and my friends, but on that evening I could see that Arkady might be the most important person in my life.

CHAPTER TWELVE

If I was any kind of a decent friend to Tess, I should be thinking about nothing except her today, but I'm in so much of a heap about Fergus I don't seem to have any time left over to worry about anyone else. I'd be no good to her, is what I tell myself. Rationalising, like.

Anyway, she's not ringing me either, is she? And it's not as if I've been doing nothing. Since I heard about her troubles, I've been sending her encouraging notes and cards and *The Little Book of Calm* and things like that. That was the best I could manage. But now, with this latest thing, all I can do is light a candle.

Rita will ring me when she knows what's happened with the police but I should have rung her myself this morning.

I'm sick of looking at the telephone. What is it about telephones? They're supposed to be instruments of communication, but every day that goes by it gets more complicated to pick it up. With Tess, for instance, it's a closed circle. The more guilty I get about not ringing her, the more difficult it gets. Then I postpone it more and then I get even guiltier. That telephone in my hall is my judge and jury.

I'll make myself ring her tonight. I'll make myself. By tonight, she'll know how things stand. It's cheaper too, after six o'clock.

In the meantime, Rita is a great friend to the two of us. Better than I am to the two of them, better than I ever will be. She's really good. Faithful. And I've given her a lot to put up with, haven't I? I keep worrying that the friendship between the three of us is maybe falling apart. It's definitely not the same as it was.

I won't think about that right now. I have to believe that there are people in this world who are on my side, even if we aren't living in each other's pockets.

Maybe it isn't such a bad thing that we're not in touch all that much. I hate the way they watch me, the way the two of them watch me.

I'm trying so hard, really I am. But they don't know how hard it is. They just don't. Sometimes I can't help feeling that the little drink is my only real friend. The only one I can really rely on. I never thought I'd hear myself saying that, or even thinking it, and I know in my heart that it's not really true, but it's how it feels.

But I'm not a drunkard, or an alcoholic, or anywhere even near it. I don't accept that, no matter what anyone tries to tell me, medical people or anyone else. For instance, I never in my whole life was in the gutter, or crashed the car, or was violent or passed out at the table with my head falling into the plate. Nothing like that at all. *Nothing.* And most days, even when I was overdoing it a little bit (all right, I admit that much!), I was able to wait until the Angelus at six o'clock before I had my first drink. It was my sad little joke on the Catholic Church. Because where was religion when I really needed it?

Sometimes I get so low and so lonely that I feel like a flat black puddle. The craving is not too bad at those times. It's more urgent when the opposite happens and a forest fire of panic is racing around inside my chest; that's happening more and more often these days.

I've been living on tea and toast. About four feet from where I'm sitting, every cup and tea-plate in the house is piled up in the sink and all over the draining-board so that I've had to use dinner plates and glasses. When I walk across the vinyl floor tiles, my feet crunch on sprinkles of crumbs.

I think it was only a couple of weeks ago – time is a muddle, these days – that I had a go at the place from top to bottom, but I'm afraid it's as bad as ever now. And my kitchen used to be so nice, even if the presses could do with a bit of updating, like. They're pine, which was very fashionable when I got them but now I'd kill for stainless steel.

No, that's a lie. I don't give a shit what they're made of. They could be cardboard for all I care. I know I've neglected my nice house so much I've turned it into a skip, but I have neither the heart nor the energy to lift that Hoover up the stairs. What's the point anyway? Who would I be doing it for? No point in doing it for myself, is there?

I've sent Colm to my mother and father in Ballineen for the summer holidays, hoping it'll do him a bit of good before he goes back to college next month. I hated the way he'd started looking at me, with those big worried eyes of his, so isn't he better off where the most disturbing discussion is the condition of this year's spuds?

After the upheaval when we got back from France, neither of us slept properly. Night after night I heard him pooching around the house at all hours. Poor lamb, he seems to have cut himself off from most of his friends and I could see he was definitely spending far too much time holed up in his room with his computer. That was why I sent him off to Cork – down there he'll at least get some fresh air and good feeding, and maybe even a bit of fun with all his cousins.

He didn't want to go, of course. We had a row about it, quite a dangerous row, as it turned out. Even though we made it up, I'll never forget the things he said. I'm trying, though, and I'm not holding it against him – of course I'm not . . .

When I suggested that he go to Ballineen for a couple of weeks until Fergus and I sorted things out a bit, he freaked. That's the only word for it.

He's normally real quiet, even taciturn. (That's a Tess word, but it fits the bill here because Colm is no chatter, that's for sure.) Anyway, I nearly freaked myself at the sight of him pounding his fist on the dining-table. I'll put it into a scene so you'll see what happened.

We're in the dining room where I'm pretending to dust and he's clicking away on his laptop. I'm so miserable I've dusted a china vase three times without noticing. Fergus won it at golf. The whole room is filled with Fergus, not only what he won, what he was given, what we got together as presents for husband and wife, but filled with his presence. I can touch him. I'm full of grief and confusion but I'm trying to keep it together.

Me (casually): 'Hey, Colm, here's an idea!'

Colm (eyes on the screen): 'What?'

Me: 'No use beating about the bush, darling. As you probably know, things are a bit tense around here—'

Colm (interrupting, eyes still on laptop) '*So?*'

Me: 'Will you stop typing for a minute and listen to me? I'm trying to talk to you.'

Colm: 'I'm busy.'

So I go over and pull the plug out of the wall. He sits with his hands still on the keyboard and his eyes on the blank screen. He starts off quiet. 'Why did you do that, Mum?'

'I did it because I'm trying to talk to you and you won't listen.'

'I was listening.'

I can see his fists are clenching and unclenching now on the keyboard and I'm not in great shape myself, so I decide to cut the preliminaries, get on with it. 'All right, here it is. Why don't you go down to Ballineen for a couple of weeks to Grandma and Granddad? They'd love to see you. And I'll send for you when things are a bit better—' I don't get any further because he takes this sort of sideways dive towards me and I even think he's going to hit me but instead, at the last minute, he twists off back towards the table and starts pounding on it. Saying nothing, just pounding.

My heart is thumping as hard as he's slamming the table. 'Your laptop!' I have to shout to be heard. 'You'll damage it – the vibrations—'

'Fuck the laptop!' His face, when he pushes it right in front of mine, is like an African mask, all pulled downwards with a wide-open mouth. 'Fuck the laptop, fuck it, fuck it, *fuck* it!' He's screaming at me and I'm stuck there, like as if I'm super-glued to the carpet. I'm frozen solid because, to my horror, there are tears pouring down his cheeks.

At least he's stopped pounding. 'You don't have to go if you don't want to.' I can hear my voice is shaky, so I get it up to speed. 'It was only a suggestion—'

'Have you listened to yourself – have you *looked* at yourself, lately, Mum? The tears are continuing to pour but the mask is all gone sideways as he tries to control himself. But he can't. 'No wonder Dad left, I don't blame him. And even though he hasn't asked, I'd go and live with him in the morning. Anything to get away from you. You just want to get rid of me too? Well, that's fine – that suits me just fine.'

He's pushing his face in at me again so I manage to unstick my feet and back off a little. 'It's not like that at all—'

'Oh, *no*?' He drives after me. 'You forced him away, now it's me. Well, I hope you're happy.'

Somehow I keep control. 'Thank you for that, Colm,' I say quietly, 'and no, I'm not happy. Forget Cork. Do whatever it is you want to. Now I'm going to leave here and go upstairs. I'd appreciate it if you wouldn't speak to me for the next few hours.'

I made it up the stairs and under my duvet. I was so shocked I couldn't cry. I had never, ever seen Colm in a state like that. It even crossed my mind that he might be doing drugs.

I heard him coming up the stairs. Stopping outside the bedroom. 'Mum?' His voice was subdued, nothing to do with the thickness of the door. I didn't answer, I couldn't. I didn't know how to behave.

'Mum?' The voice was stronger.

'Yes?'

'I'm sorry, can I come in?'

'Yes.'

The door opened slowly. The tears still streaked his face but they were old tears. His skin isn't the best and I suppose the stress wasn't helping, so even though I'm used to it, I was shocked to see, against his paleness, that many of his spots had erupted virulently. 'I'm sorry,' he said again. 'I know you're going through a hard time. I shouldn't have lost it like that. You know I didn't mean it, Mum?'

'I know, Colm.' I didn't know. I didn't know at all, but there was a new expression in his eyes. Fear. I felt so sorry for him, with his unkempt hair and his pimples and his loneliness. All the gadgets and computers in the world don't make up for loneliness. 'We all say things we don't mean. I've forgotten it already.'

'Really?' His whole body relaxed.

'Yes. It's all right. Do you want to talk about it? We haven't really talked about what's happened.'

'No!' He nearly jumped with fright. 'Definitely not. That's between you and Dad, it's got nothing to do with me.'

'It does. It affects you, Colm—'

'*No!*' He shouted it. All the horrible words, everything he had hurled at me in the dining room downstairs, evaporated and I wanted to put my arms round his skinny shoulders and kiss him better – but I knew not to do this. We had not been that kind of family. 'All right.'

'And I will go to Cork, OK?' He was rushing now, dying to get out. 'It's a good idea.'

'And you're sure you don't think I'm trying to get rid of you?'

'I said I was sorry, Mum.' He was edging towards the door.

'I'll make the arrangements,' I said quickly, 'but if you change your mind, if you find you do want to talk about it, I'm here.'

'I know that.' He fled.

I stared at a damp patch on the ceiling around the light fixture, where little flakes of plaster hung like miniature stalactites. It's been like that for years. Damp and electricity together? It's probably dangerous. Maybe it mightn't be such a bad thing if I was burned to death in my bed. I've tried to be a good mother, I really have, but . . .

I'm not sure, but I don't think Colm has told Mammy and Daddy what has happened. Right now, as far as I know, my parents think all that has happened to me and Fergus is that we're real upset about the series being axed.

They're so up in arms, like, on our behalf, they haven't twigged that Fergus doesn't answer the phone here any more. (Mammy even rang *Liveline* on the radio to tell the nation how angry she was. I was mortified, like, but proud too. She rang me in great excitement afterwards to ask me if I'd heard her. I told her I had, of course, and that it was a pity Fergus wasn't there, but I'd pass on their support.)

I can't put it off for ever. I'll have to tell them. I'm trying to build up my strength for it because there'll be murder. Mammy and Daddy are daily communicants, real orthodox. I'll go down maybe next week. (Mind you, I've been saying that for weeks . . .)

Definitely next week. When we know more about what's going to happen with Tess and Jerry and that.

Oh, God, I can't believe I made such an exhibition of myself, running away from Collioure like that. Thank God I had the passports and my driving licence in my handbag at the airport. I'm not Rita or Tess, we don't have servants, so I don't trust staff in these holiday homes and I carry anything important with me at all times. Even to the beach.

It was a lovely area and a lovely house, and we were set fair to have a great holiday, although even before we arrived I had the suspicion that, on some level, we've all grown out of our happy-gang period. I don't know if I'm the only one, though. Rita and Tess seemed shocked when I blurted it out.

Fergus and I had the whole attic of the house, huge, with two rows of the most gorgeous little windows facing front and back, and a big feather bed dressed with beautiful linen.

Not that the bed or the linen made any difference to us: we hadn't made love for months at that point and I had given up making advances to him. I didn't want a confrontation, I'm not good at them. And any time I mentioned it, he made an excuse about pressure at work and I didn't pursue it.

So, as I say, the few memories I have of the holiday this year are that bedroom, the lovely terrace with a great view of the sea, and that big beach we went to where there was a bit of a *rí-rá* about Tom going missing. That's it. That's the sum total of my album this year. If you were to ask me about the outside of the house, for instance – whether it was made of brick, or stone, or wood or whatever – I wouldn't have a clue. I was too busy watching Fergus.

So I suppose, compared to the other two, I won't have that much detail of the story to tell you, but I'll do my best.

What time is it? Rita says the police are due at around ten thirty in Arkady. Poor Tess. And poor Jerry too. He's not the worst.

But I have to look out for myself. I can't get too involved or I'll crack up totally. If they were electric wires my nerves would be short-circuiting. That's how it feels at any rate.

Mad by name, mad by nature, ha-ha!

I've lost Madeleine.

CHAPTER THIRTEEN

I met Fergus only a couple of weeks after Tess met Michael. Maybe it was catching, because she was on cloud nine and I suppose, when it happened to me, I was too.

Neither of us was as organised as Rita, though: Rita had Ricky Sleator trussed like a roasting bird and rolled up the aisle before he knew what was happening to him.

As I look back on it now, for that short while when all three of us were in love, the atmosphere in that awful Seomra a Seacht must have been something else. Hilarious, like, with Miss Santini and Miss O'Connor completely out of it, trying to keep discipline and order, and with us giggling and passing notes to each other as though we were still in school. It seems so long ago now, but I can still smell the place. It was a combination of ancient paper and dust and cigarettes and some sort of medicine. I think that must have been Miss Santini's cough drops. The poor woman had a terrible cough. A martyr to it.

When I first came to Dublin I fell for the city big-time, especially the theatres, the cinema and the variety houses. (Although no one from Cork ever admits that they could feel at home in the big smoke!) I adore theatre, or I used to. I got hooked the very first time I was taken to the Cork Opera House for the pantomime. The minute I clapped eyes on the fairy, with her sparkly tiara, her floaty net dress and her ballet shoes, I knew there was nowhere else in the world I would ever want to be. It was magic. A magic universe with no boundaries.

So straight away, when I got into the civil service, I joined one of the amateur dramatic societies around the city. I had done a bit of research and went for one in Westland Row, not because it was winning every competition, far from it, but because it was short of young women and I knew I'd have a better chance of getting parts. The plan worked, too, and before long I was being cast.

My ambition didn't end there. For a while, the only thing I wanted out of life was to join the company in the Abbey Theatre. I would have killed for an audition at that place, but unfortunately, even though I got one gig as a spear-carrier, the audition for the company never happened. I told myself at the time that it was their loss, like, but after the second rejection letter, I was heartbroken.

At that time Fergus was the star of the whole amateur movement. Everyone knew him because he had won three Best Actors in Athlone at the All Irelands. I'd seen him in *The Playboy*, where he was the perfect Christy Mahon because when he was young he was physically what we call in Cork a ladeen, with a head of tight curly black hair on him and a wicked grin. You'd want to give him your heart instantly, and you'd forgive him anything, the same way Pegeen Mike did until she was disillusioned. I think I fell in love with him when I saw him in that part, but he was so far above me in ability and experience, I didn't see how I had a hope even to talk to him.

Anyway, I was sure half the girls in the country were in love with him. Certainly the women in our group, of all ages, got misty-eyed, like, when his name was spoken. I was no exception. My crush was on a par with the secret dreams I entertained at the time about Dirk Bogarde. Fergus wasn't – isn't – a big man, but on stage he dominated. He filled the space, as the jargon would have it.

It was another small while after that *Playboy* and a *Death of a Salesman* and a *John Bull's Other Island* (he was terrific in those, too) before we met.

It was at the All Irelands it happened. We were doing *The Importance* and I was playing Miss Prism (so much for the *ingénue* roles!). I'd won Best Supporting Actress at Kilmuckridge and from other festivals we had collected a Best Actor for our Jack, two Best Directors and one Best Play, so our tails were up.

Ours was the second last show in the competition and Fergus's group, who were doing *The Crucible*, with him, naturally, as John

Proctor, were on last, so the two gangs of us crossed after our show when we were striking the set in the Dean Crowe Hall and they were setting up.

Amazingly, to us anyway, on the last night of the festival both our groups were brought down to earth because each of us got just one minor award – they got Best Set and we got Best Stage Manager. Because that year, out of nowhere, a small society from Kerry that none of us had rated swept the boards with *The Honey Spike*.

You can imagine the atmosphere in the lounge of the Prince of Wales afterwards, with the Kerry outfit whooping and singing bawdy songs and drinking their heads off, while the rest of us skulked around jealously, bonding, like, and muttering about the adjudicator being got at. (A few of them had found out, or thought they had, that this year's adjudicator was a first-cousin-once-removed of the Kerry lot's director. Ah-HAAA! QED! What would you expect, then? We all harrumphed and hoo-haahed at each other and felt a little better . . .)

Quite late in the evening, I found myself squeezed into a corner with Fergus Griggs across the table from me. There had been a lot of drinking, and as the night wore on, the noise grew deafening, so much so I was having to lip-read even what the girl sitting right beside me was saying. By two o'clock in the morning I'd had enough and I got up to go back to the digs.

Next thing Fergus Griggs is standing up, too, and miming across the table to me that he'd see me outside.

'Thank God,' he says, when we get out into the cold air. Then he flaps his elbows and screws up his mouth: a hen in a bad temper. 'Can't stand Thespians *en masse*, it's the parrot house at the zoo.' I burst out laughing.

He cocks his head further, waiting until I've finished. 'I saw you last night,' he says then. 'You're good, I liked what you did. But you need to watch your projection. I saw you in your last show, too. You need to learn what to do with your hands. And I could show you how to get your voice to carry better.'

Flabbergasted isn't in it. Fergus Griggs, Fergus the Great, offering to help me? Next thing, I hear myself saying, prim as a priest's housekeeper, 'Why not? That is, if it wouldn't be too much trouble.'

He throws up his hands. 'It speaks!'

What could I say to this? 'I really enjoyed your performance tonight,' is the only thing I can come up with.

'Thanks,' he says casually, as if he's used to it, which of course he is.

'And you were robbed,' I warm to my theme. It must have been the drink, because then don't I hear myself saying that the fella from Kerry who'd won Best Actor was shite? On and on I babble. I'm spouting for the Olympics. I can't shut up. 'He's half the actor you are, Fergus. I know he's good, but you're better. You were definitely robbed.'

It's definitely the drink.

'Whatever.' He shrugs himself into a long army greatcoat, which should make him look silly but instead gives him an air of mystery. Dr Zhivago. 'Hey! Will we go for a walk?' he asks casually.

I'm poleaxed, I can tell you. The legendary Fergus Griggs asking me to go for a walk? And he's looking at me with his head held sideways again. Sort of measuring. 'Sure,' I say, although I have only a light jacket on and am freezing. Hell or high water, though, I'm not going to let a bit of coldness stop me now.

The rest of that night, or rather, early morning, passes so quickly that it feels to me as if I must have been in a time machine. I don't know if you know Athlone but it's on this large river called the Shannon. And the next thing I know, I find myself sitting beside Fergus Griggs on a stone wall outside the town, beside where the river widens to about a hundred yards as it sweeps round a bend. I don't remember how we got there, the route we took or anything else about the interval between leaving the hotel and getting to that riverbank except that the hours simply vanished.

I do remember how I felt sitting there and everything about everything from then on. It's like a showreel. Even now all I have to do is click on it. Like right now.

Sitting there, we must have been exhausted, but my memory of it is that we are full of energy and excitement, from the shows and the adjudication. I am at any rate, the dawn is just beginning, and Fergus is talking as if he is racing a clock. He is talking about his future, his dreams, how he got into theatre, his favourite films and actors. He is jumping around on the riverbank, acting out scenes.

He stops clowning and climbs back up beside me. He lets a minute pass, two minutes. I don't know what's going on and am afraid to interrupt his train of thought. Then he says, in a very quiet voice, 'I don't know if you know, but my day job is in Findlater's in O'Connell Street. But not for long, Madeleine. Not for long.'

He then tells me, quite casually, that he is going to marry me. The Shannon flows on. He isn't even looking at me.

'I beg your pardon?'

'Madeleine. It's a lovely name. Don't let anyone shorten it.'

'I won't. But what did you say before that?'

'I said, Miss Madeleine, that you and I are going to get married.' He looks at me then.

You probably cannot credit the way it happened that night – or, rather, that morning – but it's really true. How could I make up such a thing? Such an outlandish lie? The hours might have run away up to that point, but they stopped right there, so that every second of the next five minutes was fixed into a separate bubble of crystal where, a pristine little grape-bunch, they remain lodged in my head, clean and clear to this moment. It was only ten minutes ago I rolled up the stillness in the pink sky, prised off the coldness of stone against my thighs, cushioned the sound of the racing water against the clonking of the slow goods train on the bridge about a hundred feet away from where we sat that morning.

Most of all, in the topmost sphere, more delicate and more precious than its fellows, is the feeling: the way my whole body melted when Fergus Griggs took me into his arms for our first kiss.

After a few moments he pulls back and, using the gesture I thrilled to when he courted Pegeen in *Playboy*, takes my chin in his hand. 'You don't believe me now, Madeleine, I can see that, but you and I are going to become husband and wife.'

I don't know whether to be afraid or thrilled. A bit of both, I think. The hairs still rise on the back of my neck when I imagine it. I find my voice, 'It's the drink talking, silly,' then try to laugh it off.

'All the drink in the world won't change my mind about this.' He kisses me again, even more deeply this time.

'So what do you say?' he asks then, in a tone like pouring syrup.

'I don't know what to say,' I stutter. 'This is so sudden. Would that do?'

He laughs, throwing back his head. I laugh along and the thing gets back under control. But then he grabs my hand. 'Laugh now,' he says, 'but you'll see what's going to happen.' He kisses me again. This time as if I'm his sister. 'Come on, we'd better get back. They'll have the search–and–rescue out looking for us.'

This is going to sound slushy, I know, but as we walked back towards the town along the riverbank that morning, I felt as though I was walking through the Garden of Eden. We even came across the biggest flotilla of swans I'd ever seen. They glided out of the rushes as we passed and I felt sure it was because Fergus Griggs had said he was going to marry me. And when a huge red sun came up over the fields, I felt it was there to bless us.

The next day, back at work, I was terrified. He wouldn't contact me. It had all been just *plámás*. Fergus Griggs could have picked any woman in any drama group in Ireland at that time. Probably any woman in any walk of life, of any age . . . So why would he pick me?

But it happened, it really happened, Fergus did ring me, in Seomra a Seacht. At ten past three, forty minutes after the end of the longest, most difficult dinner break my two poor pals, Rita and Teresa, had ever had to put up with.

Naturally, I've thought about that first night over and over. I've turned it inside out and analysed it to death, but I still truly believe that he was sincere. In that moment at least, he was definitely sincere.

High drama, yes, going for effect, certainly, a reaction for being bet out of Best Actor, probably, drink, definitely. All of those things – agreed. But for that one glorious night, Fergus Griggs was sincerely in love with me.

And as we reached the streets of the waking town, I told him I was confident it wouldn't take long for him to break into the professional theatre.

'Will you help me, Madeleine? Will you be my Mrs Campbell?'

'Yes.' I shivered with delight. Carried away as I was, I didn't tell him about my own dreams on that score and, looking back, I can see now that by agreeing to support Fergus's ambition I took an actual, lightning-fast and irrevocable decision to abandon my own. It didn't seem all that important any longer.

One of the immediate fallouts from becoming the Official Griggs Girlfriend was that I had great status within the drama movement. Another was that I found myself doing less and less work with my own group in Westland Row so I could help out backstage with his. The Avonree Theatre Group, as his was called, had at least five young women, all of whom had more experience than I and who had first dibs on the parts I might go up for. I didn't mind at the time, like, because they – we – were on the up and up. They had plans to do *Tom Paine*, with Fergus in the lead and a huge cast. It was a really ambitious undertaking, and it was going to take all hands on deck. On the night he told me the big news he asked me if I would help out by becoming, (officially as opposed to *ad hoc*) one of the assistant stage managers. There was normally only one, but this was such a big show they would need at least two, possibly even three.

I hesitated just a little because if I did this, it would mean dropping out of my own group's production of Lorca's *Blood Wedding*. And I had just been cast in the lead as the Bride, a real challenge.

The night he mentioned it, we were in the womb-like Trocadero, which is as much of an experience as a restaurant. Wallpapered in thick crimson, hung with hundreds of performers' photographs and wafting Sinatra, Streisand and opera through its speakers, people like us went there for three reasons. First, the owner and waiters tolerated people who could afford nothing more than a corn-on-the-cob starter and allowed us to hang around all night, consuming one cornlet at a time. Second, the place was the height of sophistication, not only for its exotics like corn-on-the-cob and its garlic, but because it had candles in Chianti bottles at a time when candles were seriously posh in Dublin.

For us, however, the third reason was the most important. We went there because it was the place 'real' actors and directors patronised after the shows in the 'real' theatres of Dublin. Since these professionals would never be caught dead at one of our offerings, we needed Fergus to be seen by them, if he was to turn pro, even for them to get to know him. There was – still is – a lot of snobbery among professionals about amateurs and so-called semi-pros.

As I dithered about *Blood Wedding*, we were interrupted by a 'real' director, a tall, untidy man who worked professionally but gigged as an adjudicator at the amateur festivals. 'How do, Fergus! What are you up to?'

'Dermot! Nice to see you!' Then Fergus introduced me.

'Charmed.' The director took my hand and kissed it. 'You've got quite a star here, Madeleine. Take care of him now, you hear? We expect great things. Talk soon.' He said goodbye and carried on down the room before Fergus could tell him about *Tom Paine*.

Despite this he was elated: 'See that? Did you hear?' He glowed. 'Could you have better timing? That has to be an omen, Madeleine! Come on, be a sport. Work with us. Rehearsals haven't even started for *Blood Wedding* so you wouldn't be letting anyone down. Please? Do this for me? Come with me to the stars!' Written down, this sounds hokey but in his mouth, the way he said it, the way his eyes shone, it was inspirational. Especially when he reached across the table and took both my hands in his: 'I'll need you with me, sweetheart. This could be the most important part I'll ever have. I just know if I do a good job it'll be the breakthrough I'm looking for. I'm going to write to the Abbey and the Gate and, of course, to Dermot there.' He twisted his head to see if the great man was watching him, which he wasn't. Undaunted, Fergus was already making a mental list. 'Even if they don't come themselves, I'll invite them all to send someone along to the production.'

I looked into his eyes, as full of honesty and pleading as a spaniel's. I wasn't as convinced as he was about his prospects with Dermot. But I squeezed his hands. 'Of course I'll do it,' I said. 'It sounds as though it's going to be great.'

So I gave up *Blood Wedding* and became an assistant stage manager with Avonree. Although it was a huge amount of hard work, I have to admit we had a lot of fun. And it paid off because the following year we hoovered up all the awards at Athlone. Including Best Actor for Fergus. And now it was our turn to whoop while everyone else in the Prince of Wales lounge was muttering. It felt really good.

A few more years had to pass before the breakthrough into the profession eventually came about, and he made it not through the amateurs but through Focus, a tiny professional company dedicated to the Stanislavski Method.

I still miss it, you know – oh, I would never have made it on the professional stage, that was a pipe-dream and I'm too thin-skinned – but I miss the buzz, the actual work. I miss the camaraderie and the sense of common purpose, the feeling of belonging, no matter what a small fry you are in the company. Each actor's good night is your good night. The director's triumph is yours.

And I didn't feel the same as Fergus did about what he mentioned that first night we met: about a group of off-duty theatre people reminding him of parrots in the zoo. To me, the after-show parties were magic.

There you are, like, tired and happy, owning 'your' show, in your secret society or private club or temple, even if you are just a lowly assistant stage manager. You sit in a flat or the sitting room of someone's parents' house and watch the actors outdo each other with stories and anecdotes and jokes, and you feel privileged to be part of it.

Party pieces were all the rage in those days and for such an extrovert group most of the songs were like dirges, the more melancholy the better. My own speciality was 'The Butcher Boy', a lugubrious ditty about early death, deep graves and symbolic turtle doves.

It was thrilling. The minute you got up to answer your noble call, a blanket of solemn respect came over the room. If anyone, even the most revered, even Fergus, whispered, drank or coughed while you were singing, all the others would ssh them disapprovingly. This was the height of it. It was holding my audience. No wonder I loved it.

These days, I teach a little speech and drama to youngsters here in the house. When Colm went to school and I found myself with time on my hands, I did my diploma and qualified, but it's not the same, like, as being part of a live show. And nobody except me takes my teaching seriously – Tess and Rita talk kindly about my hobby. Patronising, I'd call it, but of course I never say that.

That is probably why I have never told them about another 'hobby' I have. I try to write little plays.

No. Not so little. Have guts, Madeleine.

I am writing plays. Period. If I can't be an actress, my ambition is to become a playwright.

So far I haven't finished anything, but I have four separate manuscripts locked away in the drawer of the dressing-table in our bedroom.

Sometimes I ask myself if I'm writing for self-therapy, like. But I do think my themes are bigger than my own domestic dramas. My lead characters are certainly larger in life than me: one is Calpurnia, another is Elizabeth Barrett Browning. I don't care why I do it. I just do it. So what if it's self-therapy? What's the harm?

Over the years, I mentioned to Fergus from time to time that I would like to get involved once more with even an amateur crew, but he wasn't all that keen: 'You're needed at home, Madeleine. Colm needs you, I need to know that you're there for me when I get home. You know how stressful my life is!' So I didn't pursue the matter.

Thank God I have the Tricycle to go to: that's the fashion swap shop I work in three days a week, Thursdays, Fridays and Saturdays. I'm on commission, five per cent. It's not a lot, I know, but at least I get my pick of the clothes when they come in, before the clients get their hands on them. And it gets me out of the house. The days are long.

I suppose I'd better get to the nitty-gritty and tell you about that night we came back from France.

CHAPTER FOURTEEN

I knew in my heart that there was another woman. I've known for the best part of a year now, but they were clever, the two of them, and whenever I teased him about it, trying to conceal my motivation, Fergus acted all hurt. 'How can you even think such a thing? I thought we trusted each other, Madeleine.'

I didn't dun him about it: I had seen enough of these situations to realise that if a marriage is to survive, the very last thing the wife should do is turn herself into a shrew.

Anyway, there was never any real proof. Although he came home late many times, sometimes as late as five o'clock in the morning, he never spent a full night with her and always came up with some excuse for staying out: a party that his agent said would be good for him to be seen at, a cast drinking session that went on a bit . . .

So, short of playing detective and following him around in taxis (we have only one car and Fergus needs that to get across to RTE, there is no direct bus service), I didn't know what to do.

What drove me mad, however, was that I had no idea who she was. I imagined her as tall, blonde and beautiful – and, of course, very slim. Slimmer than I was (at the time, before I took myself in hand).

So how did I know he was being unfaithful?

It was not only the decline in his sexual interest in me, it was him being sort of absent even when he was physically present, if you know what I mean. We might be sitting at home watching television and I could see that mentally and emotionally, like, he was somewhere else entirely.

Then there were all the changes and transformations. First of all, he became very conscious of personal hygiene, asking me to add whitening toothpaste to the grocery list, to get him cologne as well as his usual aftershave. He even went so far as to get hair transplants, and you wouldn't believe how expensive they were. He justified them by saying it was to help him in the casting for films: 'I'm not getting any younger, Madeleine, and I need all the help I can get.' (We're still waiting, though, for him to get new publicity photographs taken.)

Then he developed this amazing interest in Irish traditional music. This might not have appeared so odd if, up to then, he hadn't listened to anything except jazz and classical and been real sarcastic about what he had referred to as 'that caterwauling'. Yet out of nowhere, like, he did this U-turn and next thing he was to be found combing the racks in Golden Discs and Walton's, asking for assistance to find 'an early version of "The Blackbird" from Martin Hayes' or 'anything from Tony McMahon, especially his slow airs.' He bought old *uileann* piper stuff on vinyl and in the car we had to listen to tapes of *sean-nós* from some ancient crone singing through her nose, or, more significantly, he would listen by himself late at night when he thought I was asleep. He began to call the button accordion 'the box' and to compare different styles of 'fiddle' players.

I couldn't stick it. But I was sort of paralysed, like. I can't explain it. I felt if I tackled him I'd start an avalanche or something.

The clincher came just before Christmas when he signed up for a credit card. It's hard to imagine, I know, how significant this was in an era when even kids use plastic the way we used to use sixpences, but during all our life together, or at least from the time we had settled to our marriage and learned each other's real nature and personality, Fergus constantly sneered at our friends for paying good money in interest to banks and credit-card companies. 'We're not going to live beyond our means, Madeleine. You'll thank me some day, you'll see.'

One evening when he made his announcement, we were having our tea, I remember. We always had it in the kitchen so I could keep topping up the teapot. Colm drinks gallons of the stuff. He had just gone back up to his room and I was clearing away into the sink. (I'd dearly love a dishwasher, all our friends have one, but Fergus said that, with just the three of us, it wouldn't be worth the money.) 'What did you say, Fergus?' I turned round. I thought I must be hearing things

'I said it's time we got a credit card.' He was staring at a pile of bills in front of him on the table. 'I'm sick of trying to keep tabs on our expenditure. A credit-card company would do all the calculations for us.'

'But, Fergus, I thought you always said—'

'Well, I've changed my mind, haven't I?' He kept his eyes on the bills. 'It's for convenience, I told you. For God's sake, Madeleine,' at last he looked at me, 'do I have to justify *everything* I do around here?'

I think he realised he had been more irritable than perhaps he should have. 'Nothing will change materially as far as you are concerned, Madeleine,' he said, in a softer way. 'We still have to behave as we always did, not like other people who give no thought to the future. But this is the twenty-first century, after all, and I suppose it's about time we joined it.'

I dried my hands on my apron and came back to the table, staring at him, bold as you like. 'Can I have a supplementary card, so? It'll be handy for me for the groceries and so on. We can keep track of those bills as well.' The question, more of a challenge, like, seemed to pop up out of nowhere.

He had not been expecting this response, but there was little he could do about it without admitting he was mean. His expression was priceless as he struggled. 'Why not?' he managed eventually, before warning me that I couldn't have *carte blanche* with it.

It was a small victory, hardly a victory at all because I have hardly used it. I got a few items for Colm, rugby gear, things like that, but the inquisition when the bill arrived would not be worth the hassle if I used it to buy things for myself. I had a system anyway and, over the years, I had become an expert in ducking and diving where my own expenditure was concerned.

To this day, I have never seen a bill for our credit card because he gave the production office of his series as his billing address. 'That's for convenience too,' he explained, 'expenses and so forth. And, as you know, we have long stand-by periods during filming when I can deal with it, any discrepancies I suspect and so forth.'

So when you take all these shifts combined, it was sticking out a mile that there had to be another woman.

Of course he had perfectly reasonable explanations for every one of them. Even his conversion to Irish music, so abrupt as to be weird, was explained away. It was, he said, because of a future storyline in his soap where, to bring in the tourists, his character was due to convert the lounge bar of his hotel into a traditional music pub. 'I need to know what I'm talking about when I get those scripts – at the beginning I was only researching, but when I began to listen to our native tunes for the first time in my life, I was blown away, Madeleine. Blown away. I can tell you that those trad players are world class, marvellously skilful. Bloody marvellous. You'd think so, too, if you'd just listen with an open mind.'

You see how deft he was?

I see now that, in the run-up to it, I had grabbed hold of that holiday in Collioure as a rock in the sea of all that change. We'd be away from 'her', whoever she was. I would find a safe opportunity to talk to him. Like, he couldn't run away from me, or make a big scene in front of our friends. Also, I hadn't been feeling all that well: I'd had dizzy spells and headaches, often a gyppy tummy. I was looking forward to a jolt of sea air and French sunshine.

Although I now know that I was a psychological and physical mess by the time we were due to leave for Collioure, I was congratulating myself on having hidden it quite well from everyone, was genuinely optimistic about the future and, except for the physical discomfort now and then, felt good about myself. I had worked really hard to slim down and I knew I looked younger and more attractive than I had for years.

It started with a crash diet. I had tried on a silk jersey dress that had come into Tricycle; it was a sheath, in a beautiful coral colour. I adored it and grabbed it before it was put out on the rails. Mary, who owns the shop, came into the changing room when I was trying it on. 'I wouldn't, if I were you,' she said.

That was all she said because the security bell on the door rang and she raced away to answer it, but when I turned back to the mirror, I was shocked at what I saw. Maybe it was because I was seeing myself through her eyes.

You see, up to then I had been quietly smug that I hadn't let myself go the way (whisper it) Rita has. But the fabric of this dress was so clingy that I could see clearly how my tummy bulged, and the awful handfuls of fat on my upper back between the bra straps. As for my upper arms, I had floppy elephants' ears hanging down under them and there were ridges on my hips above the panty line. I even had a spare tyre. Admittedly, the dress was only a size ten and it was a French label – they're always cut very narrow – but even allowing for that I was disgusted with myself.

This 'reality check' happened at around the time I was beginning to suspect that Fergus was having an affair and I decided there and then that, rather than roll over with my paws in the air and give in, I would take myself in hand.

That very night, I started my diet and also to smoke again: there was no point in living a long life free of lung cancer, I thought, if I was going to be fat, miserable and alone, trying to eke out a living for myself. If Fergus left me, what would I do? I had no qualifications for anything except the speech and drama, and unless I was to go bald-headed for that and start my own school in opposition to the well-established ones, I was not going to live on what I earned from my little classes.

This twin approach worked, because as well as the weight coming off satisfactorily, bit by bit, my appetite diminished until, thank God, the very thought of stuffing food into my nicely flat stomach appalled me. And the switch to slimline mixers was no problem at all. They taste the same as the real thing. Almost.

By the time I got to the airport for the first day of our holiday, I was in high spirits. I was even wearing a sundress to show everyone, and Fergus in particular, how good I looked. I had packed the coral dress, which I thought now looked stunning on me (you could even see my hipbones in it) and I was looking forward to wearing a swimsuit and not being ashamed. I had made all kinds of resolutions: I was going to get plenty of rest and exercise. I was going to give up spirits for the duration and drink only wine. I wouldn't eat bread, of course, remembering how on other Continental holidays I had made a pig of myself with baguettes and croissants. No need any more for mountains of starch. Instead I would eat a lot of good fresh French salads and fruit. And I would exercise to work them off. I would take long, hard mountain walks; I would swim, play tennis and take advantage of every physical pursuit going.

That was Plan One.

Plan Two, the more important one, was that I was going to have it out with Fergus. It had to be done if we were going to make a fresh start. We had a chance now to spend a whole month together without interference from 'her'. When he got into the holiday mood and let his guard down, and saw how young-looking and attractive I was again, we would be able to talk honestly to one another.

I was so happy in myself that first day and so full of resolve. I was convinced I could win him back.

Then, of course, he got this phone call about the series being cancelled and I panicked. That careful planning, those high hopes, all gone. I couldn't pretend otherwise and I showed how upset I was, which made him go ballistic.

True to form, he waited until we got on the plane before having a go at me. (Outside the house, Fergus presumed he was surrounded by viewers so never fought with me: he didn't want to give the fans the wrong impression about good old Chester Malone. In fairness, who was to know how many Irish were in the airport in Perpignan that day? With the same haircuts and clothes all over the world, it's impossible to tell until you hear the accents.) 'For Jaysus' sake, Madeleine, what are you at?' he hissed, safe because all around us the accents were English. 'What good will it do us all galloping home like a bloody army? I won't even be there, I'll be out all the time. I'll be at union meetings and cast meetings – are you trying to make me feel guilty about losing my job?'

'Guilty? How? Why?' I was taken aback. 'How is my going home with you meant to make you feel guilty?'

'Because,' he said, raising his voice, 'I'll have to be thinking of you moping around. You'll make me feel responsible for that.'

Thank God Colm hadn't been able to get a seat with us and was several rows away. 'Fergus,' I said, 'I'm going home with you because I'm your wife. For better for worse, remember?' I tried to take his hand, then realised the plastic-faced hostess was holding out a brochure to us. 'Would you like a brochure?' the girl's expression did not flicker.

'Thank you, my dear!' Fergus, the perfect gentleman, smiled at her and took it.

I grabbed it out of his hand and thought furiously while pretending to flip through it. There were two ways to go. I could stop behaving like a doormat and fight my corner properly. That way I'd risk driving him off. I could take the long view and try even harder.

Question: What do you want to happen?

I want things to go back to normal. I want Fergus to stay with me. I want to stay married to him and for everything to calm down and for the three of us to be a family again.

Question: Is challenging him on a Ryanair flight in the middle of all these people the way to go about it? Will it do any good?

No. It'll make you sound like a fishwife. It'll give him the perfect excuse to go to her. Think, Madeleine. Think!

So I read my brochure and stayed quiet.

CHAPTER FIFTEEN

The minute we arrived home, Fergus rushed upstairs, changed his clothes and then, while I was still checking that everything was sound with the plumbing and the kitchen electrics, came back into the kitchen to announce he was going out to RTE to see what the situation was. 'Don't worry about food for me, I'll eat in the canteen.'

'It's after seven, it'll be closed by the time you get there.'

'Why do you have to argue with me about everything, Madeleine?' I could see I had seriously annoyed him, but then he checked himself, made an effort: 'I'll get something from the coffee bar in the radio centre. A sandwich. I don't think I'll be late but I might be so don't wait up for me. I'll try not to wake you.' He strode out of the kitchen before I could tell him that the coffee bar in the radio centre was closed for good. Cutbacks in RTE, the same cutbacks that had led to the cancellation of his series. I had read this in an *Irish Independent* discarded by another passenger on the flight.

I waited until the front door slammed behind him. Then, with my stomach dragging as if it was filled with lead, I turned to get something from the freezer for Colm's dinner.

It was quiet in the kitchen, except for a small, tap-tap-tapping against the frosted-glass window set into our back door. I didn't turn round: I knew it was loose ivy, stirred by the breeze. When we moved into this house, I planted various ivies against the back wall to take the bare look off the concrete. I've been sorry ever since: our back garden faces south, the ivies love our soil and I have been engaged for a decade in trying to keep them from smothering the windows, doors and the entire house.

A metaphor for the silent unhappiness smothering those inside it.

'We eating dinner, Mum?'

My eyes were smarting and I realised I had been standing in front of the open door of the freezer, staring into its depths, for some time. 'Sorry, Colm.' I turned round. He was standing in the doorway of the kitchen and his expression nearly broke my heart. He was pretending to be cool, but I could see that, underneath, he was worrying his head off. He knew perfectly well what had been going on in this house. What he really wanted to know was 'Where's Dad?'

'Sure,' I said. 'I was just trying to find something you'd like. There isn't all that much, I'm afraid, I didn't do any shopping. Dad's gone out to RTE, a union meeting, I think, so he'll eat there. Do you fancy a pizza?'

'What are you having?'

'Oh, I'm not hungry.'

He hesitated and seemed to be about to say something, but instead, looking at the floor, he mumbled that he didn't feel like pizza, he'd go out to the chipper to get a batter burger.

'Have you money?'

'Yeah.' He sloped out of the kitchen.

I still had not closed the freezer door and instead of doing so I put both hands inside, rejoicing as the palms burned on the thick layer of frost. Defrosting is a chore I hate.

I remember reading an interview with the writer Frank O'Connor in which he said that a short story should be a moment of fundamental change in a person's life: an unexpected light illuminating an action or event so that everything inside the person changes and nothing afterwards will ever be the same.

That's what happened to me right then and there. As I stood in my kitchen putting myself through stupid and unnecessary pain, I knew with complete certainty that everything in my life had changed. Maybe I was ready for it. Maybe it was seeing Colm shuffle off. Maybe it was the closed, silent atmosphere of this sad home. I don't know what it was, I just know it happened.

Carefully, I peeled my hands away and closed the freezer door. I ran them under the hot tap, welcoming the way the heat magnified the freezer burn. Good, I thought. I'll get chilblains now. Proper order.

Fergus came home at about a quarter to midnight. I had passed the time with flicking through the channels on the telly – fifty-seven channels and nothing on, isn't that what they say? Canned-laugh sitcoms, movies from the eighties, police dramas, serious-faced reporters, nothing worked for me that night. I had the volume real low. I hadn't even bothered to put on the light. I was waiting for the sound of the key in the lock.

He came in, sighing and yawning and rubbing his eyes. 'Jesus, Mary and Joseph,' he said, 'you gave me a fright, sitting there in the dark. You still awake?' He snapped on the central light.

'Just about to go up.' I smiled widely. 'What happened?'

'We'll talk in the morning. It's a mess, I'll tell you that much, Madeleine. A bloody mess.'

'Did you eat? Would you like me to make you a sandwich?'

'No, don't fuss, it's all right. I had a sandwich in the radio centre coffee shop, like I told you I would.' He yawned again, very widely this time. 'God, I'm beat. I'll be asleep as soon as my head hits the pillow.'

I sat very still as he left the sitting room and went upstairs.

I stayed still while I listened to him go into the bathroom, while he flushed the toilet, while he came out again.

I listened to the sound of the filling cistern.

I waited for five more minutes until I was sure he was in bed and then I went upstairs.

He was turned away from me and breathing evenly when I slid into our bed beside him, but I knew he wasn't asleep. After all these years you get to know such things.

I lay on my back and, to remind myself of Frank O'Connor's unexpected light, raked my palms across the rough cotton of my pyjamas. The stinging was real.

It was a wild, wet night.

Like our short-lived quarters in Collioure, our own room is in the attic: in fact, it was one of the features of the house that most attracted me because the previous owners had used it as a home office, so it already had skylights and a polished wooden floor. I immediately saw it as our bedroom: 'It's so romantic,

Fergus,' this was in the early days, 'we can put our bed right under one of the skylights so we can see the stars!' It was the first and last room I got to decorate with a free hand – he insisted on choosing the colours throughout the rest of the house – and I went at it with some zeal. I chose a scheme of blue and white: blue carpet, white walls and ceiling, with a gauzy, star-patterned bedspread. I still love those skylights and not only at night. I'm an early waker and I love to watch the creamy trails piercing the dawn as the overnight airliners home in on Europe from America.

America. It was always my dream to go to the wide, windy spaces of America. In the meantime, it was lovely to lie there, imagining the hopes and dreams of the passengers racing above my house. Were they planning business deals? Meeting up with long-lost family members? On the run from the FBI and terrified of landing?

Did they know that there was probably at least one coffin containing a body in the hold beneath their feet? I had read that this was the case with a very high percentage of all commercial flights. And whose bodies were in those coffins? What story came with those deaths?

No jet trails on that night we returned from France, however, no stars, no sky, just darkness. And as the rain belted down against the glass above my head, I cast myself as a character in one of my plays:

> *The living room of a suburban middle-class home somewhere in Dublin.*
>
> *Enter MADELEINE, fiftyish, svelte, FERGUS's wife. She is troubled.*

Frank O'Connor's light grew brighter. Was FERGUS's wife to be defined by the fact that she was troubled?

Wife. Troubled. Troubled. Wife.

Was this what made me a unique person as distinct from six billion others on the planet?

The more I thought about this, the more aghast I was at what I had become. I thought back to the Madeleine of thirty years ago, the Madeleine whose breath was always in her fist because she was always in a rush to achieve something, to make something of herself; mad Madeleine who was up for any party, any devilment, who barely had time to rake a comb through her too-curly hair, who had attracted Fergus Griggs because of her vitality.

That Madeleine had enjoyed sturdy genes: from a granny who smoked a pipe and rode a bicycle around the byroads of north Cork until she was well into her eighties, a grand-uncle who was the hero of the county football team, a great-grand-uncle who had survived the War of Independence, who told hair-raising stories about his adventures in the Spanish Civil War and who had lived to be ninety-nine. Those genes had been dormant for too long. Before I had thought of the consequences, I had turned on the bedside lamp. 'Fergus?'

'Mmmm?' He pretended to be asleep, warning me off.

'I know you're not asleep, Fergus. Will you sit up, please? I want to talk to you.'

'Can't it wait?'

'No. It can't.'

'This had better be good.' He sighed heavily and pulled himself up. Then he shaded his eyes against the lamp. 'What time is it, for God's sake?'

'It's not late. It's only just gone a quarter past midnight. You've been in bed for about twenty minutes.'

I waited until he had settled against the pillow and was looking at me. In spite of the seriousness of the situation, I nearly burst out laughing. I was probably nervous and I always giggle when I'm nervous.

Because his hair was tossed, the little criss-crosses of his transplants looked absurd on top of his forehead; you could see his scalp shining as if it was a polished egg. He looked like a ventriloquist's dummy that had seen better days. I didn't laugh, of course, but, I had to look away to stop myself.

I traced one of the stars on the bedspread, faded now, of course. Well, it was more than twenty years old. 'I want to have a chat with you about something, Fergus. I had meant to have it on our holiday, but I can't wait any longer.' I curled my toes, then, waited for him to attack me, but nothing happened.

When I looked over at him he was gazing towards the ceiling. 'Fine. Fine. Spit it out.'

'I'm sorry, Fergus—'

'Stop apologising, Madeleine,' his voice was weary, 'it's driving me mad.'

I'm not quire sure what I was expecting, but it wasn't this quiet . . . reasonableness, I suppose you'd call it. In fact, I was so taken aback that I could feel a blush starting from my chest. What was I going to say next?

Then I remembered the freezer door, my son's face, Frank O'Connor's big bright light. 'I'm not happy, Fergus. And neither is Colm and neither, I think, are you.' He went to say something but I stopped him. 'No, please listen to me.' I rushed around inside my head, trying to find the right words to express the truth. 'I feel I'm drowning in shadows,' I blurted, 'and whatever is going on, please treat me with dignity and respect and tell me about it.'

'What do you mean, "What's going on?" There's nothing going on. Madeleine, for Christ's sake, will you lie down and go to sleep like a good woman? I'm tired and I'm going to sleep, if you're not.' He went to turn away but I stopped him by grabbing his arm.

The next thing came out all in a rush: 'If you're having an affair, have the guts to be honest. Please, Fergus. It's tearing me apart, but not only me, it's affecting Colm too, it's affecting the whole house. It's like a mausoleum in here. I hate it. I used to love this house, you know that, but I hate it now. I hate it when you're not here, and lately I hate it when you *are* here. It's so silent and awful and oppressive, with us all creeping around and everyone saying hardly anything. It feels like it's crushing me to death. Please tell me. At least if I know what or who I'm dealing with I'd have some chance.'

'You're a madwoman. I have to go to the loo.' He threw back the covers and walked quickly out of the room.

A month seemed to pass before I heard him come slowly up the stairs again. I forced myself to stay sitting up in the bed with my back as straight as the handle of a sweeping brush. He had not flushed the toilet.

I was expecting him to look like a stormcloud, with the words spilling out of him like hailstones, giving me the story he had cobbled together in the few minutes he had pretended to go to the loo. Instead I could see, as he walked back towards the bed, that he was very pale. And his walk wasn't aggressive, like, it was sort of resigned; looking back, it was the walk of an old horse going to the knackers.

I was shocked. *Dear God*, I thought, *he's going to tell me—*

Now that the moment of truth had arrived, I didn't want it. I wanted to take back my question. I wanted to turn out the light and go back to the way it was ten minutes ago.

I forced down the panic and waited while he sat with his back to me on the edge of the bed at his own side. 'I should have told you long ago,' he said then. 'I'm sorry, Madeleine, but I've met someone else.'

CHAPTER SIXTEEN

It sounds melodramatic to say this next thing, but it did feel like the world stopped spinning. I was expecting what he had said, but that didn't take away how it felt to hear it raw. And the world did stop. I've seen that kind of reaction described in novels and every time I'd thought it was way over the top. But it's not.

It doesn't even feel dramatic, no sensation of grinding to a halt, no crashing. It is just that everything stops, everything goes very quiet and, in my case, everything near me became like it was in the clearest, brightest photograph. For instance I saw that the hound's-tooth pattern on Fergus's nightshirt was beautifully intricate and delicate. I found myself noticing the way the small, jagged teeth dovetailed like the work of a careful carpenter.

And, you know, I even felt a dart of relief while, at the same time, anticipating the devastation to come. Right then, for a few seconds, it felt good to know that I hadn't been imagining things. I wasn't cracked, or mad, or anything else he had called me, or that I had called myself. 'Who is she?' My tone sounded conversational.

'That doesn't matter.'

'It matters to me.'

'What's the point of telling you?' At last he turned to face me, the springs of our old mattress complaining. 'It won't make you feel any better and the last thing I need is you going to her and making a scene.'

The world cranked itself up again and let go a blast of anger. It was great. Clean. Cold. After all the dithering and questioning I felt energetic but totally in control, clear-headed. 'If you don't tell me who she is, Fergus, I will make a scene. I'll start making a

scene right here. See this?' Before he could stop me I was out of
the bed, had walked calmly away from it and had removed his
framed 'Best TV Actor' award nomination certificate from above
the bed. I flung it, hard, against the furthest wall. The glass
smashed into smithereens, showering the bed. 'That felt good,' I
said.

He jumped up and backwards, spreading himself against the wall
under the sloped ceiling. 'I was right earlier. You are a crazy
woman,' he said.

'Are you going to tell me?' I reached for a figurine of a ballet
dancer on my dressing table, also glass, a gift from Fergus in the
early days. I raised it above my head and threw it, over my
shoulder this time, without aiming it at anything in particular. It,
too, smashed satisfactorily. Against Fergus's exercise bike, I guessed,
without turning to check.

I reached for a ceramic piggy-bank, a treasure from Fergus's
childhood and raised it, looking around for a target. 'Stop it, stop
it.' He rushed towards me and grabbed my arm. 'This is insane!'

He held my wrist so tightly above my head that the flow of blood
to my fingers was restricted, making them cramp. I didn't care. I
was going to smash everything breakable in the room as soon as he
let me go. 'Are you going to tell me?' The anger wasn't cool any
longer. It was hot and choking me as we stared at one another.

It could have gone either way. He was so close I could smell
drink under the scent of his cologne.

He let me go. 'Come downstairs,' he said. 'We can't stay here
anyway – there's nowhere safe to sit with all this glass.'

'And you'll tell me?'

'I'll tell you.'

I flung the piggy-bank on to the rumpled bed and marched
ahead of him out of the room. I was so flush with fury that I did
not try to go quietly down the stairs. I knew Colm usually fell
asleep wearing his headphones so it was safe to believe that if he
hadn't yet got up to see what was happening, he had not heard
anything. So far. But if he had, he deserved, as much as I did, to
be put out of his misery. Better to know than to worry.

We went into the kitchen where, like the well-drilled wife I
was, I went automatically to the sink, filled the kettle and plugged

it in. Then I sat at the table, waiting.

He had told me by the time the kettle switched itself off. And it was a feeble, clichéd little story, the kind you'd read in the *Star* or the *News of the World*:

MY PASSION FOR SOAP STAR

He needed prompting, of course.

'I don't know where to start.' He was not looking at me but at the kitchen table and talking in a low, monotonous voice as though reciting for his kindergarten teacher.

'Start at the beginning. What's her name?'

'That doesn't matter a damn, Madeleine.' He looked up. 'Why do you need to know that? It's not going to make the situation any easier, is it?'

For once I knew I had the upper hand. I just stared at him.

'Vanessa Thomson,' he said.

The name meant nothing to me. 'Where did you meet her?'

'She's on the show.'

'An actress?'

'Yes.'

'How old?'

'*Madeleine* – for Christ's sake—'

'*How old?*'

'She's twenty-four.'

I didn't want to think about the implications of this, not yet. 'What character is she on the show?'

It turned out that Ms Thomson was a mini–minor character in the series – she played the flaky daughter of the hotel porter – and flitted in and out only occasionally, usually to suit someone else's storyline.

And, of course, we got to the bottom of his Johnny–come–lately interest in Irish traditional music, or 'trad music', as it had been termed in our house in recent months: Vanessa's real–life father was a traditional musician.

'And her mother? I suppose she's a *sean-nós* singer from Donegal. Or does she play "the box"?' I was being bitchy. Oh, how I loved being bitchy. It was *enjoyable*.

'Her mother is dead.' He got up from the table. 'Why are you asking me all this? What's the point?'

'The point is, *Fergus*, that for nearly a year I have been driving myself demented with this. That's a year of my precious life. Gone.' I stood up too, 'No, I lie. It's not me driving myself demented, it's you. You have been driving me demented. Did you think you could get away with it? How long were you going to carry it on?'

'You don't understand—'

'I don't understand?' I was alight. 'What don't I understand? That you've found yourself a younger model?'

I had been moving towards him and we were now almost nose to nose in front of the sink. For some reason, he reached out and turned on the tap. The water crashed into the sink. I put my hands to my ears. 'Turn that off, Fergus. Turn it off.'

He turned it off. 'What do you want me to say? I've met someone else. It happens. I'm sorry, but I'm sure you don't believe that.'

'How did it happen?'

'If you're really sure you want to beat yourself up like this—'

'I'll be the judge of that. How did it happen?'

'Sit down, then. This is ridiculous, standing here like this.'

We moved to the table, me on legs so stiff they might have been stilts. We sat down.

The affair had started at the RTE Christmas party eighteen months previously. 'Things got out of hand a bit that night.' He was looking at the table-top again. 'There was a great deal of alcohol involved, and she and I went back to her place. I had no intention of seeing her afterwards – in that way, I mean. I would have ended it there and then. These things go on at Christmas parties, Madeleine, you know how it is.' He looked up at me tentatively, but when he saw my expression he lowered his head again.

'But it turns out she was keen, kept turning up on days when she wasn't scheduled for filming, or happened casually to be in the canteen when we broke for lunch. I suppose I was flattered. I was trying to end it by Easter but she kept coming back at me and back at me. And then—'

His voice faltered.

'And then she told you she was pregnant.'

'How did you know this?'

His amazement seemed genuine.

'I just knew. It's such a crappy little story, so ordinary. Let's just say I knew what the punchline had to be. Did she have the child?'

Had that been my voice? Was that me, sounding so businesslike? He nodded miserably. 'It was a little girl.'

'I see. What's this little girl's name?'

'Felicity.'

'And I assume you have been giving her money? Our money?'

'Madeleine—'

'Madeleine what?' I drove on. 'Are you or are you not giving this woman and her daughter money? It that why I'm wearing second-hand clothes and buying two-for-one Lithuanian pizzas in Aldi?' Aldi is the pile-'em-high German supermarket in Parnell Street, which attracts the poverty-stricken widows and single mothers, the asylum-seekers, the black and Asian immigrants, and me. His gaze slithered away. 'Not a lot. But she is my child. I have to take care of her.'

Tinkling in my ears was my own trilling, regretful voice each time I turned down an invitation from Tess and Rita to go somewhere 'because I have too much on that day'. 'I'd like you to leave now,' I said quietly.

'This is my house. I'll leave when and if I'm ready—'

'Do you not love me any more?'

Goddamn, I'd said them, the exact words I swore I would never say. In all the mental rehearsals I'd conducted with myself before the Collioure trip, I had batted them away every time they popped into the script. They sounded so pathetic. So bleating. As if the wife was a bloody defeated sheep. It is a way to lose the high ground when you're on it and now, here, I had yielded it to him. He knew it too. Gently, he took my hands in his. 'Don't humiliate yourself like this, Madeleine, you've humiliated yourself enough.'

I snatched away my hands. 'What do you mean, I've humiliated myself? What have *I* done?'

It was too late. He was controlling the game now. 'Look at you,' he said. 'Have you looked at yourself lately? You're pathetic. You're so scrawny, like a plucked chicken.'

I shot to my feet, tears threatening to let me down still further. 'Get out. Get out, please. Leave, *now*!'

'It's the middle of the night—'

'What do you care? You have somewhere to go.'

I fought tears. I was not going to let him see me crying. 'Go to *Vanessa's*.'

He watched me, uncertain for once. 'Are you sure?' he said finally.

'I'm sure,' I said. And I meant it.

'If I go I won't come crawling back.'

It was my turn to gaze at the table-top. 'I'll organise your stuff. You can ring me and tell me where to send it.'

A few seconds' silence, then footsteps. He left the kitchen.

The shaking started then, so bad that I had to put my arms round myself in case I flew apart. Then, after a minute or so, when I had got back a bit of control, I lifted the receiver of the wall phone. 'About half an hour,' I heard him whisper. 'I'll have to leave her the car – it wouldn't be fair if I took it.'

'Is she all right?' Although Ms Thomson was trying to sound grave and responsible, I could hear triumph and delight bubbling just under the surface.

'It was awful. I'll see you soon.' They hung up and I did too, very, very carefully as though to bump the receiver might be to shatter myself.

He was carrying one small travel bag when he came downstairs. 'I cleared the glass off the bed,' he said, from the kitchen doorway. 'I think I got it all, but you might check before you get back in.'

'I will.' I nodded. Except that we weren't looking at each other, we might have been discussing the cost of new curtains. After all, the drama, the break-up of a marriage can be so ordinary.

'Goodbye, Madeleine,' he said then.

'Goodbye,' I said to the table.

He closed the front door quietly.

Some time passed, I don't know how much.

When I went upstairs to our attic bedroom, his wedding ring was beside the reprieved piggy-bank on the dressing-table. It's hard to describe how I felt when I found that little circle of gold on the dark mahogany. I touched it and it was still faintly warm.

That was the worst moment, I think. I picked it up and, without undressing, got into bed holding it tightly in one of my sore hands.

It was embedded in my palm when dawn broke at just before five o'clock that morning. I believe my body was still in the same position too, I don't think I had moved at all. I hadn't slept. I was cold.

Some time later that morning, I flushed the ring down the toilet. It wouldn't go at first so I poked it with the brush but it hung around at the bottom of the water, flush after flush, until, the final indignity, I had to put on rubber gloves and manipulate it round the bend with my fingers.

It might be still there, somewhere in the pipes, for all I know.

Of course I went back on my decision, many, many times during the rest of this summer. Once I begged him to come back to me. And, to my toe-squinching horror each time I remembered it afterwards, I even offered, during one of those long, awful phone calls to him, to share him with her. I remember every word.

Scene: The hallway of MADELEINE GRIGGS's suburban house. MADELEINE, a middle-aged housewife, is clutching the telephone receiver in her hand. It is dark and MADELEINE's gaunt face is illuminated only by the light from a single table-lamp beside the telephone on the table. Through a speaker, we can hear the response of FERGUS at the other end of the line.

MADELEINE: I have a plan. Could we talk about it?

FERGUS: Look, it's late, I've got to go—

MADELEINE: Fergus, please. I just want to talk to you. After so many years of marriage, you owe me that much at least, surely.

FERGUS: Shit, Madeleine. (*Sighs*) All right, what's this plan?

MADELEINE: It's difficult to say it on the phone – could we meet somewhere for a cup of coffee, (*in a rush*) tomorrow maybe?

FERGUS: No, that wouldn't be a good idea. Not yet. It's too soon.

(*Pause.*)

FERGUS: Are you going to tell me? Madeleine? Tell me or I'm hanging up.

MADELEINE: I'm nervous, Fergus, this isn't easy for me, you know.

FERGUS (*sighs*): Look, I'm not going to jump down the telephone at you. Spit it out.

MADELEINE (*swallows hard*): Well, I thought, not only for me, but for Colm too, Colm misses you so much, Fergus.

(*Pause.*)

Fergus! Fergus! Are you still there?

FERGUS: Yes, I'm bloody here. Are you going to tell me or not?

MADELEINE: All right. Sorry. (*Quickly*) I just thought it might be a good idea. Now, don't bite my head off about this, just think about it, Fergus — but I'm sure Vanessa wouldn't object if you came home for just a couple of nights a week, even every second weekend, something like that, I'd even be willing to—

SFX: Click (*followed by dialling tone. The line has gone dead.*)

MADELEINE slowly replaces the receiver. She covers her face with her hands.

Although I was in a terrible state and was tempted many times to telephone Rita and Tess while they were still in Collioure, I resisted the urge. It wouldn't have been fair. They were on holiday. They deserved to stay on holiday.

Mary, at Tricycle, who is separated, was very good to me. Knowing that my two best friends were away, she came round to the house and let me work six days instead of three. 'Work is what you need, kid! Buckle down!'

On one of my 'strong' days, I went round to confront Fergus and Vanessa in her flat but when she opened the door with the little girl in her arms, my strength wilted. I was devastated to see his eyes staring at me from the baby's face. And although Vanessa looked tired, in all truth she was lovely. Ordinary lovely, if you know what I mean, a girl-next-door, not the tearaway I had seen on screen.

And she was so very young.

I managed to keep it together enough to get a lot of stuff off my chest. I've written down the episode in their flat; it's one of the scenes in my drawer. At least I might get some advantage from it one day if I can ever put it together with all the other disconnected stuff I've written in fits and starts. I tinkered with reality: my scene, quite dramatic, ends with Madeleine triumphant.

What really happened was that I went sadly home alone. It was three to one. But that is leaving Colm out of it. Where is he is in this?

Anyway, there were – are – no winners, but I believe I came last.

CHAPTER SEVENTEEN

What a summer!

It's not even two months since Mad and Tess and I sat together in a tight little row on that flight – such giggles we had! And just think of what has happened since then.

I wonder how they're feeling this morning in Arkady. I can't believe it has come to this, to the *police*. Tess and Jerry of all people – Jesus! Can you imagine? I can tell you I won't take my life for granted ever, *ever* again. I don't even *rate* what's happening here in San Lorenzo. It's bad enough sometimes, but it's normal bad; *minuscule* compared to what's been going on up there in Howth.

At the beginning I didn't take my life for granted, of course, especially after Ricky and me were just married. I wouldn't have called the Pope my uncle in that little house in Finglas.

And then, as we moved up in the world and transferred out to this place, I suppose I just expected the universe to keep on expanding, like Tess would say. I can see now that this feeling of being safe just crept up on me, especially after Mammy and Daddy died and there was no one left to pull me down a peg. (I can just hear Ma: 'Who do you think you are, Miss? With your big house and your so-called "chain" of shops and your bloody millions and your four daughters with their ponies and their Calvin Klein this and Nike that . . .') And Daddy wouldn't have been far behind her either in raining on my parade.

The biggest sin on our street was to be jumped-up. Daddy, whose job was in a trade union, was a dyed-in-the-wool socialist because with all us kids hanging out of him he didn't have any choice. Or maybe he did and he didn't want to compromise his principles. I never asked. Kids didn't ask much, in those days, because we would have been told to mind our own business. For whatever reason, my father was deeply suspicious of anyone who had a few bob, or who rose above what he called their station. That certainly describes me and Ricky, these days.

Except the way I see it now is that we have enough so we never have to worry about the bills. Also, we're able to look after both our families when they hit rocky patches. Yes, I do have four gorgeous, healthy daughters who are probably a bit spoiled, but so what? They'll be gone from here in a few years and they'll have a sunny childhood to look back on. And yes, I do have an easy-going old man and a house that we can all breathe in. Again, so what? I'm not hangdog about being successful, or ashamed of it, because we've worked bloody hard, Ricky and me, especially in the early days. If it all disappeared tomorrow, we'd start all over again and I'm willing to bet it wouldn't be too long before we'd get back up there.

Enough about me and mine. This is Tess's story, or it's supposed to be. I find it hard to know what to think about what's going on over in Arkady. I've been finding it hard to even *talk* to Tess and if she doesn't ring me, especially lately, I've let days go by without picking up the telephone.

I'm going to have to tell you the story of this summer the way I saw it. I wouldn't be as good, now, at storytelling as Maddy or Tess, but everything is still clear in my mind, as clear as mud, as my granny used to say when I was a girl. Some bits are going to be a lot easier than others, I suppose.

Nearly half past ten. I wonder how she's feeling. The police might already be there. That bloody Collioure! I know deep down it couldn't have been the cause of anything really, but still and all, look at what's happened to our little gang. There was probably a curse on that house, that's what I think anyway.

Like, how would you fancy living in a place with a grave in it? Tess was mad about the stained-glass windows in the chapel, but I don't care how classy they were, it just isn't natural to be living cheek to cheek with a mummy.

We should have gone to Marbella like I wanted.

CHAPTER EIGHTEEN

After we saw off the Griggses at Perpignan, the conversation Tess and I had in the people-carrier as I drove us back to the villa kept rolling around like a bingo ball in my brain all that day and the next. I hadn't meant for it to pop out like that about Fergus maybe having an affair. People's lives are their own business and the very minute I said it, I knew I shouldn't have opened my big mouth.

I could see she was shocked. God love her, she wouldn't have copped it in a million years. Oh, I know she looks sophisticated and shined up, but at heart she's still a nun from the country, that one. Signs on, we all watch our language when she's around. I don't know how she got to our age and stayed so innocent deep down. You won't believe it but it's not that long ago I had to explain to her what lesbians got up to in the privacy of their own homes.

I don't know how she got to our age and stayed so innocent. Hear no evil, say no evil, that's our Tess – but sometimes I wonder if this image of being calm and in control all the time is for real. Because if you ask me, she isn't all that calm underneath. How could she be, with what she has to deal with? That strange little boy, for instance. I can't make head nor tail of him. And as for Mr Master of the Universe – that's what the rest of us call him privately. Even Tess uses the term when she's relaxed with us. His PA – Susan Vitelli Moore, that's her name – must have a dog's life, in fairness to the girl.

The Vitelli comes from the father, who's Italian, separated from the mother and back in Italy these donkey's years. As it happens I know her slightly, or I used to. When she was in secondary school, she and her friend used to muck out the stables in the equestrian centre where my girls learned to ride before they had their own ponies. Ireland is a small world, you know, and Dublin's smaller. The same people keep popping up all the time and I immediately made the connection when Tess mentioned her last name in passing. Susan is the apple of her mother's eye; I used to meet her too – at open days and gymkhanas when we'd both be there with our kids. She owns a small shop in town.

So. Anyway. To get back to Fergus. Why did I think he was playing away from home?

Easy. There were telltale signs. Dozens of them. The guy was like a walking advertisement for those articles you read in magazines about How to Tell if Your Husband is Cheating on You. Like, he is never exactly Santy Claus when it comes to throwing money around, but about a year ago he switches his aftershave from Old Spice to Calvin Klein. I'm good at smells.

Then he gets those niggledy little hair transplants stitched into the front of his baldy head and they don't come cheap. He tells us all he did it for the job.

Then he joins a really expensive gym – for the same reason? For the job? My *eye*!

There's more. Our Kit, who's only seventeen, comes home one day just before last Christmas with a story about how she'd seen her uncle Fergus and a young one hugger-muggering in some café in Temple Bar. Naturally I pooh-poohed, didn't want her growing the idea and maybe upsetting poor Maddy. But Kitty's no dumb belle and if she thought enough about the sighting to mention it there had to be something in it.

Another of the reasons I never spilled those beans to Maddy is I didn't want to make things worse for that poor underfed kid of theirs. He is a bit of an oddball, that's for sure, but that doesn't mean you shouldn't be sympathetic. My own lot have always tried their best, but they've never been able to get any satisfaction out of him. I wonder does Maddy cook at all? I never hear her talking about food and she never invites any of us to their place. If it's their turn to have us to dinner or anything, she always suggests a restaurant. And because of yer man, it's always cheap. (Mid-range, *he* calls it.)

I'm seriously worried about her on a number of fronts. She has those little bags under the eyes, the bags *under* the bags, if you know what I mean. That's a real sign when someone's been hitting the sauce. She could have anorexia too, I'd nearly bet on it.

But, anyway, from the minute we saw them off at Perpignan airport, things got a little bit weird for the rest of us. I know there were only three people missing but the heart had gone out of us all. And especially during the first week after they left, I had a very definite feeling that we were coming to the end of something. I nearly said the end of an era, but Tess would hate that. She hates clichés.

Looking back on that holiday, I think it wasn't only me who felt that, as a holiday group, we were getting past our sell-by date. Wasn't it Maddy, on the very first day when we were on the beach, who made some remark or other about maybe re-examining the whole idea of these group holidays? That struck quite a chord with me because, sneakily, I'd already been thinking that it would be great for just the three of us girls to go off together to someplace exotic, no kids, certainly no husbands. Maybe to one of those spas. The luxury!

Is it only me, or do women put a sort of hood on themselves when their husbands are around? It's something I've noticed a lot. We can be having great fun together and then let a husband walk in or, worse, two, and the whole thing changes. We all, even the best of us, switch into Mammy mode immediately, putting them and their opinions at the top of the agenda, making sure they're OK, catering to them and their feelings.

To get back to the story, after only one day, as I say, our holiday was turning into a washout, fun-wise.

That night, the night the Griggses went home, we played cards but we shouldn't have because I really missed Maddy as a soulmate. She can be really brave when the heat comes on. She seems real timid now, half the woman she used to be when we were all young, but when she plays cards you get to see that, deep down, she hasn't lost her reckless streak. I'm good at eyeballing, but she's better, probably because of her being an actress, and without her there that night, Jerry Brennan walked all over Ricky and me.

Next day, to cheer ourselves up, Tess and I drove down the
motorway a bit, across the Spanish border and to a little place
called Pals. It has a seaside but we'd heard that the ceramics shops
in the village part were marvellous.

At first she didn't want to go – didn't want to leave Tommy after
the fright she got the day before. Jerry was gone to the golf course
and had persuaded my Ricky to go with him as a substitute for
Fergus, and my girls were going with Jack to the beach. As a last
resort, I said we should bring him with us. (You can see how
unsettled I was, can't you? That I would even *suggest* spending half
a day cooped up in a car with the little oddbod surprised even me.
I have to admit, though, that he's never any trouble. I just would
have preferred her and me, free as two swallows.)

I hadn't a bit of guilt about leaving my own lot – it wasn't as
though we were selling them into slavery. They had every possible
mod con to keep them entertained, and if they didn't want to go
to the beach, the pool was terrific. The French do things very
well, don't they? Architecturally speaking, I mean – I can't say the
same for their food. Their bread is nice, and their fruit, of course,
but I was never one for offal and as for their joints – if you can
actually *get* one! I'm always suspicious. You'd never know by
looking at it how the stuff was butchered or how long it was
hung. And don't talk to me about frogs and snails et cetera! Stop
the lights! Their duck is nice, though, when you can persuade
them to cook it so it doesn't arrive on your plate with the inside
of it looking like it's still half raw. You have to cook duck properly.
And that's well done.

I always bring our own meat on these Continental holidays.
Ricky vacuum-packs it for me and we freeze it. You'd want to see
the looks on the faces of the cooks when I unload the whole
shebang in the middle of their kitchens!

Let's see, where was I? Oh, yes, Pals.

Well, even though it was cloudy when we arrived, Pals village
turned out to be the most gorgeous little place on the top of a hill.
Real civilised, with very old stone houses, steep, winding streets
only a few feet wide, with lots of window-boxes. And not an iota
of litter, not one cigarette packet or plastic bag. I couldn't help
wondering what the Irish would do with a place like Pals. The

ice-cream vans! The chip vans! The burgers! There was also a
pretty church.

Tess is musical, and when she thought she heard an organ, we
installed Tommy on the steps outside with an ice-cream cone –
he's not *that* weird that he doesn't like ice-cream – while we
popped in for a bit of a visit. Tess was thrilled because when we
got inside we found that the organist was practising something
high-falutin. Thick as I am in these matters, even I could tell he or
she was very skilful.

I feel bad sometimes that I'm such a moron when it comes to
culture. But I can't help it if I get bored out of my tree at those
concerts she drags me to. I keep going because yer man is always
away on business and she has nobody else to go with. In recent
years, Maddy is always saying she has something else to do but we
know she doesn't have the money for the ticket and there is only
so much of the I-have-a-spare-ticket-at-the-last-minute sort of
guff you can lay on someone without making them feel like the
poor relation. She gets free tickets to the theatre sometimes and
the three of us go and sometimes that's not too boring. I love a bit
of a laugh and if the play is by someone like Bernard Farrell or
Hugh Leonard or that English fella, Willy Russell, at least I can
recognise the characters they write about as real people with real
lives; bad things might happen to them, sure, but they don't be
unhappy or staring into their navels *all* of the time. Tess's concerts,
though, leave me cold.

When we got back outside that church, the clouds had lifted so
the sun was splitting the rooftops and Tommy was still sitting
where we had left him, quite happily, arranging little bits of gravel
into what seemed to be a perfect circle. 'Good lad.' I tousled his
hair – which he, quite politely, rearranged. 'We're going shopping
for a bit, Tom,' his mother helped him to his feet, 'but not for too
long. And then we can have lunch. You're not too hot, are you?'

'I'm not.' Then, without complaint, he accompanied us to
ceramics heaven. I told you. Weird.

I soon forgot about him because you'd want to see the
merchandise in those shops – anything your heart desired. I
bought loads. Literally. Candlesticks and bowls and decorative
plates, and the dotiest water-feature you ever saw. The water pours

out of a lion's mouth and is caught in the skirt of a little girl hunkering down at its feet. It's bottle green, about five and half feet tall, nearly as big as myself, so I had to leave it in the shop for bubble-wrapping and collection later. It'll go great in the garden, I thought. Ricky Sleator's always giving out about having to pay the excess baggage after these holidays. I just ignore him.

Tess bought nothing. She's a real perfectionist. Everything is in its place at Arkady, not a bit of clutter. You'd want to see it, you'd sure be impressed. I know I always am. But for some reason I always feel really fat when I walk into that house.

Probably to please me, to take the bare look off things, she had decided to look for a tall vase or an urn. I found rows and rows of urns and vases in all the shops, but there was nothing she liked; the surface was too shiny, or not shiny enough, or the colours were too garish, or too dull, or the pattern was wrong.

I could see I was wasting my energy. To spite her nearly, I bought a goldy-coloured Buddha, about two feet tall. The exact thing she'd hate. 'Doesn't look like we're going to find anything you like,' I said nastily.

'Oh, it's out there, we'll find it. I'll put it in the hallway just inside the front door. It'll look really good, maybe with a few ornamental grasses in it.' Then she turns to the kid: 'Is there anything you'd like, Tom?'

'A yellow frog.'

'Have you seen any?'

'Yes. There was one about three shops ago.'

'Well, why didn't you say? We'll have our lunch first and then we'll go back and get it, all right?'

'Yes.'

This politeness was getting to me, it always does. Any one of my brood, even the best of them, would be whining and complaining and arguing that they wanted stuff by now and what a mean old skinflint I was. I missed it.

I was delighted to be able to kick off my shoes under the table when at last we got into a little restaurant at the very top of the village. It was full, but luckily for us, a big party got up and left a terrific window table just as we walked in so we grabbed it. Real French, the menu was, but I stuck with the pizza. I suppose they do pizzas for tourists. Tommy had one too but Tess, of course, ordered a mixed salad and when it came, immediately picked out all the olives. Too fattening. She's very keen on keeping the figure.

Every morning when I wake up I have the best of intentions but, God, we'll be dead long enough, won't we? And I seriously love pizzas – oh, the crispy bits! So again, sort of to spite her (I was hot and uncomfortable, my feet hurt and my belt was too tight – someone had to pay!), I ordered ice-cream for after the pizza. The kid was busy lining up the toothpicks into a complicated criss-cross pattern on the table. 'You'll have ice-cream too, Tommy?'

'Yes, please.'

We sat looking out at the view. A valley with green trees. 'Are they vines?'

'They're olive trees.' Tommy did not raise his eyes from his complicated game. The pizzas came then, the waitress taking great care not to disturb the kid's pattern.

'Are you having a good time, Tom?' Tess picked up a bit of asparagus from her plate.

He was carefully cutting out a wedge of his pizza and ignored her.

'We're here in a window seat in a French restaurant,' I answered for him, 'looking out over vineyards – sorry, olive trees – I've more shopping than I can carry, the sun is baking and there isn't a husband in sight. So, what more could we want?'

'I don't know,' she said slowly, glancing at the kid to make sure he wasn't paying attention, which he wasn't, 'but I can't help feeling a sense of impending doom.'

At least, that's how I remember it now. It's not really the way people talk, but it's the way Tess talks. She uses words in a way the rest of us don't; when you listen to her sometimes, you'd think you'd be reading a book or listening to a serious programme on the BBC. Probably because she went to boarding-school, and then that convent shut her off for too long from the way normal people talk. 'What kind of doom?' I say back to her, humouring her.

'I don't know,' she said again, like a stuck record. 'It's just a feeling I have.'

The kid, having eaten just that one small slice of his pizza, got up and went to stand in front of the gaming machine in the corner of the restaurant. 'Is he OK, d'you think?' I looked after him. I certainly wouldn't have let one of mine walk off like that.

'Oh, he's fine.' But I could see she was a bit on the back foot so I let it go.

'When you're talking about this feeling of doom, do you mean Maddy and Fergus?'

'Maybe.' She looked down at her plate. 'Oh, I don't know, yes, maybe it is about them. I certainly got a shock when you said it—'

She shut up and I had this sort of flash! Like you see happening to people in the soaps when they're supposed to be realising something and they frown and the camera closes in on them. 'Is it Jerry? You're not telling me he's—'

She looked at me, scandalised. 'That's the second time you've brought that up. Of course not!'

'I wasn't – I was just wondering what it was that was bothering you. Forget it!' Now as you will get to know, I wouldn't be a person who is analysing myself all the time, testing how I'm doing, the way Tess does. Sometimes she drives me mad that way but, lookit, I'm sure I drive her mad sometimes too. She's a bit complicated, I think that's the way to describe her. The best in the world, of course, but you'd never *really* know what she'd be thinking.

'It's too hot to eat,' she said then, pushing away her salad. I was so annoyed with her that I chomped my way through the rest of the pizza while she looked out dreamily at the view.

By the time the ice-cream came, I was good and full, but determined to see this through to the end. We called Tommy over. 'This looks good.' Tess picked up the kid's spoon and took a millimetre from his sundae dish. 'Mmm.' Astonishingly, to me at least, she held up a finger and called the waitress, 'One more, please.'

She saw my expression. 'Well, it's hot!'

And then Frederick Yarso walked in. Of which more anon.

CHAPTER NINETEEN

I remember the first day I saw Tess, timid little mouse that she
was, arriving into Seomra a Seacht with her handbag and her
white gloves. You'd just want to take her in your arms and hug her
to death, then bring her out to give her a good feed.

Maddy and I both took her under our wing from that first day,
brought her round, showed her what was what in Dublin, and
although for a while she stayed a bit more backward than us, she
came along nicely. She used to come with me to the dance halls –
without poor Maddy who would be working her fingers to the
bone in some bloody draughty hall with some play or other. (She
wasn't 'poor Maddy' then, of course, she was the leader of the
three of us, full of vim, the fullest. Always suggesting we go here,
there, everywhere. We had our first holiday abroad together thanks
to her because she made us all put money into the post office
every pay day for a whole year. We went to Benidorm for a week
and had the time of our lives. You couldn't keep up with Maddy
back then. It's a calamity what's happened to that girl.)

Back to the dance halls. I loved to dance. I was particular, of
course, wouldn't get up with just anyone, even though in those
days it was just not done to refuse any gouger or oul' bachelor that
flicked his quiff at you.

I did. Refused anyone that I didn't like the look of. I got
thrown out of the Ierne once, for refusing a gobshite with the
smell of drink off of him so strong it would knock you down. He
complained to the management – imagine! So instead of him
being evicted, I was. And I was told I was barred for a month!

Tess never clicked in the ballrooms. She did dance a bit, of
course – even the wall-eyed and the lame got asked up towards the

end of the night – but nowhere near as much as me. There was something about her, even then, that seemed to warn off all but the bravest.

Just as well that her first husband, Michael, was the type who wouldn't notice if you were freezing him out. If his head hadn't been in the clouds so much, I doubt that they would ever have got together.

I'll never forget the day she first told me and Maddy about him.

Apparently, he was behind her in the queue while she was waiting at her bus-stop to go home after work. Something dropped; I forget exactly what but, they helped each other to pick up whatever it was. And that's how it started.

We couldn't believe the change in her, Maddy and me. You know the way they say things like people are ten feet above the ground? Well, that's how she was, I swear to God. Our little Teresa, our little novice nun, floated into work the next day, all pink and gauzy. And she stayed like that, all through their marriage, right up until the day he died. It was a tragedy. A fecking tragedy.

I can't say the same for her relationship with Jerry Brennan. He's a completely different kettle of fish, and of course they're older, we all are. But I'm not sure I'd be able to live with anyone who seems to eat, sleep and drink work all the time.

I suppose I shouldn't be downing him so much: he's good to her, in an absent-minded way. She's totally loyal, I'll say that for her. Oh, we tease her about him, all that Master of the Universe stuff and so on, and she takes it well, but she never tells us anything seriously bad about him. Reading between the lines, though, the main problem with the tension she hints at, I'd say, is that the two boys aren't his. The soaps are full of that kind of thing and they're spot on. Those programmes have psychologists on the staff, you know, to advise them. You wouldn't need a psychologist in Arkady because a one-eyed stranger would see that Jerry's relationship with both of Tess's kids is difficult in different ways: with Jack because he's a typical bored male teenager, and with that strange little Tommy because, well, he's Tommy.

What you see in those reruns of *The Brady Bunch* – his three, her three, all cute together – is not real life: in real life, in Ireland

at any rate, having step-children is a minefield and I've never heard
anything to make me think otherwise.

So, anyway, there we were in Pals, quiet enough, looking out at
the scenery, when the next thing, this American guy came in.

Let me paint you the picture. He's tanned, like as though he's
been working outdoors or on holiday for a long time, carrying a
camera bag and backpack by the straps, and he's looking around as
though he's getting the feel of the place. We're sitting at this
window table, as I said, just the two of us, Tommy is standing
beside his mother getting coins for the gaming machine. All the
other tables, much smaller, have people at them, so I suppose it's
understandable that he comes over and asks us if we'd mind if he
joins us. Americans are like that, forward. They must be the
friendliest people on the planet.

They're also the nosiest. I suppose it's just a different culture
from ours but I've noticed they think nothing of asking you in the
first few minutes of any conversation where you're from, who's
your seed, breed and generation, what you do, even what you
earn and how much your house cost you. This guy, Frederick
Yarso, is no exception.

Tommy goes off, back to the machine, and yer man sits down to
join us. And, of course, when we all introduce each other, we find
that in spite of the name – which is Scandinavian, he tells us – he
has a bit of Irish blood, like half of America. 'What county are you
from, ladies?'

'I'm from Mayo.' Tess is doing her bashful bit. (I don't mean that
bitchily. Underneath all that sort of detached sophistication, she's
genuinely shy.)

'Well, how about that?' He sits back in his seat. 'My great-great-
grandmother was from County Mayo. Her name, I guess, was
Sullivan?'

'What part of Mayo?' Tess is delighted. 'I'm from Ballina, do you
know it?'

'Afraid not. I guess she was from some little place near Knock
shrine? My mom thought it was called Ballylin, Ballyline,
Ballysomething?'

Tess shook her head.

'Whatever.' He grinned. 'I'll find her. I'm planning a visit there real soon, maybe even next vacation, go through all the old parish records.'

'Well, if you do go, you have to see the Céide Fields. That's an excavation in the north of the county, showing more than five thousand years of farming. It's wonderful, well worth a visit.' Tess, who was getting carried away, caught me looking at her severely and rowed back a bit. 'My husband was an archaeologist, you see,' she said meekly, as if this explained everything.

'Five thousand years of farming!' He's nearly pushing the charm down her throat. 'Older than Giza. But who am I telling this to?' His smile is about forty million candlewatts and she blushes.

'And you, Rita?' He turns the megawatts on me. 'Where are you from?'

'Dublin,' I say shortly. I'm really resenting the intrusion. I was enjoying just having Tess and me there. And I want to talk about myself when *I* decide to. Yanks and their bloody questions.

'Well, when I do come over, I'll have to make Dublin my first stop.' The charm offensive doesn't get any less but he can see I'm not half as impressed as Tess is and turns back to her: 'You say your husband was an archaeologist, Tessa? You know, that's my field! I'm not eminent, I have to confess . . .' he witters on.

Turns out, would you believe?, that this guy is a bloody archaeology lecturer at the university in Chicago. Or somewhere near Chicago – I forget. Of all the bars in all the world, et cetera, an archaeologist with Mayo ancestors has to walk into ours. Tess, of course, is thrilled. I can see the shyness dropping off of her like icing off of a cake.

'Has your husband retired from archaeology?' he asks then.

'He's dead,' she says simply, and leaves it at that. Next thing, he's all sympathy as she tells him about Jack and her Tom and how Tom was so young and all that, and he listens as if this is the most important thing he has ever heard. He shows her a picture from his wallet of his two sons aged five and seven. He's divorced, apparently.

Now, is it just me or do you think it's peculiar that she doesn't at that point tell him her second husband is very much alive? But she doesn't. So I don't either. And then the two of them launch into talking archaeology. I mean *really* talking. Her face lights up and her eyes light up and she smiles a lot and he smiles a lot, too, as he tells her about digs he's been on and places he's seen. 'So tell us, Frederick,' I ask him, 'now that you know all about *us*, where are you from?'

Again I forget what he said, although he did tell us some place with a real funny name. I forget because from then on I might as well have been another sugar lump in the bowl for all the notice they take of me. I just dig into my ice-cream and try not to sulk. I find it hard.

I mean, what's going on here? I'm not a one hundred per cent fan of Jerry Brennan's, as you must know by now, but at the same time she should have mentioned him. Once at least. Because I can see this guy is very taken with her.

I can't blame him. Our Tess is a looker and, even on holiday, she's always immaculate. This day she's wearing light khaki, a cool, well-pressed skirt and blouse that wouldn't look out of place in that film *Out of Africa*. She already has a bit of a tan – although I suspect a touch of the Egyptian Wonder there – and not a hair out of place. The sun is behind her too, which always helps, not only with the hair-shine thing, but also with not highlighting any little facial wrinkle or imperfection.

Yarso is good-looking too, in a sort of Nick-Nolte-meets-Jeremy-Irons way: the weather-beaten face and the ashy hair are Nolte but the long thin body is Irons, and I can see she's looking at him in that special, considering kind of way women do when they are, well, *considering*.

I look him up and down myself, but a bit more critically, I have to admit. I reckon he is in his early to mid forties and for my taste he's a bit too superficially attractive. I prefer my men to be like onions: you peel off the layers until you get to the real nice juicy bit. You only have to look at Ricky Sleator to know I don't go for the macho look. I'm more a Danny de Vito woman!

Tommy comes back then. 'Can I get a yellow frog?'

'Sure. How much was it? Do you remember where it was and could you go by yourself? This is Tom, by the way,' she says to Yarso. 'He's my son.'

'Hi, Tom!' Yarso holds out his hand but Tommy just looks him up and down.

'I want the big one, Mum,' he says then. 'It's a hundred and twenty-six euros.'

'*Tom!*' Tess shoots an embarrassed look at Yarso, then rummages in her handbag and gives him the money. 'Bring me back the change.'

'I will.' He takes the money.

'Sorry about that,' she says, when he's gone. 'I'm afraid he's a bit lacking in the social graces.'

'Don't give it a thought, Tessa!' Yarso is comfortable. 'If you had to deal with the bunch of little slackers I have to put up with in my lecture hall – and they're supposed to be university level!'

What happens next, you wouldn't put it in a book.

'Any decent places to stay around here that won't break the bank, ladies?' he asks, including me in the question. So I tell him we can't really recommend anywhere because we're visitors ourselves. 'I've just come from Barcelona,' he says, 'and I was curious to see around this area. You know, Tessa,' he beams at her, 'there are all kinds of sites along this coast, through Perpignan, relating to Hannibal.' He has drawled her name as if he was Marcello Mastroianni or someone. Whether he had misheard the introductions or not I don't know. I wait for her to correct him and she doesn't.

'Perpignan?' she says – and I swear to God she blushes. 'We're staying half an hour south of Perpignan, in a lovely little village by the sea called Collioure.

'As it happens, Frederick,' she says then, glancing at me, 'we find ourselves unexpectedly with two spare rooms. It's a lovely house. You'd be very welcome if you should find yourself passing through. That's if you don't mind having a whole lot of young people around. Rita has four, and there's my two.'

He smiles at both of us with his American teeth. 'What a lucky break. Are you sure you wouldn't mind? You must let me pay you.'

'We wouldn't hear of it.' Tess was scandalised.

'OK, but I will earn my keep.' He points to the camera bag. 'And I do take good pictures! I'll send you both copies. Promise!'

'It would be all right with you and Ricky, wouldn't it, Rita?' Tess chimes in. 'After all, the rooms are paid for.'

I'm so flabbergasted at this development it feels like my kidneys are down around my ankles. Yarso, who is sharp, picks up on this. 'Is this cool with you, Rita?'

'Sure, sure,' I say. Well, what else *can* I say? She's already invited him. 'The more the merrier.'

'Great,' says Yarso. 'Just for a few days, of course, I wouldn't like to impose. But if it's OK, there's no time like the present, is there? Have you ladies a car?'

He was polite, I couldn't fault him on that, insisting on carrying all my pucks and parcels to the Voyager, even fetching my water-feature from the shop and placing it carefully on the back seat between himself and Tommy, alongside the frog, which turned out to be three feet tall and a hideous shade of mustard. 'Don't worry, Rita, we and Kermit here will look after it, won't we, Tom?' Tommy responded only with a curious look, which didn't faze Yarso even though Tess hadn't yet given him the tutorial on the kid. He seemed to accept that Tommy was just Tommy and let him be, and although he did try to engage once or twice during the trip, he didn't push it. Instead, he 'entertained' us with jokes about Romans and Greeks that I didn't think were funny but had Tess gurgling like a drain.

He was definitely knowledgeable about the area. For instance, when we were passing through the checkpoint between Spain and France, high up in the mountains, he was able to tell us about all the border wars that had gone on over the centuries and pointed out so many hill forts and lookout posts, never mind hermitages and old ruined monasteries, that I was permanently in danger of going off the road trying to see them. He was interesting about Hannibal and his elephants, I'll give him that. Even I knew about Hannibal and his elephants.

Apparently Hannibal had marched his army all the way from south-eastern Spain, 'That was ancient Carthage, you know, Tessa', across the very mountains we were crossing right then. 'Col de Perthus,' he says. 'Nothing as daunting as the Alps, of course, but with such a huge fighting force, it should not be underestimated. And by the way he was a terrific negotiator, the George Mitchell of his day.' Then he gave us the blow by blow, with the fighting and 'negotiating' Hannibal had to do with hostile tribes all the way through the South of France, before managing to do his famous crossing-the-Alps thing into Italy. 'All the towns and villages along this coastal strip are associated with him in one way or the other. I've wanted to see these places for myself for a very long time. Thank you, ladies.'

'I've wanted to see them too.' This was Tess and it was the first I'd heard of it so I shot her a dirty look. She ignored me. 'Michael,' she said, 'my husband, was more interested in the prehistoric sites of Africa than of Europe, but for myself, I would have preferred it if he had opted for somewhere like this. The conditions in Africa were not all that conducive to having small children around.'

'I hear you, Tessa, I can imagine that,' says yer man, before launching into another long joke about the Horror of Delphi or someone.

I tuned out. We were coming off the motorway in any case, so I had to concentrate on the roundabouts, although when Tess said something else about Michael and his favourite sites, I was sorely tempted to ask her straight out what sites her *second* husband favoured?

When we pulled up in front of the villa Jerry and Ricky were unloading the golf clubs from the other car. I watched for Tess's reaction, but there was nothing much to see. 'Oh, great,' she cried. 'Good timing, they're back.' I checked Yarso in the driving mirror but I have to say his expression seemed just normally interested, as far as I could tell. *Back off, Rita!* I said to myself. I can be a bit of a nosy-parker and it was something I was trying to get out of.

There was no sign of any of the kids around the pool, but as we got out of the car, we could hear the thump-thump-thump of Beck, or whoever was the Anointed at that time, so they were around all right.

Tess hurried over to Ricky and Jerry. 'Guess what, we have a guest.' She turned to smile at the American, who was strolling across after her. 'This is Frederick Yarso. He's an archaeologist. We met him in a restaurant and he was looking for accommodation and I said he could stay with us because we have spare rooms now. Don't we?'

I could see both husbands were gobsmacked. Then Jerry put on his chief-executive face and stuck out his hand. 'How are you, Frederick? Of course. Delighted to have you. How long will you be staying?'

Yarso smiled easily and said something about not being quite sure. 'As long as you guys can put up with me, I guess. A few days, a week, who knows? I don't have to be back in school until September, thank God. I have no specific plans. But I am house-trained, I swear.'

I could see Ricky and Jerry looking at each other and there was a little pause. Then Jerry heaved his golf bag on to his shoulders. 'Let's see how it goes, shall we? You're welcome anyway, Frederick. Do they ever call you Freddie or Fred?'

'I'll answer to anything.' The grin stayed easy.

'I'm Jerry, and this is Ricky Sleator. The wives, I see, you have already met. See you at dinner.' His tone told us he was already thinking of something else, much more important than a mere American backpacker. Then, to Tess, 'I'm going to have a nap and then a shower, OK, darling?' and he walked off into the house, leaving us and Ricky to take care of the details regarding Yarso's accommodation.

Good old Ricky Sleator took up the slack. 'Howya, Fred.' He held out his hand. 'It's a big place, there's plenty of rooms. You don't even have to see us if you don't want to. What part of the States are you from?' He picked up the backpack and walked with it towards the house.

Yarso followed and we could hear him telling Ricky that he was from Wisconsin, originally. 'Oshkosh, but I've been out of it so long I consider myself a city slicker now.'

When they were safely in the house, I turned to Tess. 'What are you at?'

'What do you mean?' She put on this puzzled look, about as genuine as a three-dollar note.

'You know what I mean. You're only short of kissing his feet. We don't know this fella, Tess, he could be a murderer or a rapist, and you're bringing him in to live with us. What about the kids?'

This brought her over all huffy. 'Do you think I would invite him as our guest if I didn't think he was kosher? I think I'm experienced enough to tell the difference between a murderer and a career archaeologist and, if you remember, I did consult you before I invited him.'

I held my tongue. Because she had done no such thing. I was

'consulted' when the damage had already been done. There was no point in arguing at this stage, though. 'I'm sure it'll work out,' I said, as I went back towards the car to collect my parcels. 'But if it doesn't, if he trashes the place or runs off with all our jewellery, don't blame me!'

'I'm sorry, Rita.' She hurried after me. 'Maybe I did jump the gun a bit, but it was so nice for a change to be able to talk to someone about something interesting.'

'Thanks a lot!' I was getting annoyed now and, with my water-feature still half in and half out of the Voyager, I turned to her. When I saw her face, I relented. 'Oh, for God's sake, it's probably going to turn out great. I'd trade Fergus Griggs for him any day.'

'Thanks.' She touched my arm. 'You're a pal.'

'You know what I think – and don't bite my head off about this. I think this guy reminds you of Michael.'

'So?'

It hadn't taken Einstein to work that one out, but when I saw the flush creeping up her throat, I realised it had been a cutting thing to say. There was no taking it back, though, without making things worse. 'So nothing,' I managed a smile, 'it was just a thought, no big deal. Just be careful, that's all.'

She opened her mouth to say something else but I turned away to wrestle with my water-feature. By the time I had the rest of it out of the car, the subject was closed and she helped me carry it and the rest of my stuff into the house.

CHAPTER TWENTY

Ricky was in the shower when we deposited everything inside the door of our room, and it was only when I saw it all piled up against the wall that I realised how much I'd bought. 'He'll kill me.'

'No, he won't.' Tess leaned over and gave me a hug. (Now, there was another turn-up. She's not the huggy type.) 'He adores you. It's a game you two play, we all know that. See you at dinner.' And she floated off.

When he came out of the shower, Ricky Sleator was all tubby and pink, with a towel tucked round his tummy and his hair up in spikes like Worzel Gummidge. He stopped dead when he saw the pile of ceramics by the door. 'Jeez, Reet!' He put his hands on his hips so the towel fell off. 'How much did that little lot set me back?'

'You'll love them! They cost a *fortune!*' Dramatically I kicked off my sandals, threw off my top, then my bra and, keeping one eye on him, spent ages peeling down my skirt. Then I sashayed towards him wearing only my knickers. He loves it when I do that kind of thing. The more showily I do it, the better he likes it. It's just a bit of gas. I wouldn't make a fortune as a stripper, I've no illusions about that, not with *my* figure, girls, but Ricky says my enthusiasm makes up for my lack of subtlety.

And Tess was right, we do play these games: this was an example of them. He pretends to be furious at my extravagance. Then I pretend to be giving him sex in return for the gew-gaws I buy on his money. We both get a kick out of the deal.

After we'd made love, we plumped up the pillows, cracked open a couple of beers and settled down beside each other to have a chat. The bed was massive, an antique brass thing that you could fit four people in quite comfortably. (Eight, if you were a member of my family in the inner city when I was growing up!) The room was lovely in every way. Like the drawing room downstairs, it was full of little ornaments and mirrors and antimacassars on the chairs and lacy runners on everything else. Three floor-to-ceiling windows with wooden shutters, a wonderful, faded old carpet that felt like silk under your bare feet and probably was silk. I felt very contented. There was no need to check up on the kids: the thump-thump-thump of the hi-fi was going strong somewhere in the background. That's the beauty of these holidays. We know they're safe.

'So, what's going on with this Fred guy?' Ricky asked.

'I don't know what's going on,' I told him back. 'Tess invited him. It wasn't me, honest!'

He considered this for a minute, then took a swig from his bottle of beer. 'That's gas. It's hard to believe,' he said slowly. 'Don't get me wrong now, I like Teresa, you know that, but she's so uptight most of the time you'd want to take a corkscrew to her—'

'Ah, that's not fair,' but I did know what he meant. She had been pretty tense this last while.

Ricky ignored me and kept on: 'It's not like her to do something on the spur of the moment like this, is it, now, Reet?'

I had to admit that it wasn't, but I didn't confide in him that I thought Tess was seizing on this guy as a way of reliving her love affair with Michael. That's none of my business, any more than it was my business to blab about what Fergus Griggs might be up to. So I moved the spotlight on to Yarso and confided in Ricky that I wasn't convinced he was as on the level as he seemed to be.

'Why do you think that?'

'I don't know. Women's intuition.'

He pooh-poohed this. 'Yeah, right. Why not give the chap a chance? What does Teresa think of him?'

'You know her. She's not Mary Poppins, but she's still not streetwise, Rick. Ask Maddy.'

'Ah, youse two don't give her enough credit. Listen, it's early days. And women's feckin' intuition or no women's feckin' intuition, sometimes what you see is what you get, Reet.'

We batted it forwards and backwards for the next few minutes but came to no conclusions, and then it was time to start getting ready for dinner.

When we got out to the pool, in which Tommy was doing his fierce, swimming-up-and-down thing, Yarso was already there, chatting to my Carol and my Alice, who were sitting right on the edge of the water. He was hunkered down in front of them taking their pictures. Well he might: they were posing for him, done up to the nines and plastered with makeup. Carol was wearing a navy and white polka-dotted shift minidress with a matching scarf round her forehead like a sweatband and huge dangly holly-berry earrings. Alice, who is naturally blonde, the only one of my girls who is, was sporting shocking-pink hipster jeans with spangles across the hip band and a lime green belly-top. Her earrings were in the shape of big yellow daisies. Poor little Patricia, looking so young in comparison, was sitting glumly a little apart from them, banging away at her computer game thingy.

'That's great, ladies.' Yarso stood up when we arrived. 'That'll do for now at least.'

'When can we see them?' Alice simpered up at him as the two of them stood up too.

'I'll get them developed as soon as I can,' Yarso smiled his great big Yankee smile down at them, 'and don't worry, I'll catch you guys again!' He had changed outfits: his jeans were khaki rather than blue and his white T-shirt was freshly ironed. He looked cool and relaxed and hip, and compared to him, me and my husband looked as if next stop was Shady Pines Retirement Home. I certainly felt decrepit – that's a good word, one Tess would use, I think. I suppose the three of us are all taking on a few of each other's words and ways of talking, it's only natural. Anyway, the belt on my shirtwaister was too tight – I could have sworn that dress fitted me. I couldn't be putting on holiday weight so soon, I thought, but then had to admit, dammit, that I probably was, to judge by the discomfort. I only have to look at food and I pile it on.

'Want a beer, Fred?' Ricky and I sat down with our own replenishments.

'No thanks, maybe later.' He crouched down by the pool again, this time to watch Tommy swimming. He seemed totally comfortable – I wouldn't be able to hold that position for two seconds without falling over or getting a cramp in my legs.

Tess, cool and perfect in a cream linen trouser suit, opted for a gin and tonic when she and Jerry joined us a few minutes later, but drowned the gin in so much slimline tonic that she might as well not have bothered. By contrast, Jerry poured enough whiskey into his glass to ossify an elephant. I wondered about this. He never used to be a drinker. First Maddy and now him. Was I getting a thing about drink? (By the way, did you know that elephants are the only land animals that can't jump? One of my brothers sent that fascinating fact to me in an e-mail from the States.)

There was still no sign of Kitty or Jack. Hmm, I thought. 'Your Jack joining us?' I asked Tess.

'He's locked into his bathroom. The smell of aftershave would knock you down.'

'Kitty's not here either. I have to say that the same is going on in her bedroom. When I checked there were at least seven discarded outfits on her bed. Are you thinking what I'm thinking?'

'Come on, girls!' Ricky scoffed into his beer. 'For God's sake, yiz'll have them married off next!'

We all settled down. It was that time of the evening I like, when the sun is gone but it's not dark yet and the air turns kind of blue.

A hint of a thing going on between Jack and Kitty wouldn't have been the worst thing in the world. He's a decent young fella. A bit quiet. But they all are around adults. Anyway, even if there was some spark, it wouldn't be serious. There'd be plenty more romances for the two of them before they settled into something for real.

She'd better not get pregnant, though. I'd kill her if she did. I know we're all supposed to be modern and tolerant about this kind of thing but my view is that any chance of a decent carefree youth goes out the window when you have a child outside the sheets. It's not that I wouldn't support her, of course I would, but I'd murder her first.

Going the whole way was not on the agenda with Ricky Sleator and me before we were married. It was nothing to do with morality or what my mother said or the bishops or anything like that. He was a little goer, in those days, and it wasn't that he didn't try and it wasn't that I didn't want to do it either. But I thought it was better to keep him at arm's length until I had the ring on my finger. Sounds calculating now, when I say it like that, but it worked out, didn't it? Anyway, it wasn't all that long. We were married within six months of us meeting.

I remember the first night I saw him. It was in the National where the Cadets were playing and the smell of Intimate, that week's special offer in Hayes Conyngham Robinson in O'Connell Street, was so strong it would choke you. I was pissed off that everyone else had bought it the same as I had.

I spotted Ricky almost immediately when I went in that night. He was with a gang, who were roaring at each other's jokes and seemed to be having a high old time. He was the only one who wasn't falling about. He was standing on the edge, with a smile on his face and taking part in a sort of a way, but not making a show of himself like the others.

If he hadn't given himself that little bit of distance, I would probably not have noticed him because, physically, he wouldn't have stood out from any crowd. He was lower than average height, for instance, but there was something about the way he carried himself, some kind of purposefulness, if there is such a word, that made the lights go on for me. So did the way he was dressed. Not in a suit like so many of the eejits who thought suits, no matter how greasy, would impress girls, but in a nice brown sports jacket with a white shirt and a brown and white striped tie. Showed he had a bit of respect for himself, that did.

I stayed with Tess during the first dance so I could watch him. The minute the music started, he was up and dancing a quickstep with a girl who was wearing glasses. The points were mounting up in his favour: the fact that he would ask out a girl with glasses was a good sign. Light on his feet too.

When he left the girl back to her friends, I excused myself from Tess, who wanted to hang about against the wall as usual, and went over to stand in front of him. 'I know this next one is not a ladies' choice,' I said brazenly, 'but I would like you to ask me to dance.'

The other fellas in his gang nearly died of shock, but he didn't. A lesser man would have been afraid of being jeered at, allowing himself to be hen-pecked. Instead, like a little gentleman, my Ricky just crooked one elbow and held it out to me. I took it, and he escorted me on to the floor.

During that first dance, he answered all my questions and, for some reason, he didn't mind me asking them so I learned very quickly what he was doing and what his plans were for the future. I remembered a phrase that had stuck with me from some book or other I was trying to read at the time: *a man of substance*. Even though most girls would probably not have given him a second glance, I soon found out that inside that ordinary-looking body and face, Ricky Sleator was a Man of Substance. During that evening we talked and talked, even getting pass-outs so we could walk round Parnell Square and listen to each other properly; poor Tess, I completely abandoned her.

I apologised later and she forgave me. She was excited for me, because she could see as well as I could that it was game, set and match for me and Ricky.

And here we were all these years later in the South of France, still together, with three of our four smasher daughters in front of us. I leaned over and planted a smacker on his cheek. 'What's that for?' He was surprised.

'Nothing,' I said. 'I just felt like doing it, that's all.' Tess and Jerry took no notice, although I thought I saw Jerry's eyebrows twitch.

We settled down again. It was very silent on the patio where we were sitting and all we could hear was the little splish-splash as Tommy continued to go about his business in the pool.

Yarso was on his feet again now, taking more snaps, of us, of the general scene, of the house and the swimming-pool. His camera looked good, one of those where he kept snapping off the lenses and putting others on. Only Tess protested, skittishly, in my opinion, although no one else seemed to notice anything different about her.

Then this really amazing-looking bird landed near us. I had never seen one like it: it was about the size of a big duck, but slimmer, brown, with black stripes, and it had this big feathery plume on its head. 'It's a hoopoe,' Tess whispered to me. 'I saw a picture of it in one of the books in our room.' The bird just looked at us and we looked at the bird and then it flew off.

This is going to sound stupid. But I can't get it out of my head so I might as well tell you. At the time those few seconds seemed to me to mark the end of one thing and the beginning of another. They still do. While we were looking at the bird and the bird was looking at us, I definitely felt something, a little flash, as if the world had taken a photograph of the scene for a keepsake because nothing was going to be the same ever again. (I told you it would sound stupid.) I turned to look at Tess to see if she had noticed anything peculiar, but she was standing up. Tom was climbing out of the swimming-pool.

As she walked the few feet to put a towel round him, it was so quiet we could hear her feet on the tiles and also what Yarso was saying to young Tommy. He was making a deal with the kid: he would teach Tommy the proper butterfly stroke if Tommy would pay him back by teaching him the right way to kick his legs in the front crawl. 'I've never been able to do it properly, Tom,' he said, in his soft American accent. 'Will you show me?'

Astonishingly – to me at least – Tommy, whose usual reply to any adult request is nothing at all or 'No', said he would.

Tess looked up at Yarso, and although I couldn't see her face, I didn't find it hard to imagine the expression. She put the towel round Tommy and came back. 'Did you hear that?' she said to me. Her eyes were shining.

'I heard.' I stole a quick look at Jerry, but he was staring into his glass. He hadn't said a word since he came out. 'Enjoy the golf today?' I asked him, at the top of my voice.

'What? Oh! Sorry. Yes, the golf. Grand. It's a fine course.' He had obviously been miles away. I felt like jumping up and thumping him and telling him to look to his wife. Instead, in a temper, I said I was going inside to see what was keeping our dinner.

But on the way into the kitchen, I gave myself another good talking-to. Tess was a grown-up, so was Jerry, and although the jury was still out on Yarso, so was he. Once and for all, I was to keep my nose out of other people's business.

You can't go against nature, though, and I stayed on the alert for the rest of that holiday, for no reason I could put my finger on. Maybe it was because our new friend became and remained the ideal guest. He was as good as his word with Tommy, for instance, and they spent hours in the pool.

Frederick Yarso kept his room spotless, although he didn't have to: the villa came supplied with maids for that. He played cards, badly; he was eager that Jerry and Ricky should show him how to play golf; he was always the best fun at the beach. He babysat Patricia and Tom a couple of nights to let the four adults go out alone and free up the teenagers to do their thing. He fell in with every plan. That was when he and Tess weren't driving around in one of the cars looking at 'sites of interest'. All in all, he was the life and soul of the bleeding party. He didn't put a foot wrong, and maybe that was it. I guess, being an Irish woman, I was too used to Irish men!

We never found out much about him. Although we tried our best, Ricky and me anyway, all we got was bare bones, no flesh. He had little contact with his ex-wife and he had his children only for Easter, Thanksgiving and two days during the Christmas holidays. He expressed no emotion about this, despite me trying to find out how he felt about it. (I would have thought any father would be bitter about this but he told it to us in the same way as he told us he was an only child and that both his parents were dead.) I was launching into more questions when I saw Tess warning me with her eyes to back off. I wasn't about to, but she changed the subject back to bloody archaeology.

At one point I tried to talk to Ricky again about him. 'Can't you see she's falling for him? I can see it if you can't – I tell you, Rick, it's dangerous.'

He scoffed at me: 'Women! You can't blame Fred if your imagination is running away with you. The chap is so polite he could be a waiter! He doesn't even flirt with the girls – and, by the way, speaking of those girls, have you seen the get-ups they're going around in these days? Are you not going to do anything about it? Bandages, they're wearing. Me ma would turn in her grave, she would!'

I ignored this. Such as it was, Ricky always left almost everything to do with the girls to me and in my opinion they were dressed no better and no worse than the French young ones all around them on the beach. 'Yeah,' I said, 'but they're not interested in him. Tess is.'

'Give us a break, Rita.'

But even though he wouldn't give me the time of day on this, I continued to think the whole set-up was really weird. I mean, we were supposed to be on holidays with our families, our two husbands were here and very much part of it, and Tess had invited a very big cuckoo into the nest and they all loved him. It beat me how Jerry Brennan didn't wake up to see what was maybe happening under his nose. She was going around with a smile on her face as big as the Amazon river.

I'm not saying she set out to do anything wrong or bad, I doubt if she even realised what was happening. And, to be fair, they did invite me, and anyone else who might want to go, along with them on their outings, but none of the rest of us ever went.

I tried the light approach, teased her about it but she didn't bite. All I ever got out of her was that Frederick was such a great teacher. He made archaeology so interesting.

Yeah. Right. Archaeology. And my name is Twiggy.

CHAPTER TWENTY-ONE

The fog has not lifted from the water below and Jerry has not moved from his chair. Nor has he touched the coffee I made him. 'They're late,' he says, hunching his shoulders. Although he has made an effort to sound indignant – as he would have only two months previously in his 'boss' persona – his tone is so flat that, despite everything that has happened between us, I want to rush over and hug him. Instead, I look at my watch: 'They could be caught up in traffic – they're only twenty minutes late.'

He does not respond.

'Would you like me to bring you another cup of coffee?' I ask. 'That one must be cold by now.'

'No, thank you.' His gaze slides to the carpet.

I made sure that Jack stayed in Rita's – or, rather, as he calls it now, Kitty's – last night, even though he was somewhat reluctant. He has no inkling – I hope – of what has happened. Not yet anyway, although of course I will have to tell him in time. I had entertained hopes that this visit by the police would be simply a formality and that everything would be cleared up. But instinct – and Jerry's demeanour – seems to say otherwise. He is pessimistic, I can see that. In his position, he has fairly good contacts and he has used them to the full. However, the person – he would not tell me of what rank – with whom he was put in touch had apparently remained quite formal. All he would tell us was that the best thing to do in circumstances such as these was simply to tell the truth.

As for myself, having run the gamut over the last few weeks since we returned from Collioure, I suppose the word 'numb' would best describe the way I am right at this moment. Only three times has my life seemed 'real', when I knew what it was to be alive and fully present, with every nerve and brain cell operating in unison, every organ, bone and blood vessel filling every inch of skin. This may be the fourth.

The first time was when I was visiting my mother on her death-bed, the second was on the day I was received by my congregation as a novice, and the third was on the instant I saw Arkady.

Is it odd that I have not included either of my wedding days or the birth of either of my children? I think so, but there is little point in telling this story if I am not to be honest.

Now, with Arkady drawn up protectively around me, I can hear the sound of a car engine climbing our hill. On a quiet, windless day like this, we always know when someone is coming to our gate.

I look across at Jerry. He has heard it too. The car stops and, instinctively, we both turn to watch the drawing-room door; the pause while we anticipate the sound of the doorbell reminds me of those Second World War scenes where the inhabitants of London wait for the explosion after the engine of the doodlebug cuts out.

Although we are waiting for it, when the bell rings, we both jump. 'I'll go, will I?' I stand up.

'Thanks.'

There are two of them, in plain clothes, man and woman, very polite, youngish. 'Mrs Brennan?' asks the man.

'That's right.'

'Detective Nugent,' he flips open a little card-holder and shows me an ID, 'and this is Detective Marsh.'

'Naomi,' says the woman, shrewd-eyed and softly dressed in polo-necked sweater and slacks under a windcheater.

'How do you do?' I open the door wide. 'Come in, won't you?'

'Cold day,' says Ms Marsh, as they wipe their feet carefully on the coir matting.

'It is, yes.' I close the door behind them. Then, indicating the double doors, 'My husband is through here, in the drawing room.' As I walk, I can feel them behind me, their eyes swivelling, assessing.

Our hallway is a treble-height atrium. We gave up a couple of rooms on the first floor and some storage space in the attics for it but the sacrifice paid huge dividends: it is as imposing as any I have seen anywhere and my plants are as thrilled as I am with the light from the clerestory we put in. I can just imagine these Gárdaí's thoughts about fat cats.

Jerry is standing when we get into the drawing room. After the introductions, all four of us stand around awkwardly as though not knowing what to say next. 'Coffee, anyone?' I manage to sound matter-of-fact.

'That would be lovely, Mrs Brennan,' says the one called Nugent, sitting down on the nearest sofa. The woman sits beside him as I leave the room; Jerry resumes his own seat. I move quietly down the hallway, but although I can hear voices, I cannot distinguish what is being said.

We had agreed beforehand that, after serving the coffee, I would stay in the room with Jerry during whatever was to transpire – if they allowed this. No matter what was going on privately for us, to show marital solidarity in public might have been a beneficial psychological influence, we thought.

The coffee tray, complete with chocolate biscuits (I had assumed Gárdaí would like chocolate biscuits) is on the kitchen counter nearest the door. As I fill the cafetière with boiling water and place it beside them, I experience another of those out-of-body moments with which I have been afflicted lately. In this instance, it is as though everything in my kitchen shrinks, while I, looking in from outside, remain life-sized, a giant peering through the window of a doll's house.

The miniature coffee tray is as I had set it; I, in miniature, am standing beside it, dressed in my doll's grey linen skirt, black cashmere sweater and tiny black court shoes. My doll's hair is pulled back in a black Alice band and my little eyes are as dead and shrunken as currants.

The illusion passes as quickly as it had arisen but my hands shake as I press the plunger of the cafetière. Up to now I had thought these occurrences were of no moment, but for the first time, I wonder if I should make an appointment with our doctor. For instance, could these hallucinations, if that's what they are, indicate a brain tumour?

Quickly, I arrange my face into blandness and hurry back

towards the drawing room. All three are in position as I left them, but on seeing me enter, the two Gárdaí stand politely.

Jerry's expression is unreadable. 'Please sit.' I place the tray on the coffee table. There is profound silence as they obey.

The sound of the coffee being poured is as intrusive as the electrically controlled splatter of a hideous fountain Rita brought home from a shopping trip we took to Spain. 'Thank you, Mrs Brennan.' Delicately, Nugent picks up his cup. 'No, thank you, no biscuits. Watching the old figure these days.' Then, to Jerry, 'Before we do anything else, perhaps we'll take a look at your computer, Mr Brennan.'

CHAPTER TWENTY-TWO

To backtrack again a little, here is what happened after I got home from Collioure.

It was no surprise to find that Jerry was as immersed in work as ever, but what was different, and pleasant, was how well we got on during those first few days after the holiday. When he was here, or even on the phone, he was attentive and pleasant; we even made love two nights in a row. And on the first Saturday after our return, he brought me roses. An enormous bouquet. 'What are these for?' For a moment I thought I must have forgotten some anniversary.

'For putting up with me, lass.' He stroked my cheek. 'I know I was bad company in France. I'm sorry.'

It occurred to me that now was a good time to find out what had been wrong, but I didn't want to destroy his gesture so I just thanked him. We would have time enough for post-mortems. 'Let's go away for a weekend,' I said impulsively. 'Just the two of us. To Paris, or even Rome!'

'We'll see.' He smiled at me. 'Maybe. Now, if you can do without me for a couple of hours,' his tone became brisk, 'I think I'll get the mower out. It's a lovely day, might as well take advantage of it, they're so few and far between.'

I was taken aback to say the least. We pay a gardener to come in once a week and Jerry has never once shown the slightest interest in our lovely gardens. But who was I to demur? 'Great,' I said. 'See you later.'

I hummed as I distributed my roses among a number of vases. I had made the right decision in not picking over old bones. I was just going to accept and enjoy this *volte-face*.

His good humour continued for those first few days after the holiday so life was pleasant in Arkady and promised to remain so, even though Jack was feeling his oats, as I believe the phrase is. He surfaced from the chaos of his bedroom around noon each day to go into Dublin. This led to repeated, wearying conversations between us.

'Where are you going, Jack?'

'Out.'

'Where "out"?'

'Just out. I'm not a baby, Mum.'

'I know you're not a baby. I keep telling you, it's not a challenge – I don't demand to know, but I'm your mother, not some sort of housekeeper. I'm only asking. I'd *like* to know where you're—'

'Town. Where do you think I'm going? I'm going to town, all right? Same place I went yesterday. And the day before. Same place I'll be going tomorrow.'

'Jack, don't speak to me like that. Have some respect—'

'Well, *you* don't speak to *me* like that. *You* have a bit of respect for *me*. Leave me alone, Mum!'

'Jack! I'm only—'

'And before you ask, I don't *know* what time I'll be home and I don't *know* who I'll be meeting. Just some of the gang. And, yes, I *will* have my mobile with me and it *is* charged up. All *right*, Mum?'

I was usually left looking at the inside of a slammed door. The consolation was that, when we compared notes, Rita was having conversations along similar lines with Kitty.

In fact, neither of the two boys was at home all that much. Tom, having watched some of Wimbledon on television, decided that tennis was his latest all-consuming interest and – despite the appalling 'summer' we were having – took to leaving for the tennis club every morning immediately after breakfast and not reappearing until supper time. I was delighted, too, that he seemed to have a new friend, a boy named Colin. 'He's only ten, Mum, but he's cool.' ('Cool', a word I thought had vanished, seems to have been resurrected this year.)

Then there was Frederick.

I haven't told you yet about Frederick, have I? He is an American, a maverick type we invited to stay with us in Collioure,

a couple of days after the Griggses left. Although, to my recollection, the invitation was not for an open-ended visit, his days with
us stretched into weeks, right up until the end. It was actually
quite nice to have him: he was the only adult male we had as
company after first Ricky, then Jerry left the villa.

Rita and I met him in a hilltop village in northern Spain where
we had been shopping for souvenirs. We were having lunch and it
is no exaggeration to say that he lit up the room when he walked
into the restaurant. Does that sound like a cliché? If it does, I can
think of no better way to describe it. The room, clattering with
trade, was sunlit at our end where a big picture window overlooked a little valley planted with dusty olive trees. Yet somehow,
when Frederick came in, the light seemed to intensify as though
someone had turned it up. I know this could not have happened
in reality, but that is my recollection. It might have had something
to do with the way the sunlight reflected from his hair, which is
longish and wheaten in colour. It may simply be that memory has
enhanced the moment.

After looking around the restaurant, he spotted that there were
vacant places at our big table, came over and asked if he could join
us.

He and I clicked immediately, so much so that Rita was left out.
I made an effort to include her in that first conversation, but
Frederick is an archaeologist, as passionate about his subject as
they all are in that discipline, and she has neither the interest nor
the knowledge to participate. So as he and I rabbited on, we
unconsciously excluded her and the two of them got off on the
wrong foot. Although she agreed with inviting him to stay with us
and was not openly uncivil, she never warmed to him.

After he arrived, Frederick and I began going about without the
others, none of whom were interested in visiting sites. I know I
have told you that going on digs with Michael was soul-
destroying, but I was not talking about archaeology *per se*. What I
was referring to were the long, hot periods of *ennui* when poor
little Jack and I were confined to some third-world hotel while
Michael and his colleagues were miles away, scraping in the dirt
with their little trowels. The excursions Frederick and I took were
entirely different: they were day trips for one thing, so there was

no time to get bored, and awaiting us at the end of each day was the prospect of our lovely villa, with its wonderful power-showers and *haute cuisine*.

He guided me around places like Elne, which has a five-thousand-year history, and it was fascinating to hear him speak about Perpignan and Carcassonne, ancient places in the Pyrenees and, further west, the Basque region.

He made the latter sound so amazing (the Basque civilisation is the oldest in Europe) that I wanted the whole group to take a trip to Bilbao.

Again, no one else could be bothered. 'Come on, Tess.' As usual, Jerry took it upon himself to speak for all. 'We're not here a wet week and you want to drag us all off again. Settle down.' We were about ten days into our holiday. We adults were sitting on the calm, warm terrace after dinner, the air lit and scented with the citronella candles Maddy had brought with her, and that we had decided to burn in her honour. 'What do you think, Ricky? Want to go trekking through the Pyrenees and into Basque territory? Get blown up by ETA?' He turned for support to Rita's husband, due to leave for Japan in ten days' time.

'Hey!' Ricky protested. 'Leave me out of this. I'm not going anywhere, I'm conserving me energy for that bleedin' flight, thank you very much.'

I turned to Rita. 'How about you, Reet?'

She glanced at Frederick, who was nursing a glass of the local rosé. 'I don't think so,' she said slowly. 'Sorry.'

'So I guess not.' Jerry picked up his wine. 'We're all perfectly happy here. If you're restless, Tess, go shopping or something.'

'That's not fair and it's insulting.' I was mortified at this marital patronising.

'All right, sorry,' Jerry apologised. 'Maybe it was. Why don't you and Frederick go if you want to? We can manage here with one car.'

I was so angry and embarrassed I very nearly retorted that this would suit me fine. But I have to admit that, by the time this spat occurred, I had recognised danger. I was becoming aware of Frederick as a male. Although I conscientiously invited Rita, the boys, her girls, even Jerry to come with us on every one of our archaeological outings, I found myself pleased each time they refused.

He fitted in well with the group but, for me, the best time was when I was alone with him. I don't mean this to sound as if there was a romance between us, certainly nothing happened. All I mean is that, compared to Jerry (and even my darling Michael), Frederick was so open and easy, so accommodating in that American way of his, that I found myself confiding feelings and experiences to him I had not fully exposed to anyone else. He was fascinated by my convent stories, for instance, and I was so relaxed with him that, bit by bit, I began to talk about them.

But neither of us could ever be accused, *ever*, of stepping over the line.

Here is one small anecdote to illustrate what I mean.

One afternoon, we were strolling around the cloister of the medieval cathedral at Elne, a few kilometres north of Collioure. The place was deserted, it was mid-afternoon and the air drowsed in the type of heat that sends most sensible people to the beach.

I was admiring the Romanesque stone carvings on one of the entrance doors from the cloister into the body of the cathedral when I sensed Frederick very close behind. He wears an aftershave lotion or cologne with a tang of citrus, distinctive and pleasant, although probably cheap. (It became clear early on that Frederick's funds were limited. I did notice him using a credit card but that was hardly significant in this day and age.) Quickly, I turned round to find him smiling at me in that slightly lopsided way of his. 'What?'

'What?'

'I asked you first.'

'But I didn't speak!'

'I know you didn't – but you have something on your mind. Why are you smiling like that?'

'Jeez, Bibi, can't a guy smile these days without someone making a federal case out of it?' He had begun to call me 'Bibi' early on, making fun of my two surnames.

'*Frederick!*'

'Whoa – chill!' He put up his hands in mock defence. Then, dropping them, 'Okay – walking behind you, I was thinking that if you let down the hems on those shorts you could call 'em jeans!'

Modesty, long ingrained, is hard to dislodge, and even my tennis shorts are always Bermuda-length. I gave his chest a little push. 'By all means feel free to comment on my shorts.'

We were standing virtually nose to nose, so close I could see perspiration lying like a string of seed pearls along his hairline. For one mad moment, I thought we might even kiss.

We didn't, of course. And, in all honesty, I cannot remember which of us turned away first. For my part, I went back to my arched doorway, muttering something banal about the way stone remains so well preserved in this climate.

I tell you only to show how nothing happened and that the mood between us remained light-hearted. The episode might seem significant when it is put down in black and white – and it was significant, I suppose, or I would not have mentioned it. I cannot speak for him, of course, but afterwards he behaved as always. As for me, even with the memory of temptation lying like a shed snakeskin round my neck for the remainder of the afternoon, I continued to enjoy myself like a giddy schoolgirl on the mitch. We wandered round the cathedral confines, sipped from our lukewarm water bottles and ate Magnums under the shade-trees of the village street.

I can hear you say that I protest too much, and you may have a point. There was indeed something consequential about that episode in the cloister – and others similar – in that they acted like a ring of little lighthouses warning against the one rocky area in a friendly sea. But I am a married woman, and my marriage vows are as sacred as the vows I would have taken in the convent, had I been professed.

So in this roundabout, long-winded way (sorry!) I am explaining why I kept my mouth shut that evening about Bilbao, despite Jerry's provocation.

I see now that it was easy, in that golden, seductive sunshine, to think that the friendship with Frederick could have remained exactly as it was. And when the time came to leave Collioure, it felt natural to invite him to visit us in Ireland on his way back to the States.

The invitation arose spontaneously, on our last night in the villa.

Having eaten, the young people went off about their own business and, depleted in numbers as we were, we adults – just Rita, myself and Frederick now – were sitting by the pool having a last drink together. Rita, whose indifference to our guest was still obvious to me, swivelled to him. 'So, where do you go from here, Fred?' She had persisted in calling him 'Fred'.

'I'll take a ride as far as the village, if you don't mind,' he replied equably, including the two of us. 'I haven't decided yet where I'll go from here. Into northern Italy, maybe. See where the road takes me.'

'Why don't you come and visit us in Ireland on your way back home?' This was not something I had planned to say, yet the moment I said it, I knew it had not been spontaneous at all.

CHAPTER TWENTY-THREE

I did not really believe that Frederick would take me up on the invitation. I had overlooked the fact that, unlike us, Americans usually take such gestures at face value. Less than a week after we arrived home, I was on my way to the Dart station to pick up Daddy, who was coming to stay with us for a few days, when I saw this unmistakable figure toiling up the hill towards our house. We spotted each other at the same instant and I was so surprised that I swerved in to the kerb too quickly, denting a hub-cap. Ever after, when looking back on the catalogue of subsequent, runaway events and the way my life sped out of my control, that sighting of Frederick would be the starting-point. But, of course, I did not know that then. 'What on earth are you doing here?' I lowered the passenger window.

'You did invite me! I can see you drive in Ireland as well as you cook in Collioure!' He touched the hub-cap with the toe of his walking-boot. My burning of toast and incinerating of bacon, when I had tried to prepare American BLTs using the unfamiliar appliances of the Collioure kitchen, had been a source of much merriment to everyone.

'Thank you. And, if I may return the compliment, you look terrible.' He was unshaven, red eyed and sodden, courtesy of our incessant Irish downpour.

'Is this my fault?' His wave took in the thunder-grey sky and the streams pouring through the overflowing gutters. 'And how come no one thought of laying on a goddamned bus from the station to your house?'

'Get in!' I leaned over and opened the passenger door.

'Thanks!' He threw his backpack on to the back seat, then

scrambled in beside me, grinning through wet corkscrews of hair. 'Glad to see me?'

'Shut up! And behave! I'm going down to the station to pick up my father. You'll have to come with me, I've no time now to bring you into the house.'

'Great. I love relatives. And I even have a way to ingratiate myself – I'll show him my pictures.' He settled back.

'What pictures?'

'There's a great one of you by yourself on the terrace by the swimming-pool – and a really awesome one of all the kids together. Remember that evening when Jack jumped in with all his clothes on because he was pissed that you were nagging him to get changed for dinner? And then all the girls jumped in too?'

'Can't wait to see them!' I turned on the windscreen demister to deal with the steam filling the car and drove off.

He had instantly re-established the atmosphere of the holiday. I well remember that evening, far away in time and space now that our Irish 'summer' was in full flood.

I had mixed feelings about Frederick's timing because I had no idea how Daddy and he would get on. I adore my father, but it is easier to love him from a distance. He can be demanding and pernickety, especially if he thinks he is not the main attraction. He is also old fashioned: discipline and routine are paramount and I was not sure how he would react to Frederick's casual ways.

On the other hand, having Frederick around would give us an excuse for outings, despite the appalling weather. Everyone in Ireland seems to forget, year after year, that we don't have summer here, just a small variation on winter. Every spring we unearth the linens and the straw hats and the deck-chairs and plan barbecues as though we were Californians. Then, when we are driven miserably indoors clutching flaccid paper plates, we complain bitterly that this must be global warming because we've never seen anything like it in our lives. This summer had, to date, surpassed itself. It was sneaky too, because many of the very early mornings were delightful, sunny and enticing, but by the time I had breakfasted and was ready to go outside, cold silvery sheets were again pouring from Arkady's eaves.

'We're all pinning our hopes on an Indian summer in September,' I said now to Frederick, as we approached the village. 'How did you get here?'

'I hitched.'

'All the way from the South of France? You couldn't have.'

'I was lucky. I met a couple from England when I was eating lunch in that café in Collioure we liked. They had a girl of about Tom's age and a boy a bit older. The woman reminded me of you, as a matter of fact, Bibi, although she wasn't a fox, like you are!' He grinned.

'Go on.' I was flattered.

'Well, I could see these people were dressed for travelling – big serious bum-bags, jeans instead of shorts, that sort of thing – so I joined up with 'em, asked if I could share the table and, in the course of conversation, asked where they were headed. Turned out they were leaving within the hour for the north, driving all the way without a stop to take the Channel Tunnel. I really lucked out. They were on one of those deals with one car and a certain number of people free, you know? After a bit of discussion at the terminal, they let me join them and I didn't even have to pay for my ticket.

'It was simple on the other side. I got rides from tourists – English too. They're so polite, aren't they? Anyhow, I got to Holyhead in one piece. And that ferry was wild! I hooked up with a youth soccer team on the boat, they were great!' He smiled reminiscently. 'Boy, can those kids drink beer!'

'Aren't you supposed to be doing a research sabbatical or something?' The details of his thesis had remained vague: something to do with an attempt to connect the ancient civilisations of East and West involving threads of language. 'I thought you were going to northern Italy?'

'I was.' We were pulling into the tiny car-parking area in front of the Dart station, watched dully by three tourists who were sheltering under the awning over the outdoor tables of the coffee shop. 'But then, when I met those guys, it seemed like fate. Same way I met you and Rita in that little place in Spain, eh?' He grinned again. 'I feel I've done enough research to last me a lifetime, Bibi. What I need to do now is get on with the actual paper. That's the crappy bit. *Mañana* sounds pretty good to me right now.

'Don't worry,' he said then, 'I'm not going to be a slacker while I'm here. I'll help earn my keep. I'll garden, I'll continue the great swimming experiment with Tommy, or I'll fix your roof.'

'Chance would be a fine thing.'

'You don't think I can fix a crummy little roof?'

'You haven't seen the size of Arkady's roof. Or roofs. There are several of them.' As I slotted the car into a parking space, it occurred to me that Frederick had made an art form of finding benefactors. 'How long are you planning to stay?'

'Depends.'

'On what?'

'On when you throw me out.' I looked at his cheeky face and didn't know whether I wanted to kiss it or slap it. 'You're a lunatic, do you know that?'

'Takes one to know one, Bibi.'

'Ssh! Now, listen to me, Frederick, the train's due in two minutes and there are a few things you need to know . . .' I took him quickly through a potted guide to the dos and don'ts of how to deal with my father.

He listened intently. 'Sounds like a real swell guy,' he said, when I had finished. I didn't know how to take this and opened my mouth to protest, but he covered it with a gentle hand. 'Don't worry, kitten, I'll be the perfect wallpaper. He won't know I'm even there.'

I could hear the train squealing into the station. Flustered, I opened the door of the car. 'I'm serious, Frederick! One false move and you're out on your ear – oh, and by the way, his name is Paddy Cahill. He's quite straight-laced so I'd appreciate it if you'd call him Mister Cahill for the time being, until he says otherwise, OK? And by the way, we pronounce it "Ca-al" here, not "Cay-hill".'

'Yes, ma'am!'

As I dashed through the rain and up the steps into the station I was conscious that he was watching me. Although I had been genuinely surprised at his unexpected arrival, I discovered that secretly I was thrilled – *Stop it right there, Tess Butler Brennan!*

The train had just halted and its doors were opening. I arranged my expression into daughterly anticipation.

'Hello, Daddy!' As usual, he had emerged from the lead carriage. My father had been known to stand all the way from Connolly station to Howth rather than sit anywhere but the carriage in which he always travelled. 'How are you?' As we embraced, I was shocked to discover how thin he had become. He had last visited us less than three months previously and I did not remember him like this.

However, he was eighty-three, people of that age do shrink – but somehow I had missed his ageing. His shirt collar was standing away from his neck and even his tweed cap seemed too large for his head. 'Are you feeling all right, Daddy?'

'What do you mean?' He warned me off with his tone. Daddy could always do that.

'Here, give me the luggage.' I went to pull the bag from his hand but he wrestled it back.

'I'm not in an invalid carriage yet, Teresa. Don't fuss.'

The electric engine of the Dart cut out and, in the ensuing quiet, I realised we had both been shouting. 'Daddy, listen,' I said urgently, 'before we get to the car, I need to warn you that we're having another visitor besides yourself. His name is Frederick Yarso and he's an American we met on holiday.'

'I see.' When something unexpected happens, my father has always kicked to touch.

'As a matter of fact, he's in the car, waiting for us. He was on the way to the house when I met him and in all this rain I thought it was better . . .' I trailed off. Those bushy eyebrows, grey now, were meeting in the frown that had always intimidated me.

'What's wrong with you, Teresa? Why are you babbling? You're entitled to entertain any visitor you like in your own house. I daresay we'll rub along together well enough.'

'He's a bit, well, unusual.'

'I see. Black, is he?'

'Daddy, no!' I was taken aback. 'He's not black. He's an archaeologist. An academic.'

'A friend of Michael's?'

'No. I told you, Jerry and I met him on holiday in France.' I gathered myself together. 'Oh, never mind, you'll meet him soon enough.' I took his elbow, noting again how bony it was. 'But as I mentioned, he's absolutely soaked to the skin and he's been travelling for days so you won't really see the best side of him right now.'

Frederick had ensconced himself beside his pack in the rear of the car. The introductions, conducted over the headrest of the front passenger seat, were cordial to the point of obsequiousness. 'Good afternoon, Mr Cahill.' The pronunciation was perfect and the tone utterly respectful, 'I've been dying to meet you. I've heard *soo* much about you from your daughter and her husband.'

'Very nice to meet you, Mr Yarso. Frederick, if I may?'

'Of course!'

'I hope you will forgive us our climate, Frederick.'

Both were acting as though it was the most natural thing in the world for a middle-aged married woman to be hosting a wet, hairy hitchhiker in her husband's absence. (Jerry was in Stockholm at a media conference.) I leaned over and attempted to pull the seat-belt across my father's chest. 'Let me help you there.'

'Please, Teresa.' He waved me away. 'I asked you not to fuss. I am not a child, don't treat me like one.' As much as his arthritis would allow, he twisted his head so that Frederick could see him throw his eyes to heaven. In the mirror, I saw the gesture reciprocated, along with our guest's most beatific smile.

I fired the engine.

Frederick's reaction to Arkady was gratifying, to say the least. 'Bibi! What a place! This knocks the Taj Mahal for a home run!' The three of us were standing in the entrance hall and, dripping on my Victorian tiles, he was gazing upwards through pearly light at the clerestory.

'Don't be silly, Frederick.' I tried to keep my satisfaction from showing, the novice mistress's exhortations about pride and falls not having been in vain. 'It's nice, but I'm sure you've seen some wonderful houses on your travels.'

'Yeah, I have, but this stands up to the best of 'em. Right, Mr Cahill?' He turned to Daddy.

'Yes, it's very nice.' Daddy wasn't looking up: he was carefully removing the waterproof covering from his cap. It pained me to see how slow he had become. When had that happened?

'Nice?' Frederick shrugged off his drenched denim jacket, exposing the equally wet shoulders of his white T-shirt. 'I want to ship it brick by brick back to Oshkosh.'

'Enough! By the way it's just the three of us for supper tonight, I'm afraid, the boys are eating out at various friends' houses.'

'What about Jerry? Is he working late?' Frederick was unlacing his walking-boots.

I took his wet jacket from the end of the banisters where he had hung it. 'He'll be upset to have missed you,' I lied. 'Let me put this in the warm room in the laundry. You wait here, Frederick. When I come back I'll show you to your room. Daddy, you know where to go. Everything's ready for you up there.'

I walked away down the hall towards the kitchen and laundry room. 'Jerry's away again, Frederick,' I called over my shoulder. 'He's at a conference this time.' This had been an announcement for Daddy – who already knew that Jerry would not be here during his visit. It was one of the reasons he had chosen to come: he liked to have me to himself. But I needed him to know that Frederick's timing was not deliberate.

We ate supper at eight o'clock.

Our menus change dramatically when Daddy comes to Arkady. His culinary tastes had not changed since he was ten years old. He despised the modern trend for 'smothering good food in sludge', would not eat pasta, barely tolerated rice, and fish only if it was either sole or plaice, fried in egg and breadcrumbs. Before she left at lunch-time, Mrs Byrne had given me a hand with an old-fashioned shepherd's pie. One of my inheritances from the house in Ballina is my mother's old Spong mincer. I am impatient with its slowness, fiddly little parts, and the physical effort required to use it.

Mrs Byrne loves it. Her childhood, like mine, had included the task of mincing Sunday's leftover lamb or beef for Monday's pie and she revelled in assembling it, clamping it to the worktop in the kitchen, pressing the individual cubes of meat into the funnel on top and then exclaiming extravagantly as it re-emerged in little pink worms: 'Oh, my! Look at this. You can keep your food chefs and your choppers, Mrs B, they don't make machines like this any more!' (Mrs Byrne and I mutually call each other 'Mrs B'. It is our small bonding joke. For me it serves to assuage the guilt in having a servant. For her it signals that she is as good as me. At least I think so, we have never discussed it.)

Given that I had worried more than a little that Daddy might be sniffy with Frederick – a cuckoo in the nest demanding my attention – the meal was remarkably free of tension. In some part this was thanks to the same Spong because, not surprisingly, the American was eating his first real shepherd's pie. 'This is delicious!' he said. 'You must give me the recipe.' I looked hard at him, but he seemed sincere. So I was able to fill at least ten minutes of conversation time with memories of shepherds' pies past and detailed description of the workings of the peerless mincer.

My father, to give him his due, did his best to contribute. When, towards the end of the meal, the conversation hit a sticky patch, he piped up, asking for Frederick's 'expert opinion' on the achievements of the Romans and, in particular, on Caesar's Gallic wars, a subject he remembered from his Latin classes at school. 'I have a reason for asking about this, Frederick. What I believe is that, like the Roman Empire two thousand years ago, our own western civilisation is about to collapse, and for the same reasons, we face corruption and a decline in morals.' He placed his knife and fork side by side on his empty plate and sat back, folding his hands, Monsignor-like, in front of him on the table. 'Would you agree with that, now?'

Our guest did not blink. 'You may have a point there, Mr Cahill. We have certainly lost our respect for some of the old-fashioned verities.'

After Frederick had helped me clear away the dishes, the three of us went into the television room and Frederick produced his holiday snaps, which proved to be of very high quality. I have always hated pictures of myself and glossed over my own frequent appearances, but as well as the action sequences of the clothed kids in the pool, there were some terrifically informal shots of the whole group – a particularly fine portrait of Jerry in pensive mood, a gorgeous, coquettish one of Carol and Alice, and two superb studies of Tom, the best I have ever seen. Frederick had caught him beside the swimming-pool at the villa, in light that slanted obliquely and turned his skin to pale gold. 'I'm surprised he let you take these,' I said, pleased. 'He's usually very camera shy. Could I have copies of them?'

'You can have copies of 'em all! And I don't think he knew I was taking them at the time. You're right, Tessa, the kid hates posing. You have to be clever to catch him – or very quick.'

'Yes, they're very good, Frederick.' The photographs then received the Patrick Cahill seal of approval. 'Young Tom is a great swimmer, I believe.'

'He is indeed, Mr Cahill.' Frederick glanced at me and grinned: *Told you I'd get on with him!*. 'And a good little teacher, too. He improved my front crawl big-time.'

My father replaced the photographs in their envelope and handed them back.

'Would you like me to get a set made for you too, Mr Cahill?' Frederick put them back in his camera bag.

'No thank you.' Daddy shook open his newspaper to the television-listings page. 'I'm getting too old now for collecting any more photographs. I must have thousands in the house.' He smiled. 'I'll keep these in my brain.'

I was surprised. Daddy had always persecuted me for photographs, which he filed meticulously in chronologically ordered and labelled albums.

Having perused the listings in the newspaper, my father decided there was nothing worth watching and that he was going to bed. 'Can we go for a walk on the pier tomorrow morning, Teresa? We could go early – before anyone else is up and about, get a jump on the day.'

Despite the casual tone, I knew from experience that this was not a request but a command. 'Sure, Daddy, I'd love that.'

He looked at Frederick. 'I'm sure you'd like to sleep on a bit?'

Frederick had stood up respectfully when my father had. Trim in fresh denims and sweatshirt, he took the hint. 'I sure would, Mr Cahill, I'm pooped. Travelling, these days, is getting less and less glamorous.'

'I wouldn't know much about that, of course.' Daddy picked up his *Irish Independent* and folded it carefully in its original creases. Although he stocked all the national newspapers in the shop, coming from a rock-solid Fine Gael background, he had been a diehard supporter all his life and never read any of the other 'propaganda sheets'. I have always believed part of his standoffish-ness with Jerry was due to his stewardship of the rival Sentinel Group. 'Goodnight to you both,' he said, inclining his head, ever the gracious patriarch. 'See you in the morning, Teresa, bright and early.' He stuck the newspaper under his arm and walked stiffly towards the stairs, leaving Frederick and me to our own devices.

CHAPTER TWENTY-FOUR

Frederick watched Daddy go, then sat down again on the sofa. 'What a great old guy.'

'Yes, he is.'

I, too, sat down and turned on the television, flicking from channel to channel without really noticing what was on any of them. Outside, rain still dripped from the eaves and the heads of the hollyhocks in the flower border in front of the window drooped miserably.

Our sofa in the television room is sectional and very large; Frederick and I were at opposite ends, with more than eight feet between us. Yet although I was staring straight ahead, his long legs and canvas running shoes seemed to grow across my vision until I could see nothing else. He was not wearing socks. Those small hairs above his tanned ankles caught the light like threads of gold . . .

Colin's mother had telephoned during supper to ask if Tom could stay the night. Jack would not be home, I knew, until midnight or thereabouts. I would be alone with Frederick at least until then. I clicked off the television. 'Nothing. Daddy was right.'

I made heavy weather of walking to the window and pulling the curtains. 'What would you like to do now, Frederick? As it happens, I'm tired too.' I forced a yawn as I turned back to him. 'I wouldn't mind going up myself.'

'Hey, I have an idea. Where's your cello?'

'It's in the attic.'

'Get it down. Play something for me.'

'You must be joking. I haven't played for years!' I was sorry I had told him about it during one of our jaunts.

He persisted. 'It's gotta be like riding a bicycle.'

'No, it isn't! It isn't at all like riding a bicycle, Frederick, it takes practice. A lot of practice.'

'It was only a suggestion, Bibi.'

I looked at his amused expression. 'Sorry,' I mumbled. 'What I mean is that I would be ashamed of how badly I'd play now. I'd need at least six months of retraining.'

'Whatever.' He was still amused.

' "Whatever" what?'

He sprawled, spreading his long legs. 'Whatever, nothing . . .'

'Stop this, Frederick.'

'Stop what?'

I could not exactly say to him that what I meant was that he should stop affecting the speed of the blood hammering through my veins. Nor could I confide the appalling truth that when I made love to my husband the previous week it had been to my memories of Frederick's body. (I had been consumed with guilt afterwards, but Jerry hadn't noticed anything amiss, so it was between me and my confessor.) 'Just stop it, all right?' I walked across the room and turned on a table lamp.

'OK. I'll stop it.'

When I turned back, he was smiling happily. 'Anyway,' I said heatedly, 'after all these years, there isn't the remotest chance that the strings would be intact.'

'Not intact.' His smile grew broader. 'Of course they wouldn't.'

Seriously agitated, I crossed to the cabinet housing the television, opened it and peered inside. 'I'm exhausted so I'm going to bed, but I think the boys have some DVD films in here. I could set it up for you. Would you like to watch one?'

'I'm not in the mood for a film at the moment. But if you're not going to entertain me to a musical evening, do you have a computer I could use to access my e-mails? I haven't checked them since Collioure.'

I straightened up to face him. 'Actually . . .'

He mistook the reason for my hesitation. 'Don't worry. I can easily wait until tomorrow. Go to an Internet café.'

'No. Please don't do that.' I turned back to close the cabinet. 'It's just that Jack locks away his laptop in case Tom might get at it

– and unfortunately I never use the one in Jerry's study. You see, I'm a bit of a Luddite when it comes to technology.' I could feel the onset of verbal diarrhoea. I was also dicing with the truth. It is a source of semi-amused irritation for Jerry that I have refused to have anything to do with the computer at home, privately on the basis that the more you know, the more you're required to do. I have no intention of becoming an auxiliary, unpaid staff member of the Sentinel Group.

In any event, I do consider myself a technological dunce, the exception to the rule dictating that a talent for music is an indicator of an aptitude for mathematics and computers. But even Rita talks now about shopping on the Net and how handy it is to be on e-mail, so some years ago I bowed to universal pressure and took one of those capsule computer courses run by the *Irish Times*. I tried to learn, honestly I did, but I found it difficult to remember my Power Point from my Excel, probably because I had no real interest in it. I retained the rudiments from that course, however, certainly enough to recognise some of the jargon, to turn on the machine and to locate the Remote Access icon.

'Is it Jerry's office computer?' Frederick asked now. 'I wouldn't like to—'

'He has his laptop with him, of course,' I interrupted, still babbling, 'but I think they're linked in. He prefers a big screen when he's working. I know he's been talking about upgrading it, getting docking or something, but it hasn't happened yet. In a way, Jerry's quite old fashioned about some things. Don't worry, I'm sure he wouldn't mind at all.' I was fiddling with the television cabinet as though it required a locksmith's genius to close it. It had become imperative that I escape right this instant from Frederick's presence, from his citrussy smell, from his height. From the curling softness of his hair. But I was the hostess. I could not wave vaguely up the stairs and leave it at that. Any doubts I had about letting a stranger loose on Jerry's computer were buried in confusion and the desire to get away from this man as quickly as possible. 'I'll show you where it is and make sure you're up and running, all right?'

If he was aware of my agitation, his voice did not betray it. 'Thanks,' he replied easily, 'that's great. I won't tamper with any of the software or settings. I'll just log on if I can, and if I can't suss it in the first ninety seconds, no harm done. That's if you're absolutely sure it's OK.'

'Of course it is.' I turned towards him at last, staging another yawn. 'Sorry about this, I don't understand why I'm so tired all of a sudden. This way.' I had to pass him on my way to the door, and although I took as wide a course as possible, I felt as though I was travelling through a forcefield.

I practically galloped down the hallway and up the stairs ahead of him but then had to wait for him just inside the door of Jerry's study.

'Wow!' He stopped dead on the threshold and whistled through his teeth. 'How cool is this!'

'Thank you.' During the last revamp of Arkady's interior, I had given a lot of thought to how this room should look and had ordered bespoke bookcases, work-station and a large worktable in solid maple, with chairs and couch in soft, buttery leather and a deep pile cream carpet. I had softened the film-set, captain-of-industry effect with accessories: personal photographs of Jerry's children and mine, good-quality art prints in vibrant colours, and small vases of fresh flowers for which I had placed a permanent weekly order with a florist in Sutton. As a final touch, I had given him Marmalade, my rocking-horse, the battered but still beloved companion of my childhood and so-called because his paintwork was orange.

Frederick moved over to him. 'What a great horse! This have some special significance for Jerry?'

'No. For me, actually. It was mine when I was a child. I brought it from the house in Ballina when Jack was born.'

'Look at him.' Lovingly, he stroked the pale mane of string. The backs of his strong hands were covered with the same fine hair I had noticed on his ankles. Why had I not been affected as acutely as this in Collioure?

No point in speculating. I had to get away: I was in and out of Jerry's sanctum on a daily basis, but being in it in this state with Frederick felt like infidelity. 'He's a palomino,' Frederick said now, 'a golden horse, did you know that? He appears in works of art and even wall paintings all over the ancient world. The Crusaders first saw him in reality when they came up against the forces of Saladin and he was—'

'This one was made in Hong Kong, Frederick. There's the computer, over there.' I backed away a little. 'As I said, I'm afraid you're on your own with using it, but I'll wait until I'm sure everything is working for you.'

'Sure. Thanks.' Frederick seated himself and hovered briefly over the keyboard, searching for the 'on' key.

He found it immediately and I stood a few feet behind him as we both watched a cerulean sky spread across the screen. He twisted his head round, twinkling at me. 'Are you sure you don't want me to show you what you're missing? In five minutes I could have you surfing.'

'No, thanks,' I said fervently. 'My head is filled with enough information I don't need and will never use.'

My brain told me to leave but my body, held as if by grappling hooks, insisted on hovering behind his chair during the hissing and howling of the modem connecting. 'You'll be all right now,' I gabbled, 'I'll be off. Goodnight, Frederick.'

I was turning to go when I saw, among the unopened messages, that one from Jerry's PA was flagged with a red exclamation mark, meaning it was top priority. 'We should probably open that one.' I moved closer to the screen and put my finger on it. 'His assistant mustn't have been able to get him on the phone. It's probably something I should tell him about when he rings later on.'

Frederick clicked on the message.

It opened.

'Hey-hey! Look at this! Go, Jerry!' His spontaneous reaction was to chuckle delightedly. Then he looked back at me. 'Oops! I guess you weren't meant to see that.' Swiftly, he closed the message, then swivelled on his chair and touched my frozen arm. 'Hey, come on, Bibi,' he said softly, 'don't get upset! It's not a big thing, boys' stuff, it don't mean a thing. We send each other junk like that all the time! Pretty juvenile, huh?'

I have told you before there were three occasions in my life when all elements fused and when the world became real. This was indisputably the fourth as I stared at the purring computer, its screen restored to the display of its desktop.

'Bibi? Tessa?' Frederick half rose from his chair but I pushed him down again.

'Carry on, Frederick.'

Funny the kind of thing that pops into your mind on occasions like this. *The digital camera.* 'I'm grand, don't worry. You're right, it's nothing . . .' I turned away from him. The previous Christmas, Jerry had asked my advice about what gift he should buy for Susan. He wanted something impersonal yet thoughtful. My suggestion had been a digital camera.

'Are you sure you're not upset?' Frederick stood up again. His expression was one of serious concern. 'Will I delete it?'

'No, don't. As you say, it's not meant for me and I'm fine.' I walked to the door and turned round. I even smiled. 'Goodnight, Frederick. I'll see you in the morning.'

I found my way to our bedroom and into the bathroom, where I threw up the shepherd's pie.

The urgently flagged message to my husband was a photograph, no head or face, just a close-up of a cleavage visible through an open-necked white blouse. In it nestled a silver Alan Ardiff pendant I had chosen for Susan's birthday. At the bottom of the photograph, under the breasts, a hand was pictured holding an oblong, lettered placard:

WE MISS YOU!

CHAPTER TWENTY-FIVE

So we survived the holiday, making the best of it, although after my Ricky left for the World Cup in Japan and Tess's Jerry to go back to work, sometimes I felt that the villa was like an enormous bleeding morgue, with just the two of us adults rattling around with the kids. I couldn't count Yarso as one of us, I just couldn't, at least in my heart and soul, although my brain kept telling me that my dislike of him was unreasonable. Very unusual, because generally I love a crowd.

At the beginning I told myself I was worried about his influence on Carol and Alice who followed him around for the first week like a pair of lovesick poodles. You know how it is, these days, with all the perverts and child abusers going the rounds. But I have to admit that although I watched him, beady-eyed, there wasn't the smallest sign of anything you'd be upset about: he behaved absolutely properly towards them all the time. He was so proper, in fact, that the two of them found him boring and soon moved on to gaze at the beautifully tanned French and Dutch boys on the beach. And I have to give him his due: he continued to have endless patience with that young Tommy.

Then I examined my conscience to see if I was jealous of him taking Tess's attention away from me and eventually decided that maybe this was it, especially in the last week or so when they went off on at least two occasions to view 'sites', leaving me alone in the villa. When he went off on his own for a few days, into the Pyrenees, while she and I quickly fell back into our old girly ways, I could see she was dying for him to get back . . .

I know, I know, it's childish. (This is looking back: at the time I didn't think I was jealous but, then, who's to know what's in the sub-conscious?) I stayed civil to him, of course, for Tess's sake, but I could hear my voice being false and that irritated the shite out of me. So when, after all my efforts, I still couldn't warm to him, I called it quits. Some feelings you just can't explain.

Towards the end I was so pissed off I even found myself trying to bribe Kitty to come with me in one of the cars on a twenty-four-hour trip to Andorra: 'Come on, it'll be fun. It's a shopper's paradise, I hear, all duty free. I'll get you the best pair of rollerblades money can buy. And a Gucci watch. How about that, now?'

'No. Thank you, Mother, but no. And Gucci? Yuck. That's so last year!' The 'Mother' thing is recent, a clear 'back-off' signal. Kitty had become moony about Jack and was telling me she now had grown-up secrets. I was sad, but thrilled too. I envied her the excitement.

And I was glad Jack was her first real crush because, as I think I said before, he's a good kid. He gives his mother and stepfather a lot of crap, sure, but he's had plenty to put up with, what with his real father being killed. And then, so soon, having to accept this interloper – as he probably sees Jerry – coming in. And *then*, to cap it all, he had to move away from their cosy little place in Sallynoggin. Arkady is gorgeous but it isn't where he had built up all his friends and where he went to school.

As for the other kids, during that holiday they had soon, as usual, found new friends and were doing their own thing. Our Patricia had been semi-adopted by a Dutch family, who had a pair of really well-behaved twins; even weird little Tommy had palled up with a local girl, Marie-Claire, who was eight years old and didn't seem to find anything odd about him. Maybe because he couldn't speak French and she couldn't speak English! He met her in the kiddies' playground fronting the harbour beach, apparently; she was playing house with her little sister in the playhouse and invited him in to be the papa. He must have been a hit because next thing, apparently, he was telling Tess that he wouldn't be home for dinner, that he was going to eat at Marie-Claire's house.

You can see, then, how I could be fed up. I was sorry I hadn't agreed to go with Ricky to the Far East: after the big hoo-hah about Roy Keane – he was sent home from the training camp in

Japan – settled down and the team began to do well, the telephone calls were so ecstatic I sometimes couldn't make out what he was saying. And when we found a pub in Collioure that was showing the match between Ireland and Saudi Arabia – with a French commentary that none of us could understand – I was slating myself even more. Because, would you believe?, at one point the camera showed, right in the middle of this huge group of Irish fans, my Ricky and his gang holding up their green-white-and-gold banner: 'MOCKTON'S ON TOUR, 2002'. Mockton's is their darts local. They all seemed to be having the time of their lives.

All in all, for the first time ever after one of these holidays, I was glad to get home.

It didn't take me long to want to go back, I can tell you, loneliness or no loneliness. The worst summer in Ireland since 1985, they're calling it. Maybe even since records began. Rain, rain, more bloody rain. You have to wear wellies just to walk the land because it's full to the gills, and you should see the state of Ricky's store cattle. Manky. We had to keep the horses inside, would you believe (in July!)?, because they were sinking into the mud up to their bums. And as for my lovely garden, it looks like a building site. One night, Patricia's Shetland somehow got out of his stall and headed straight for it, turning it into a pig-sty. This climate would put years on you.

Ricky's mood didn't help the atmosphere. Although Ireland went as far as the last sixteen in the World Cup (and, of course, he went with them from Japan to Korea) he was in a queer humour for the first while after he came home. Very quiet and into himself.

I made allowances because, of course, he was completely knackered, slept for the guts of the first twenty-four hours and even after that kept falling asleep in the middle of the day. He even took to coming home from the shops early, before closing time.

I picked my time to tackle him. We were having a takeaway in front of the telly and watching *Big Brother*. (He couldn't be bothered with it, but even though it was well under way and there had already been a couple of evictions when we got back, I had become hooked.) It was raining outside as usual but we were real relaxed and cosy in the TV room, the curtains were pulled and I had put on the gas fire.

He fobbed me off, of course. Didn't I know he was tired and hadn't he a right to be? 'I'm shagged, Reet, and so would you be. Them flights'd kill anyone.'

Well, tell me something I don't know! I wasn't put off. 'There's something else, Ricky, I know there is.'

'There isn't, Reet.' He shook his head from side to side slowly, as if trying to find something in it that would satisfy me. 'It could be the friggin' football! It's certainly not going to be worth going half-way round the world for without Roy. Thank God the next two big competitions are in Portugal and Germany.' He adjusted his recliner and stared gloomily into the food on his lap tray. 'That's if we friggin' qualify without Roy.' Ricky has a season ticket for Old Trafford, Roy Keane is his hero and, in Ricky's opinion, what had happened between him and his manager was a 'frigging silly little argument in the heat of the moment' and should just have been sorted. It was a 'travesty' that he was sent home. 'For a friggin' shouting match, Reet! What age is Mick McCarthy, might I ask?'

'Sure what age is Roy Keane?' I asked him back. In my opinion, there were two of them in it. But for Ricky Roy is whiter than white. It was the press people, who blew the row up out of all proportion, and the 'suits', who let it get out of hand, and the manager, who should have managed his star player. Ireland could have gone all the way, he says, if Roy had been with us. There wouldn't have been any penalty shoot-out with Spain in the quarter-finals: there would have been no need for one.

'So it's just the football, then?' I wasn't convinced.

'Don't talk to me any more about it, Reet. It makes me sick just to think about it.' Viciously, he speared a chip and shoved it into his mouth.

I decided to let him get away with it this time. That's the best thing with men: I find. You can wear them down gradually. Anyway, Jade, the big blonde girl on *Big Brother*, was in the middle of one of her spectacular bust-ups with the housemates and I wanted to enjoy it. But as I settled back in my own recliner, I made a mental note to have another go at him, and sooner rather than later.

One evening, about a week after we came home, I was in Maddy's. It was the first time I had had the opportunity to bring her luggage and Colm's over to her. Poor thing, I should have gone earlier. Tess and I had rung her a couple of times from France, but you know how these long-distance phone calls go; they weren't very satisfactory and she sounded so completely miserable it was hard for the two of us to keep any kind of a conversation going. And although her news about Fergus hit us like a ton of bricks, neither of us had been all that surprised.

The minute she answered the door, I could see she had been hitting the bottle: her skin was grey and dry and her eyes were bloodshot. In fact, she looked like a thin little old woman of sixty-five instead of just barely fifty.

She asked me in, and within a very short while she was crying and going on about 'I said this' and 'he said that' on the fateful night he left her. 'It was my fault for confronting him, Rita. If I hadn't, he'd still be here. I just want to die.' She looked at me with big, sunken eyes. 'There's no point in living any more. My life is over.' Maddy has always been the most dramatic of the three of us.

We were sitting side by side on their soda, each of us with a G and T in our hands. Their sitting room is nice enough with a good-sized bay window and a Dralon suite she got a few years ago in Arnotts' sale. All the colours, though, are variations of beige. The Hand of Fergus again. His theory, which we've all heard many times, is that you can live with 'discreet' colours for a long time without getting tired of them and without having to spend good money on redecorating. I can hear him in my head. Pontificating.

Well, they may be practical but those safe shades do nothing to make a room seem inviting, especially when it's raining outside.

Arkady, by contrast to Maddy's house, is a mansion, but Tess has brilliant taste and every single room, furnished and decorated to the tune of zillions, is a treat to walk into. You feel instantly at home in it, as if you're in your own cottage with your feet stretched out by your fireplace. (Except, as I think I've told you, I always feel like a rhinoceros in the middle of all that delicate china and stuff.)

There was more to the misery in this room, though, than just bland colours. It made me uneasy to see how she had let the place go: there were stains on the carpet, there was a horrible, stuffy smell from full ashtrays, there were butts in the fireplace and on the hearth. And it was obvious she hadn't dusted or Hoovered. This was very unlike Maddy.

She had good reason, of course, but in general, I thought, Tess and I had been right to worry about her health in every sense. 'Come on, Mad, don't be like this.' I put my arm round her shoulders. 'Your life isn't over. That's not you talking, that's the hurt. After all, you have Colm to take care of. I'm sure he's very upset too, he'll need you more than ever now.'

'Colm – oh, God! I'm a rotten mother – he'd be better off without me.' She buried her face in her hands.

I gave her a little squeeze. 'You're heartbroken, and you've a right to be, but stop beating yourself up. You're not a rotten mother, Colm adores you. He'll be OK. He's safe where he is, you'll talk to him when you feel up to it and, after all, he has his own life to lead.'

'Should I take him home, Rita?' Her tear-stained, red little face reminded me of an anxious monkey's. 'Would that be a good idea?'

'All in good time. You're buried in this avalanche right now, Maddy, so you can't see anything straight. Maybe some time soon the two of us will go down to Ballineen to see him.'

'When?'

I thought fast. She was in no condition to talk to Colm now without driving him crazy. 'Very soon. But think about the big picture, Maddy. If you do you might even see this as an opportunity. It's your time now. You can do anything you want to, go back to acting, even go to university, and without a by-your-leave from anyone.'

'I don't want to act,' she cried. 'I don't want to go to university, I want Fergus.' She cried harder.

'Hey, hey, Maddy, listen, *listen*!' I said loudly, to make myself heard. 'Don't be like this, make an effort. It's dreadful, of course it's dreadful, but it's happened and it seems there's no point in hoping he's going to come back.'

'That's what you'd all like, isn't it?' She threw my arm off her shoulder and blazed up, bubbles coming out of her mouth through the tears.

'What?'

'Don't think I haven't noticed the little looks between you and Tess. I never said anything because I didn't want to cause friction but it was always very clear to me that the two of you never liked him.'

I opened my mouth to protest but the storm had gathered strength so she was almost screaming: 'Don't lie to me, Rita. Don't even try!'

Shit! I thought as I sat there, Bigmouth on the sofa. I couldn't just have left well alone, could I? I couldn't just have listened and patted her and said, 'There there' . . . Oh, no, I had to play Mammy as usual. I watched her distorted face and heard her go on and on, and on the one hand I felt like shaking her out of her stew of self-pity, but on the other I knew that, never having gone through it, I had no right to be judgemental.

One thing was for certain: I had been right to worry about her mental health. A couple of days before this episode, I'd put down the phone to her after she'd been carrying on like this and seriously considered contacting the little shite out in RTE or wherever he was hanging out to tell him to get his ass in gear and look after his wife – she was still his wife, after all. He wouldn't be too hard to find, if I put my mind to it. I didn't, though. I figured I might make things worse for her in the short term because he would think it was a scheme she'd put me up to so she could get his sympathy. He'd have a go at her.

It was getting dark outside and while she continued to weep, although less violently, thank God, I looked secretly at my watch. It was about five minutes to ten. I hadn't planned on spending the whole evening there. 'Here.' I pulled a tissue out of the box, now nearly empty, on her lap. 'Calm down, Mad. We won't talk about Tess and me and what we think about Fergus right now. Dry your eyes with this.'

'I was right, though, wasn't I? You two never liked him.'

'We had problems with him, Mad, with the way he treated you. It was nothing personal.'

She opened her mouth to say something else, but changed her mind and blew her nose. 'Sorry, Rita. You're the best friend a person could have. I'm sorry.'

'You've nothing to be sorry about, Mad. We love you, you know that. Listen,' I made a great play of looking at my watch, 'I have to go soon, but before I do, I want to talk to you about something else. Something really serious.'

'Is being betrayed and abandoned by your husband not serious?'

It looked like she might fire up again and I grabbed her hands. '*Maddy.*'

'Sorry!'

I let her go. 'Of course it's serious, but there's something else I'm worried about. And not only me. Tess and I are both worried about it.' I took a deep, deep breath. 'We're worried about your health.'

'My health?'

'You're so thin. But it's not only that. We're upset about your drinking, Mad.'

'I beg your pardon?' She went as stiff as a telephone pole. At least I had her full attention. I tried to make my voice sound gentle and caring. 'That was a bit bald. I didn't mean it to come out like that. Has Fergus never said anything to you about this? I'm sure he—'

'Mind your own fucking business, Rita!'

'I know you don't want to hear this, Maddy.' I reached out to take her hand again but she snatched it away.

I tried to stay calm. 'Do you think I'd be saying this for my own entertainment?' I could see she was icily furious now, despite the drink she'd had, but I ploughed ahead regardless: 'Would you consider going for a bit of help to a clinic? Or maybe, if you couldn't face that, to an ordinary doctor? That could be a first step. I'd go with you – Tess would too. We'd be with you all the way.'

'How dare you? How dare you come in here—'

'Maddy—'

Ring! Ring! My bloody mobile went off.

'Dammit! Sorry, Mad, I should have turned it off.' I pulled it out and looked at the screen. 'It's Tess. I'll just say a quick hello and tell her I'll call her back, all right?'

'Oh, yes,' she said stiffly. 'St Teresa of the Roses. Mustn't discommode St Tess!'

I was now seriously losing my patience. Even, perish the thought, feeling a twinge of sympathy for Fergus. 'Will you shut up, Maddy? I'm here with you, amn't I?' I pushed the answer button on the mobile and barked into it: 'Hello?'

'Oh! Hello, Rita – is this a bad time?' Although she sounded quite calm, even cold, I knew instantly that something was wrong with Tess.

'No, it's fine, sorry if I sounded a bit grumpy, go ahead. As it happens,' I forced myself to sound lighter, 'I'm in Maddy's house, we're just having a *chat*.' I emphasised that to let Tess know what exactly we had been talking about. At the same time, I smiled at Maddy, so she wouldn't feel we were talking about her behind her back. (Jeez, life gets complicated sometimes, doesn't it?)

Maddy, however, had curled herself into a little ball in the crook of the settee. 'Oh,' Tess's voice wobbled a little, 'give her my love, will you? How is she?'

'Are you all right? You sound weird.'

'I'm fine.'

Then there was this pause.

'Tess? Are you there?'

'Yes.' Her voice cracked now.

'Tess, tell me, what's wrong?'

'I'm not really fine. I'm not fine at all, Rita, that's why I rang you. I'm sorry to be bothering you with this, but something's happened, I can't—' She burst into tears.

CHAPTER TWENTY-SIX

'Tess, what – what, love? Tell me.'
But for the next minute or so I couldn't make head or tail of what she was saying. I was appalled. I had never, in all the years we'd known each other, heard Tess Butler Brennan lose control like this. Not even in her worst moments after Michael was killed. 'Ssh, dear – Tess! Listen! Listen to me, you have to slow down, darling. I can't make out what you're telling me!'

Maddy was gawping, her pinched little monkey face screwed up with disbelief equal to mine. She could obviously hear Tess's wailing. '*What's wrong?*' she mouthed.

I mouthed back that I didn't know. Then I thought I caught something about Frederick.

'Hold on, Tess. Tess! *Tess!*' I got through finally.

The crying stopped. She coughed a bit and blew her nose. Then: 'I'm – I'm sorry, R–Rita—' She had the hiccups. 'I'm so sorry. I'll ring you again tomorrow.'

'No, don't!' I was shouting. 'Don't ring me tomorrow. Tell me now. Did you say something about Frederick Yarso?'

'He's here.'

'*What?*'

Hiccuping all the way, she spilled it out then, a whole saga about Frederick and a computer and a bloody e-mail.

You know, sometimes I wonder about all this technological revolution and so on. Maybe we were all better off with the Pony Express. It'd cut down half the heartbreak in the world.

But Susan Vitelli Moore? I was shocked. She seemed like such a nice girl. 'Are you sure it was Susan who sent it?' I asked.

'Yes—' I could hear her gulping and swallowing, trying to keep it together. 'I'm certain. She was wearing—'

Then she couldn't continue. 'Tess,' I said quickly, 'maybe you shouldn't jump to conclusions right away. There might be some really simple explanation for this. You'll have to talk quietly to Jerry about it. Quietly, do you hear me? Give him the benefit of the doubt until then at least. Isn't it possible, just possible, he didn't know this was going to happen? That he could be completely innocent? That it could all be her doing? A sort of fantasy thing?'

Mind you, I didn't for a minute think that was the case. *'We miss you?'*

There was silence at the other end. 'Tess? Are you all right, Tess?'

'Thanks for listening, Rita.' She was quiet at least. 'You're a brick, and I'm sorry to disturb you. How's Maddy?'

'Maddy's fine.' I glanced at her, and smiled.

'He's away,' Tess said, after another pause. 'I don't know what I'm going to say to him when he rings—' Her voice broke again and, although I knew the worst was over, this was still so unlike the cool, *sorted* Tess I've known for more than twenty-five years that I couldn't stand it. I wanted to get into my car immediately, drive to Howth and give everyone over there a box.

But I was stuck between the two of them. I couldn't leave Mad in the state *she* was in. 'Get in your car right now, Tess,' I made myself sound really fierce, 'and come over here to Maddy's. This is an emergency. The three of us need to have a council of war.'

She protested a bit – it was late, it was too far, Jack wasn't home yet, all the usual crap – but I could hear she wanted to come and insisted until finally she agreed. 'But don't forget, Rita, it'll be about forty-five minutes before I get there. And I'll come for only half an hour.'

I looked across at Maddy, hunched over her tissues. *In a pig's eye, half an hour*, I thought. 'That's all right,' I said out loud. 'The time doesn't matter. We're not going anywhere.'

While we waited for Tess, I told Maddy what had happened, doing my best not to embroider. Apparently Susan Vitelli Moore had photographed her own breasts and sent them electronically to her boss. You'd think it was hilarious if it hadn't happened to one of your best friends, and I have to admit that, although I was 100 per cent with Tess in this, I could see the funny side of it too. I mean, how did she do it? I had visions of her lying on a photocopying machine after hours, carefully lining herself up . . .

And for stuffy old Jerry Brennan! Jeez, I thought, the mind boggles.

Maddy was roundy-eyed with excitement. She couldn't wait for Tess to arrive. Misery loves company.

We were in for a long night, and I decided to stay. When Maddy went to the lavatory, I rang Ricky to tell him what had happened. He was fine about me sleeping over. 'Stay as long as you like, Reet. Is she hitting the sauce?'

'A bit.' I had discussed Maddy's drinking with him because, over the years, he has had a number of alcoholic friends. His advice had been to watch her and wait until we thought she was ready to help herself – or until she asked for help. It was only then that we could do anything effective, he said. My efforts tonight had proved his point.

'Thank Christ I'm not there,' he said. 'I can't cope with cryin' women. But tell them both I was asking for them, all right? Godalmighty, Jerry Brennan! Who'd have believed it?'

He sounded gob-smacked, Real Ricky rather than Depressed Ricky, so perked up in fact that I decided to tackle him for the second time. Maddy . . . Tess . . . I was on a roll. 'Yeah,' I said, 'it's all happening here. So, listen, Rick, Maddy's gone to the toilet. And to get back to what we were talking about the other night, are you all right?'

'I'm fine, topping.' Then he immediately went all defensive again. 'Why do you keep asking me that?'

'Women's intuition. You have to admit you've been a bit quiet. Ever since you came home from the Far East. And you're sleeping so much. That's not like you.'

'Give it a rest, Reet. This is gettin' on me wick. You're lettin' yourself get infected with that carry-on over there. Once and for all, I'm fine.'

'But, Ricky.'

'I'm *fine*, Rita!'

I could hardly conduct the Spanish Inquisition on him from Maddy's sofa. 'All right,' I said. 'I won't ask you any more, but I am definitely going to make an appointment for you with the doctor

– and as soon as possible. You're not yourself, Ricky, whether you can see it or not. You might even have got one of them weird bugs people get from foreign travel.'

'Rita!'

'I'm making that appointment! And no arguments, right?'

He groaned. 'You're a terrible woman, Rita Corcoran.' (Corcoran was my maiden name.)

Maddy came back then so we said goodnight to each other. As soon as I clicked off, I realised there was no point, with Tess coming, in trying to run a temperance meeting tonight. Tonight it was her house, her drink, and she was going to drink it anyway, with or without me. So I did a complete U-turn and told her to break out the gin again.

I'd had two more by the time we heard Tess arriving at about ten minutes past eleven. 'Come in, love,' I said, when I opened the door. She, too, looked terrible, but in a different way, and not quite so dramatic. She is usually so tidy about herself, but her hair was all over the place, her eyes swollen, her nose red. 'You poor old thing!' I hugged her as tightly as I could. 'It's not the end of the world – yet.'

'You should see it from my side!' She attempted to laugh but the joke was a clunker.

Maddy rushed into the hall and fell on her neck. 'Can you believe it? The two of us in the same boat at the same time!'

'Oh, God, oh, God, Maddy, I'm really sorry I wasn't sympathetic enough when it happened to you. I should have been over here the minute we got back.'

They were both crying and talking on top of each other. It was bedlam. I felt like blowing a whistle to cut across them. 'What we all need is a stiff drink,' I said, catching their arms and marching them towards the sitting room and Maddy's drinks trolley.

'I'd better not, I've to drive.' Tess let Maddy go and sat down.

Even when she is in bits, our Tess can't dream of doing something illegal. 'Drive, schmive,' I said firmly. 'You can get a taxi, you can certainly afford it. And you can also afford for you to get a taxi back in the morning to pick up your car. That's if you don't stay the night and I think you should.'

'And if you're right,' I was really getting into my stride, 'if that bastard is giving his secretary one, you'll drive around Dublin in a Cadillac for the rest of your life. I'll personally see to it. So you'll stay here with us and there's an end to it. It's time we three had a good bitch.'

'But I've to meet Daddy early in the morning. We're going for a walk and if I'm not there—'

'Ring up. Tell him.'

'Nobody'll answer the phone. Frederick wouldn't, I don't think, and Daddy is already asleep.'

'Now, listen, Tess . . .' I was fast losing it with her and what I've always felt is her oversized sense of responsibility. Daddy, Tom, Jack, Jerry and now Frederick – you could sing it if you had a piano. I splashed gin into three fresh glasses. 'Here! Have a bloody drink.' I added tonic and handed them round. 'Now,' I said, 'chins up, and I mean that literally. We can hold our heads high. We're the best we have and we'll have the best. *Sláinte!*'

After all the protesting, Tess, understandably enough, really went for it, glugging the G and T as if it was water. 'Attagirl,' I said. 'Give me that glass.' I refilled it, then raised my own in a toast. 'To us!'

Over the next three-quarters of an hour, while the two of them got locked into their stories, Tess drank three more gins, Maddy drank four so they were literally locked as well, even though, despite my macho guff, I was doing the old trick of giving them less of the spirit in each glass. No benefit from driving them into alcoholic poisoning, I thought, and, anyway, they didn't notice.

At this stage I was drinking tonic only. I'm a lot bigger physically, and I eat a lot, so I drink more than either of them can with less damage. But I'm at that age when I think about the brutal hangover before I take a sip of the first drink. As well as that, although I've never believed the old *piseóg* about gin making women maudlin, I knew that one of us had to keep a grip in case things got out of control.

I had had enough, though, to be feeling no pain, just that lovely warm, full, false sensation you get right before you're drunk, where all that exists is what's around you right at that moment and you can solve everyone else's problems with a wave of your hand.

Here's the picture. At the beginning, Maddy is all agog for Tess's news, every bleeding detail. I suppose her going on and on about her own situation had bored even her so fresh disaster was a godsend. And after the first two gins, the edge is off the horror for Tess herself, so she is able to answer Maddy and to speculate about what the next step should be.

My role is to be the quiet, listening auntie, indulging them, and for that first while, anyone coming in from outside and not knowing what their chat was about would think the three of us are three normal buddies on a drinking binge.

Maddy moves on to Yarso. 'So tell me again,' she says, lighting a cigarette, 'you were in your car, were you? And he was coming up the street towards Arkady? Just like that? You had no phone call, even?'

'None!' Tess shakes her head.

'What's he look like?' Maddy holds out her glass for me to refill it.

'Well,' Tess says, 'he's tall, thin, thin face too, curly fair hair—'

'He's a ringer for Michael Butler,' I give Maddy her fresh drink and sit in the chair opposite them, 'except for the colour of the hair.'

They turn to me. They'd forgotten I was there as Rita, not as bar-person. The penny drops, late, with Maddy, whose gestures had become wider with each drink. 'Ohmigod! *Tess!*' She attempts to clap one hand over her mouth but it's the one holding the cigarette. Fortunately, her aim is off, her grasp is weak and the cigarette falls on to the sofa between herself and Tess.

'Jesus, Maddy!' I jump up out of my chair.

'Wha?' First she looks at me, then she looks down at the sofa, her head wobbling on her neck, but does nothing to retrieve the cigarette. I can't even see it. Great, I think. Now we're all going to be burned alive.

I go across quickly, scrabble for it under a scatter cushion and manage to find it before it does any damage. I am pinching it out when I hear sounds. I turn to find that Tess has covered her face with her hands and is crying again. 'It's a judgement,' she says, then something else, but she is blubbering so it's hard to understand.

'Judgement?' Maddy lights another cigarette and blows smoke.

She pats Tess's shoulder. 'You cry all you like, love. I know what it's like. But what's a judgement?'

I sit down for the nth time. I don't mean this to sound harsh but I am fed up. I feel like the designated driver at a surreal Christmas party and all I want now is to get my head down on a pillow. 'What do you mean, "judgement", Tess?'

She hiccups. 'Excuse me. It's a judgement on me. The judge-judgement of God.'

'Why?' I'm mystified. 'What have you done?'

'I've actually *done* noth-nothing, but I've *thought* lo-lots – excuse me. I've com-committed adultery in my heart.'

It's on the tip of my tongue to tell her not to be so ridiculous, (and I don't need to be Columbo to know who she had committed it with) but she's really distressed and it would have sounded too sharp. So I curb my tongue and instead of snapping at her, tell her quietly not to be so hard on herself. 'You've done nothing wrong, love.'

They both look bleary-eyed at me. 'But she's right, Rita. In your heart is just as bad as the real thing,' Maddy says solemnly.

Tess's mobile goes off. She struggles to retrieve it from her handbag. 'Give me that.' I lean over and grab the handbag, finding the phone just as it rings off and the *Missed Call* notice flashes on to the screen. I turn it off altogether.

'I'll take it, Rita.' Tess holds out her hand. 'It's prob-probably – excuse me – Jerry.'

'Do you really think you should talk to him at the moment? When you're like this? Wouldn't it be better to wait until the morning?'

'Do you think I shouldn't?' The tears are still pouring down her face. It's like she's looking for direction from the school counsellor and my impatience evaporates.

'I do.' I nod gravely. 'Tomorrow would be better. It's always better to give these things a few hours.'

'All ri-right. Excuse me.'

'Good girl.' Maddy is slugging again. I'm no saint and I've had enough. I stand up. 'Bedtime, everyone. We can talk more tomorrow.' Maddy protests but I detach the glass from her fingers, collect Tess's too and put both on the mantelpiece. Tess gets up under her own steam but I have to help Maddy off the couch.

We parted on the landing. Maddy hit the wall as she walked to her own room but I left her at it and opened the door of the hot-press to rummage through its jumbled contents. I could find only one nightdress and gave it to Tess – it wouldn't have fitted me anyway. I took out a pair of Fergus's pyjamas. 'Will you sleep, Tess?'

'I – I hope so.'

I hugged her. 'Things will look much better in the morning. I promise. And I'll be here for you. OK?'

'OK. Thank you so much, Rita. You're a great friend.'

'Shut up. Now, go to that room over there, get into bed and count backwards from a thousand.'

'I will.' She smiled a watery smile and went off.

I didn't take my own advice as I lay, sorting and re-sorting things in my head. The bed was comfortable enough but Maddy's spare rooms are just that, 'spare', with bare walls, cheap, ready-made curtains, the minimum of furniture and empty suitcases piled in corners. You would know that they are not used: my sheets were clean but the smell was musty. They'd clearly been on the bed a long time so now, on top of everything else, I had damp to worry about. I longed for my own bed and Ricky's snoring, hot little bod beside me.

What to do or say next? With both of them. The whole thing was doing my head in.

Easy enough to be headmistressy in the heat of the moment, harder when it's a matter of what's best to do in the long-term. If you gave the wrong advice and people follow it, they'll blame you for ever.

CHAPTER TWENTY-SEVEN

It was dark.

I rarely drink spirits, and once in bed, I had fallen instantly into a heavy, alcohol-induced slumber from which I had just woken with a lifting head; I must have been snoring because I also had a very sore throat.

Worse, however, was the clenching fear in every nerve as, like meteorites, images from the night before crashed all about me. Breasts, for instance. I turned on the lamp beside Maddy's spare bed and checked my watch. It was only five minutes to three in the morning, I had been asleep for less than three hours.

I continued to stare at the watch, Raymond Weil, last year's birthday present from my husband. A beautiful watch, delicately crafted in white gold with a discreet diamond on its bezel. Dulled by fatigue and drink as I was, I had nevertheless to resist the urge to take it off and grind it underfoot because he had probably sent Susan to buy it.

After Michael died and my world plunged into chaos, Daddy came to Sallynoggin to help me through the formalities and gave me a piece of advice. Born of his own methodical personality, it was elementary by any standards, but I had been thrashing around in a fog of incomprehension and would have grasped any lifeline. 'Deal with what you can, Teresa,' he had said, 'and postpone the rest. Be practical and that will save you. Make a list of what you have to face. Put the most urgent item at the top, the least urgent at the bottom, but deal with at least one item every day and put a tick beside it on the list. That way you'll feel in control and find your way through.'

I dredged up that advice again in Maddy's Spartan room. Tried mentally to make a list.

So. Number one. What was most urgent?

The concept collapsed immediately because I discovered there was no number two. My list began and ended with only one item; I had to confront my husband, who was not due home from Stockholm for two days. I could not wait for two days. Not in this state.

I knew I would not be able to sleep any more so I eased myself out of the bed, stripped it – institutional training again – and dressed quickly, wincing each time the ice pick stabbed the inside of my skull. Then, guiding myself by touch through the darkness, I crept slowly downstairs and towards the front door. The click as I closed it sounded like a small explosion in the profound silence of this dead time of morning. The cobble lock of Maddy's driveway was wet, but the rain had stopped and the air was full of the faint scent of neglected wallflowers and sweet william spilling through the weeds in her window-boxes.

I was conscious that I was probably still way over the alcohol limit and therefore should not drive. But if I was careful, I should not pose a danger to myself or anyone else because, at this time of morning, I would have the city to myself. This proved to be the case and so, trying not to become hypnotised by the steady shush of my tyres on the slick pavements, I drove very slowly, alert to traffic light sequences and trying to keep the needle steady on the speedometer.

Mammy had always said that trouble comes in threes: we had Fergus being unfaithful to Maddy, now Jerry being unfaithful to me. What or who was next? Rita and Ricky?

Thank God for Rita and Ricky.

Having crossed O'Connell Bridge, I turned right along Eden Quay, heading for the roundabout at the Point, but my hangover was intensifying with every yard. Just before I got to the turn, I felt I might be sick, so I pulled over to the right-hand side of the road and stopped beside the river. I cut the engine and lowered the window, keeping my hand on the door-handle in case I had to make a dash.

The Liffey was swollen but peaceful, the scent of cold clay lying on its breath, its quick brush against its wall scarcely audible. I swallowed repeatedly and closed my eyes, allowing my face to bathe in the coolness until, gradually, the nausea subsided.

When I opened my eyes again, I saw I had company. A seagull had balanced on the kerb beneath my door; it inclined its head for a few seconds and, with one eye, contemplated both of mine. Having decided I was not worth its time, it crouched and flexed, then took off on unhurried, silent wings downriver towards the sea. I watched it fly until I could no longer pick it out against the pencil line of light drawn on the horizon between the docksides.

Was Jerry bidding for proof of personal freedom and virility with his infidelity? (To me it did not matter whether or not they had done the actual deed.) I doubted that such a substantial person as he could stoop to such a cliché.

Was he unhappy? Could my busy, always rushing, in-charge husband be hurting in some way that I had never considered? It had been a long time since I had fitted myself into his skin to sense what he sensed, feel what he felt. The thought was insidious, four-o'-clock-in-the-morning weakness: if I muddied my resolve with his point of view at the outset I would be lost.

The other possibility was that he loved her. I could not face that bleakness, not yet at any rate, and forced myself to concentrate on what I could see: river, building sites, lightening sky, bridge, ships at rest.

Momentarily soothed in the mouth of the relaxed city, I leaned my head against the door pillar of the car. Wordsworth, in his poem about London, could have been writing about this part of Dublin at this moment, I thought, fragments surfacing from my school poetry book:

> The river glideth at his own sweet will:
> Dear God! The very houses seem asleep;
> And all that mighty heart is lying still!

'Mighty' was one of Daddy's highest accolades. On the football pitch, a mighty victory for Mayo. At a funeral, the deceased had been a mighty man. That mighty heart of Dublin would continue to beat without me. If I were to vanish now, cranes would continue to swing, ferries and container vessels would come and go to timetable; there would be new generations of pop stars and tenors to fill the Point with applause and cheers, the East Link bridge would lift to let the yachts through. And the river would rush to the sea as it had rushed for thousands of years. Did it really matter that, in one microdot of time, Susan Vitelli Moore and Jerry Brennan were lovers?

It did.

It did, it did, it *did*. . . My gorge rose.

I made it to the quay wall just in time and vomited painfully, staining the brown shoulder of the river. Gasping as I straightened up, I looked around: thank God no one had witnessed my shame. On the far bank, however, I could see the toll barrier rising to let a white van through.

Shaken, and cold now, I got back into the car and rinsed out my mouth with some of the Evian I always carry in the glove compartment. While keeping an eye on the van, now moving at a leisurely pace across the bridge towards me, I spat discreetly into the gutter. Then, with a hand that felt like a collapsed balloon, I raised the window and started the engine. Although my head continued to throb, I felt marginally better: at least the queasiness had subsided.

As I turned into East Wall, I remembered the contract to walk the pier with my father in just a few hours' time. What were we going to talk about? How could I conceal the one and only thought in my mind? I wouldn't be able for it, I wouldn't . . .

Settle down, Tess. I jabbed the accelerator so hard that the car leaped. I had to face it and get on with it.

By the time I turned into our driveway, it was half past four and the windows of the house were pinkening in the rising sun. Instead of going inside immediately, I pulled down the visor mirror to interrogate myself: 'I love my children,' I said aloud to the haggard, wan face I saw reflected. 'I love my husband, my father and my friends, but I love Arkady too. It is my husband who has betrayed me, my house hasn't and never will. If this casts me as a decadent, stone-hearted materialist, so be it.' Then, feeling silly, I pushed the visor back up.

I postponed going inside for another while by walking around the side of the house and into our back garden, where I made for the primitive summerhouse left by the previous owners. It is nestled under the canopy of an ancient copper beech and we call it the shack. I have done nothing to improve it so it has remained exactly the same as it was left to us. Furnished with just a bench seat and rattan table, it is my personal haven; I love to come here to read, especially on days of bad weather, when the rain rushing through the russet leaves makes a xylophone of the corrugated-iron roof.

Whoever had named our house, although misspelling it, had named it well; Arcady, I discovered, when I looked it up in Collins', is another term for Arcadia. 'The traditional idealised rural setting of Greek and Roman bucolic poetry', and that morning, my lush, damp garden lived up to the description. To sit there was to be part of a calming aviary where pigeons cooed, a pair of tits was busy in the dense ivy covering the back of the house nearby and a blackbird in full song led the rest of the sleepy, twittering crowd in greeting the sun.

With Arkady's arms around me, and its reassuring bulk to lean on, I was reminded of what a presenter of a television documentary about antiques had once said. The exact words escaped me but he had been musing about the attraction of antiques and said something about the comfort of continuity or the illusion of permanence . . . Something along those lines.

Whatever his words, the sentiment had rung true for me. Taking it in tandem with those few minutes I had spent beside the river, when I had set my insignificance in the world against the world itself, it was comforting to know that objects, whether precious or utilitarian, can live in their original form long after higher human, animal or plant life has turned to dust.

Yes, I do believe that, spiritually, we go on, but not in the form in which we were created.

A house is at the zenith of artefacts. I get so sad when I see a cottage in ruins because of human neglect, while knowing that buried among the nettles and scutch will be an iron kettle or a leather shoe, created, ignored but enduring. Arkady will survive me. It will survive until human indifference, or greed, decides it should not. In the meantime, it will be my guardian, it seems, rather than the other way round—

God! I was now aghast: what kind of a woman was I if, at the height of such an emotional crisis, I could be comforted by stones, mortar, wood, slates and glass?

I am not sure how long I sat there, but the sun was fully risen when I rose and crossed the steaming grass towards the house. I got upstairs, thank God, without incident, although I almost stumbled when tiptoeing past Jerry's study where that e-mail, in all its tawdry horror, seemed to pulsate inside the wood of the door.

I had intended to have a long hot shower, but when I got into the bedroom the sight of the huge bed with its snowy linen proved irresistible. I'll just lie on top of it for fifteen minutes, I thought. I won't even get in.

Next thing I knew, my father was shaking my shoulder. 'Teresa! Teresa! It's a quarter past seven!'

'Thanks, Daddy!' I jumped into a sitting position. 'I was up earlier, but I didn't want to wake you—'

When my father is disapproving, his lips tighten to the extent that they are barely visible. He did this now. 'If you say so, Teresa. I'll be waiting downstairs.'

'Oh, God.' I groaned as I lay down again. Now I had blown it with Daddy too. How was I going to face this day?

In the bathroom, Jerry's ordered sets of colognes and aftershaves, different scents for different occasions, ranged themselves like a jeering enemy army against me. How dare he? How dare he go off to work in the morning as if he was preoccupied only with acquisitions and ratings? *How dare he bring me roses?* It all made sense now – the roses, the tension and bad humour in Collioure, the good humour when he got back to her.

The lovemaking with me two nights in a row. Guilt or sympathy? Daddy or no Daddy, I rushed for the telephone.

He answered on the second ring. 'Yes?' His voice was hushed. He was obviously already in a meeting.

'Something's happened, Jerry. You have to come home.'

'What? Are the kids all right?'

'They're fine. But you have to come home – today!' I was holding on, just about. 'I can't tell you why over the telephone.'

'What—' His voice rose slightly.

'We'll talk when you come home,' I interrupted him. 'Just *come home!*' I hung up.

Then I took the telephone off the hook again in case he tried to ring me back.

I gargled straight from the bottle of mouthwash, pulled a brush through my hair, put on a pair of trainers and went downstairs. Arms folded against his chest, my father was standing inside the door, cap on, coat belted. 'Just a sec, Daddy.' I had heard cartoon sounds from the television room. When I peered in, an equally absorbed Frederick and Tom were eating cereal. 'Good morning!' I said.

Only Frederick looked round: 'Morning, Bibi! Sleep well?'

I looked closely but could discern no irony. 'Fine,' I said, as lightly as I could. 'How about you? Was your room all right?'

'AOK,' he responded cheerfully. 'I think I've died and gone to heaven.'

'When did you get back, Tom?'

'Colin's mum drove me home late.'

'I thought you were staying the night over there?'

'I changed my mind.' He did not move his gaze from the television.

I was flooded with guilt. I hadn't been here, and that probably explained the thin line on my father's mouth when he woke me: he sleeps lightly. 'Your dad is outside waiting for you,' Frederick said, as though he was a mind-reader. 'Would you like me to make pancakes for us all when you come back?'

'Thank you very much,' I said faintly. He certainly seemed to have made himself at home.

'See you later, then,' he said cheerfully. 'About an hour?' He turned back to the screen.

'Do you always allow Tom to watch television this early in the morning?' My father picked up his umbrella when I came back into the hall.

At that moment, I did not need his opinion on child-rearing. 'He's on his holidays, Daddy.' I plucked a jacket from behind the cloakroom door and shrugged it on.

'It was only a comment. Nothing to do with me, Teresa, it's your business.'

We drove to the pier in silence. Commuter rush-hour was in full swing, although it was not yet a quarter to eight. 'Tsk, tsk!' Daddy shook his head as a two-seater sports car swerved round us and broke an amber just as I was slowing down before turning into the main street. Normally I would have jumped to the errant driver's defence – purely to be contrary. Today I did not have the energy. I just had to get through the next hour and then I would be back home and safe.

I helped him out of the car, but I could see that he hated it. 'Well, finally, we might have a good day!' He took several steps away from me and jammed his cap further over his ears. 'Saving Frederick's presence and all that – he seems like quite a nice chap, Teresa – but I blame the Americans for all this bad weather. It's climate change. Did you read in the paper about them not wanting to sign the Kyoto Agreement? Tsk, tsk! All those gas guzzlers belching into the atmosphere.'

I knew it was his way of saying sorry for interfering earlier. He always changed the subject and became quite chatty when he felt he was in the wrong. 'They should sign it, Daddy,' I said.

'Of course they should. Did you know that forty per cent of the cars in Texas are now those enormous off-roaders?'

'I didn't . . .' We headed off on our walk, having re-established not only communication but the proper pecking order: he with the knowledge of the world, I the learner.

The pier in Howth is lined for a lot of its length with buildings, warehousing, fish shops, and lately a couple of restaurants. On the open side, some of the trawlers were berthing after their overnight trips so even though I was feeling so poorly and battling with the image of that damned e-mail, it was not difficult to make conversation. 'Oh! Come here, Daddy – look! The box near the wheelhouse of that boat there, look at the size of that big weird thing on top of the cod! Is it a monkfish?'

Or: 'What do you think of this, Daddy? Look at the size of that conger eel . . .' indicating the creature, mouth smashed and bloody. In this way, we made our slow progress.

When we got to the end of the pier, two hardy souls were already ensconced on the sea wall, lines cast into the open sea.

One of the attractions of Howth pier for my father had always been to shoot the breeze with the anglers: to swap boasts, his concerning salmon exploits on the Moy river. Even in the absence of fishermen, in very bad weather, he never missed climbing the steps on to the end wall to gaze into the sea.

But now the worst thing happened. As we got to the base of the wall, he hesitated. Then, sniffing the air: 'Uh-oh! I think I can smell rain.'

I raised my head and pretended to scan the sky. In truth, after such a promising start in the early morning, it had again clouded over, but the clouds were high. 'Gosh! You're right, Daddy,' I said, broken-hearted, 'we should head back.'

'Well, if you're sure . . .'

'Yes. These early mornings give you such false hope, don't they?' I linked him and felt him stiffen, but this time, to add to my alarm and misery, he did not reject my assistance.

CHAPTER TWENTY-EIGHT

We did not speak on the way back. Anyone seeing us would have thought: Father and daughter in step and in harmony, out for an early-morning stroll. But this was far from the truth because, through the entwined sleeves of his coat and my jacket, there was a crackling interchange of unexpressed feeling. My father and I inhabited a partitioned island and, on my side, I was bowed with sadness.

I have always skipped the feature articles in newspapers where adult children write about a parent, about the formative years and how they were now best friends, so close, could tell each other anything. I felt envious when I saw a television drama where the daughter fled an abusive husband and confided in her understanding father; or even when I watched a daughter who was comfortable enough to cry in her dad's presence, prompting him to put an arm round her. As I moved to his left side to shield him as best I could with my own body from the wind whipping coldly from the north-east, my father, I knew, was struggling too.

What we both wanted to say, of course, was that most simple and most complicated phrase in the English language: *I love you.* Neither of us had ever uttered it and I knew it was unlikely that either of us would ever do so now. As a substitute, we barked at one another irritably, or customarily exchanged euphemisms. We asked one another if we were all right. I offered him food and treats and tried to spoil him when he came to stay. His substitution was advice and dry admonitions.

Behind it all, he offered unconditional support. No matter what ill-advised (in his view) path I took or choice I made, my father had always simply been there.

That Daddy would die some time had been a notion always with me in the abstract, but seeing his tired, bleached eyes and feeling the thinness of his arm brought it jolting home to me that his time to be 'there' was running out.

About ten yards short of the car he stopped abruptly and, given the way my thoughts were running, I was disturbed. 'Are you tired, Daddy?'

'I'm fine.'

'Are you sure? You've gone pale.'

'Just let me get my breath for a minute.'

'Are you feeling all right?'

'I'm grand, grand. Probably something I ate yesterday on the train.'

'Have you a pain?'

'No. Not a pain, as such.' (Even while suffering, Daddy had to be precise.) 'It's more a tightness.'

'Where's the tightness?'

'Across my shoulders. As I said, it's probably something I ate. Now, don't fuss. Just let me stand here a moment.' Something about his tone – resignation – worried me further but, the good daughter, I waited as instructed. He was panting slightly, and I resolved to call the doctor as soon as we got home. 'Teresa,' his voice was faint, although his colour was returning, 'would you help me to the car, please?'

I must not cry. I must not cry in front of Daddy. Mutely, I took his arm again and clicked the car door open with the key remote.

When we were both inside and belted, before starting the engine, I turned to him – and surprised a look that, despite my resolve, siphoned tears from depths I had thought sealed after Michael's funeral.

I managed to hold them inside although I knew something was dreadfully wrong. I was afraid to find out but the words came anyway. 'Daddy,' I whispered, 'tell me what's going on.'

'Here – I have something for you.' He reached into the inside pocket of his coat and withdrew a business envelope. It was very bulky. In its Cellophane window I could see part of a hundred-euro note. 'I don't want it, Daddy,' I cried. 'Please, I don't need it, you need it yourself, for the future—'

'Your mother asked me to look after you.' I saw his lips tighten in that expression I recognised so well but this time, I knew, it was not from disapproval. 'Take it.' He held out the envelope. He would not meet my eyes.

'No. I don't *want* it.' If I took this money it would be some sort of admission.

'Take it, take it, Teresa, *take* it.' He was frantic, pushing the envelope repeatedly against my hand, almost hitting me with it. I had no choice. In my hand, the money was warm from his breast.

'Good girl. That's not for the family.' His voice was a little stronger. 'You're to put it away. It's for yourself, just between you and me. Jerry need know nothing about it. I've looked after you, of course, and Jack and young Tom, for their education – McCarthy's in the town has my will. But I want you to have that from me now to buy yourself something. I wouldn't know what you'd like – you seem to have everything.'

I had listened with mounting horror. McCarthy and Co. had been the family solicitors ever since I could remember. 'Please, Daddy,' I croaked, 'I don't want to hear you talking like this.'

'Teresa, we may not get another chance on our own without making a big hoo-hah out of it. We have to be practical here. Life goes on. So,' he became brisk, almost himself, 'I've sold the shop. The deal will close in two weeks' time and McCarthy's will have that money too.' His voice vanished then re-emerged. 'Joe McCarthy will know what to do.'

'Sold the shop?' Stupidly.

'Do you have a problem with that? Did you want the shop?'

'Of course not – but, Daddy?'

'Yessy?' A cut as if from a stiletto dipped in sugar. When, as a child, I had called to him, this had been his response.

'Are you telling me you're going to die? Is this all because you're going to die?'

'Everyone has to die, Teresa.' He brushed the creases of his trousers, although they were thin, clean and sharp. 'I have cancer,' he said firmly. 'There's nothing to be done. I've refused treatment – I'm eighty-three years old, what's the point? Pain, sickness, hospitals, everyone's pity. Losing my hair. No, thank you.' Daddy had always been vain about his hair, now iron-grey but still a thick and wavy sweep from forehead to nape of neck.

I felt he was speaking from the far side of the world. I have always hated the few seconds' telephone delay when Jerry is in Australia on business; right now I was still receiving the word 'cancer' and I gaped at him, no longer tearful. My insides were frozen. 'Cancer? What kind of cancer?'

'Does it matter? Prostate, if you must know. Spread to my bones now.' Finally, he looked directly at me from behind the fashionable, titanium-framed glasses bought at my urging during one of his visits to me. They were anachronistic, I could see now, on his long, countryman's face. 'I'm sorry to be the bearer of bad news, Teresa, but you mustn't worry about me. I've made arrangements to be looked after, good arrangements, and I won't be a burden to you. Thank God there's enough money.'

'Why didn't you tell me, Daddy? You should have told me.' Everything was clanging around and inside me. This was why he did not want copies of Frederick's holiday snaps.

'Why?' He looked away from me to where two fishermen were hosing down the deck of their boat. 'What could you have done?'

Overwhelmed, I looked at him, at the father who had minded me for fifty years. Howth, the car, the trawlers dissolved. I was a little girl, and he, with clumsy hands, was trying to tie a plaid bow into my hair. 'We have to be nice for Mammy. She has to see that we're managing grand. She mustn't be worrying about us.'

'Ow, Daddy, that hurt! You're pulling—'

'Sorry. I haven't got the hand of this yet.' He was wearing his dark blue Sunday suit and a snowy shirt, crackling with starch, that one of our neighbours had washed and ironed for us. I was too little to do the laundry but I was good at getting the tea. Especially beans on toast or boiled eggs. And when the meal was ready, I always felt really important when going to the door connecting the house with the shop, just like Mammy always did: 'Daddy! Come on! Tea's ready!'

He had always come in wiping his hands on a linen tea-towel. 'Look at this! What a treat! Good girl!'

I didn't want to go to the hospital that last day. I was afraid to see her the way she had been the previous Sunday, pierced with needles and tubes. With few televisions in Ballina, the paraphernalia of hospital drama had not become familiar and was therefore frightening. But Daddy had insisted. 'You're a big girl now, Teresa. Mammy wants to see you. And you have to smile and be good, and say hello to the nurses and don't fidget.'

Behind his head, the first raindrops splattered on the glass of the car window, fuzzing the images of trawlers beside us. 'How – how long?'

He shrugged. 'Only God knows that.'

'You must have asked.'

'I didn't, actually.'

I was stunned but I believed him. He implicitly trusted doctors, lawyers, teachers, Gárdaí, all professionals, anyone in legitimate authority. And I knew that, having decided against painful, invasive treatment, he would carry out all other instructions to the letter, faithfully follow any regime, swallow anything prescribed. But whether he needed to or not, I needed to know how long he had, how long we had. 'We'll talk about this again, Daddy.'

'All right.'

I had been expecting an objection. Something along the lines of 'We've talked and that's the situation, Teresa.' His quiet acquiescence was seismic, reversing our places so that we were no longer father and daughter, or instructor and learner. We were adult and dependant and, just like that, I was in charge. Beside me in the car, he said something I didn't catch. 'What, Daddy? What did you say?'

'Put that away safely, now, won't you?' His voice was still old but strong again.

'Put what away?'

He indicated the dashboard where I had placed the money. I had forgotten all about it. To please him, I put it in the glove compartment.

I started the car and backed out of the parking space, looking over my shoulder as far as my neck would allow. Then I drove to the edge of the car park, stopped, waited to cross the traffic, looked right, left, right, left, anywhere but at him, my mouth full of all the things I could not say. A motorcycle screamed past at high speed, weaving in and out of the cars in its path. 'Tsk, tsk!'

He shook his head in displeasure. 'Would you look at that!' He craned, glowering in the direction of the bike, already gone from sight. 'Where are the Gárdaí, I might ask? One of these days, that young man will kill himself or somebody else.'

A gap opened in the traffic and I drove across. 'Just one thing,' I said and, as though it was the most casual invitation in the world: 'I want you to come up and live with us.'

There was no response. 'Did you hear me, Daddy?' I glanced across at him.

'We'll see.' He was my father again and I thanked God for His respite.

When we got back, he went up to his room for a rest. I was numb. I believe now that we are given the capacity to absorb shocks of enormous magnitude in manageable doses: that the brain, like a sophisticated circuit-board, trips out from time to time to save itself from overload.

I was about to go up the stairs to shower and change when I heard murmuring from the kitchen and went in to find Tom and Frederick hunkered on the floor, heads almost touching. They were so absorbed they didn't hear me. 'What's going on?'

'Look, Mum! Look what we found!' Tom's face was more animated than I had seen it in years.

I walked over to find a black and white puppy, a ragged bundle of wool and eyes, squirming on my tiles. 'I found her in the garden. I was looking out the window and I saw something moving under the bushes. Can we keep her, Mum?' His eyes were shining. 'Frederick says she might be sick, but we don't know. We have to take her to a vet. She'll need an injection for – what's it called?' He looked up at Frederick, who was now standing.

'Parvovirus. And other things.' Frederick shrugged apologetically at me. 'We couldn't leave her out there, Tessa, she was shivering. Less than six weeks old, maybe five, I'd say. We've been trying to give her milk, but she won't take it.'

'She's frightened.' Tom put his head to the ground right beside the pup's. She recoiled from him, curling herself up like a hedgehog. I picked her up, feeling her heart beating rapidly against my fingers like a little drill. This too? On top of everything else?

'I'll feed her, Mum.' As he scrambled to his feet, Tom's excitement was so intense he was short only of hopping. 'I'll be in charge of her, I'll bring her for walks. I'll do *everything*, Mum. Please let us keep her. Anyway, we can't just throw her back into the garden.' He was working himself up. 'She might *die*.'

Knowing that I would be left to look after a pet when the novelty had worn off, I had always resisted rabbits, kittens, gerbils, hamsters, even, on one occasion, a white rat Jack had brought home, claiming he had 'rescued' it from the school laboratory. 'She might be lost, Tom. Some other boy might be out looking for her right now.'

'Mum, she's not lost, she was *in our garden*! She couldn't have got there by *herself*. She's too *small*!' He was working himself up again. 'She's been *abandoned*.'

I could not summon the energy for further resistance. 'All right.' I handed over the limp pup. 'On condition that you do everything you've promised, Tom. Including house-training her and cleaning up after any accidents. I mean it, now. She'll have to go if I find I'm having to do it.'

'Oh, thanks, Mum, thanks.' Instantly, his mood changed as he stroked the puppy's head with the utmost gentleness. 'You won't have to lift a finger. I *promise*!'

'We'll bring her to the vet after breakfast, eh, Tom?' Frederick's voice was cheerful. 'They'll have advice as to how to get her to eat and what we should get for her. We'll need a collar and a little bed, for instance. What should we call her?'

'I'm calling her Norma.' Still stroking, Tom walked across to a chair and settled the pup in his lap.

Our guest turned to me, eyebrows raised in amusement. 'Well, that's a good name for a dog! So where's the nearest veterinary office, Bibi? Walking distance?'

'I don't know. Look up the *Golden Pages*. It's in the cabinet under the telephone in the hall.' I had spoken more sharply than I had intended: *Did he not know what had happened on the pier?* But there was something else too: I found that Frederick's physical presence no longer disturbed me.

He seemed to sense that something had changed, and his eyes widened briefly. 'I will,' he said quietly. 'In the hall, you said?'

I felt the imminence of release, of something lifting off me and escaping from the house. *No*, I thought, refusing to be tricked into another of those out-of-body moments. 'Yes,' I said firmly, 'in the top drawer.' Then, 'If you'll excuse me, I'm going for a shower.'

I fled the kitchen, leaving the two of them and Norma to continue getting acquainted.

Upstairs, I knocked on Daddy's door. No answer. Heart pounding, I knocked again. He was a light sleeper, he should have heard. And I didn't hear anything from his bathroom. The walk had been too much for him—

Melodramatically fearing the worst, I opened his door as gently as I could. He was lying on his back on the bed, snoring slightly through an open mouth.

I ground my fist into my own mouth to prevent myself crying out; his upper denture had slipped a little so the teeth protruded from between his lips, giving the illusion of flesh eaten away, as though he had been dead for a number of days. I backed out slowly.

Trembling, I picked up the bedside telephone in my own room and dialled 1811 to get the number of our ancient but sharp-witted GP in Ballina.

He told me that my father had anywhere from two to six months. 'I won't lie to you, Teresa, it's bad. But he's a strong character and instinct tells me that he'll carry on until he decides he's had enough, I've seen it a thousand times. Quality of life is what we're aiming for now. God knows, he deserves it. There's a lot of respect for Paddy Cahill in this town.'

'What should I do? He's going to be with me for the next few days. Should I contact my doctor up here?'

'There's nothing you can actually do, Teresa. Tell your doctor by all means, if it makes you feel more secure, but he has his tablets with him and he knows how to use them. He's fine at the moment, in the sense that I don't think there is anything going to happen tomorrow or even next week, but a process has begun in his body, it's well advanced, and without chemo and radiation we can't halt or even delay it. There will be options down the line, you and I will talk about them when the time comes although, of course, everything will be his to decide. But you should feel free to ring me at any time, day or night.'

He hesitated. 'I know this is going to sound trite, Teresa, but in a way, you know, you're lucky. Treat this as an opportunity. We don't all get a five-minute warning. Your time with him will be precious. Make the most of it.'

For a long time, or so it seemed, after we broke the connection, I sat on the side of the bed with the receiver in my hand. The dial tone wavered constantly in my lap, indicating that there was a message in the service.

Dully, I punched out the retrieval numbers. *You have five new messages in your mailbox . . .*

They were all from Jerry. The first four wanting to know what the hell was going on. The fifth to say he was at Stockholm airport and would be in touch from Heathrow.

I had been worrying about my list containing only one item – well, I certainly had another now, had I not?

Was Daddy's terminal illness another punishment for my attraction to Frederick?

I sensed someone in the room. Jack was standing at the door, rubbing sleep from his eyes. 'What's going on? Who's cooking?'

Faintly, from the kitchen, I could smell pancakes.

CHAPTER TWENTY-NINE

Maddy's house was deadly quiet. It was ten o'clock and we had all overslept. Or I thought so until I looked through the hall window into the driveway and saw that Tess's car had gone.

I rang home and the only person I could get was the chap who looks after the stock for us. 'They're all still in the scratcher, Mrs S,' he said cheerfully, from the yard phone. 'The curtains are still pulled on all the windows. Do you want me to go inside and call one of them for you?'

'No, leave them, Cyril. There's nothing urgent.'

Ricky was harassed when I got him at work. The main office for all the businesses is at the back of the original butcher's; our accountants are there, for instance, and it's normally quiet, but I could hear a lot of loud voices in the background. 'What's going on?'

'Jimmy caught someone walking out the door with two sirloins under his jumper. He saw the bloodstains and tackled him. The kid resisted and now he's screaming blue bloody murder that he was assaulted. The cops are here.'

'For two steaks?'

'Don't talk to me!' He sounded exasperated. 'The effin' complication is that the kid's black. He's told the cops it was a racist attack and now there's three of them. I think the other two are his brothers or his cousins or something. They must have been waiting outside and called the fuzz. It's like the bleedin' United Nations in here.' The voices in the background increased to serious shouting level and he went off: 'Keep it down, will yiz? I'm trying to run a business here!' Then he was back on: 'Listen,

Reet. I have to go – everything OK your end?'

'As good as can be expected. I'll see you at dinnertime.' Ricky made a point of coming home to his dinner, 'like my father did, Reet, and his grandfather before him.'

'Take it easy,' he said then. 'Good luck.'

'You too.' I couldn't help smiling as I put my phone back in my handbag. Jimmy is one of our security guards; he's been with us for years and Ricky promoted him to so-called chief of security, but it's gone to his head. All the regulars know him and tease him about *LA Law* and *The A-Team* and stuff. He's supposed to be looking out for the money in the back office but he gets bored and thinks he's Superhero protecting Ricky's kingdom from all thieves, robbers and varmints. This isn't the first time he's gone over the top about a joint or a half-pound of sausages – he doesn't have to because we build a bit of thieving into the budget. We complain in public about having to do it but in private Ricky's and my attitude is that people wouldn't be stealing meat if they weren't hungry.

It's a different matter with the DIY shop. There we have to chain up the power tools and spades, even the hoses, would you believe? And our policy is to prosecute everyone caught with even a handful of screws or a dog lead. They'd rob you blind otherwise, because the word would spread that we're a soft touch. (You wouldn't believe what people lift: a woman was caught going out of the pet shop in the Midlands with a pocketful of fish food and it turned out that she didn't even own a fish. She was rumbled because one of the assistants saw the empty tube on the floor.)

It was now a quarter past ten and I debated whether or not to ring Tess, but decided to postpone it until this afternoon. She knew I was supportive. She would be in touch if she needed to talk earlier.

I could hear movement upstairs. Poor Maddy would be feeling pretty sorry for herself.

I looked around the messy kitchen. If I cleaned up, would she be insulted? Ah the hell with it, I thought, and looked under the sink to see if there was any Jif, or Cif, as they're calling it now. They changed it because people who speak Spanish couldn't pronounce the J. Spent millions on marketing that. I didn't believe it when Ricky told me, but apparently it's gospel.

I had made good inroads into the cleaning – at least, you could see the draining-board and some of the counters – when Maddy finally came in. She was dressed but looking ghastly. I peeled off the rubber gloves. 'I was killing time, hope you don't mind?'

She shook her head and I could see it hurt like hell.

'Come on, sit down, the kettle's boiled. Have you any bread that isn't mouldy? I've thrown out what was in the bread-bin.'

'In the freezer,' she whispered.

'Toast, then – mind if I put on the radio?'

'No.'

The radio is great for covering awkwardnesses. Marian Finucane was on her summer holidays from Radio One so I twiddled around until I found a bit of decent music on Lite FM. 'There. That'll keep us going.' For the next few minutes, to give Maddy a chance to get herself together, I hummed along with the music and didn't exactly hustle while I made tea, popped and buttered toast. 'Here we are,' I said, when I brought it to the table. 'Get that down you, chicken, it'll help.'

Her head was in her hands. 'Nothing will help.'

'Mad . . .'

'Nothing will help!' She looked up. She had obviously cleaned her teeth but her lips were cracked, the corners red and sore. She's so thin, you see, she has no reserves and that's why her skin looks so terrible. Me, I could live for three months on water only and hardly anyone'd notice the difference. I poured tea for the two of us.

'This has to stop, Maddy,' I said softly. 'Even if you want to get Fergus back – and you know my views on that – you won't if you keep on the way you are.'

'I know.'

'Do you remember what we talked about last night?'

'Vaguely.' She tried to raise the cup to her lips but she had the shakes and slopped tea all over the table.

'We talked about you maybe getting help.'

No answer. She was staring at the half-empty cup as if it could talk to her. 'Maddy?'

'Yes, yes, I remember.'

'Well?'

Instead of answering, she got up and tottered across to the draining-board where I had placed a fresh roll of kitchen towels. 'Maddy, did you hear me?'

'All right, all *right*! Stop *nagging* me!' Raising her voice was obviously torture because she groaned and put her hand to the side of her head. She was so bad, I thought, she had to have drunk even more after Tess and I had gone to bed. She must have had a stash in the bedroom.

While she was blotting up the tea with the paper, I chewed my own toast and thought furiously. It was all very well playing Mammy to her. Now I had to come up with something she would buy, something concrete and immediate: she was in such a state she just might agree. I said a mental prayer to St Laurence O'Toole to help me handle this right. He's the patron saint of Dublin and my favourite because hardly anyone I know uses him and he has to have time on his hands. (Ricky's favourite saint is St Eligius. He's French and he's the patron saint of jockeys! And taxi drivers, jewellers and coin collectors! He found him on the Internet when we were opening up the first bookie's shop a few years ago.)

Maddy finished blotting. She crumpled up the paper and took a sip of the fresh tea. 'Eat your toast too, Maddy. You need to line your stomach.'

'I can't.'

'Try. Just a few bites.' It was like dealing with a toddler.

'I really can't. It's no use.' She stood up, but was so unsteady on her pins she had to catch on to the table. 'Sorry, Rita, but I have to have a drink.'

'That's the last thing you need!' I jumped up and caught her arm. 'Be realistic, Mad. If you're going to get help, you have to be in your full senses.'

'I will be in my full senses,' she pleaded, trying to arm-wrestle out of my hold on her. But she was too weak and gave up. The tears began to flow again.

Although I didn't want to sound unsympathetic, I was sick of people crying. 'Maddy, don't cry,' I said to her. 'It's not going to do you or me or anyone any good.' I let her go.

'I can't help it.' She sniffed, but reached for the paper towels and blew her nose. Then she sat down again. 'Listen, Rita, I'll make a deal with you.' She was begging, making me feel like a right heel. 'One G and T, just one, and then no more. Ever. I promise. I've learned my lesson, you can be sure of that. One drink will sort me out. The hair of the dog, like, it's a proven cure.'

'No.' I folded my arms. 'If you lay a finger on that gin bottle now, I'm leaving and I won't come back. I mean it, Maddy – you're on your own.'

'But I promise—' She realised I was serious and shut up. It was touch and go for a few seconds while we stared at each other. She made one last try. 'But I haven't been drinking that long. I couldn't need *treatment*, Reet, I'm not an alcoholic, I couldn't be.'

'It doesn't matter how long. Addiction is addiction, love. You can get addicted in twelve months. Less, even. Especially when you're a woman. Our livers are much smaller, Mad.'

My phone rang. I ignored it but she grabbed the opportunity. 'Aren't you going to answer that?'

I glanced at the screen. 'I'll ring back later. It's only Carol, she probably wants money.' I continued to stare her down while mentally saying another quick ejaculation to give Laurence a gee up: Laurence, Father, hear our prayer, Guide us with thy royal care . . . It worked because Maddy hung her head like a little girl.

'All right,' she muttered. 'Tell me what to do and I'll do it.'

'We'll finish our breakfast,' I said, sitting opposite her, 'and then I'll drive you.' I was winging it now. 'I've been thinking about going to your GP like we talked about – but then, I thought, sure he'd just give you a letter to take to one of the hospitals anyway, wouldn't he? So I think the best thing is for us to go right to one of the hospitals. Straight away. Might as well cut out the middle man, eh?'

'A hospital?' She was horrified.

'You know what I mean, Maddy. A clinic, if you like, whatever you want to call it. That's where the help is. Specialists. There's no shame in it any more – sure they're boasting about their detoxes all over Dublin, I've heard them myself. You must have heard them too.'

Then I lied. I took her hand with as much sincerity as I could find and, although I had every intention of trying to get her admitted as an in-patient, I reassured her that all we'd do today was have her checked out. 'We'll get someone to give you the once-over and some tablets and stuff to make you feel better.'

'That's all? You promise that's all we'll do? We'll just talk to a doctor and get me something to help me?'

I couldn't look her in the face any longer and removed the hand holding hers to scratch an imaginary itch on one of my eyelids. 'You want to feel better, don't you? At least, better than you do now?'

'Are you being sarcastic?'

'No,' I said lightly, rubbing away, feeling like Judas Iscariot, 'I'm just thinking ahead.'

Quick now, I thought, and dropped my hand. 'So, where'll we go? The only places I know about are the Rutland Centre, St John of God's and St Roland's. They're all very good, I believe, but Roland's is just down the road. Or is there another one you know about yourself?' I held my breath.

'No.' Her misery almost undid me but I kept my tone light and my heart hard. 'So, will you try the bit of toast?'

'I can't.'

'In that case, will we head, then?'

'What? Now?'

'What's the point of postponing it, Maddy? You'll feel even worse later, you know you will . . .' I didn't want to give her time to think. Roland's was definitely the nearest by my calculations and I was hoping they would take her in straight away; I could come back to the house and fetch her clothes and toiletries later – my family would have to do without me for the day. 'Where's your handbag?'

'In the hall.'

'Are your keys in it? You go on out to my car – don't worry, I'll make sure the front door closes properly.'

She was too ill to protest as I shepherded her up from the table, through the hall, gathering up her coat and handbag as we went, having to curb my instinct to push her into a run. Once we were inside and in the hands of the professionals, I reckoned, I could back off. They would know how to handle her: falling off a log for them. As gently and quickly as I could, I installed her in the front seat of my car, her little thin body like a broken sweeping brush inside the seat-belt.

As we drove out of her estate, I kept up a running commentary, I'm good at that. I tried to distract her by talking about Tess and her problems, about how Ricky was probably handling his situation in the shop, about asylum-seekers, Kitty and Jack, anything I could think of. She didn't speak, but when we stopped at a set of lights, I saw that, despite her thick coat, she was shivering. 'Are you cold?'

'Like an iceberg.'

I turned the heater full on. 'Some summer, eh?' That drew a little smile but within minutes her head was drooping and she was having a doze. My heart went out to her but I couldn't let that influence me: alcoholics are very manipulative, you know, and if I weakened at all, I knew she'd try to get round me. So as we drove along, I kept telling myself that this was for her own good.

Yet I dreaded what was ahead. For all my big talk, I had no first-hand experience of anything like this; all I knew was what I had seen in the movies and what I had picked up over the years from Ricky and his mates. Although we've been lucky, touch wood, there aren't many people in Ireland who don't have an alcoholic as a friend or in the family. That's why we all know the lingo, the names of the hospitals, and what happens inside them. What I did know for sure was that Maddy had to go inside of her own free will; they probably wouldn't take her if they felt she was being pushed, especially by someone like me, who wasn't even a relation.

This was going to be delicate. She looked so vulnerable, with her head bobbing about; I could imagine what she must have been feeling and thinking before she nodded off. She knew we were doing the right thing but at the same time she was terrified and would probably do or promise anything to avoid it. I was sweating in the blast of the heater, but I didn't dare open the window or turn down the heat because I wanted to keep her asleep.

CHAPTER THIRTY

The traffic was free enough and we made good time so that we were driving up to the hospital within twenty-five minutes of leaving the house. The car parks, however, were so jam-packed I had difficulty finding a space. By the time I'd got one I was cursing and swearing under my breath. Maddy stayed asleep, thank God, hanging over the seat-belt. Gently, I cut the engine: the last thing I needed now was for her to wake up and make a dash for it.

I got out of the car, walked round to her side and pulled open the door as quietly as I could, at the same time blocking any escape route. 'We're here, Mad,' I said softly, shaking her shoulder.

She came to and looked at the cars and the trees around us. 'What—'

'This is the hospital, chicken. We're here.'

Her expression grew wild. 'I don't want to. I've changed my mind.' She struggled against the belt and scrabbled wildly with the release button.

'Ssh. Remember what we talked about? You can't change your mind now.' I leaned across and undid the belt for her.

'Please, Rita, I'll change.' Her tone was pitiful. 'I'll take the pledge, I promise.'

I was nearly in tears myself now and had to remind myself what I was doing and why. 'Don't be silly, Mad,' I said, as if I was a parish priest. 'There's nothing to be afraid of, we're only going for a consultation. You know you need help, you said it yourself – you asked me!' I stood back a little as though I was really cross. 'You're not going to tell me I've wasted my whole day like this, are you? I have better things to do with my time, Maddy.'

'I don't remember asking you to do anything for me.'

'Well, you certainly did. Last night.' Another lie, probably a mortaller because I was using it to get my own way. I put my hands on my hips. 'It's not my fault you don't remember. That's called a blackout, Maddy, and it's very, very serious.'

'Is it?' She leaned her head against the dashboard and the tangled, thin hair moved me so much I very nearly surrendered. Instead, I made myself sound really tough. 'All right, Maddy, which is it to be? Are you going to get help or not? Make up your mind, please. I haven't got all day. I've wasted enough of my time on you already. You don't have to go in here – I'll take you anywhere you want – but I'm warning you, Maddy, if you don't do something for yourself, you needn't coming whining to me any more.'

This got through to her and she stared at me, shocked. Then she moved to climb out of the car. I rushed to help her – she weighed nothing at all.

When she was out, I hugged her very tightly. I was so sorry – but of course I couldn't let her see that. 'You're great,' I gushed. 'I promise you you're doing the right thing.'

We set off. Slowly, because she felt she might vomit. As we came in sight of the hospital's entrance, her hand crept into mine. 'Look, they have a really nice garden,' I chirruped, and hated myself with a passion. 'Aren't those roses really terrific?'

The place was old fashioned but clean and airy, and in the end the procedure wasn't as bad as I had expected. Not a totally smooth ride, naturally, and there were a few minutes when I thought she'd bolt as she realised this wasn't going to be the just-in-and-out I'd promised and that I'd tricked her. After getting through Reception, we were seen by a doctor then put into a waiting room, furnished with a few shabby fireside chairs and coffee tables. That was the most dangerous time when she rounded on me.

But then the system kicked in. The woman who came in to us with the forms to sign was superb. She spoke in a calm, matter-of-fact way, as if hospitalising drunks was in no way a source of embarrassment any longer but the most everyday occurrence – to her, of course, it was. 'You've come on a good day.' She smiled. 'I don't know why but we have a number of beds today. We're usually full – and we'll probably be full tonight like always. We can even give you a single room – you're lucky. Do you have a medical card or VHI, Madeleine?'

I produced Maddy's VHI membership card out of her handbag. (She's the total opposite of me. Every time we go abroad, I have to turn the house upside down looking for all my documentation.)

'Next of kin?' the woman asked. Another sticky moment. Then Maddy surprised me. After a short hesitation she gave, in a firm voice, not Fergus's name but the name, address and telephone number of her father in Ballineen.

'All we ask, Madeleine,' the woman went on, as she wrote this down, 'is that you're serious about this and that you co-operate with the doctors and therapists. And, of course, no alcohol or drugs while you're here.' She smiled. 'Our patients drink a lot of coffee. Sooner or later someone's going to have to open a caffeine-addiction facility. We'll give you a thorough medical work-up and we'll be detoxing you over the next day or so. You'll find you'll sleep a lot. Now,' she pulled yet another form towards her, 'when did you have your last drink?'

'I'll head off, Mad,' I said. 'You're in good hands. I'll be back in an hour or so with your case packed for you. OK?'

The tears sprang into her eyes then and, like a kid being left in school for the first day, she clutched my sleeve. But then she saw what she was doing and took away her hand. 'Thank you, Rita. See you soon, then.'

But when I got back to the hospital with her clothes and toilet bag – and flowers and a box of Cadbury's Roses – she was in bed, deeply asleep. The hospital nightgown, what I could see of it, was too big for her and fell away from her neck and chest, exposing the bones.

Carefully, I left the gear on the floor beside her, then kissed her cold, damp forehead. Her eyes opened briefly, but registered nothing and closed again.

Poor Maddy.

Now I have to ring bloody Fergus, I thought, as I drove away. He had to know. I certainly wasn't going to alarm her poor unfortunate parents or Colm. They'd find out sooner or later, but that had to be Maddy's call.

In our house, daylight hours during the school holidays, particularly when it's raining – as it was (again!) by the time I got home that day – are trying. Televisions compete with stereos at top volume and the girls, plus whatever friends they've had in for sleepovers, clatter around in dressing-gowns or their latest gear, with me nagging at everyone not to be a wimp because of a drop of rain but to go outside and get a bit of fresh air or exercise the ponies.

Today was no exception. It was nearly dinnertime when I let myself in and the house rocked with the thumping and screaming of the hifi in the sitting room. I heard it even before I opened the car door in the driveway.

Only Kitty was still in bed; the rest of them, plus assorted pals, were shoulder to shoulder around the kitchen table, scoffing cereals. The floor looked like a sandpit. 'Somebody turn that music down!' I shouted, from the doorway.

'Oh, Ma!' Alice threw her eyes to heaven. 'We can't hear it from in here if we have to turn it *dow-un*!' My third daughter, who used to be the most biddable of all four, has taken to calling her father Rick and has developed this awful whine. A lot of words have one more syllable than they should have.

'If you don't turn it down,' I yelled, 'I'll turn it off altogether. And I'll take the fuse out of the plug.'

'I'll do it, Ma.' Patricia jumped up and ran out of the kitchen. Thank God for Patricia. But if she gets to be like Alice in a couple of years, I swear to God I'll tie her into a Moses basket and put her into the rushes.

While we were waiting for a bit of hush, I surveyed the faces turned in my direction. I recognised two of Alice's pals and one of Carol's, but there were at least four I had never seen before. I don't bother asking the names unless they're here more than three times because, quite often, their visits are once-off. Girls can be fickle. 'That's better,' I said, as soon as the music was lowered to manageable proportions.

'Hello, everyone,' I said then, as if I was a Butlins Redcoat, 'you're all very welcome, but I'd appreciate it now if you'd all skedaddle and let me get on with cleaning up here and making dinner. Who's staying?'

They all looked at each other and then, one by one, they all confirmed they would be our guests for the meal. 'Thank you very much, Mrs Sleator,' said one of the ones I didn't recognise, 'but I hope you don't mind, I'm a vegetarian.'

'Me too,' pipes up the one beside her.

'That's not a problem,' I was used to this, 'but it's just pot luck here, all right? So, how many?'

I counted. With Kitty and Ricky, if he came home, we'd have fourteen. 'Yikes! It's an army kitchen I need!' I sighed, but it was for effect. I didn't really mind even though I was on my own and there would be a mountain of potatoes to peel. Betty, my home help, was on her holidays in her sister's in Sligo, but what else did I have to do on a rainy day? The freezer was well stocked and, as I think I said before, I love a crowd. 'You rang me, Carol?' I asked, as they dislodged themselves from the table.

'I can't remember what I wanted, Ma. I'll think about it soon.'

'Right. So, go on, shoo, all of you!' I said, and they scattered to the four corners of the house. San Lorenzo is homey but very big, with plenty of room for each of the girls to have her own space, her own stereo, even her own TV.

And the neighbours can't complain – because they aren't within earshot. One of the things that attracted me to the house when we began to make a few bob and were able to stretch our wings a bit was that it was plonk in the middle of its own land. Unless times got hard and we had to sell sites, we would never be crammed in like popcorn in the middle of estates.

I'd had enough of estates, thank you very much. I was reared in a place where neighbours thumped walls if they didn't like what was going on in the house next door, or even your choice of music, and where if you sneezed, everyone on the road said, 'God bless you!' This old barn of ours has nine bedrooms. It had had only six when it was built 150 years ago, not counting servants' quarters, but all these original bedrooms had been enormous – murder to heat, even though they all had fireplaces. The people we bought it from were trying to pay the bills by running it as a guesthouse and had divided three of the bedrooms so it went from six to nine in one go. I only redecorated, didn't bother putting them back, so we had four spare rooms, which was real handy when the girls had pals to stay. In fact, the place is so solid we had very little to do with it, and the only structural change we made was to add on a conservatory. I love light, I do.

I went into the scullery, put on an apron and slit open a four-stone bag of Queens. You might ask why I don't get my daughters to do the potatoes. Well, this is probably mental but I don't set chores for the girls, purely because they are girls. When I was growing up, only the girls in our family had chores, the boys got off scot-free. Two of us plus Ma, six of them plus Da. And I was determined, absolutely bloody determined, that I wouldn't rear any daughter of mine to skivvy for men.

Lookit, I know there's no logic in what I'm doing because here I am skivvying not only for a man but for the girls too. I can afford to pay someone to do this or I could force it on the girls, but I *choose* to do it myself for my own family in my own house and nobody is telling me I have to. That's the difference.

I miss my sister. She lives in Florida now, with her brood. The telephone just doesn't do it, does it? As for my brothers, there's only one of them left in Ireland, the youngest. He's in an indie band – not very successful – and not interested in family at all.

Christmas is the only time we'd have a chance of any of us meeting. Sad, after such a crowded growing-up.

I set to work. I wouldn't be popular for saying this these days, I suppose, but I enjoy manual housework, doing dishes by hand, peeling potatoes. There's something earthy about it, if that's not a bad pun. Kitty showed me a poem she came across recently. It's by Séamus Heaney, and it's about watching his own mother at the sink doing the spuds. 'This reminds me of you, Ma! Listen!' When she was finished, she gave me a quick little thump. 'There. Isn't that you exactly?'

I can't remember any of it now except one word he used about the knife: something about it being 'fluent', I think it was. I was pleased that she had noticed because it was exactly right. You get into a rhythm and your mind goes free. I was pleased about the thump she gave me too.

At this time, my mind could go only so far before bumping up against what I should be doing. Instead of enjoying myself here in my scullery, I should be ringing Tess and St Roland's and Fergus

Griggs. They were all going round in my head like the camels in Duffy's Circus. But I couldn't face breaking up this lovely bit of peace and quiet. Not yet. I let myself off the hook by promising myself that I'd ring every last one of them after the dinner.

Well, after the dishes were done.

When I had a pyramid of peeled potatoes on the counter, I tipped them into the sink to wash them, then opened the freezer door to see what we'd have. We have a ginormous freezer – Ricky's always bringing meat home, naturally.

Steak, I thought. Girls always like steak, although they don't like to admit it. As for the two vegetarians, I had a few Lean Cuisine packets for my next diet. (I usually end up throwing out the packets when they go past their best-before dates.) The two girls would have to make do with vegetarian Lean Cuisine and potatoes. Pity about them.

We have two microwave ovens and I shoved the first lot of steaks into both of them on defrost. As I was unwrapping the second heap, the wall phone rang. Phones, phones, phones, I was sick of phones. 'Yes?'

It was Tess. Very quiet. 'Are you busy, Rita? I know you eat around this time, should I call back?'

'Not at all.' I braced myself for more about Jerry and maybe another guilt trip on what she's been imagining about Yarso. 'Fire ahead,' I said, 'no problem. I can keep on doing what I'm doing while you're talking. How're things?'

She told me about her father. I couldn't believe it. Jesus. All right, he's eighty-three and this is a natural disaster, but hey! What did she do in a past life? Someone sure has it in for her.

I sat down with the half-unwrapped steaks in my lap. 'Oh, God, Tess, I'm so sorry. Is there anything I can do?'

'No. There's nothing anyone can do.' Her voice was flat. 'Jerry's on his way home, I don't know what time he's going to arrive but he'll be here.'

'Does he know?'

'No, I haven't been speaking to him, I just yelled at him to come home and hung up. This was before—' her voice wobbled.

'You poor, poor thing, it must be awful over there.'

'It is. But I can't let Daddy see I'm upset. I have to act as if everything's normal. We even had pancakes for breakfast. Frederick cooked them. Thank God he's here, he's taken Tom to the vet.'

'I beg your pardon?'

'Sorry.' She actually laughed, although there were a few high notes there. 'You won't believe it, but we have a pup now.'

'Look, Tess, you can't go through all this on your own. Do you want me to come over?'

She hesitated. Then, 'No. It's not your problem, it wouldn't be fair. I bent your ear enough last night over in Maddy's. How is Maddy, by the way?'

I decided not to add to her concerns. 'Fine, a bit hung-over.'

'Me too. I feel like I've been hit by a train. Thank you for listening, Rita. I'm sorry I rang you, it just bubbles up every so often and I have to talk to someone.'

'Listen, no arguments. I'll come over this afternoon. I'm afraid I have an army here for feeding at the moment, but when I've done that, I'll be there. All right?'

She hesitated again. 'But that's not fair.'

'Shut up! I should be there between half-three and four.'

After I hung up, I stood looking at the wall phone. By what right had I escaped trouble when my two dear friends were up to their necks in it?

The microwaves pinged, one after the other, and I set about organising the gang meal.

Three-quarters of an hour later, as I looked at all the faces around our huge kitchen table, Little Ricky and his Harem, I decided that Laurence O'Toole had taken a special interest in me because I had named the house after him. I was protected.

I had, therefore, to look after my friends. But, dear God, would it never end?

CHAPTER THIRTY-ONE

By contrast with our house, Arkady was very quiet when I got there. First thing I did was give Tess the biggest, hardest hug she ever got in her life. 'You poor, poor bitch,' I said.

'Don't. Don't sympathise, Rita, or I'll start to blubber.'

'All right.' I let her go. 'Where's everyone?'

'Frederick has taken Tom off swimming and Daddy's in the television room, there's racing on.'

'Did you say anything to the boys?'

She shook her head. 'He'd kill me if I did. He'll tell them himself if he wants to. Jack's in there with him.'

'Frederick?'

'Of course not.'

'So how is he?'

'The same as he was this morning – oh, Rita!' She covered her eyes. 'I always knew this day would come but I just don't know how I'm going to cope – and, funny, it's bringing Mammy's death all back again.'

I hugged her again, but quickly. I didn't want to start her off, poor thing. 'I'll go in and say hello to him in a minute. In the meantime, come on into the kitchen.' I led the way. 'I'm gasping for a cuppa.

'That the pup?' As I walked to the kettle, I pointed to a corner of the kitchen where something that looked like a ball of wool lay in the middle of a huge, brand-new dog basket.

'That's her.' Tess barely glanced at the animal. 'Norma.'

'Norma? Why?'

'Search me. Tom's decision.'

When we had installed ourselves with our tea on the high stools at her island unit she filled me in. 'And there's no hope?'

'None. Not if he continues to refuse treatment, which he will.'

'That's your father all over – but it would be just a postpone-
ment anyway.'

'Yeah.' Her eyes filled with tears but she blinked them back.
'And Jerry – how am I going to deal with that situation now?' She
looked into her cup. 'He rang from Heathrow about two hours
ago, but I was crying so hard about Daddy I couldn't talk to him,
so not only does he not know about the – the thing – he doesn't
know about the cancer either. I don't mean to be acting like a
baby, but I'm all over the place, Rita.'

She didn't look all over the place: she was dressed in a designer
tracksuit in a pale grey that made her look real stylish. I wanted to
tell her that she was bearing up very well, in my opinion, but I
thought it wouldn't make any difference. For once, I had no
advice to offer. 'I'll stay until Jerry comes, all right?'

'Thank you, Rita – again.'

'Any biscuits in this kip?' I got off the stool and crossed to the
cupboard where she usually kept the tin. Crawford's shortbread,
wouldn't you know? None of your Fox's custard creams.

I had this awful feeling of time passing too quickly; I wouldn't
be the most imaginative woman in the world, not like Maddy – or
Tess herself – and I've probably been watching too many films on
the TV, but right then I got the clearest picture in my head of
Jerry getting closer and closer, a big black crow cutting out the
light with his gigantic wings. 'I'll stay as long as you like,' I said
quickly, grabbing a handful of the shortbread, 'but your dad is the
main priority, Tess. The other stuff . . .' I tried to think of
something suitable to say, or some way to refer to the e-mail
'. . . well, it's just stuff, isn't it? I'm sure it'll sort itself out. He loves
you, Tess, I'm sure of that.'

'How sure are you?'

'Sure as eggs are eggs?' I got back on my stool. I wasn't at all as
convinced as I had tried to sound. But then I thought: Who
knows what goes on behind closed doors? Just because they
weren't kissy-kissy in public, and he was so involved in his job . . .

But I also remembered the strange conversation Tess and I had
had on the beach during the holiday when she seemed to be

questioning the meaning of her whole life. And her confessions about bloody Frederick Yarso.

He had to go sharpish. If she wouldn't do it, I would. She and Jerry had been together for ten years. That had to count for something. And they didn't need complications in the house like attractive, footloose Americans. 'Look,' I said, 'you've an awful lot going on, would you like me to take Frederick off your hands?'

She shot me a look but I couldn't tell if it was gratitude or what. 'Oh, no, Rita, it'd be too much.'

'You know we have about a zillion spare rooms. He'd be a novelty for the girls and their gangs of friends. A trophy, even.'

'You're so good. Maybe in a few days, when I get my act together and I know what I'm doing . . .' She was about to say something else when she seemed to hear something and turned towards the kitchen door. 'Oh, God, Rita, that's him!'

'Frederick?'

'Frederick doesn't have a key—'

I hadn't heard anything but next thing the kitchen door was thrown open and Jerry was standing there. 'What's going on? Oh, hello, Rita.' He turned back to Tess. 'Tess?'

Funny the way a person's mind works, isn't it? Despite all the trauma, and that I should be hating him on Tess's behalf, I noticed for the first time in years, how good-looking Jerry Brennan is. At that moment, you could even have said he looked a bit like the dishy film stars the tabloids call 'rugged'. He was wearing a trench coat and because of the downpour, which had begun again in early afternoon, his hair was wet as if he had come through some disaster, saving the world or something hunky like that. 'I'll leave you two to talk.' Once again I slid off my stool.

'No, please, Rita. Stay?' Tess's eyes were wide, as if she was afraid to be alone with him. She wasn't, of course. She was just afraid, full stop.

'All right,' I climbed back up. I'd get welts on my bum at this rate. I was praying she wouldn't go into the e-mail thing first off, I wasn't sure I could handle that.

'Will someone please tell me what has happened? I left a very important meeting—' I could see Jerry was getting angry now.

'My father's dying. He has terminal cancer,' Tess said quietly.

'Oh, my God . . .' In fairness, he was genuinely upset. 'When – what's wrong? How did you find out?'

'He told me this morning and our doctor in Ballina confirmed it.'

'That's dreadful – but why couldn't you tell me on the phone, Tess? Did you know last night? I rang you—'

'I didn't hear the call, we were in Maddy's, she asked us to go over, she's in trouble as you know.' Tess looked towards me for help.

'It's been a terrible shock, Jerry,' I said. 'He hasn't got long, you know. Tess doesn't know whether she's coming or going, she's finding it hard to think at the moment, as you could well imagine.'

'Dear God!' He walked over to the kettle. 'Is this hot?' He shrugged off his coat and threw it across a little cane couch they have in one of the kitchen alcoves and we watched while he made himself a cup of instant coffee. 'Christ! What was that?' He jumped away from the counter as though he had been stung. The pup, Norma, had somehow managed to crawl out of her basket and had brushed against his toe.

After all that was dealt with and the little dog had been dispatched back to her proper place, Jerry made his coffee and turned to face us, cup in hand. 'Where's your dad now?'

Even though she was three feet away from me I could feel the tension in Tess as if she was gearing up to tell him about the other business. Please, please God, I prayed, please, Laurence . . . Not now. Not yet. Wait until I've gone . . .

My prayer was answered. 'He's in the television room.' Tess's voice was as high as Patricia's. 'But you mustn't say anything, Jerry. You know him, he doesn't want us all to be making a big thing of this.'

'But it is a big thing, lass. It is a big thing.' He walked across and touched her cheek so tenderly that for a second or two I thought the e-mail had to be some kind of awful misunderstanding. By the way she was flinching, though, while trying not to show him, I could see she didn't think it was a misunderstanding. Oh, how I wished at that moment I was snug in San Lorenzo with Ricky and the girls. I'm long on talk and hugs, it appears, but short when it comes to putting my money where my mouth is.

'Well, we shouldn't all just hang around here, he'll think we're talking about him. Let's go inside.' Jerry moved towards the door.

'Are you sure you want me to stay, Tess?' I was hoping against hope she'd excuse me. 'I could just go in and say hello to your dad, like I said?'

'Please, Rita . . .' She signalled again with her eyes.

Naturally I was dreading what I would see when I followed the two of them into the room, but I needn't have. To be sure, Mr Cahill was thinner than when last I had seen him, much thinner, but he got to his feet without too much difficulty and after saying hello to Jerry – expressing no surprise at seeing him – came across to me immediately. 'Rita, how nice to see you! How are you? And how's the family?'

We shook hands. 'Grand, Mr Cahill. Growing fast.'

'And your husband?'

'Grand too.'

'Business good?'

'Thriving.'

'Yes. They say the Celtic Tiger is dead and all the rest of it, but don't you believe it, there's plenty of money around.'

'I'll head, Mum.' Jack stood up and walked towards the door. I noticed he hadn't acknowledged Jerry's presence.

'Where are you going?' Tess was still just inside the door.

'Town, Mum, is that OK?' His tone was just short of cheeky.

'Try not to be too late?' Tess flashed a look at Jerry.

'I won't.' Her son snaked round her and left.

Mr Cahill was still standing, looking from one to the other of us. I smiled but he didn't smile back. 'I see,' he said to Tess, 'you've told everyone.'

'Only Rita and Jerry. Honestly, Daddy, no one else.'

'Well, we all know now, so there's nothing more to be said, then, is there?' He returned to his seat.

'Paddy.' Jerry sat down on a chair at right angles to him and leaned forward as though to engage him.

'Not now, Jerry.' Mr Cahill waved a hand in his son-in-law's direction. 'I have a tip for this one. One of my customers has a horse running.'

To give him his due, Jerry handled him great, immediately sitting back into his chair and settling in to watch. 'Have you money on?'

'A modest bet.' Using the remote control, Mr Cahill turned up the volume. 'Sit down, Tess,' he said irritably, 'you're making me nervous, hovering at the door like that. Come in or go out. One or the other.'

She and I sat together in the middle of their big sofa. Their television room is decorated in white and yellow, usually real cheery. Today, though, it seemed dark, first because the curtains had been pulled to help with the glare on the television picture, but also, of course, because of what we were all thinking.

I, for one, didn't hear a word of the race commentary because I was too busy watching the 'condemned man' out of the corner of my eye. I felt ghoulish about it – is that the right word? – as if I was waiting for him to keel over there and then. My own mother and father died quietly of heart-attacks, my mother in her sleep, Daddy while he was out shopping for a new hall carpet, so thank God I never had to go through that awful business of watching them in pain and fading away in agony and on drugs that addled their brains. How bad would the next few months be for this poor man? And for Tess?

He was watching the race with deep concentration, his body bending more and more until he was nearly double. When his horse won, he didn't whoop or cheer like Ricky or I would have, he just sat back and let out a big sigh.

'Congratulations! That was wonderful. What odds?' Jerry reached over and gave his elbow a little squeeze. I have to say that this was a side of Tess's husband I had not seen in all the ten years. I had seen him be nice to Tess, of course, especially in their honeymoon period, but I had always felt he wasn't interested in any of the rest of us, or even in her family.

'I got fourteen to one!' Mr Cahill was as proud as if he had ridden the horse himself. 'What do you think of that now?'

'Pretty terrific!' Jerry stood up. 'We'll go out for a pint later, eh? Just the two of us. The drinks are on you.'

'Of course. I'll look forward to it.' Tess's father beamed as Jerry gave him another pat, then went to leave the room.

'Where are you going?' Tess, too, stood up.

'I won't be more than a few minutes.' He paused by the door.

'I'm just going up to check on my e-mails, and I need to ring Jeremy from the Swedish office. I was supposed to be a rapporteur during one of the break-out sessions and I left him a little in the lurch when I dashed off without warning.' He smiled again at Mr Cahill. 'See you later, Paddy. Get your wallet ready!'

Tess and I looked at each other as he left the room and I saw a completely different woman from the frightened, confused person who had let me in earlier. 'I have to go up!' she said quietly. 'I can't let him delete it before I confront him. Wish me luck.'

I glanced at her father but he was absorbed in the racing pages of the *Irish Independent*. 'Yes,' I said. 'You have to. Good luck. Ring me later if you need to.'

She slipped out and I went across to her father. 'Cheerio, Mr Cahill – I'll see you soon, I hope.' I held out my hand again to shake his.

'I'll be selling tickets,' he said dryly, then looked around. 'Everyone gone to the moon!' Then, settling in again to watch the next race, he looked up at me, very serious. 'Look after her, won't you? She'll need all the help she can get.'

'I will. Don't you worry.' I had been about to throw my arms around him but I checked myself. Where he was concerned, that would have been going too far.

Outside, I zapped the car and got in, looking back up at Arkady's grey face. I couldn't bear to think what might be going on behind those innocent-looking windows and wheeled around the gravelled turning circle in front of the house as if I was Eddie Irvine. One thing was for sure – my resolve hardened; Tess would have to get rid of Yarso. What a nerve the guy had.

My offer to take him had been genuine and remained on the table but I was half relieved she hadn't taken it up. I tell you, he would have got short shrift in my house, no matter how charming he was or how much house or garden work he offered to do. Maybe, at rock bottom, what I had against the guy was that I hate spongers, always have – probably comes from my own background where if you didn't pull yourself up by your bootstraps you died young. Literally.

While I was driving home I checked up on Maddy. We're going to be penalised for using mobiles in the car shortly, so I was going to make hay while I could. 'Are you a relative?' The nurse, or orderly, or whatever he was, was cautious.

'Yes,' I lied. 'I'm her sister.'

He put me on to her unit. This second person was nice, but just as leery with information as the first. She did tell me, however, that Maddy was still sleeping and was expected to be out until the morning.

'Can I come and visit her? Maybe tomorrow?'

'I'd say leave it for a few days. We'd like to give her a little while to settle in. Maybe Wednesday? Give us a call on Wednesday morning.'

'Thank you.' I was secretly glad I had a few days' reprieve. I thought then that I should ring Fergus, get it over with, but I couldn't face the palaver of getting his number, much less actually talking to the little weasel. I would ring him first thing in the morning, I promised myself.

It had been quite a day.

That evening, I sat very close to Ricky in front of our television but I was on hot coals all the time, waiting for the phone to ring with some new crisis in Arkady. Thankfully, it didn't.

And when we were in bed that night, I hugged him and hugged him and hugged him until he protested. 'What are you doing, Reet? Are you trying to smother me or what?'

'I am. I feel like smothering you to pieces. I love you, you big lug, do you know that? I love you, I bleedin' *love* you!'

CHAPTER THIRTY-TWO

While climbing the stairs towards Jerry's study, I could not make up my mind whether I was glad or sorry that Daddy and Frederick were with us as house guests. It would be difficult to conceal a cataclysmic row from them and the atmosphere in the house would be riddled with tension. Leaving Frederick out of it, however, in present circumstances I doubted if Jerry would let himself down in front of Daddy, whom he liked and respected, and I also doubted whether he, any more than I, would want to upset him. So it might be possible, I thought, to manage the situation in a civilised fashion.

This may sound as though I was calm but I was far from it. Brain was racing against Anger and Fear, and Brain was temporarily in the lead.

His door was ajar and I could hear him opening and closing drawers. I could also hear the computer booting up. 'Hi.' I stood in the doorway.

'Oh, Tess! Hi.' He turned, surprised. I didn't hear you.'

'I've only just arrived.'

'Something I can do for you?' He was holding a bulky file in his hands. He put it down and came towards me. 'What a stupid question! Look, this must be terrible for you. I'm really sorry, but I'll be there, we'll all rally round. How much time does he have?'

I was looking over his shoulder towards the computer screen, on which the blue sky had just appeared. Puzzled, he turned round to look at it. 'What is it?'

I waited until he turned back to face me. 'Are you having an affair, Jerry?'

'What?'

'You heard me.'

He frowned as if I had said something completely outlandish. 'Of course not. What's got into you, Tess? What's this all about?' He attempted to touch my arm but I pulled away just out of reach. 'Look,' he said then, 'you're overwrought naturally – of course I'm not having an affair.'

'Oh, really?' Everything – bones, muscles and organs – exploded into action and I raced to the computer. Blinded by fury, I scrabbled at the keys, crashing, missing, hitting them in groups, causing the screen to flicker and strobe.

Now Jerry was behind me, pulling at me, trying to protect the keyboard. 'What are you doing? You'll damage it – Tess—'

'If you're not having an affair, then explain this!' I blocked his access to the computer with my body while my hands continued to bang about, ineptitude fuelling frustration and anger. 'Damn, damn, blast, where is it?'

'Tess, stop that at once!' He grabbed my left hand but I resisted and redoubled my efforts with the right, still to no avail.

'What are you doing? Leave that alone!' With considerable force he succeeded in pulling me away.

'Yes, you'd like that!' I was struggling in his grasp, virtually screaming. 'You'd like me to melt away, good little spouse, and leave the two of you to it, pretend I never saw anything!'

'What are you talking about? And stop behaving like a fishwife, will you? What are you looking for? What's in there?'

'I'm trying to find the fucking e-mail from Susan!'

There was a brief, scandalised pause. In all the years Jerry has known me he has never heard language like that from my mouth. He rushed over to the door and closed it. 'Calm down, Tess! Think of your father.' He grabbed me again. I struggled again.

'How very convenient for you that Daddy's here – how very convenient that he's dying! What a distraction – what a gift.'

But mention of my father had opened up a chink of reason. I stared up at him, hatred pooling in my cheeks. Hating his composure. Hating her. Hating him. He let me go. 'What's this about an e-mail?'

'Look it up. It's from Susan.'

'Susan?'

'Susan!' I watched him carefully.

'I think you should go downstairs.' He did not even blink. He was good at this. 'Or, better, go into our bedroom and compose yourself. You're in no state to deal with anything at the moment. I'm sorry about your father, Tess, and of course you're upset about him but there's no reason to take it out on me.'

'This is not about my father.'

So far I could not be said to have handled this well, the understatement of the year, but I was more or less in control of myself again. 'Open the e-mail from Susan,' I said icily.

He glanced at the screen. 'I don't know what you're talking about. There's no e-mail from Susan here. There'd be no need for her to e-mail me, Tess. I was speaking to her less than an hour ago from Dublin airport. All that's there at the moment is stuff from the out-offices.'

Yes, of course. That would be the first phone call, wouldn't it? Then memory dredged up a fragment of knowledge from my IT course. 'You're looking at the unread messages. Open the read ones.'

'No.' For the first time, his eyes flickered with doubt – or was it fear? 'I won't give in to tantrums. Especially unwarranted ones. This is outrageous. I won't stand for it—'

'Open the read messages, Jerry! If you won't I will. And I'll stand here all day if necessary until they are opened. I also know, by the way, that nothing is ever permanently deleted from a computer and can be retrieved, so you needn't bother trying. I'm not a complete dodo.'

'Tess, you're behaving like a lunatic. Are you cracking up? It's understandable—'

'Are you going to open that file?'

'No.'

'Very well. I'll have to get Frederick in on this. He saw the message.' I turned to go but he came after me. 'Yarso? Yarso was messing about with my computer?'

'Our computer, Jerry, in our home. Husband and wife, remember? What's mine is yours and vice versa – and there was nothing sinister in it, no "messing" as you call it. He asked me if he could check his own e-mails. I came up here to show him where the computer was. And I don't care whether you believe me or not, when I saw that – that *thing* from Susan, I opened it because – oh, stupid me! – I thought it might be important and that I should telephone you to tell you. Big laugh on me, eh?'

He was so still I could see a strand of his hair moving in the draught from the side of the monitor. 'All right. You've seen it, whatever it is. What's in it?'

'Open it.'

'I've told you I won't be bullied. You're the one exercised about it, you tell me.'

I nearly balked at the last fence but, in glowing detail, the computer image rose in front of me and I could not withstand it. I chose my words, hammering each one as if it was a steel nail: 'What it is is a picture of breasts. Susan Vitelli Moore's breasts. They miss you, apparently.'

'I beg your pardon?' Incredulously – to this day I believe his shock was real – he ran his hands through his damp hair. 'That's ridiculous, Tess. You're imagining things. It's some joke someone from the office sent me.'

'She was wearing the pendant you bought her, I bought her, for Christmas.'

He imploded – that is the only word for it – on to his work chair. It told me all I wanted to know. 'You're pathetic!' I said, with all the dignity and venom I could muster and left the room.

The victory was Pyrrhic. Because as I sat, seething, at my dressing-table, staring at this Gorgon version of myself in the mirror, I had no idea what should happen next.

I picked up a Swarovski crystal butterfly, a conciliation gift from Jerry after a brief, unimportant row, and I was back in 1993 on the cemetery island of San Michele in Venice. A weekend was all Jerry could take off work; it was also the maximum length of time I had felt, in conscience, I could be away from the boys. Rita had offered to mind them in her house.

San Michele is one of the sights recommended in all the guidebooks and the autumn weather, misty, grey but warm, was perfect for visiting a graveyard as atmospheric as that one. Slowly, contented in each other's company, we wandered among the graves of the famous and the loved, stopping occasionally to peer at their speckled sepia photographs.

I found these images dreadfully sad. Many were from the nineteenth century, when photography was becoming universal. They would have to stand in stiff, Victorian poses for eternity now, these husbands and wives, mothers, aunts and siblings, unvisited except by people like us who were merely curious. They would become unknown to their descendants except by the few who might be interested, not in who they were or who they loved, only in tracing their own roots. 'You won't forget me when I die?' Impulsively, I had kissed Jerry – a proper kiss on the mouth – to the obvious disapproval of an old woman, dressed entirely in black, who was hobbling past us, laden with plastic bags and a watering-can. 'Will you put my photograph on my grave?'

'That depends on how you behave before you die.'

We walked on, and passed a middle-aged man sitting on a flat gravestone of dark-coloured marble into which was set the picture of a girl in First Communion gear. His head was bowed over the paid of faded pink satin ballet slippers he was clutching. 'Spare me,' Jerry said. 'Listen, Tess, when I die, I want none of this stuff, I find it macabre. I want to be cremated.'

'Oh, Jerry, that's selfish. Funerals are for the living, not the dead.' I stopped in the middle of the avenue. 'If you die before I do, and I sincerely hope you don't, by the way, I'll want to be able to visit your bones, not some wall.'

'You won't be able to visit me at all, lass. I'm going to be scattered at sea. I've made my mind up this very minute.'

'*Jerry!*'

We bickered about this on and off for hours that afternoon, all the way back in the *vaporetto* to our hotel, where we made up by falling into bed. Afterwards, while I slept, he went out for a walk and returned with the butterfly. 'Thought you'd like this. And I've changed my mind. I'll be cryogenically frozen if it makes you happy, Tess.'

Only people who really love one another would fight about such matters, I had thought then – and still think. But what had changed in recent years was the way we communicated and lived with each other. That had been a period when my opinions about his new job mattered, when, despite the demands of the office, he came home most evenings to be with me when I was putting Tom to bed. When he bought Jack his first fishing rod.

When, because of his commitments to his first family, money had not been as plentiful for us as it was now – although we had not been poor.

He had been a good man then and, angry as I was, I knew nothing was fundamentally different about him.

Should I fight for him? I put the butterfly back on its little mirrored stand on the dressing-table. And what about the boys? What about Arkady? Was I really bent on turfing him out now, flinging us all into the path of Krakatoa, thereby pulverising everything I had worked for? I had spent so much time and creative energy in the attempt to glue the four of us together as a family – should I undo all of that because of a sexual fling?

If that was all it was. And if it was the only one . . .

What was I thinking? He had to go. I had to make a stand, for how could I ever trust him again? He had stood there and lied blatantly. 'No,' he had said, when I asked him straight out if he was having an affair.

I looked up. He was standing in the doorway. 'I saw it. Can we talk about this?'

'Do we have something to talk about?'

'Obviously.' He hesitated. 'Do you mind if I come in?'

'It's your bedroom too, your house. I can't stop you.'

'What's mine is yours?'

I did not smile. I was not going to be talked down or mollified. I picked up my brush and dragged it through my hair.

'Can I tell you what happened?' He sat on the side of the bed.

'If you insist,' I brushed harder, 'but, please, I don't need any of the sordid details.' That had hit home. I could see in my mirror that he flushed.

'It wasn't, isn't sordid. Whatever else it is, it isn't sordid.'

'No, it never is, is it?' I was brushing so hard now, the bristles stung. 'It's the romance of the century.'

He bunched his fists by his sides. 'Are we going to talk about this,' he asked, in a low voice, 'or are you going to continue to act and talk like we're characters in a cheap novel?'

I put down the hairbrush. Jerry is not one to trifle with and I knew he was close to walking away. I had to give him some latitude. Injured party or not, I discovered that, subconsciously, I had already decided Krakatoa was not in my best interests, or in anyone else's – always provided his dalliance was not serious. But I was not going to conceal how hurt and angry I was. 'So tell me.' I turned round to face him. 'I'm all ears.'

'It happened when we were in Paris for a conference.'

'The one two months ago or the one last year?'

'I thought you didn't want any details?'

'That's an important fact, not a detail.'

'All right. Two months ago.'

'I see, just a couple of weeks before we went on holidays, then. That would explain the so-called extra work at the office on the day we went to Collioure, the missed flight and so on. You stayed at Heathrow, she went with you to London for the night, didn't she?'

He reacted to the sergeant-major tone by lowering his gaze to the floor. He hated this. I hated it too, hated the way I was behaving, but I could not help myself, although I had found a glimmer of hope in the knowledge it had been going on for such a short time. Everything is comparative.

'Is this the way it's going to be? Because if it is . . .' He shifted his weight as if he intended to leave.

'What do you expect, Jerry?'

Instead of answering right away, he walked to the window, looking out towards the sea or, more precisely, into the rain beating on the trees at the end of Arkady's garden. 'I wonder if you have noticed that you pay more attention to strangers than you do to me, Tess?'

'You mean Frederick?' Instinctively, I bridled. 'Is this all about me not paying you enough attention? Perhaps if I saw you more often, if you were actually here—'

The rest of the sentence never got said because he turned to look at me with an expression of such sadness my throat closed over. 'I don't expect you to understand what it's like to be a man more than half-way through his life,' he said softly, 'with one failed marriage and another perilously close to it. Whose wives, both of them, think of him only as a cash machine, whose children don't ring him because their mother has convinced them they've been abandoned, whose step-children despise or ignore him, who lately looks into the mirror every morning and wonders what is it all for?'

'I don't think of you as a cash machine . . .' but I had been thrown off my sense of righteousness.

He turned round and perched his long body on the window-sill. 'Don't you? What is it for, anyway, Tess? I work to keep you in shoes? To keep two wives and four children in funds and this house maintained? Is that why I go to conferences that bore me, and stay in dreary interchangeable hotel rooms and talk the same bullshit in crap cocktail bars with the same people and hold meetings in my office that take five hours and should be over in thirty minutes? Why I am so lonely?'

I was dumbstruck at the turn this was taking. 'We were talking about you and Susan,' I said feebly.

'Yes, we were, but if you would come down off your high horse for a moment, and give me one moment of thought or under-standing, you would see exactly why I took advantage of Susan. And yes, that's the truth, hurtful though it must be for you. She let it be known she was more than willing, she made advances to me, and I resisted for a while, but finally it was I made the move. And – again before you ask – it happened exactly twice. And I am *not* going to go into detail about that aspect of the matter. It's of no relevance. Because the sex was incidental, Tess.'

It was not incidental for me, of course, and I got busy with mental callisthenics. He had been in France with us for three weeks, the Paris conference where it first happened was two weeks previously . . .

But then I saw the defeated expression in his eyes and my brain stilled. 'Why didn't you say any of this to me before? I don't mean about Susan, but how depressed you are about your life.'

'I gave up ages ago. You weren't listening.' He rubbed his eyes. 'I'm not pitching for the sympathy vote or feeling sorry for myself, I'm a grown-up. I did wrong, I have to deal with that. And I am very, very sorry you found out about it – especially in such a crude manner and at such an awful time for you.

'But if you've been listening – at last – you'll know now how much I hate my life. She was a vivid distraction, a distraction that told me my existence mattered a bit. That I mattered a bit. She is a lovely, intelligent person, who listened to all my elderly anecdotes without interrupting me – and I know you'll say it's because she hasn't had to listen to them forty times over and you're probably right.'

That was exactly what I had been thinking.

He eased himself off the sill and half turned again towards the window. 'She respected me, Tess, hung on my every word. She thought I was wonderful and, for a short while, she convinced me that I was. I found it intoxicating. I fear it's been a long time since you thought I was anywhere near wonderful.

'I know all of this makes me sound like a wally. Most likely I am. I probably conform to every cliché in the book concerning men of my age. It's ironic that you should have found out now because I am actually in the process of disengaging from her. I thought about the situation deeply while we were in France and I have told her that there is no future in the relationship, although of course she thinks there is. That's probably why she sent me the e-mail – it was her way of trying to appeal to me to change my mind. Or to find out if I really meant what I said.'

'When did you tell her?' I launched again into mental arithmetic.

'Tess, don't flay yourself like this.'

'When did you tell her?'

He sighed. 'A few days after I came back from holidays.'

'Before I came home?'

'Yes.'

'I see.' That was at least one small positive. I became aware of a strange silence in the room, then realised that the rain had stopped. 'Do you love her?'

He hesitated. 'I love her, yes, but not in the way you mean. I love what she represents. Hope.' He walked towards me and, for a moment, I thought he was going to try to take my hand. 'I'm not very proud of what I've done, Tess, and I'm seriously pissed off with her too. She had no right to do what she did. But she's young, and the young think they can get away with things, that they're invincible and, God help her, she thinks she's in love.'

'Are you making excuses for her now?'

'No.' His tone frosted over and he stiffened.

'How are you going to continue working with her?'

'That's something I'll have to handle. She's a great PA. But I know you'd find it difficult.'

'You bet I would!'

'Whether you accept it or not,' he said, almost formally, 'the affair is over. But I don't know whether our marriage will survive it, not because of a few rolls in the hay with a girl half my age, and not because I don't love you, but because of how entrenched and uncomprehending you are, how neither of us understands the other any more. And if that doubles up the clichés, I'm sorry. I'm taking full responsibility for this mess. And for the moment, at least, I think it's better that I sleep in one of the spare rooms, don't you?'

'Yes. Yes, I do.' I did not want him to sleep in a spare room. I wanted him to stay so I could thrash this out, thrash it and thrash it until I had no strength left. But he walked out of the bedroom and my pride would not let me call him back.

My first instinct was to rush to the telephone to confide in Rita, but I stopped myself: that would not be fair. I had to deal with this myself. I had to take charge.

Anyway, I was too upset to move. I was upset for us all, for Jerry, for myself, even, briefly, for Susan, who was going to be hurt too – because I believed him when he said he was ending it. He is a truthful man.

More truthful than I. Would I have confessed my virtual infidelity with Frederick? I agree with Maddy that it is every bit as damning as the real thing and I doubted I would have admitted it to Jerry, even if he had suspected anything.

What is more, my attraction to Frederick did not even any scores, even retrospectively. I was just as hurt by Jerry's betrayal as though I had been as pure in mind and body as one of the virgin martyrs. Life, as Forrest Gump might have said if he had had a different scriptwriter, is not a tennis match.

To keep myself strong, I needed an enemy but, right then, could not find one. Instead, I fell back on my truest, most stoic friend. Knowing it was crass even as the thought occurred to me, I tried to concentrate on what I must do so that the boys and I could remain in Arkady in case the worst came to the worst.

CHAPTER THIRTY-THREE

In my dream, or nightmare, more like, Fergus's head was three times bigger than his body. And when I woke and tried to sit up in the bed, my muscles didn't seem to work properly.

Like, I knew that I had sat up, but when I looked at my arms they were lying on top of a bedspread beside my prone body. I didn't recognise this bedspread; I didn't recognise anything about where I was, walls, wardrobe, the door of the room. I could see flowers on a window-sill and a box of chocolates – Cadbury's Roses – but they were blurred, a watercolour of chocolates and flowers left out in the rain.

Then someone knocked at the door and, without being invited, a woman came in: 'Hello again!'

Again? I'd never seen her in my life.

'I'm Louise,' she said. 'We met yesterday, but I'm not surprised you don't remember. How are you feeling? I'm your counsellor.'

'Couns—' I couldn't say the word. My tongue wouldn't move properly and had got too big for my mouth. I tried again to sit up but my legs and arms continued to defeat me.

'You're probably feeling a little bit muzzy,' this woman said. 'You've been asleep on and off for a couple of days. Don't worry about that. A few belts of that coffee out there, a decent meal, and you'll be back to normal. I have your programme here.' She put a ring-binder on a little table beside the bed.

It was when she said the word 'coffee' that I remembered.

People here drink a lot of coffee . . .

The door to this room had opened and closed a lot and someone in a white coat was checking my blood pressure and giving me an injection and someone else was holding out tablets for me to swallow. I was here because people thought I was an alcoholic. I was in a clinic for alcoholics.

This time I did sit up, but it made me dizzy. Nevertheless, I managed to croak out a full sentence: 'There's – there's been some kind of mistake.'

'Why don't you get yourself organised and we'll have a chat later?' The woman smiled as if she hadn't heard me. 'I'll be around this afternoon. The common area is just to the right, along the corridor. Take your time, there's no rush today – your programme doesn't start until tomorrow morning.' She smiled wider and left the room.

I lay back, trying desperately to piece things together. Then, emerging from a sort of whirling kaleidoscope involving Tess and myself in our sitting room, I saw a central image, very clear, of Rita towering over me in a car park with trees in the background.

It was Rita who had put me in here. This was all Rita's doing – thanks a lot, Rita.

I was out of here—

I threw back the bedclothes but the action made me dizzy again and I had to wait until the room stopped heaving. Then, gingerly, bit by bit, I managed to get off the bed and stand upright. I took my bearings. I was wearing some kind of disgusting floral bag.

I had to get someone to come and rescue me. Where was my handbag?

Nowhere to be seen.

I tested my feet to see if they could move. They did and I walked over to this wardrobe thing, a lash-up made from plywood, and found the handbag inside, neatly stashed in a corner. Some of my clothes were hanging there too, and some underwear folded on a shelf, and my toilet bag.

When I searched the handbag, my wallet, makeup and all my documents were in it, but I couldn't see my mobile phone.

I panicked. I always carry my mobile with me, ever since I got it. I had to find it. No point in ringing Rita, obviously, but Tess would help me. I tipped the contents of the bag over the bed, but the mobile was definitely not among them.

With all this exertion, my head was thumping so I hunted now for my Solpadeine. I never set foot anywhere without a supply but the little packets weren't there either. I riffled through the documents, shaking them out individually, looking for tablets and mobile. What was going on? Had I been robbed while I was asleep?

I found out smartish that I hadn't been robbed. *They go through your things.*

'Sorry about the Solpadeine but we'll give you back your mobile, of course,' says this Louise person, more smiles – this woman could smile for the Olympics – after she came back into the room to see if I was ready now for 'our chat'. (I wasn't. I was sitting on the bed wearing this godawful *thing*, which was hanging off me.)

'It's just that we would like you to focus on the programme, and for the first few days we encourage patients not to have much contact with the outside world.'

She kept talking but I couldn't get a proper handle on what she was telling me because I was so angry at the gist, which was that I was apparently in some kind of gulag. When you come into a place like this, they search all your luggage for pills, alcohol, razor blades and anything that they, in their wisdom, think you shouldn't have, did you know that? People should be told about this . . .

'I think I'll be going now.' I attempted to stand up but the lightheadedness kicked in again. Meanwhile she just continued her monologue as if I was a waxwork dummy: 'But if you need to make an urgent call, there's a pay-phone at Reception.'

Yeah. So they could hear what you were saying.

I was not only angry now, I was outraged. 'Could I have my mobile, please, *now*? I'm out of here – this is all a mistake, someone got hold of the wrong end of the stick and I'm taking up a bed that somebody else needs. I don't have a drink problem. I'm going to ring my friend and she'll come and get me.'

She kept on with the smile. Like a Barbie. In fact, she looked a bit like Barbie, I thought, with her long blonde hair in a ponytail and a little slide in the shape of a seahorse over her left ear. 'Who's in authority here?' I pulled the wretched nightgown tightly round me.

'I am, Madeleine, but if you'd like to talk to the doctor on call—'

'I would, please. And be sharpish.'

'Certainly.' She tucked the file she'd brought in, another one – *my file?* – under her arm. 'I'll bleep him. He's doing rounds at the moment, but I'm sure you won't have to wait too long. Would you like to have coffee while you're waiting? Are you hungry, Madeleine? There are biscuits, I believe. Some of the others are out in the common area, there's a break at the moment.'

Now that she had said it, I discovered I *was* hungry. It was an astonishing feeling, which I had not experienced for some time. As I came to terms with this I could see she was making judgements on me: it was obvious that those blue Barbie eyes were shrewd enough. Well, I was not going to give her any satisfaction. 'No, thank you,' I said stiffly. 'I'm not hungry.'

'When did you last have a meal, Madeleine?'

I hated that she used my name in almost every sentence, but the question threw me and, temporarily, I forgot my antipathy as I tried to remember when I had eaten. I honestly couldn't – the last memory of my house was of Rita and myself sitting in the kitchen this morning – yesterday, the day before? Had we had food then? Toast, maybe? I seemed dimly to remember fighting with her about toast. But I hadn't cooked since I sent Colm to the country.

Barbie Louise was watching me struggle. 'You missed breakfast this morning, and I understand why you wouldn't want to go right away into the sitting room with the others, it's all strange and new at the moment, but would you like me to rustle up a cup of tea and a few scones while you're waiting for the doctor? It'd be no bother, Madeleine. We have homemade strawberry jam, I think, if there's any left, but I have to warn you it's very sweet – the patients seem to like it that way. Perhaps you would prefer marmalade? Or raspberry?'

How did the bitch know I craved something sweet? My tongue salivated at the thought of the red, sugary softness of strawberries.

The hell with it, I thought, I'd humour them for a couple of hours. 'Thank you.' I tried to sound as if I was ordering afternoon tea in the Shelbourne Hotel, as if I was the one in control here. 'The strawberry will be fine. By the way, I should like to wash. I don't seem to have a shower with this room.'

'The bathroom is two doors down. You'll probably have it all to yourself at this hour. You'll find towels in the linen closet beside it. We'd appreciate it if you'd take any you use back here to your room and hang them on the radiator to dry. And by the way, Madeleine, we do expect our patients to look after their own rooms. See you in a minute,' and she was gone again.

Madeleine, Madeleine, Madeleine – I was beginning to hate the sound of my name.

I spent a long time in the shower, which was dingy but functional. Amazingly, I felt calm as the water ran quietly down my back and front, gurgling away in an everlasting stream between my toes. I wanted to stay in there for ever, warm and safe and not having to face anyone.

Because a lot of things were starting to emerge from behind the barrier of what Barbie Louise had called 'muzziness'. Flashes. The filth of my house. The pain in Colm's eyes when I burned his dinner – pain that had little to do with the food, the row we had had . . . The loneliness of the empty gin bottle.

I couldn't cry so I had the shower cry for me. I closed my eyes and let the water play on my skin. I allowed it inside my pores and into my heart.

But in what seemed like an instant, my mood switched and, in that close, consoling shower stall, my mind ran as clear as the water. All right, I had probably overdone it with the booze. I *had* overdone it, no 'probably' about it – I could certainly admit that much.

It was understandable, though, because – hello? – I had had such a lot to contend with. My husband had left me, for God's sake, not to mention that long period when I had worried myself sick about him having an affair. Literally sick. So I had let myself slip into bad habits, yes, I would buy that. It was because I had overreacted. That's what had happened and – although I probably wouldn't get Fergus back no matter what I did now – to make things right again with my own life I had to give up alcohol. QED.

I would have no problem with that, none at all. Alcoholics are violent and get sick in public and don't wash. I was nothing like that, not even in my darkest moments. I could give drink up overnight.

In fact, I thought, stretching my toes in the healing water, *I have made a decision*. With full knowledge and consent. I have had my last drink, ever. If they were all worried about my drinking – if Rita, God bless her, was worried enough about me to inflict a *clinic* on me, well, then, I'd have to show them that they had nothing to worry about. I'd just stop. I would be the best, most reformed, most non-alcoholic in Dublin.

But that was going a bit over the top, since I hadn't been an alcoholic to start with. I amended the decision: I would become the most teetotal teetotaller in Dublin.

That had been quite easy, I thought, as I turned off the shower.

When I got back to 'my' room, the tea and scones were on a tray on the rumpled bed. With just 'my' towel around me, I dived ravenously on it. The tea was cold but the jam was to die for, and I have to say that the scones, homemade obviously, were also good; I scoffed every last crumb. I felt extraordinary now, clear-headed, powerful and full of energy. I hadn't felt this good in years—

I stopped myself in my tracks. This high could not simply be the result of scones and strawberry jam, could it? No, of course not. They must have slipped something into my tea. Something to make me feel positive. An upper or something. How dare they? How *dare* they?

I was appalled. Seriously angry again. I would ring *Liveline* to tell the nation how they treated people in these hospitals . . . I'd go to the newspapers . . . I might even sue . . . Holding the towel in place over my breasts, I paced the ten-foot room, planning my revenge. Exposing this place would be completely justified because if they were doing this to people here they had to be doing it everywhere. They were all in collusion. They were writing books about it and they all went to the same case conferences and bolstered each other up. The public had the right to know—

Abruptly, I caught another image from the night before. She had said I'd been here, sleeping, for 'a couple of days': was this image from two or even three nights ago? I had dropped a cigarette on my lovely couch and Rita had been mad at me because I was going to set the house on fire.

Rita. Oh, God, had I alienated Rita? My best, bestest friend?

Had I said something to her that upset her? Did we have a row and was I hateful and was that why she had driven me here? As quickly as I had soared, I swooped again. I had completely messed up my life, no wonder my husband had left me—

'Ready now?' That woman was back, without even knocking this time. 'Oh, I see you're not—' She glanced at the empty tray. 'Enjoy that, Madeleine?'

'Yes.' Huge, fat tears came out of nowhere and squeezed themselves past my eyes.

'Good. I'll give you a couple of minutes to get dressed.' She hadn't reacted to my tears. She hadn't noticed that the world had crumbled to nothing. People were supposed to react when you cried. What was going *on*?

When he came a few minutes later, the doctor was far from a Marcus Welby. In fact, he was brusque to the point of rudeness when I tried to explain to him that I wasn't an alcoholic and that everything was going to be all right now that I had made my decision to abstain. I was calm again, although feeling pretty grim. 'I would strongly advise you to stay here,' he said – although 'advise' was the wrong word for the tone of voice he used. 'Command' would have been more suitable.

He went on to inform me, at length, how the 'alcoholic brain' works and the latest thinking and research about 'this disease'; and about how it should be treated as an illness like any other. At least he didn't keep inserting my name into every sentence like his sidekick did.

And at least I was dressed in my own clothes this time, so I was able to stand – or sit – on my dignity. (We were both seated on the side of my bed. The furnishings in this palatial guest room didn't include a chair.) 'Thank you, Doctor,' I said, when he got to the end of his monologue, 'but you don't understand. I – am – not – an – alcoholic. Why can't I get people to understand me?'

'Do you remember everything you did during every drinking bout?'

'I strongly resent that phrase. There were no drinking bouts.'

'Let me rephrase the question,' he said comfortably. 'How many units of alcohol would you consume per week? Now, a unit of alcohol is—'

'No need to tell me. I know how much a unit of alcohol is,' I said stiffly, 'and I also know how much is recommended for women and for men. I read the features pages of the newspapers.'

'So, how much, Madeleine?'

I stared at him. 'Depends,' I said then.

'On what?'

I took evasive action. 'I admit my consumption has gone up lately. But my husband left me and I've been under a lot of pressure.'

'How much? You can lie if you want to, we call it minimising in here, but you're lying to no one except yourself. You thought you were drinking too much or you wouldn't be here.'

'I came in here—' Then I stopped. I wanted to tell him it was none of his business. I wanted to slap his carefully shaved face or throw a glass of water against his carefully open-necked shirt, but he was right. There was something about his patience, his demeanour, that made it impossible for me to escape the truth.

Another image rose: of Tess crying on my sofa. Hazily, I remembered something about her being in trouble the same as me. It was the first time I had remembered that. It gave me no satisfaction, though, not with Dr Crippen looking at me from under his white eyebrows. 'You're not a prisoner here, Madeleine, you're free to go at any time – and, believe me, it's no advantage to us if you stay. If you're not serious about this, now would be the best time to discharge yourself. We don't like to waste our time or our resources, which, God knows, are scarce enough, these days. And we're never short of customers, unfortunately.'

I stared at him. For the first time, he cracked a smile. 'So, do you think you'll stay and see how you get on? I have to warn you, it won't be easy.'

CHAPTER THIRTY-FOUR

Four days after the seminal conversation Jerry and I had had in our bedroom on the night he came home from Stockholm, I was in the kitchen with Frederick. At just after nine o'clock in the morning, the room was suffused with sunlight, a phenomenon of late, and while he ate breakfast, his hair, still wet from the shower, glistened under one of the Velux windows. Dressed in his usual jeans and T-shirt, he was percolating coffee for himself while I was fiddling around with a lump of pastry in a half-hearted effort at baking. I could hear Mrs Byrne on the rampage with the Hoover in the drawing room, Tom was watching something in the television room, Jack was still in bed, and so was Daddy, whose breakfast tray had returned untouched to the draining-board.

Outwardly, Frederick and I were in quiet harmony together; what he did not know was that I was trying to work out the most tactful way to ask him to leave.

Contrary to my hopes of managing the chaos that now surrounded me, I had found it increasingly difficult to behave in the house as though the only serious problem I had to contend with was Daddy's illness. And while Frederick continued to be a model guest in every respect, as good as his word in that he had helped with chores in the garden, the presence of a stranger, however agreeable, had somehow become anachronistic.

There was something else too: being around him now reminded me of what a shallow person I am, not only frivolously lustful but fickle too. One moment, it seems, my blood can run hot at the sight of someone, the next, when real life intervenes, I cast aside these feelings like a torn glove.

So my lust had not even been honest: I had deliberately

whipped myself into a false fever, for what reason I did not dare to imagine. Advancing middle age? To prove something to myself? To others? To my husband? Looking at Frederick now I embarrassed myself.

Jerry had not expressed an opinion of our guest's continuing presence during these trying times, except when he had accused me, correctly, of paying more attention to a stranger than to himself. Neither did the boys seem to find it difficult or distract-ing; while they were both obviously upset when I first told them about their grandfather's illness. Tom had uncharacteristically burst into tears and Jack, according to Rita, had wept too that night, on Kitty's shoulder, so that she had come home from town almost as upset as he was. (I did try to talk to him of course, but he warded me off. 'Leave it, Mum. You're just making things worse, watching me all the time and asking me if I'm upset. I'm upset. There. I've said it. Are you happy now?')

Within twenty-four hours, though, they both seemed to have come to terms with it. Jack mooched around as usual and, on the surface at least, Tom again became his ordinary detached self, looking after Norma, playing tennis or swimming with Frederick. For them, it appeared, life simply chuntered on. Granddad was going to die – that was sad, but that's what everyone's granddad did eventually. Meanwhile, we had a friend staying with us, no big deal.

In parallel for me there was what I had now tagged in my mind as 'The Susan Situation'. Since the night of the row, my husband and I had behaved very politely to each other and while we did discuss my father, about whom Jerry was deeply upset, Susan had not been mentioned again. By tacit mutual consent, it seemed, we had prioritised Daddy, with all else put off until later.

He had not been at home all that much anyhow, which made things easier on the one hand, more difficult on the other because I alternated between wanting to kill him and wanting to talk this through, even to reach out, difficult as that was to believe in the circumstances. What he had said about his own life had hit home, hard. He had been right. I had been blinkered, even complacent.

So between the Susan Situation and Daddy, I had felt mangled during these last few days, by turns angry, frantic and desperate, self-conscious too, because I was sure Jerry's move into the spare room had not gone unnoticed by others in the house. Life under Arkady's roof had become too complex. 'There's something I need to ask you, Frederick.' I ceased messing with flour and pastry board.

'Shoot!' His coffee was percolating on one of the counters and he was seated at the island unit near me, his mouth full of Coco Pops.

'This is awkward for me, and I hope you won't be offended, but as you know, our circumstances have changed dramatically since you first arrived, with the dreadful news about my father. We may be getting round-the-clock nursing care quite soon and we'll need all the rooms we have.' It had only that moment occurred to me that this was the way to ask him to go without seeming rude or inhospitable.

He was full of sympathy. 'Of course I'll vacate my room, I understand completely.' He hesitated. 'Maybe I could sleep on one of the sofas? I wouldn't mind that. Jeez, the places I've slept in my life!'

'I don't think so, Frederick.'

This was difficult. I had not made myself clear enough. 'It's not just the room, it's, well, I feel we have to pull in together now, as a family—'

'—and I'm not family.' He finished the sentence for me.

'That's right.' I was relieved. 'I'm so sorry, but I'm sure you understand?'

'Sure, sure, of course I understand. I'll go upstairs right now and start getting organised—' He broke off. Then: 'That's if you don't think I'd be any use around here? Won't you, in particular, need a friendly shoulder to help get you through all this? Jerry's so busy all the time.'

'Thanks, but I'll be fine. You've become a great friend, Frederick, but right now I can't even explain why I need to be alone with family, it's something quite deep.'

'That's only natural.' He lowered his head and thought for a moment. 'Let's see . . . I'll head for London, I think, I have a couple of buddies there and an open invitation—'

'Hey!' His head came back up with a jerk. 'I've just thought of something. Why don't I take young Tommy off your hands for a few days? You'll have enough on your mind and the poor kid shouldn't have to go through this kind of thing at his age, especially since he's been through it once already. However young he was, I'm sure his dad's death has left its mark.'

'I don't know . . .' I was touched that he would offer, but wondered aloud if Tom would not be better off in the long run for 'going through it'. 'I can't shield him from the sadder side of the world for ever, Frederick.'

'True enough, but why don't we ask Tommy himself? One of my buddies is married with a little boy – I think he's around his age, I could check. I'm sure he and his wife wouldn't mind if I turned up to stay for a few days with another kid in tow. And from what they've told me,' he was becoming enthusiastic about the idea now, 'the London Eye is just a couple of stops away on the Tube from their flat. Tommy'd sure enjoy that!'

I was tempted. On Tom's behalf and on my own, I was also deeply grateful, even moved, not only because of the generosity of the gesture but because it was a validation: someone besides me took my son at face value when almost everyone else I knew thought he should be in some sort of treatment. I tried to force my tired brain to think straight, to see the flaw in the offer. 'But how would he get home?'

'No sweat! I'd put him on the plane myself. See him right to his boarding tunnel.'

I thought for a moment while he watched me expectantly. 'Thank you very, very much for offering to do this.' In gratitude, I touched his arm but I felt sure Tom would not take up the offer and said so. 'You can't have missed that he has his own ideas about how to live his life.'

'No problem, it was just a thought.' He shrugged.

'I'll tell you what, I'll ask him, all right? I'll let the decision be his. And if he does want to go, of course we'll pay for both air tickets, yours and his.'

'No – please – I couldn't.'

I could see his refusal was out of politeness. 'If he says he wants to go, then I insist.'

'Oh, God!' He rolled his eyes to heaven. 'I hate taking your money, and after you and Jerry have made me so welcome. You both must think I'm such a slacker.'

'Don't even dream of saying such a thing. We loved having you. I'm only sorry I've had to cut your visit short like this. Now, I'd better go and ask Tom, all right? If he's going to London with you, we need to gear ourselves up for it – and I would like to talk to your friend's wife, the boy's mother, if that would be in order? Just to make sure it wouldn't be an imposition. Are there other children?'

'Another son, I think, but just a toddler. I'll be upstairs. Let me know what happens. And I'll root out their telephone number.'

Tom was wearing the glassy expression he slips into when engrossed in a television programme. Norma was squirming around on the sofa beside him; he had placed his duvet under her in case she had an accident. 'Tom? There's something we need to talk about.'

'I'm watching a programme, Mum.'

'What is it?'

'It's about how to train your dog.'

I walked over to the television and switched it off. In Jack, this would have provoked outrage. Tom merely looked at me as though I was wearing some unfamiliar headdress. 'Frederick has invited you to go with him to London for a few days.' I put Norma on the floor and sat beside him. 'He has friends there who have a boy of your age and apparently they live very near the Millennium Wheel, that's this big Ferris wheel that's higher than anything else in London. You go up in it and—'

'I know about the London Eye, Mum. Is this to go to Evan's house?'

'Evan?' I stared at him.

'Frederick told me about Evan. His dad works in a bank. He's in charge of billions of pounds. Evan is allowed into the vaults to see the money.'

'Well, I don't know. I didn't ask what the boy's name is. Would you like to go?'

'Would they bring me to see Madame Tussaud's?'

Ever since he saw a programme about it on TV, Tom had been fascinated by the wax museum; he was particularly intrigued by the way the impressions were taken of people's heads and faces

(It'd be a good way to kill someone, wouldn't it, Mum?). But I was surprised at his ready interest in the trip. I had been expecting a 'no' but, then, since he could walk and talk, Tom's reactions had always been uniquely his own. 'So, anyway, it's up to you, Tom,' I said, 'no hassle if you'd prefer to stay here and not to go.'

He gazed at me with mild eyes. 'Is this instead of tennis camp?'

'Oh dear! I had forgotten about that.' In the confusion of the past week, it had slipped my mind that, at the urging of his new friend, Colin, Tom had enrolled in one of the summer tennis-coaching schemes run in the public parks. 'I guess it wouldn't be either-or,' I said. 'The camp starts on Monday, doesn't it? This is Friday. You'd certainly miss the first day, but you could catch up. Why don't you discuss it with Colin?'

'I don't play with Colin any more.'

'Why not?' I was taken aback. Tom made so few friends, I had seen it as a good sign that this summer he had made two: the little girl in France and now Colin. Then I remembered his premature return from the sleepover in Colin's. 'What happened, Tom? Did you two have a row that night when you were meant to stay in his house?'

'I don't want to talk about it.' He was watching the blank screen of the television as if it were alive with pictures, and his tone was as level as always.

I knew from experience that there was little point in interrogating him. 'All right, but you've got to make up your mind. Frederick is upstairs right now, packing. He will probably go today. So is it a yes or a no?'

He turned to look at me. 'Who'd mind Norma?'

Yet another thing that had slipped my mind. 'I would. It's only for a few days.'

'OK.'

'You're sure you want this? You don't have to go.'

'I said OK, Mum. Will I pack now? And can we bring Norma to see me off?'

'All right. Just one thing, I'll have to talk to Evan's mother, just to make sure it's OK. But, yes, you could make a start on the packing. Ask Mrs Byrne to help you.'

After I ascertained that Aer Lingus had seats available to

Heathrow in the early afternoon, I told Frederick about Tom's decision. His response was a simple 'Great!' Then he asked, carefully, watching me, if he could use Jerry's computer one more time to e-mail his friend in London. 'Give 'em the good news.'

'And can I have their telephone number so I can talk to the mother, please? By the way, is the boy's name Evan?'

'Yes!' He was astonished. 'How did you know?'

'Oh, when you tell Tom Butler something he's interested in, for instance Evan's dad being in charge of billions of pounds in a bank vault, he doesn't forget the details.'

'What a kid! But listen, Tessa, I can't seem to find their telephone number. It must be in my old address book. I was sure I had it but all I have is their address and e-mail. I'll mark the e-mail "urgent" so they can send the number right back. OK?'

'Or if that doesn't work, we can get it from Directory Enquiries.' I backed away, the mirage of Ms Vitelli Moore's cleavage hovering between us.

When I knocked on Daddy's door and opened it, he was sitting propped up on his pillows, staring vacantly through the window. Without his glasses he looked exposed and unprotected. 'You all right, Daddy? Do you need anything?'

'Nothing at all, thank you. I'll get up now in a minute. I find I'm a bit tired this morning.'

I dealt with the choking sensation at the base of my throat by telling him about the trip to London. 'That's marvellous,' he said. 'Young Tom will really enjoy that.'

'I should be back at about half past three. And if you do need anything while I'm gone, Daddy, or if I'm delayed in traffic, Mrs Byrne will be here until about half past four.'

'London is a great city. More than seven million people, you know, Teresa, more than one and a half times the population of Ireland according to the last census.'

Evan's dad, whose name was Stewart, rang our house in response to Frederick's e-mail just before we left for the airport, when I was getting to the stage of maybe aborting the trip. After all, what did I know about these people? But when I spoke to him, he appeared to be very nice, and totally unconcerned about the short notice of his friend's arrival with a strange child. 'No worries,' he said, in a broad Australian accent. 'It'll be great. We'll show him a really good time. Sorry about your dad, by the way,' he added. 'Freddie told me you're having a rough time right now.'

'Thank you. How about Evan's mother? I don't like to impose – maybe I should consult with her?'

'Mel? Oh, not at all. She's an Essex lady, laid back, you know? I'll give you her number, if you like, but she works for Americans in her bank and you know what they're like about personal phone calls. Talk to her tonight, eh? But I can assure you she'll be easy, we've the whole weekend off, as it happens, and Evan's a sociable kid.'

'Thank you. You're sure it'll be all right?'

'Don't give it another thought, Tessa!'

As I handed the telephone back to Frederick, I wondered if I would have been so hospitable in similar circumstances. But then, as I had already discovered, Frederick seemed to have an amazing knack of discovering an international network of people prepared to offer him hospitality.

An hour later, with Norma safely locked into the car, the three of us, Frederick, Tom and I were walking across the airport car-park towards the terminal. More doubts about sending my son off like this were tugging at my consciousness: he had never been further than two miles from home on his own. Suppose he didn't like these people? Suppose he got sick, even homesick, in the care of people I'd never met?

All right, I trusted Frederick himself, in as much as I had seen he did not drink to excess or take drugs, but what about them, no matter how together or friendly they seemed? 'You're sure your friends are not just being polite? They're happy enough about this?' I could not in all propriety ask him out straight about these people's recreational habits. But if they were bankers, I reasoned . . .

He caught the nuance. 'Perfectly happy, and perfectly respectable, Tessa. Stop worrying, they're solid citizens. As solid as you and me!' His wide grin made me feel stupid.

We were almost at the terminal door. 'I'd like to talk to the mother. Men don't know what having visitors really entails. I'll ring tonight when she's at home, OK? In the meantime, please buy some kind of gift to thank her. It'll be a bit impersonal from the airport, I suppose, but I'm sure she'll understand.'

He looked at the two hundred-euro notes I had pressed into his hand. 'Smoked salmon, maybe?'

'You'd get a fair amount of smoked salmon for that. Maybe a piece of Irish linen? And buy something for the little boy too.'

'Oh, God,' he groaned, 'I'm useless at shopping.'

'*Quel surprise!* You being a man and all!' I gave him a gentle dig in the ribs. I would miss him around the place, I thought.

'Well, if you trust me.' He put the money into the top pocket of his jacket. 'I'll do my best. But don't blame me if I panic and all I can find is two dozen green leprechauns.'

I laughed and put an arm around Tom's shoulders. 'Now, you be a good boy, all right? And it's still not too late to change your mind, eh?'

He looked up at me with the interested expression that drives everyone else mad.

'So, what are you looking forward to most?' This was Frederick.

'I dunno,' Tom replied calmly. 'Maybe Madame Tussaud's.'

'Anyone in particular you'd like to see there?'

'Mrs Thatcher.'

We looked at each other over his head, both having to curb our laughter. 'You're an original, kid, that's for sure!' The American cuffed him gently on the head.

Tom smiled up at him and my fears were eased. This was going to be OK. I was fussing. Being a mother. 'You take care of him, Frederick,' I said none the less.

'As if he was made of eggshells.' He grinned. 'Don't you trust me not to lose him on the Tube, Bibi?'

'Of course I do – and listen, Frederick, I'm very sorry I had to ask you to leave like that. But you understand?'

'Chill, Tessa. Not another word. You and Jerry have shown me what a true Irish Céad Míle Fáilte can be like. I'm very grateful.'

'And you'll stay in touch? Maybe we'll get together in better times.'

'Yes.' He glanced down at Tom, who was waiting without any sign of impatience. 'Now, this young man and I have a plane to catch. Thank you again. And I'm so sorry about your dad. That's a real bummer.'

This felt like a cue for us to hug each other, but it did not happen. One instant the possibility was there, the next it was not. 'Goodbye, so!' I rushed to cover up the hiatus and bent to hug Tom instead. 'You be good now, as I said. Don't be a nuisance in the house and do everything Frederick tells you, OK? We'll talk tonight when I ring Evan's mother.'

He wriggled out of my grasp. ''Bye, Mum.'

Frederick turned and waved as they entered the steel maze leading to the departure area. Then he bent down to whisper something in Tom's ear. Tom turned to wave too. 'Ring me, Tom!' I called. 'Ring me any time!' Frederick ushered him towards the security aperture and they vanished. I waited, straining to see if they might pass the opening again, but they were lost from view. I was choking again. *Don't be ridiculous, Tess. He's only going for four days.*

When I got back to Arkady, Norma was nosing around on the floor of the television room, which she had appropriated as her home. Daddy, smartly dressed as always in suit, collar and properly knotted tie, was ignoring her and doing the *Irish Independent* crossword. The TV was on, but with the sound muted and – I was clutching at straws here, I knew – I thought he looked marginally healthier. 'Everything all right, Daddy?'

'Grand, Teresa.'

'Did you take all the tablets you're supposed to take?'

He glared at me.

'Let me take the dog,' I said hastily, scooping her up. 'She probably needs to go outside.'

About an hour later, Mrs Byrne and I were tidying out the fridge. She is vigilant about sell-by dates and we had been trying to decipher the date on the label of a salami. A trivial exercise, you might think, especially with my father only yards away, but life has to continue. I hadn't told Mrs Byrne about him. I could not have faced the daily long face as she came in avid for bad news. Mrs Byrne likes nothing better than a good tragedy. 'How's Derek?' I turned the salami this way and that. Derek was Mrs Byrne's husband, who does our gardening; he had been off sick with a bad back for the past ten days.

'Agony, Mrs B,' said Mrs Byrne, with great relish. 'He's a martyr to it. Them tablets and painkillers he's taking is useless. I want him to go to the House of Prayer in Achill but he won't hear of it – won't *hear* of it.' She snagged a jar of beetroot and slapped it on the counter. 'This one's for the bin anyway.'

'Ssh!' I held up my hand. I thought I had heard a key turn in the lock of the front door. I put the salami back on the shelf of the fridge. 'Who could that be at this time?'

Seconds later, Jerry stood in the kitchen doorway. He was ashen-faced and home four hours before he would have been expected. Beside me, I could feel Mrs Byrne, scenting trouble, stiffen with excitement.

'What's wrong?' I closed the fridge. I noticed something else about him: a non-smoker of years' standing he was carrying a lit cigarette.

'Good afternoon, Mrs Byrne.' He glanced at her. Then, to me: 'There's something I have to tell you, Tess.' Even his voice sounded fragile. 'Could you come upstairs, please?' He withdrew from the doorway, leaving Mrs Byrne agog and me shattered. I was convinced he was going to tell me he had filed for divorce.

'You carry on here, Mrs B,' I said quickly, wiping my hands on a piece of kitchen roll. I had to keep it together in front of her, at least. 'I'll be back.'

When we were in our bedroom with the door closed, Jerry told me that Susan Vitelli Moore had not turned up for work that day. Instead, she had gone to see the chairman of the Sentinel board and had brought a solicitor with her; she is alleging that Jerry sexually harassed her and abused his position of power to the extent that she felt pressurised into sleeping with him in order to keep her job. She is taking a case against the company.

In light of this, as 'best practice', the chairman told him, and 'in adherence to the company's internal guidelines', my husband has been suspended on full pay pending investigation. 'Sorry about this,' the chairman had said then, apparently, 'but I have no option. I'm sure it will blow over.' He did not give an opinion as to when it would blow over however. And Jerry says that throughout their meeting the man's eyes were fixed on the edge of his desk directly in front of him. The only time he lifted them was when he advised Jerry to get himself a good solicitor and offered the name of his own.

CHAPTER THIRTY-FIVE

Have you heard of Family Day? I hadn't either. But let me assure you that in St Roland's it has nothing whatever to do with discounts on fairground rides.

I had made no friends in the few days I had been there. If I had, I might have been warned about Family Day by others who had been through it, but when my fellow inmates were colloguing and topping each other's lurid stories of drinking binges and car crashes, passing out at weddings, hitting and being hit, gambling the rent money and being barred from every pub in town, I kept strictly out of it. I just wasn't interested in these people, although if I had met them in other circumstances, I would probably have enjoyed the company of one or two, especially the woman who owned a small business in Galway. She seemed vivacious enough, although she had a lot of problems. A *lot*. Like, she had been raped. One of her kids had died in a swimming-pool.

The others in our group of seven were all men. Two were priests, one ran a pub, two were unemployed and one was a kid of only nineteen. As for the final guy, who was about seventy, he was retired but I never found out what he had done when he was still working. All human life, you might say.

Family Day occurs once every two weeks in St Roland's, and when I heard it mentioned, it was in low tones. What I gathered was that, while nobody liked it, it was essential to 'the healing process'. Apparently it was something like a convention where we would all sit around with our counsellors and selected family members in a big room. Our part was to listen to what our families had to say about how our drinking affected them. 'And you're not allowed to interrupt,' said the Galway woman mournfully.

'So who will you be inviting, Madeleine?' My counsellor's face was glowing with the steady, maddening smile I had come to detest. I noticed that instead of a seahorse in her hair, she now had a dolphin; the woman obviously has a thing about fish. 'We have your father down here as next of kin.'

'But they're in Cork!' I protested. 'I couldn't expect them to come all the way up here just to visit me. Anyway,' I looked down at my hands, 'they don't know I'm here.'

The woman smokes, thank God. She offered me a cigarette now and we both lit up.

We were sitting in the office she shared with the other counsellors, a large, depressing room littered with files and furnished with scarred desks, crowded memo boards, ageing thank-you cards bearing illustrations of kittens and teddy bears, and two sad, yellowy rubber plants. 'So who, then? The idea is to get those who are closest to us to come. That usually means people we have lived with.'

'What about friends?' I asked, reasoning that in some ways Tess and Rita knew more about me than anyone else. I had certainly confided more in them than in anyone in my family.

She considered this, holding her cigarette upright at shoulder level, as if it was a little flag and she was waiting for the Pope to pass in his Popemobile. 'That has occasionally happened, but usually our friends don't see the real us, Madeleine, do they?'

I thought for a minute. Much as I hated to admit it, she was right. I had let my guard down in front of Tess and Rita but never completely. As I said, they knew more about me than most, but underneath all three of us knew we were pals by choice and could terminate the friendship at any time.

Fergus? In the last while, I had been so set on keeping him that I had been over-nice, over-eager. He hadn't seen the real me lately. As for my parents, I was Miss Super-cheery on every visit.

So, by a process of elimination, it was probably poor Colm who was most qualified. With nowhere else to go and no livelihood, he had little choice but to put up with my vagaries. This admission was terrifying – but I certainly wasn't going to make it aloud here in this room.

I opted for Fergus. Why shouldn't he see what he had driven

me to? This might be the way to sort things out. Although I rejected the notion that I was an alcoholic like the rest of the deadbeats in my class – sorry, 'group' – when Fergus saw how sincerely I was trying to re-examine my life, that to do it I was even willing to endure the stigma of voluntary imprisonment in a place like this, he might realise the mistake he had made in leaving me. 'My husband,' I added helpfully, although I had filled her in on my marital situation during my first one-to-one session with her. 'And maybe we should ask Vanessa too.'

'Vanessa? Is Vanessa your husband's new partner? What would you hope to achieve by that, Madeleine?'

I stared at her. The woman was a menace. A bloody witch. Because, for one millisecond, what I had hoped was that if Fergus was faced with direct comparisons between me and Vanessa in the same room, being more substantial and, for obvious reasons, having far more claim, I'd win out. 'Forget it,' I said, 'it was just a thought. Fergus on his own.'

'Fine.' She wrote something on her notepad. 'It's your husband, then.'

'When do you ring him?' I got nervous.

'I don't.' She smiled. 'You'll have to do that, Madeleine. And it's your choice of course, but what about your son? Shouldn't he be included?'

Again I stared at her. The thought of putting Colm through something like this was appalling, yet somewhere deep down I was conscious of a niggle that he deserved to be taken into the process. 'All right,' I said reluctantly. 'But when I ring them, what'll I tell them?'

'The truth. That an important part of your treatment here involves your family. How will your husband feel about it, d'you think?'

I shrugged my shoulders. 'How do I know? He'll hardly be jumping up and down, but I'm sure that in his heart he still loves me.' Mixed with the nerves now was excitement: I had a legitimate reason to telephone Fergus. Yet the more I thought about it, the more aggrieved I got. I had every right to summon him here – he was the one drove me into this place with what he did to me: he had to take responsibility for that.

She was watching me. 'You know, Madeleine, Family Day is when the families get to tell their side of the story. On that day, you get only to listen. Some people find it very bruising to hear what their drinking has put their loved ones through.'

'Yeah, I know.'

But I didn't. Not at that stage. I was barely listening because I was already planning what I was going to say to Fergus when I rang him.

Throughout the rest of that dreary day, consisting of so-called 'workshops' where we gazed into our navels and were outright bitchy if one of us thought someone else was trying to 'minimise', i.e., get away with something, I was hanging back as usual, my mind busy. The counsellor challenged me from time to time, but to little effect. I was setting up scenarios and dialogue.

(Ring ring!)

Hello?

Hello, is this Vanessa?

Yes.

May I speak to my husband, please?

No. No 'please'.

May I speak to my husband?

Pause.

(Off: footsteps receding) Fergus! You're wanted on the phone.

Hello?

Fergus?

Yes?

It's me. Sorry to drag you away from whatever it was you were doing with, or to, Vanessa. I don't know whether you know that I'm in St Roland's—

No. Too weak.

You may or may not be interested to know that I'm in St Roland's.

(Pause while he takes this in.)

What are you doing there?

What do you think I'm doing? Are you stupid? I'm having a fucking holiday! I'm in here because everyone's been telling me I'm drinking too much. Your drove me in here, Fergus. Your philandering drove me in here. Rita and Tess could see what was happening to me and they were worried about me. Unlike you, of course.

'Madeleine? Have you left us again, Madeleine?'

I broke off my drafting. They were all staring at me, pained, in their ancient jumpers, their trainers and tracksuits. (Even if my fellow woman patient's sportsgear was from DKNY – it said so on the front of her chest in letters two feet high – she looked every bit as much of a loser as the rest of them.)

Since I was technically free to leave at any time, why, you might ask, was I staying there?

At rock bottom, I think I was having a rest. The place was organised in such a way that I had no responsibilities to anyone except myself. The physical work we were required to do, vacuuming the carpet in the common areas, keeping our own rooms tidy, washing up after we ate and so on, was mechanical and quite soothing.

In a way, it was like staying in a rundown penal hotel on full board, and I thought more than once that this must have been what it was like for Tess in her boarding-school and novitiate. With this exception: here I had blanket permission to be self-centred. I had been so tired, mentally as well as physically, that it was almost pleasant not to be worrying about other people all the time.

Health-wise, however, there was one astonishing aspect to the place: although there were distinct no-smoking areas and they paid lip service to weaning us off cigarettes, their attitude to this was 'One evil at a time, Sweet Jesus', and we all went around the place under a thick blue cloud of smoke. My own consumption had ratcheted up to twenty-five a day. But, despite this, I had to admit I was physically healthier and more clear-headed, even after a few days, than I had been for years. And when I had regrouped and recharged, I was out of there. Greased lightning.

Tess, as it happens, was on my conscience. Although I couldn't remember very much, I had had flashes of that last night in my living room when she was spilling her guts out to Rita and me. Something to do with Jerry and his PA? Although, no matter how hard I tried, I couldn't imagine poker-straight Jerry Brennan having an affair. (Like, what did they do when they were in bed together? Collate their adding-machines?) But Tess is not the type to exaggerate. I made a vow to ring her at the earliest opportunity.

First call that evening was to Tricycle. I planned to come clean, to 'out' myself as a sort of practice run for coming clean with Fergus. At the last minute, however, the words wouldn't come and I found myself speaking through my nose. 'It's some sort of virus, Mary.' I sniffed loudly. 'I'm stuffed with antibiotics.'

'You poor thing.' She was full of sympathy. 'Where are you ringing from? It sounds as if you're at the bottom of a bucket.'

'I'm in a shopping centre. I've just picked up my prescription.'

Tess wasn't there when I got through to Arkady, but I left a message with Jack, who appeared to be in a hurry. 'Be sure and tell her I rang and that I send my love.'

'I will, Mrs Griggs.'

'You won't forget now?'

But he had already hung up.

A crowd of butterflies launched a carnival in my stomach while I was punching out Fergus's – or Vanessa's – number. I had rehearsed and rehearsed what I was going to say to him. (It would be different with Colm. With him I'd just have to be honest. At least, I'd try.)

Contrary to what I had planned in my scenarios, I had revised my Fergus-strategy and now, with my eye on the long ball, I was going to be calm, regretful, magnanimous, even humble. And if Vanessa answered, I would be quietly polite with her too. No point alienating her, it might rebound on me.

But all this planning and rehearsal proved to be a waste of energy because Fergus answered the telephone, knew where I was and, to my amazement, agreed without any argument to come to Family Day.

'How did you know I was here?'

'News travels fast. You were spotted in the coffee bar. Vanessa was in there visiting someone.'

So much for anonymity, I thought. 'Who was she visiting?'

'Leave it, Tess. Some relative of hers.'

'And you didn't think fit to contact me?' All my good intentions fled. 'To come in and see me? I'm your *wife*, Fergus! Till death do us part, remember? Do you care one iota about me any more?'

There was silence at the other end of the line. I became conscious that a queue was forming behind me. 'Sorry,' I said quickly. 'I didn't mean to fly off the handle like that.'

'What time is this thing on? What day?'

'You'll come?'

'I have no choice, have I? Otherwise I'll never hear the end of it.'

It was my turn to be silent. This was hopeless, there was no point if he was going to come in under duress, he would resent me totally. I was almost in tears. He seemed to sense this. 'Look,' his voice softened, 'I want to help, if I can. And I'm glad you're getting treatment, Madeleine, I really am. I was actually quite worried about the amount you were drinking.'

I told him where and when and we hung up. At least we had been civil.

He had been more than civil. He wanted to be helpful. I was now buoyed up. He was actually worried about me! That was a good sign surely.

Colm, when I got him, sounded low. 'I'm sorry I haven't been in touch, darling, but something's happened. I'm trusting you not to broadcast this, all right?' He listened in silence while I told him where I was and why I was ringing. The silence continued after I had finished. 'Are you still there, Colm?'

'Yes.'

'Do you understand what I'm asking? Is it OK?'

'I don't think I could go through with it, Mum. Do I have to?'

'Of course you don't, darling. I just thought it would be good for you, for all of us. And your dad will be there, of course . . .' I faltered. For the very first time, despite my keening about being a rotten mother and all my protestations, I realised properly, with no sheaths or fences between me and the truth, how difficult it had been for my poor son. 'Listen,' I said quickly, 'just think about it. You don't have to decide right away. I'll ring again tomorrow night. The – the thing isn't until Thursday.' For some reason I couldn't bring myself to say 'Family Day'. 'I mustn't hold you up, and there's a queue here for this phone. I'll talk to you again tomorrow night, darling. All my love to everyone down there, all right?'

'Mum?' His voice was strangling.

'Yes?'

'I'm glad you're doing what you're doing. It's the right thing.'

I hung up quickly before I betrayed myself to him. Or we betrayed ourselves to each other.

But when I did ring him next night, he was a different person, firm, apologetic but adamant. He couldn't face it. He was sorry, but there it was. I didn't push it and we left it with a promise that I would call him on the night after 'it' to tell him what had happened. 'Good luck, Mum,' he said quickly, at the end. 'I mean it. Good luck.'

CHAPTER THIRTY-SIX

Family Day dawned, and through the morning I could sense the tension growing amongst the members of the group. But not having forged any relationships with anyone, I maintained my aloofness. They weren't going to see that I was rattled.

Underneath, however, I was as nervous as the rest of them. God knows what would happen in that room – I couldn't even begin to imagine the humiliation of speaking to your husband about private things in front of strangers. The only way I was going to get through it was with the knowledge that after I got out of there I would never see any of these people again.

Just before lunchtime I peeped into the room where the meeting was to be held, a big parlour where the hospital grandees and do-gooders held parties and fund-raisers. To my surprise, it was furnished with big sofas, chesterfields and Queen Anne armchairs, even a couple of garden recliners with deep, squashy cushions. Everything had seen better days, of course (and – shades of Louise and her aquarium – the four sofas were covered with loose Indian throws to cover the threadbare upholstery) but the set-up looked comfy, even inviting, all drawn up into a big circle.

Huh. So well it might look inviting: it was designed to lull us into a false sense of security – because what those counsellors do when they bring in the husbands and the wives, or the brothers or the mothers or the kids, is encourage them to let rip. To let us have it with both barrels.

Fergus met me in the poky, smoke-filled second-floor coffee bar, by arrangement, ten minutes before the meeting was due to begin. I had been waiting for him there for half an hour, afraid to

miss his entrance, afraid, full stop. We saw one another simultaneously. I waved, he didn't.

'Jesus.' He flapped a hand in front of his face, then pulled out a
chair to sit opposite me. 'Has no one here ever heard of
air-conditioning?'

I bristled, 'Hello to you too!' and was immediately sorry for
snapping at him. The last thing I needed to do now was create a
row, but with a lit cigarette in my hand and two butts in an ashtray
in front of me, I nevertheless felt it was my moral duty to make
light of the heavy fug. 'It's part of the deal, they're probably trying
to drive us out to free up a couple of beds.'

'So what's the deal here?'

He wasn't interested in being lighthearted about anything. He
seemed to have put on a little weight. And the transplants were
wearing thin. 'You're looking well, Fergus.' I tried again for
contact.

'Thank you.'

Then he sat back, with his head to one side. 'I have to say the
same for you. You're obviously able to sleep in here?'

'Yes, I am indeed.'

I saw some of my fellow victims trailing miserably out of the
coffee bar with equally miserable-looking strangers, obviously
relatives, following them like apprehensive sheep. So, quickly, I
filled him in as much as I could about what was to happen.
'Apparently, these occasions are meant for the families, not for us.
It's to confront us with the damage we've caused to others. I think
that's what they're for, it's my first.' My heart was popping as I
talked, with nerves about what was to come, obviously, but also
because I was trying to charm him, like. And I was giving him all
kinds of openings so he could say, 'What damage?' He didn't.

Maybe he didn't hear properly, I thought, because he was
shifting in his seat uneasily, obviously aware that people were
covertly staring at him. He had been recognised.

I watched him, trying to be clear-eyed. Now that I was
confronted with him in the flesh, and in cold, sober day, did I still
love this man?

I did love him, I did, I did . . . I wouldn't entertain any other
thought. 'Will we go in?'

By the time it came to Fergus's turn to have a go at me, I was shell-shocked. I had thought some of the quarrel scenes I had written for my plays were pretty tough, but they didn't come within an ass's roar of the stream of real-life anger and bitterness that flowed from the mouths of these relatives. The mildest-looking ones, the silver-haired grandmotherly types, were the worst. In their soft, milky voices, they poured out litanies of neglect and disaster and pure bad behaviour. (Naturally they were all long-suffering saints and martyrs.) As I listened to it, I thanked God over and over again that I hadn't subjected Colm to this. Or myself to what he might say.

What was completely disgraceful, in my opinion, was that the three counsellors in the room did nothing to stop it. In fact, the only time one of them opened her mouth was when my woman colleague tried to defend herself against a particularly vicious attack from her daughter. 'I think you'll find, Charmaine,' said this particular counsellor, cutting into the woman's shaky resistance, 'that if you listen, rather than speak, we'll all be able to move on.'

I didn't dare look at Fergus, who was sitting in the chair next to me. The dismay and upset was building up like a volcano inside me and I was afraid that if I moved even an inch it would all spill out and I'd make a show of myself. I didn't care about any of the others now or what they thought of me, all I cared about was getting out of here as soon as possible. I forced myself to tune out from the venom. I was going to get up and say I had to go to the toilet. And not come back. The only thing that was stopping me was how to get Fergus out of there too – throughout, he had kept his eyes firmly on the floor, although I could see that the coffee bar hadn't been the only place he had been clocked and that many of the others in the large circle were flicking looks at him from time to time. For the first time, I realised how difficult it had to be for him to do this. But there was no time to develop this thought: there was a changing of the guard. Louise was turning to him. 'Fergus? I'm sure there are a few things you want to say to Madeleine?'

I stared straight ahead, holding on to my sanity by a thread. Beside me, I felt him gearing up as the rest of the sorry crowd honed in, fascinated. 'Well,' he began, 'as a matter of fact,

Madeleine hasn't been drinking all that long, not excessively, anyway, but—'

'Stop!' I stood up. I turned to face him. 'I'm sorry, Fergus. I'm sorry I've put you through this torture. I'm sorry about everything, everything, everything. But I'm not sitting here to listen to any more of this. I can't.'

My face was burning but I didn't care now. Some, mostly the relatives, seemed mesmerised; a few were looking at the floor, a couple of the other drunks were looking at me with a queer expression on their faces – I suppose they wished they had done this. 'I apologise to you all,' I said to the room in general, 'But I can't cope with this. Goodbye and good luck.'

I walked towards the door through a silence so thick you could swim in it.

I wasn't aware that Fergus had followed me out until he caught up with me in the corridor. 'What was that all about?' His voice was low and venomous. 'I didn't give up my valuable time so that you could bottle out. I did this for you, you thick bitch, I had a lot of things to say to you and I thought this time you really were serious about things.'

I was shocked into silence. He saw the depth of the hurt and calmed down. 'Look, is there anywhere in this kip we can go and talk privately? And not up in that hole of a coffee bar.'

'I am serious. Why would I be putting up with staying here?' I found my voice.

'I don't think you're serious. Everyone else in there is being honest, Madeleine, but you think you're above them all, don't you? Ah, the hell with it,' he threw up his hands, 'I shouldn't have come in the first place.' He walked away from me towards the door at the end of the passage.

'Wait, Fergus, please don't go!' I ran after him.

He stopped and turned round. 'Why not? What's the point in staying, Madeleine? We're just going to go round and round on the merry-go-round.'

'I promise we won't. I promise.'

'All right. Come out to the car. I got parking quite close to the building as it turns out.'

Something happened to me as I followed him through the

corridors and out towards the car park. I saw myself as others must see me, certainly as Vanessa must see me and probably Fergus too: a sad, middle-aged woman trailing meekly after her estranged husband, while trying desperately with every means at her disposal to entrap and cement down something that was no longer hers. How had I come to this? Where was my dignity or pride in that, come hell or high water, I wished to be with someone who did not wish to be with me?

Perhaps it had been the vitriol in that room that had torn away my veil, perhaps it was merely timing, but for whatever reason, the revelation took my breath away, quite literally. I found I could not draw enough air into my lungs as, without thinking, I walked towards the beige Vectra at the end of a row of cars. 'Where are you going?' He had stopped at a battered silver-coloured Micra. I had passed him without noticing.

Of course. I still had the Vectra. He would be driving Vanessa's car.

When I got into the passenger seat, first having to clear the seat of an open box of Pampers, I automatically scanned the first floor of the building for my own window and found it. My magnifying hand-mirror has a red casing and there it was, a brave little red flag on the inside sill of the fourth casement from the left. 'That's my room up there.' I pointed.

'I see.' He didn't look up but stared at the dashboard.

My breath returned and I found strength I did not know I had. 'Thank you for coming today, Fergus.'

He shrugged.

'I mean that, and before you launch into whatever it is you have to say to me — were going to say to me in that hateful room — will you listen for two minutes while I say something to you?'

He looked across at me. Uncertainty, not a state I associate with Fergus, was written all over his face. 'If this is going to be another diatribe—'

'No, it's not.' I was finding this surprisingly easy. 'I just want to tell you my version of how we got to this horrible place. Certainly how I got here.'

'Shoot.' He folded his arms. 'But I'm out of here if things go out of control again.'

'You're referring to my throwing things? I'm sorry about that. At least I didn't smash your piggy-bank.'

That brought a small, wry smile, so I plunged in, careful not to think. For once, I was going to say what I meant, without worrying about how he would react. 'I was so in love with you, Fergus, I would have done anything for you, I would have followed you to Outer Mongolia, and I think that's why we got off on the wrong foot. I drowned all my own ambitions and dreams and hopes, all the things I wanted for myself—'

'Like what?' He was astonished.

'Like I would have liked to try my hand at being a professional.'

'You?' His amazement was almost comical. Then he saw my face. 'Sorry, Madeleine, but do you really think you could have cut the mustard on the professional stage?'

'I would have liked the opportunity at least to try.'

'Well, who was stopping you?'

He frowned but I cut in before he could launch a defence: 'You were, Fergus. You were stopping me.'

He took an angry breath but I put a hand on his arm. He glared down at it, but although I took it away, for once I wasn't intimidated. 'Please, Fergus, just listen. I need to get this off my chest. I don't know why, maybe it's these last few days in this place where I've had very little to do except think about myself, but I can now see very clearly what has been festering for a long time. I was a very discontented woman, *pretending* to be a supportive wife, *acting* being a housewife.'

His frown deepened but I rushed on: 'In a minute, Fergus, in a minute. You can have your say in a minute. You sat on my ambition. You were so determined yourself to succeed, and so needy of my support, that it damaged me. I didn't think it did at the time. I didn't think, full stop. And on my word of honour, my support of you was with a full heart all the way along the line. It's only now I can see that I was seething with resentment. Not on the surface — I wouldn't let it come to the surface. And the resentment was not only about my lost hopes, although that was bad enough, but because you never even seemed to think they were there, you never appreciated what I had done for you, you certainly never referred to it.' I took a deep breath to control my anger. 'Sorry, I got carried away a bit there. And it has to be said, you were not entirely to blame, Fergus. I should have fought you for my dream.'

Heavy silence filled the little car, adding to the claustrophobia. I could smell baby-sick, overlaid with the detergent used in an attempt to clean it. He brought his head round to face me, his expression guarded. 'But why didn't you say something?'

'Would you have let me?' At least I had got through to him. 'Would you have believed me?'

His mouth set in a grim line. 'So everything is my fault?'

'If you were listening, you'll remember I've accepted some of the blame. You were the stronger character but I allowed it. I let you and your dreams dominate me and mine. I almost invited you to keep me down. The plain truth, Fergus, is that I should have stood up to you and I didn't. I suppose I thought subconsciously that, once you were up and running, I could turn my attention to myself. But it never happened and your career and your ego ran the show.'

'But, Madeleine,' he looked puzzled now, 'what's the point of telling me all this now when it's finished between us?'

I considered this. Up to that very moment, as you know, I hadn't accepted his premise that the relationship was over. I still didn't, not completely, but now was not the time to argue that point. 'I'm not quite sure why,' I said slowly. 'I suppose I'm being honest for the first time in a very long while. I needed to say it for me. But I accept it's not going to make very much difference now.'

'You've got that right.' Although not sneering, he was recovering the high ground and perhaps I should have challenged it. But the dignity and pride I had so belatedly discovered kicked in.

'Will you at least admit that there might be some truth in what I've said?' I asked quietly. 'You've nothing to lose and I won't hold it against you. Honest!'

He thought about it. 'All right. I will say that I was pretty single-minded in going after what I wanted. But I didn't deliberately stamp on your dreams, or whatever you said so dramatically. I couldn't have. You were an amateur, Madeleine, amateurs stay amateur. If you had told me what you wanted to do, I wouldn't have stood in your way.'

'Wouldn't you? "Amateurs stay amateur"? What about you? You started as an amateur yourself.'

'*Touché.*' He looked across at me. 'So this is all about your not being on the stage?'

'No.' Abruptly I wanted out of there. I had achieved my breakthrough, even a victory of sorts, and there was no point in belabouring him, or inviting a row, *you did, I did not.* 'It's about a lot more than that, about your moods, and my pandering to them, your belittling me, and my craven trying to please you all the time and never fully being able to – all my weaknesses. I don't blame you, Fergus. Not any more.' I grabbed the car door. 'I have to go. We've nothing more to say to each other right now. And I certainly don't want to fight or argue. I'm sure you don't either. After all, there's Colm to consider. We'll have to be in communication about our son and it's best that we do so not as out-and-out enemies. Just give me the satisfaction of the last word for once, will you? And the dignity of thinking honestly about what I said.'

I jumped out of the car and, not bothering to close the door after me, hurried back towards the hospital building. I had certainly turned the stated purpose of Family Day at St Roland's firmly on its head.

But it had felt good. I didn't want the feeling to end.

In my room, I was half-way through packing, shoving willy-nilly the few things I had in the hospital into my bag, when I became aware that Louise was in the room, standing in the doorway. 'Yes?' I turned to her.

'I don't like to state the obvious,' she said, in her smooth voice, 'but you're making a mistake.'

'Really?' I turned away to take my mirror from the window-sill.

'You're a classic case,' she continued remorselessly from behind me. 'You are an alcoholic, Madeleine, and you are in denial.'

I wasn't listening. I was watching Fergus. Through the window of his car I could see him talking animatedly on his mobile phone.

'I know you are determined to leave,' there she went again, 'and you will, but take it from me, you'll be back, if not here to some other facility.'

'No, I won't,' I said automatically.

'I hope not. Everything's possible and you have had a serious fright here during your time with us, that's true. Maybe that will be enough, but I doubt it. The statistics show—'

'I'm not interested in your statistics.' I was watching Fergus throw back his head, laughing heartily and, for the first time in many years, showing me the boy I had fallen in love with. In doing so, he was also showing me definitely that I had lost him.

CHAPTER THIRTY-SEVEN

Maddy had signed herself out of St Roland's before I could get across town to see her, the bitch. I had got sucked into San Lorenzo, you know how that goes, there's always some crisis: someone's jeans go missing, someone's red blouse ran into someone else's *best* white T-shirt in the wash, no other T-shirt would do, of course, so we had to rush out to buy a packet of Colour Run; then someone needed new Reeboks, *now*, Mum, necessitating a trip to the Pavilions shopping centre in Swords.

They had to be driven to their pals' houses, then picked up again, and running through all this we had had a scare with BSE in a young cow. Thank God, it came to nothing.

All in all I had a hectic few days, so much so that I made Ricky's doctor's appointment and then forgot to tell him.

I didn't get to see Tess either, although we talked to each other on the telephone. She rang me after she had seen Yarso and young Tommy off to London. Her father was bearing up to the strain well, she said, better than she was. I suppose it comes to us all, the death of our parents, I mean, although it doesn't make it any easier. Especially when people tend to say, as they do when an old person is on the way out, that he'd had a good innings. 'That's driving me mad, Rita,' she said. 'How long is a good innings? What's the standard for a good one?'

Nobody's ever ready for it, are they?

And Jerry? Well, I didn't like to pry too hard about Jerry, but from what I gathered, things were pretty rough between them, as you'd expect. At least she'd got rid of that Yarso — that had been really complicating things. Grudgingly, though, I suppose I have to hand it to him that he took young Tommy off her hands for a few days to give her a bit of breathing space. I suppose his heart is in the right place, after all. Bet she paid for the trip, though.

Ah, no. That was mean!

But poor old Tess, she doesn't deserve all this hassle. Never done a bad turn to anyone in her life.

So, anyway, without knowing she had checked out, I had cleared the decks to get myself over to St Roland's to see Maddy. It was like organising a military campaign. Who wanted to come, who wanted to stay, who wanted to be dropped here, there and everywhere in town on my way through. Plus I was planning to take advantage of the trip to do my monthly shop in Musgrave's: we're entitled to a cash-and-carry card because we have our own shops, so we can buy in bulk. My girls might look slim, they are slim, but they eat nearly as much as their ponies, and as for the amount of tissues and toilet paper they get through! And these days I never know how many are going to sit down with us for dinner. Thank God, I thought, the holidays will be over soon.

Armed with my shopping list, Alice and Carol already installed in the car, I was pulling the front door behind me when the hall phone rang. Lately, that phone had brought nothing but bad news or hassle so I dithered. Ah, shit! I said to myself then. It might be important.

It was Maddy, ringing me from home. She had discharged herself the day before.

I couldn't believe it. I was speechless. All that fuss and I turn my back for a few days and she swans out of the place.

She was in a weird mood, half apologetic, half bolshy, being belligerent with me one moment because I had no right, et cetera, et cetera, then, in the next breath, trying to explain to me why and how she left. After telling me she was furious with me, followed immediately by how sorry she was for putting me to so much trouble, she launched into what had happened to her at Family Day: 'It wouldn't happen in a gulag, Rita. Psychological torture, that's what it was. Well, I wasn't going to let them work it on me . . .'

As she continued yakking away nineteen to the dozen I got the impression that something had changed. It was the tone of her voice, I think. It's hard to explain, but as she went on and on giving out about St Roland's (at least it had had quite an effect on her!) I felt it was almost like she had rehearsed it, and that underneath there was something she wasn't telling me.

It occurred to me then that she hadn't yet mentioned Fergus. 'Was Fergus there?' I asked, when I was able to get a word in.

'Yes.' She hesitated. 'I'll tell you about that in a minute.'

As she carried on, I remembered the conversation I had had with Maddy's husband when I rang to tell him about her going into the clinic. He already knew, as it turned out, but at that point he had seemed less interested in her well-being than in justifying his own walking out on her, giving me a load of bullshit about how he didn't expect me to be jumping over the moon about him and his new girlfriend, but that at last he had found out what true happiness was, blah-di-blah.

Maddy's relationship was a dead duck. Had she finally copped it? Was that what was different? I tuned in again. She was still on about Family Day. '. . . you'd want to hear it, Rita, you'd want to hear what they said. It's all right for you, you never had to go through that kind of humiliation, it's all very well for people like you to be judgemental—'

'Hey! Hey! Steady on, Maddy, I'm not judgemental. What did I say to make you think that?'

She stopped and I could hear her pulling on a cigarette. 'All right,' she said, sort of subdued. 'I thought I could hear you thinking it.'

'Well, you didn't. All right?'

'Sorry.'

The sound of the car horn came from outside the front door. But I didn't feel I could cut her off. 'Look, Maddy,' I offered quickly, 'I've to go, but why don't you come out here, stay a few days, get your bearings? You'll have to take pot luck and so on, but it can't be good for you to be rattling around over there all by yourself.'

The car horn sounded again; one of them was really leaning on it now. I'd murder them when I got my hands on them. 'Excuse me, Maddy,' I rushed to the door and screamed at the two of them to stop it or they'd be sorry.

'Apologies, Maddy,' I panted into the phone when I got back to her. 'They're right little wagons, these days. I really will have to go now, but will you come?'

Another hesitation. I expected her to say no, or that she had to stay in in case Fergus rang. Instead, slowly: 'I'd love to. Have you been in touch with Tess? I rang the other day but she wasn't in.'

'We can have a good chat when you come, Maddy.' We made arrangements for her to arrive at around half past four that afternoon.

I hung up and raced outside, and ate the faces off the girls when I got into the car. 'Don't you dare sound the horn at me like that ever again. There are other people in the world besides youse two selfish little cows.'

'Selfish?' Alice geared up for a fight. 'It's not me that spends all my li-uf on the telepho-un!' I turned round and glared at her so hard that she sat back into her seat and shut up. And, thank God, neither of them said another word until I shovelled them out of the car at Moran's Hotel at the end of Gardiner Street. Alice, predictably, whined about that too. 'We're going to Henry Stree-ut – it's mi-uls away!'

'Yeah,' Carol chimed in. 'These shoes hurt, Ma, they're killing me!'

With traffic building up behind me, I was at the end of my tether. 'Stop this, the two of you, and get out this minute or youse'll be walking a lot further than bloody Henry Street! I didn't have to come into town, you know, Musgrave's is in Ballymun now! Out – *out*!' They got out.

As you probably know, they're demolishing the Ballymun flats, which does not make it any easier to drive through the place, with all the cones, and barriers and temporary roundabouts. Traffic was fierce and I was in a right old temper when I got to the cash-and-carry.

But, then, who was getting into the car next to the parking space I found but Mrs Vitelli, Susan's mother. Of all people! The last person on earth, probably, I'd want to talk to right now. She had cut her hair short and was a bit fatter since the last time we'd bumped into each other, but it was her all right.

I tried to act as if I hadn't seen her, and after I'd cut the engine, I picked up my mobile and pretended to be talking on it.

She had seen me, though, and now, dammit, here she came, tapping on my window. I smiled at her, and waved, all the time nodding furiously into the dead mobile but she wouldn't take the hint. Instead, she just stood there, waiting.

What the hell was she doing in Musgrave's, anyway? She's not a bloody trader like us. This place was a cash-and-carry, it was supposed to be for trade only.

I had to give in, finally, because it looked like she was prepared to wait for ever. I finished up my pretend conversation. 'See you soon now, mind yourself!' and put the mobile away. I lowered the window. 'Mrs Vitelli, how nice to see you again! How are you keeping, these days?'

'Fine! And you?'

'Oh, pulling the divil by the tail as usual. Are you a customer here?'

'I've taken a job with a computer company. Well, I was bored at home, the days were very long. Anyway, I've been trying to persuade everyone in this industrial estate to switch to us. I suppose you know what's happened with Susan?' This last bit came in a big rush, which of course, Big Surprise, was why she had waited to bend my ear.

'I just heard a little bit,' I said, putting on my most innocent expression. 'I've been very busy. It's been some awful summer, hasn't it?'

She wouldn't be diverted. Then she told me that Jerry Brennan had now been suspended because Susan was taking a case against him and I couldn't keep up the pretence that I knew hardly any details about the situation. 'But he didn't force her, Mrs Vitelli! She's over twenty-one, after all, she's not a child, and what about—' Just in time, I stopped myself spilling the beans about the e-mail. She went cold on me all the same.

'You seem to know more about it, Mrs Sleator, than you let on.'

'His wife is a great friend of mine, Mrs Vitelli.'

'I see! So in your opinion, it's all right, then, for a young girl's boss, twice her age, to abuse his power over her in order to seduce her?'

Something in my head was warning me not to say too much more. I was helped by a big tipper lorry that roared into the car park, making so much of a racket as it passed us that it gave me a few seconds to think.

'Tess, that's Jerry's wife, is my friend,' I said, when the noise had died down a bit, 'so naturally I'm sympathetic to her because she's very, very hurt. But I have to say, from the little I do know, my impression is that there were two of them in it and your daughter was not seduced, as you call it.'

She became really angry then. 'I'm sure your friend is hurt, but so is my daughter. He's getting full pay, of course, while all this is being investigated. And, of course, they're trying to keep it all hush-hush – they do look after their own, don't they? Well, we'll see what public opinion has to say about that! I have friends in the media, you know. See you, Mrs Sleator!' She marched away, leaving me hollow. God, I couldn't bear to think what Tess would make of this. If she knew. Maybe she didn't, she hadn't rung me, and it certainly wasn't my business to tell her.

The nerve of that girl! After sending him that e-mail?

I didn't blame the mother. I'd be like a tigress defending one of my own in a case like that. But to tell you the truth, I had changed my mind about Mrs Vitelli. I had thought she was a very nice person until today, when I discovered that I had never really liked her. You have to take sides and I knew which one I was on.

Maddy drove into the gravel forecourt at San Lorenzo as Betty and I were taking advantage of a short break in the rain to unload the last of the twenty-four packs of toilet rolls from the car. ('Scattered showers and sunny intervals, some of them heavy and prolonged', they had called this Noah's flood on the weather forecast this morning, ha! In a way that's the story of our lives as well as the weather this awful summer; for us too, there had been far more prolonged showers than sunny intervals.) Betty went inside but I waited while Maddy parked her little car: she could probably have fitted it inside mine if we'd had a ramp. Sometimes I feel silly driving a monster Land Rover through the choked streets of Dublin, but it does come into its own for shopping. 'Howya!' I called to her as she got out. I was still officially cross with her for not staying the course at St Roland's, but I had to get over it. She wasn't looking too bad, I had to admit, so the few days she had spent there had done her some good.

'Hi, Rita.' She came across to me and pecked me on the cheek. Close up, I could see even more improvement. Amazing, actually, the human body. Less than a week off the sauce and the skin clears up. So do the eyes. I was about to compliment her when I spotted Jack Butler slouching up the pathway towards us. When I say 'slouching' it's a vast improvement on the way he used to walk. He and Kitty are getting on very well and she's obviously having an effect on him. Even his patchy designer stubble has a sheen now.

'She's inside in the conservatory,' I called to him.

'Thanks, Mrs Sleator,' he called back. Even his manners had improved.

Maddy and I didn't get a chance to talk properly until after tea. Tea in our house is not like dinner, where we all sit down, it's more like a short-order buffet, where they all come in in their own time and graze off whatever is available. I usually have one core thing, like a big tuna and egg salad or a bowl of chicken wings or ribs, that they can add bread to, or pasta, or rice, or salad, whatever they like. The disadvantage is that, at tea-time, our kitchen gets to look like Croke Park on All-Ireland day as they scrum around cooking this, that and the other. I know the modern fashion is for dinner to be in the evening, and Betty, who is a bit of snob, doesn't know why I keep on doing it this way, but Ricky is still able to get home in the middle of the day. Plus, the rule is that we all have to clean up after ourselves at tea-time, so I get the evenings for myself and my soaps.

That evening, the core food was a platter of pizza slices and I noticed that Maddy wolfed hers, along with nearly half a loaf of garlic bread and salad. She ate chocolate ice-cream too.

Big change from the last time we'd been together when I couldn't even get her to look at a piece of toast. I was delighted with her. It was early days yet, however, and I know that no alcoholic is ever cured. It'll be tough going for her, poor lamb.

And maybe Tess and I had been alarmist about anorexia. It's a fashionable disease, in the sense that it's always being written about and talked about on the radio, and maybe we had been too quick to jump to conclusions.

Ricky went out to play darts with his team at the local, and the two of us girls settled down peacefully in front of the wide-screen television, both already in our dressing-gowns. I had put Maddy in the nicest guest room, having warned off Patricia and six of her pals, who had planned to have a pyjama party in it.

'I feel like having a fizzy orange,' I said during an ad break in *EastEnders*, 'how about you?' I usually had a G and T at this time of the evening, but I felt this would be rubbing her nose in it.

'No, thanks,' she was a bit sheepish about it, 'but do you have any Coke?'

I brought in the drinks. 'Look,' I said, as I gave her a glass, 'I don't want to go on about it but I have to say what's on my mind and I think you shouldn't have signed yourself out like that.'

Afraid she would fire up, I went on quickly: 'But all that's history now. I mention it because I want to let you know that if you need help, day or night in the next few weeks, you only have to ask. I know it's not going to be easy for you.' Then, to head off any further discussion, I told her about the latest in Tess's saga, including the threat to go to the media. Her reaction was to put down her drink.

'We should go over there, right away. We have to tell her—'

'No. She'll tell us when she's ready.'

'Are you sure?'

'Absolutely sure. We'll help when we're needed, which we will be. Jerry's not normally a subject for the gossip columns, as you know, but he's head of the Sentinel Group here. Bad news for them is great news for all the other rags. It'll be all over the place.

'Speaking of gossip columns,' I added cautiously, 'I saw some reference to Fergus last Sunday. Did you see it?' It hadn't been that bad. Just a couple of snide lines about him and his 'new squeeze' at the opening of some play or other. He hadn't rated a photograph.

'No, I didn't.' The way she said this cut off further discussion. She realised she'd been abrupt. 'Look,' she said, 'it's very soon to say this, and maybe it's temporary, but for some reason, I feel much stronger in that quarter just now. I'm not out of the woods, but I got the chance to get a lot of stuff off my chest. I said things that I never thought I'd hear myself say to him, stuff I'd been storing up for years and years. The reason I feel chary about talking about it too much is because I haven't worked it all out yet, but while I won't say I'm not heartbroken, it's sort of a quiet heartbreak right at the minute.'

She smiled sadly at me. 'You'll be glad to know that, at any rate, I'm no longer frantic to get him back. Certainly not at any price, the way I was up to now. Sorry, Rita. You and Tess had a lot to put up with.'

'Rubbish. Not at all.'

She gazed into her drink. 'Yes, you had,' she said slowly. 'You were right. I'm wasting my life, have wasted it, certainly the last couple of years. It's almost as if venting all that gunge and bile and disappointment opened up my eyes to what is available as opposed to what is shut off. What you were saying to me that night in the house came back to me in little bits and pieces. You were right. Sorry I was so rude to you, Rita.'

'Stop saying sorry, will you?'

'Yeah.' She smiled again. 'That's something I'm going to have to work on too, isn't it?'

'What a relief for us all!'

'As I said, don't celebrate yet. I haven't fully accepted that I'm a separated woman. That's too hard right now, too harsh and final. I'm still confused, but mostly sorrowful, and that's a more peaceful feeling, more natural, in a sort of way, than the terror I felt up to now, where my stomach was in knots all the time. The bottom line is I can see, dimly enough, mind, that what's happened to me is not the end of the world.

'There's something else,' she added quietly. 'I saw him chatting and laughing on his mobile after he'd left me in the hospital. He was obviously on to Vanessa and when I saw the way he was with her I knew I'd lost him. But, Rita, it's dawning on me that he's the one who's lost me.'

For once I was stuck for words. She saw this, put her arms out and we hugged each other. Then, with nothing more to be said – how could I top that? – we both turned our attention to *Fair City* followed by *Off the Rails*, even managing to moan about the outrageous prices of the shoes they were showing. (I mean, over three hundred euros for a pair of Jimmy Choo sandally, strappy things? I don't care if they were by Jimmy Choo-Choo, there wasn't enough leather in them to make one glove.) She went quietly off to bed at about half-past nine, after the news.

In my own bed that night, I couldn't sleep. It wasn't just Maddy's new mood: I couldn't take in what Susan Vitelli Moore had done. Sexual harassment? Surely that couldn't be. Although I didn't know the full ins and outs of it, it simply did not seem fair or just. I know you read that it's always the man next door, the pleasant neighbour, but hey! I know Jerry Brennan. And I know what Tess told me about that e-mail Susan sent him . . .

I couldn't hold the news in any longer. 'Hey, Rick, you asleep?'

'I was until now.'

'Listen, I have to tell you this. I can't sleep, I'm bursting with it.'

He listened without comment until I had finished. 'I'm not surprised,' he said then.

'What?' I turned on the bedside lamp so I could see his expression. 'What do you mean, "not surprised"? He shouldn't have committed adultery, Rick, that's for sure, but she's not a baby, now, is she? And I told you what she did.'

He sighed. 'That doesn't change things, Reet. These days, if you're someone's boss, or in a higher grade than them, you don't sleep with them and that's the holy all of it. She's out for revenge and she'll get it, simple as that. I'm sorry for him but, let's face it, he was a pure eejit. He had to know the way the land lies as well as anyone. He's a CEO, for God's sake.'

I was pure flabbergasted. Just because he was her boss? 'Listen, do you want a cup of tea?' I threw back the covers.

Ricky sighed again. 'I'm awake now. All right, why not?'

As I went down the stairs, I thought about Ma. My ma worked nights in a factory in the weeks coming up to Christmas. She did it because we needed the money but she actually looked forward to it every year, because, she said, there was great crack to be had in the place. And not only with her mates, she used to have all of us kids, even my da, in stitches with yarns about the tricks the fellas, even the foremen, used to get up to, spying on the girls in the lavatory, pinching them, grabbing them, giving them big, beery Christmas kisses while everyone else on the assembly line roared laughing . . .

She'd turn in her grave, she would.

I'm not excusing it when it goes as far as adultery, but in this case they both did it, for God's sake. She went to London with him to do it. And she had to have enjoyed it, otherwise why did she send him that effin' e-mail?

The law is the law, Ricky said. God – is there no fun to be had any more between the sexes in Ireland?

CHAPTER THIRTY-EIGHT

'Were there others? And has she anything in writing? Anything incriminating?' It was after three in the morning. Jerry and I were still downstairs, having talked ourselves hoarse since the revelation about Susan and the sexual-harassment case.

'No.'

'No, there were no others? Or no she has nothing in writing?'

'No to both questions.'

'How can you be sure? Not even an e-mail?' I could not stop the asking.

'I was very careful. Please, Tess, leave it, I can't discuss this any more.' His voice was weak and exhausted. 'I can't reassure you any further. I can't discuss Susan, or sexual harassment, or even the Sentinel Group. Please, let's change the subject.' He got up and paced slowly around the drawing room.

Although our lives had turned into 'daymares', as Mammy used to call traumatic situations, oddly, or perhaps not, we had talked more that afternoon, evening and night than we had cumulatively in the previous year.

It might have been due to exhaustion, but at one point during that extraordinary evening, it had occurred to me that the barriers might have come down because we now had a common enemy. It even occurred to me that I might owe SVM, as I now thought of her, a debt of gratitude for breaching the communications dam my husband and I had together erected between us; shows you how worn out I was, and how sad about Daddy, and how much coffee I'd had.

I watched Jerry's slow gait, so unlike his customary briskness, as he continued to pace; although apparently we had come to a sort of lacuna in hostilities, for me SVM had not been pushed away.

'So? Here's a subject, Tess.' He stopped his pacing. 'What about you?'

I crimsoned because for a heart-stopping moment I thought he had discovered my 'virtual' adultery. His tone had not been accusatory, however, and I calmed down. 'Me?' I managed. 'What about me?'

'Well, there are lots of things I don't know about you any more, or that maybe I've lost sight of.'

'Like what?'

'How you feel, how you think about the world.'

'That's a tall order.'

'Well, let's talk about early experiences. For instance, you've never told me much about your convent days.'

'Convent days?' I was puzzled. 'I find that hard to believe. Of course I've told you about them.'

'No, you haven't,' he said patiently. 'Not me. You're probably confusing me with Michael, you would have told him.'

I had Norma on my lap, her warm body like a little muff in my hands, and I stroked her fluffy head as I thought about this. Michael was not a subject I wanted to discuss. 'What brought this up? My convent days are hardly appropriate as a subject at the moment, surely?'

'What is?' He flopped into a chair. 'Oh, never mind. Just for a moment there . . .' He seemed to change his mind. 'You should go to bed, Tess, you must be tired, and your dad will need you tomorrow.'

'You have to be just as tired.'

'I wouldn't sleep.'

'Me either. Look, are you sure there's nothing we can do to head this off? Should we talk to Susan?'

His glance told me what a daft idea that had been. 'I'm sick thinking about it, and nothing's going to be solved tonight. If we're not going to go to bed, let's at least have a drink?'

'All right. I'll have a Southern Comfort.'

'What?' He was amused more than shocked. Although we have it in the house for the occasional guest who might ask for it, I *never* drink Southern Comfort, or whiskey of any sort. 'Southern Comfort,' I insisted. Nothing would have surprised me that night because the word 'bizarre' was too weak to describe this. 'So to get back to your question, why the convent? And why now?'

'It just occurred to me, that's all. Maybe as a distraction. The human brain is a mystery. So, come on,' he smiled as he handed me my glass, 'tell me about it. Was it as sexy as we're led to believe?'

'Sexy?'

'You know, a bunch of young lasses cooped up together, covered up to their tonsils but broiling underneath with unbridled passion. It's the top of all male sexual-fantasy lists, you have to know that.'

I actually laughed. 'I don't know what comics you've been reading, but it wasn't like that at all. It was mundane, really. Ordinary. If you're looking for headlines,' I hesitated, 'think frog spawn.'

'What?'

'Frog spawn. My abiding memory of the convent, both as a boarder and as a nun, is of being fed tapioca as a great treat.'

'And that's it? Come on, Tess. Prayers. Lights out. Breaking silence – I've seen *The Nun's Story*. . . ' He sprawled on the sofa opposite mine, one long leg draped over the arm.

Bit by bit, he drew me out to reminisce about those days of innocence in the novitiate, which occupy the cleanest, most tranquil part of my memory. We had been little girls trying to act like grown-ups, earnestly performing the most gruelling and unpleasant tasks, cleaning toilets, scrubbing stoves, washing sheets by hand, all for the greater good of God and the Blessed Virgin. Aspiring with all our hearts to the holiness encapsulated in our copies of *The Imitation of Christ*, pinning back our veils to play basketball during recreation. Meditating on our knees until they hurt, singing Office in a chapel so plain it begged the imagination to soar. I found myself talking about my reception. 'I can't tell you how thrilling that day was, and how sad.'

'Try.'

What was happening? This was my husband. I was not used to telling stories to him: my confidantes were Rita and Maddy. But tiredness and the cloying sweetness of the whiskey had coated my tongue, loosening it. So I did try, shyly at first, to describe the day of my reception into the order as a novice.

Apart from the sly questions about chastity – *you must have missed it, did you never have fantasies about it?* – I have found that what most people instantly want to know about nuns is how it feels to have your hair cut off.

Well, here is the scoop. It does not happen all at once: a symbolic cut is made when a single lock is taken from under your bridal veil when you are at the altar in full finery. The rest is taken when you are robing, or being robed, in the white habit, prior to coming back into the chapel. And, yes, it did feel like a small torture to hear from behind you that dry chop-chopping from the scissors wielded by a novice mistress who gave no thought to the end result. It was probably far worse than watching it. We had no mirrors.

There were three of us being received, each of us excited and nervous as any secular bride (and far more thoroughly prepared). Our identical wedding dresses that day were of plain white satin but beautifully full-skirted, and after the months of postulants' serge, felt like cool water against our skin each time we moved; our headdresses were made of fresh white roses.

From inside the chapel, we heard the harmonium wheeze into 'Jesu Joy Of Man's Desiring', the novice mistress flung open the double doors and we started our walk up the aisle towards the altar and our Bridegroom. We entered in order of age and, the youngest of the three, I was first.

The chapel, in which a heady mix of Brylcreem and 4711 overpowered the customary blend of Mansion polish and incense, was filled to capacity with respectful relatives in good suits and boots, Sunday-best costumes of stout tweed, and glistening, country faces. As I walked, slowly like we had rehearsed, I immediately sensed the communal conflict between pride and melancholy: the air frizzled with it.

When we were mere postulants, they could visit us and we could visit them, even be taken out for lunch to the local hotel. This day they would lose us. When today's celebrations were over, contact between us and our families was severely restricted and controlled because we no longer belonged to them but to Christ and the order. Notionally, of course, a novice can leave any time before profession as a full nun, but in that era they rarely did, so this day was a serious leave-talking, immigration to a place where they could never follow. We had been fully apprised of the depth of 'never'.

When I was half-way up the short aisle, I saw the face of my father among the sea of others turned towards me. He was smiling proudly, his head high. But as I reached him and deliberately met his eyes – although I had been warned not to – he, pillar of respectability and restraint, burst into tears.

'Sorry, Jerry, that's all . . .' I took a large mouthful of Southern Comfort. I could not continue, not with Daddy lying upstairs.

'No, I'm sorry,' Jerry said quietly. 'I'm sorry I'm not Michael.'

I looked across at him, stunned.

'You're still in love with him. I can't live up to that. I don't think any man could.'

'No, I'm not.'

'It happens. You were in love with him when he was killed, the mundane had not yet set in, so you didn't let him go.'

'Jerry, please.'

He got up. 'It's all right, lass. It's not your fault.' He cupped my chin in his hand and kissed me gently on the forehead. 'I'm all talked out now. I'm sorry I hurt you, I'm sorry about your dad, I'm sorry about everything.'

'Jerry . . .' I was becoming upset.

'Ssh!' He kissed me again, perfunctorily this time. 'Now I have to go to bed. I won't sleep, but I'll rest. I'd recommend you do the same. Thank you for that magical story.' He left.

In my lap, Norma snuffled and then yawned, showing her pink tongue. I picked her up and nuzzled her against my neck. Sleepily, she gave me a little lick before settling back to sleep in the curve of my shoulder.

Still in love with Michael?

Words are very important. Once spoken they cannot be withdrawn, and what he had said acted now like a seed, burrowing into my perceptions and memory, germinating, suddenly. I had forgotten, or suppressed, the memory of Michael's immaturity. His sulkiness.

A sunny day in our kitchen in Sallynoggin. I was protesting vigorously that he was about to choose attendance at a lecture on Pompeii over Jack's school sports. 'This woman is a *world expert*, Teresa, she'll never be in Ireland again, probably.'

Then, his anger growing: 'All right, I'll go to the bloody school sports. And then will you be happy to let me spend our money going to hear this lecture in Texas? Because that's the only other place she's giving it this year. Maybe ever!'

I gave in and he went to the lecture.

The memories tumbled back into place. I had given in a lot. To Michael's career – for which read single-minded selfishness in the search for more sites, better experiences, and the hell with the rest of us.

To his profligacy. For years I had conveniently forgotten that my first husband could have been capable of letting us starve while bidding in an auction room for a Bronze Age dagger.

To his casual love. Even his proposal to me, now that I thought of it, had been almost an afterthought. He had wangled an invitation to attend a conference in Athens. 'Why don't you come with me? You could certainly do with a holiday and we could share a room and expenses.' Although passionately in love, I was still a virgin and shocked at the notion of sharing a room. He saw this: 'Sure why don't we get married, so? What's the point of waiting until we're pensioners?'

With his death, I had sloughed off the reality of him, and had woven into a tight ball only those aspects of his personality that I chose to remember. I scrambled to reassert them now: the fun, the wild yet tender lovemaking on our wedding night and subsequently, the spellbinding torrent of words when he was enthusiastic about a project. The wonderful litheness of his body, every small muscle, which I could still recall at will.

I had covered this memory ball with an impermeable layer of gold but Jerry's words had somehow worked their way into it, leaving sly cracks.

I seemed to have specialised in unromantic marriage proposals, I thought: in Jerry's case, for instance, it remained unclear as to who had been asking whom. We had been discussing the purchase of Arkady. He had seen it, liked it, but was hesitant about its size and cost and the huge renovations he faced: 'I have very little time to supervise builders and decorators, and although I'm being paid handsomely, I have an expensive family, Tess.'

We were in the Trocadero, the lights were low and I had had quite a lot of wine. I took a breath. 'I could contribute—'

'What do you mean?'

'My house. In Sallynoggin.'

He took a second to register this, then threw back his head and laughed. 'Well,' he said finally, when he had regained his composure, 'that's a peach. That really is.'

There was a mix-up then. I had been offering merely to help with the purchase and move in with my children as a sort of housekeeper/companion. He had assumed I was proposing marriage. And when that was cleared up, we looked at one another across the red tea-light on the Trocadero table. 'Well, well!' he said then. 'Wonders will never cease. But what do you actually have against marriage? How about two months from now? Would that give you enough time? I'll have a bit of a lull, then, in the company.'

And so, without the words having been spoken, we became affianced.

Outside the drawing-room window it was almost fully bright now and the dawn chorus, subdued though it was because this was high summer, was already in gear. Hearing it was becoming another habit of mine, I thought, as, wearily, I got to my feet.

The pup protested a little as I carried her to her basket in the kitchen, but I gave her a biscuit and she settled into enthusiastic gnawing. I rinsed my empty glass and placed it carefully on the draining-board.

My heart, unused to the strength of whiskey, thumped uncomfortably as I climbed the stairs, and when I got to our bedroom Jerry was not there. He had stayed in the spare room.

I undressed and lay tidily on my own side of our six-foot bed. Then, as I was spiralling into sleep, what had evaded me for so many years came rushing back.

I had never been able to remember what I had said to Michael at the door on that last day of his life. In my memory, we had kissed and he had gone off.

That was wrong. He had left our house when we were in the

very eye of a storm: we had been fighting all morning about money.

We frequently fought about money – as in, there was never enough. He was not paid well as a junior lecturer and what he did earn was soon eaten and consumed by bills. Or an axe-head.

So when I went to our grocery shop in Glasthule and discovered from the discreet but stern proprietor that my last cheque had been returned by the bank, I was furious. I had inherited my father's budgeting nature and, as far as I knew, there should have been enough in our joint account to cover what I had spent. There could have been only one explanation.

I flew home to confront him, finding him absentmindedly feeding Tom with one hand while reading a book balanced on his knee. It was a very old book and I knew instantly where the money had gone.

He was guilty, but rationalised at first: this book was rare, it would pay for itself eventually. It would appreciate in value. He would sell it for a fortune when the time was right. Arguments I had heard many times about other books, about spearheads, about what looked to me to be a rough, dented rock, but which for Michael was part of a primitive mortar-and-pestle.

The fight raged for over an hour, right up to and including his leaving for college to give a lecture.

Up to this morning, so many years later, my memory had held a picture of me kissing him gaily on the lips at the front door while holding Tom. I did have Tom in my arms, that much was accurate, but both of us were crying as we watched Michael slam down the short concrete path to our front gate.

I stared at the ceiling. At least I had learned something. I never fight with Jerry, at least I never did until I saw Susan Vitelli Moore's e-mail. He had remarked on it, many times.

Now I understood why. Fighting gets you nowhere. It gets your husband killed crossing the road.

CHAPTER THIRTY-NINE

Mrs Byrne was peppering to know what was going on in the house. She did not have the courage to ask directly, but as she swiped at the counter tops in the kitchen, I could see she was watching me covertly for indications of my state of mind, or any chink through which she could get information. 'Mr Brennan busy, these days?'

'Very,' I said. I was sitting at the island unit, covering Tom's schoolbooks with strong brown paper, a requirement at his school: he would receive a demerit for every day he arrived into class with bare covers. I glanced at the clock over the cooker: right at this moment, Jerry should be sitting down in front of a solicitor.

'It was strange to see him yesterday.' Mrs Byrne stepped back critically to assess the shine on 'her' counter tops. 'They're grand now, aren't they? I think I'll take down them dry plants from over the presses, will I? They've been up there for a year, we should put up some fresh.'

'Yes, do that. That would be a good idea.'

She took the step-stool from its alcove and dragged it over to the foot of the first press. 'Yeah, I haven't clapped eyes on Mr B for ages. Until yesterday, that is. Everything all right with him?'

Rather than endure continual probing, I decided it would be better to give her a morsel. 'He's very tired, you know. He's been working far too hard, and the office politics in Sentinel are murder. I've been trying to get him to take it a bit easier.'

'Yeah.' She was all sympathy now. 'I don't know how you put up with it, Mrs B. Sometimes I get really annoyed with Derek – he's nothing but a lazy lump, even though, of course, he's a martyr to the back, but when I look at the two of youse, I have to say!' She climbed on to her stool and began ripping down the strings and garlands, placed over the cupboards to absorb dust and grease. 'At least my Derek's home to me for his tea after his day's work. Sure isn't that what we get married for?' Perched like a pullet on top of her stool, she turned and folded her arms across her thin chest. 'And your poor da! Did he get off all right?'

'As well as can be expected.'

'Cancer's the hob of hell.'

To head her off on this subject, I made a lot of noise shearing a square from the roll of brown paper. She seemed to take the hint and turned back to concentrate on chucking at the withered festoons.

Although I had tried my utmost to keep him at Arkady, my father had been adamant about going home to Ballina. On that morning, unlike me, and Jerry for that matter, he had risen early and, when I had dragged myself downstairs, I discovered him eating toast and a boiled egg in the kitchen. 'Daddy, what are you doing up? I would have taken you up your breakfast.'

'Good morning, Teresa.' He broke off a piece of the toast, dipped it into the egg and popped it into his mouth. He even sounded chipper. 'I've made a decision. I need to go back home now.'

'Daddy, you can't—'

'Yes I can. I'm over twenty-one. Who's to stop me?' He sounded as tranquil as he was determined. 'It's not as though I don't appreciate your hospitality, I do. You couldn't have done enough for me and it was a tonic to see the boys again, but I have some life left to me, and however long that turns out to be, I want to see it out in Ballina. I have good friends there and it's my home.'

'But I'm your family, Daddy – we're your family!'

He looked at me, his expression inscrutable. 'You have your own problems, Teresa.'

I was rocked. Did he know? Had he heard? But we did not have the kind of relationship that would invite a confidence.

I tried again to convince him to stay but he was unshakeable and I had to give in. 'At least let me ring the doctor and make sure it's OK for you to travel?'

'It doesn't matter what he says. And before you make any other damn-fool phone calls, I have already arranged to be met by Vincent off the train.' Vincent was the hackney driver who has had our business since I can remember. 'All I need, Teresa, is a lift to the station in Dublin, if you would be so kind? I don't think I could manage the transfer from the Dart this time.' He levered himself carefully off his chair. 'Now, if you don't mind, I'll go upstairs and have a little lie-down. I'll be ready to leave at about half past ten, if that's all right. Would you be free to drive me?'

All I could do was nod.

Having had – on yet another night – little sleep, I was groggy and disoriented as we drove to the station two hours later. At least he allowed me to help him negotiate the slick, tiled floor leading to the platform – I was terrified he would fall. He was travelling first class and the loud throbbing from the diesel engine beside us helped cover whatever emotions were going on because I had to shout as I helped him mount the steep step into the train. 'You understand why I can't go with you, Daddy? There's a lot going on here at the moment.'

Unexpectedly, he leaned forwards from above and grabbed my shoulder with bony fingers. 'I have one thing to say to you, Teresa – thank you for everything. And I think you're a mighty girl. Mighty.' Before I could react, he released me, turned and walked as quickly as he could into the carriage and out of my view.

I did not move along the platform to wave through the carriage window. I stayed where I was, pretending to be rooting through my handbag. My father had said goodbye to me. In his own way, he had told me he loved me.

'I'm going upstairs to lie down, Mrs B.' Having finished the last of Tom's books, I built them into a neat pyramid on the counter top. Jerry had promised to telephone as soon as he left the solicitor's office but I was so tired I could barely keep my eyes open. 'I think I'm coming down with the flu or something. Maybe a nap would do me good.'

'You do that, Mrs B, I can manage here. I'll have a go at the laundry room next, I think. Is this where that dog is going to be all the time?' She pointed to the puppy, snug in her basket beside a radiator just inside the French windows. Mrs Byrne did not approve of animals in a house and, since Norma's arrival, had made this very obvious, referring to her always as 'that dog'.

'Yes,' I said, 'that's where she's going to live.'

'All right.' She sighed. 'We'll just do the best we can. You go on up. Sleep is the great doctor, as we say in our house. Do you want me to call you in an hour?'

'I'll set an alarm. And when Jack gets up, would you mind telling him that Kitty rang him three times already?' In the totality of what was going on in my life, the relationship between my elder son and his girlfriend ranked low, but I was becoming aware that all was not well in that quarter. Kitty's second call that morning had been sharp-toned, her third I would have labelled 'somewhat frantic'. But it was something I could not deal with right now. He was old enough to deal with his own love-life. Even if he would have tolerated any intervention or even advice, I had no energy left over to give either.

I lay down under the duvet and fell immediately into a deep, dark sleep. I dreamt that a fire engine, huge and threatening, was bearing down on me. I was tied into the middle of the road and could not get away. The bell was getting louder and louder—

It stopped. Relieved to find I had been dreaming, semi-awake and unwilling to accept full consciousness, I was drifting off again when someone called my name. Jack was standing in the doorway of the bedroom. 'Mum! *Mum!* Tom's on the phone.'

I struggled to sit up, sleep drifting around my head like gauze. 'Hello?' My voice croaked and I cleared my throat. 'Hello, Tom?'

'Mum, I'd like to come home now, please.'

'But you left only yesterday.' I shook my head violently to dispel the remnants of sleep. Had it not been yesterday that I had driven him to the airport? 'Shouldn't you give it a little more time, Tom?'

'I don't like it here. I want to come home. You said I could ring you. You said.'

'Of course I did.' Although I had detected no sign of distress in his voice, I was fully awake now. 'Did something happen, Tom? Why don't you like it? Did you have a row with the other boy?'

'No. But I want to come home. Will you tell Frederick to bring me to the airport?'

I heard sounds of the receiver being passed over and then Frederick came on. 'Hi, Tessa.'

'What's happened, Frederick?'

'I'm perplexed!' He sounded genuinely so. 'We had plans for today. We've already been swimming and we've booked the London Eye for late afternoon, but young Tom here is insistent that he wants to go back to Dublin.'

'Did he have a row? Is everything OK in the house?'

'As far as I'm concerned, I'm not aware of anything, although . . .' I could almost hear him shrug '. . . I have tried to find out what's bugging him, naturally. And I promise you, I did try my best to dissuade him from ringing you – you have enough to handle at present – but I couldn't change his mind. Maybe you could? Do you want to talk to him again?'

'Give me a second.'

I covered the mouthpiece and lowered the receiver to my lap so I could think. I knew my stubborn son: when he made up his mind like this it stayed made up and an earth-mover could not shift it. I uncovered the mouthpiece. 'Hello, Frederick?'

'It's Tom.'

'Oh! Are you absolutely sure about this?'

'Yes.'

'All right. Give the telephone back to Frederick and we'll make the arrangements.' Again the sound of the telephone being passed over. 'I'm sorry you've been put to all this trouble, Frederick,' I said, when he came on, 'but I know of old that if he's this decisive, there's no point in forcing him. I'm really sorry.'

'Me too.'

We made the arrangements. Frederick would take Tom to Heathrow within the next hour or so in the expectation of getting on a late-afternoon flight. He would telephone me on my mobile as soon as he had ascertained the time and number. Luckily Tom was on a full fare, flexible ticket, but because he was under twelve and travelling alone, I would have to make some calls to Aer Lingus to have him looked after as an unaccompanied minor. So that he could fill in the forms, I made sure Frederick had our proper address and telephone numbers, including my mobile, then said goodbye to him, along with more apologies. To give him credit, considering the inconvenience, he remained even-tempered about the whole thing. On the other hand, I reasoned, we had been very nice to him too. He probably felt he was paying us back.

As I was snuggling back under the duvet Rita rang, 'Just catching up, Tess. How's your father?'

I filled her in on that score, and when I had finished, she hesitated. 'And you? How are you bearing up?'

'I'm fine.'

'You don't sound fine, have you a cold?'

'Maybe, maybe I'm coming down with one.'

'Or have you been crying? How are things between you and Jerry? Have you sorted out that little lot?'

Was it my imagination or had there been something knowing behind that question? Could she somehow have heard about the latest twist in the saga of Jerry and Susan? 'No, but we're working on it. There are bad times ahead, but somehow I have a feeling that, at the end of it, things won't be too bad.' I hoped my tone would deter her from asking any further questions: this was something that, for the moment, I needed to keep private, at least until I had sorted out my own feelings properly.

'She took the hint. 'Good. Tom get off all right yesterday? Did you talk to the parents?'

I didn't even want to share with her that Tom was about to come home again. I was short on energy or enthusiasm for a long, speculative discussion. 'Yes, I got the mother late last night, just before I went to bed. She sounded OK, a bit formal, but she assured me there was no problem about having Tom there with them. I don't know if she meant it or not, I'd have needed to see her expression. The husband says she's laid back, but you know how that formal English accent sounds to us. They're usually being perfectly nice and ordinary but we think they're being standoffish. It's a cultural thing. He's Australian, sounds much more friendly.'

She gave the latest news of Maddy, apparently staying with her for a few days. 'Why don't you come out for an hour? Do you good, with Tom off your hands and your dad gone home. It might take your mind off things.'

'Thanks a million, Rita, but right now, I don't think I could even turn the key in the ignition of the car.' I had withheld too much information to face her breezy interrogations face to face.

'Well, maybe tomorrow, then,' she said kindly, and we signed off with a promise to talk again the following day. Rita is the best in the world, truly she is, but right now, all I wanted to do was curl up like a snail inside its shell.

I turned my head to gaze through the window at the canopy of beech, sycamore and birch rising to the crown of a huge weeping willow. The roots of that monster were probably undermining Arkady's foundations right this minute, I thought, but I would never allow it to be cut down.

I looked at my watch: less than an hour since I had come upstairs. Even so, it occurred to me that Jerry was taking a long time with the solicitor. I could hear water running through Arkady's old veins; in the laundry room, Mrs Byrne was obviously being true to her word and all the machines were in operation. Perhaps a shower might wake me up.

I had just stepped under the water when the telephone rang again. This had to be Jerry.

All along, I had refused to have a phone put into the bathroom, on the grounds that there should be one place in every home that was inviolate. But I regretted it now as I raced to get a towel around me and then across to the instrument beside the bed. 'Hello?' I was breathless.

'Is this Mrs Brennan?'

'Yes.' My heart thumped. More bad news. Was she a policewoman?

'My name is Dearbhla McBree, I represent a company doing a survey and your telephone number was picked at random by our computer. I wonder could I take a few moments of your time?'

I sagged on to the bed. 'No. Thank you very much, but no. Not now.' I replaced the receiver quietly and sat there, water dripping coldly down my back. Then I saw the funny side and laughed. Poor Dearbhla.

I took the receiver off the hook. The world could do without me for five minutes, I thought, and went back into the steamy bathroom.

CHAPTER FORTY

'I was trying to get through, the phone was engaged.'
'Sorry.' I was surprised that after such a long meeting with the solicitor Jerry did not sound bitter or upbeat or exercised in some way, as I might have expected. 'The phone never stopped ringing here – what happened?'

'I'd prefer not to launch into the whole thing over the telephone. Would you meet me in town, or in Howth village, or somewhere away from the house?' This new Jerry sounded flat, almost supine. 'We need to talk.'

I knew better than to ask why. 'Sure. But I'll have to keep my mobile on . . .' I explained what was happening with Tom. Then, tentatively, because I was not sure whether his suspension from his job meant he was barred from the office: 'You won't be going in today?'

'No.' Tersely.

'Give me two hours. I've to make a few calls to Aer Lingus. And how about at the airport? If we meet there I won't be looking at the face of the mobile or my watch all the time.' I got flustered. 'But not at the airport proper, it's too noisy. Say in the lobby of the Great Southern Hotel?'

'Fine.'

I was there about three minutes ahead of him and was settled into one of the couches in the sparsely populated lobby when he pushed through the glass doors. He looked upset.

I caught myself. I was a cuckolded wife. I had to stop worrying about Jerry Brennan's mood. I should worry about my own mood. I was the wronged party. But when he came over and I saw how grey his face was and how bloodshot his eyes, my resolve melted away. 'Hi,' I said quietly. 'You look very tired.'

'You're right there.' He did not sit down. 'I haven't eaten, would you like to have a meal?'

'All right.'

The dining room of the hotel was empty, except for one large table occupied by a group of men; all the others had been cleared and were being set for dinner. Jerry asked the waitress who approached us if we could have something other than a sandwich. 'Even egg and chips would be fine. All right with you, Tess?' I nodded assent, but the waitress was back within a minute or so to tell us that the chef would be happy to cook us rashers and chips rather than eggs.

'Rashers would be fine. Open a tin of beans too, and you have a deal.' He smiled as though to charm her – public habits do not die – but she looked at him uncomprehendingly and he told her that the chef's original suggestion would do.

We took a table in the corner, away from the group, who looked as though they were settling into a long, liquid afternoon.

Whether because of tiredness or pessimism, I had arrived at the hotel fully prepared, or so I had thought, for the worst case. Whatever else he was, Jerry was a gentleman and he would never talk to me on the telephone about what had happened with the solicitor because he had really bad news: he was going to tell me face to face he was leaving me and going with Susan.

He would tell me that work was his life: he would be made to give up such an exciting job.

He would explain to me then that Susan's sexual-harassment charge had been merely a ploy to pull him to heel; he would fall in with this, for my sake.

I would scoff at this, of course, leading him to explain that although he himself could shrug off public opprobrium it would not be fair to me. (Actually, it was astonishing to me that the news of his suspension had not yet leaked out to the media. Perhaps it had within his own group, I thought, but the board had put a gag on it.)

He would then tell me gently that, although he had tried his best to end it with her, he had discovered that life with Susan was infinitely more exciting and enjoyable than with me. He hoped I would understand. He wished me well. He would utter platitude after platitude . . .

The more I put words into his mouth the firmer my determination became. I would fight for Arkady, that was for sure. 'So,' I arranged my face, 'you asked to see me? I'm here.'

All that speculation could not have been more wrong. He came straight to the point. 'Would you be very upset if I resigned and didn't fight this, Tess?' Incongruously, the group at the big table guffawed loudly as I tried to take this in.

'You mean leave the Sentinel Group altogether? Is that what the solicitor advised?'

'No. The advice is that, although it will be very difficult, I could fight it. In fact, he's quite gung-ho, and I get the impression that he would relish making his name on this, but the more I listened to him, the more I realised that, with the odds so stacked against me in the present climate within Irish society, I have no stomach for it. And even if I did win the case, my personal judgement is that I would never be credible within that company again. In the meantime, I'd have put you and everyone else, myself too, through the wringer.'

He was sitting very, very still, watching me. I had to come up with something quickly.

'Surely we have proof that you did not force that girl to have sex with you? What about the e-mail? You didn't send that to yourself. We can retrieve it – that's cast iron!' My indignation was growing.

'Susan sent that when we had already had an affair,' he laughed bitterly, 'although to call it an affair is to dignify it. It's my word against hers that she went to bed with me under pressure. Like,' his face twisted with distaste, 'the implications of her affidavit are that she gave in to me because she felt that if she didn't I'd find some way to block promotion for her, to make life difficult for her within the company. The solicitor explained to me that these charges are quite plausible since I had such power. Also, I am so much older than she is, therefore the onus had been on me to control the situation.'

'But you did try to control it. And, anyway, that's not what happened.'

'No. But I've no way of proving that. Think about it, Tess. How do *you* know it wasn't what happened?'

I stared at him.

'QED,' he said quietly. 'And she's suing the company, remember, not me personally. That's the way the law operates. The process has started. It winds its way through internal procedures and then, most likely, to the Labour Relations Commission and then, if she doesn't like what happens there, she's free to go to the High Court.'

He looked off into the distance. 'So am I, of course.'

The waitress brought the rashers and chips. No beans, but some mushrooms. We waited until she had left. 'Well, then, that's your best chance, isn't it? With any judge, tribunal, court, anywhere, when you produce that e-mail?'

'That's not the way it works, these days, apparently. But I don't have an appetite for all of that and it will take months, even years. I'm sick and tired of the world I've inhabited for what should have been the best part of my life. In a way, this happening at this point is like a signal, almost an omen.

'Do you know I had lunch with Sentinel's corporate legal adviser the other day? Nothing to do with this, of course, just general stuff, but that man, whom I had always considered to be a stuffed shirt, confided in me that he'd always wanted to be a dancer but his parents wouldn't pay for the dance course. My world is full of people like that, but none of us ever speaks about it, let alone admits it to each other. I've discovered, and not lately, that I'm one of them.'

'A dancer?' I repeated stupidly. 'But what do you want to do?'

'I don't know. But I want the chance to find out.'

It was too much so I went back to worrying away at the harassment case. 'But if you do resign, isn't that almost like an admission of guilt?'

'Do you really care about that? Because I sure don't. You know the truth, Tess. And I can make it a condition of any severance settlement that there are no media leaks – although, of course, I can't be sure it won't happen.'

'Have you talked to Susan herself? Rita says, or said, that she's quite a nice girl. Maybe she'd change her mind and withdraw the case when she realises how serious it is for you. Maybe she just decided to do this in the heat of the moment. Naturally she was hurt and even humiliated when you told her you didn't – didn't want to see her any more.' Although the words had threatened to stick in my craw, I got them out without gagging.

He speared a bundle of chips and put them into his mouth. 'The solicitor says that's the last thing I should do,' he said, chewing. 'If it went wrong, any approach from me could be added to the list of intimidatory behaviour. Her side could say I was trying to influence her, even bully her again.'

'But on the other hand it could go right.' I pushed the plate away. I was no longer interested in eating. 'Surely it's a risk worth considering? After all,' and this really did choke me, 'you have been – been intimate together. That has to count for something with Susan.'

'God love your innocence, lass.' He smiled sadly for a moment, then became deadly serious. 'I doubt if she would withdraw the case. She couldn't, because it would appear then as if she had been lying, or had been acting out of malice. How would she continue in the company then? It's one thing to lose a case, it's another to withdraw the charges. No, the hare is out of the trap and it can't be stuffed back in. I'm ninety-nine per cent sure the case will go ahead anyway, whether or not I am still employed by the company. It's Sentinel she's suing, remember.

'But there is something I have definitely decided now.'

I braced myself. This was it. That whole business of being a square peg in a round hole was a softening process. He was going to tell me he was leaving me in any event. Even if it was not for Susan, he was heading off to an ashram to find himself. 'Tell me. Please.'

He shot me a curious look, then: 'Regardless of this case, regardless of anything, even of how you feel, I'm afraid, Tess, I've made an irrevocable decision now. I'm going to quit work.'

'And do what?'

'You'd be surprised. Join the circus!'

I was stunned, relieved, mixed-up. I did not know what I felt, really.

He seemed to relax, leaning back in his chair. 'Nothing for a while, maybe. Quite a long while. Then maybe I'd like to study – what, I don't know yet. Italian, maybe, or philosophy, I've always regretted that I didn't go to university. I'd also like to travel. I'd like to go to Bayreuth and hear the *Ring* in its entirety the way it's supposed to be heard. I'd like to learn limbo dancing in the Caribbean, salsa in Mexico. I'd like to see a rodeo in Alberta and attend a hoe-down in Texas. I'd like someone to teach me to fish in Alaska. I'd like for us all to go on a world cruise.' He stared at his plate. 'That's if you and Jack and Tom would come with me, of course. Big "if".'

I could not believe what I was hearing. 'You never mentioned any of this before. Not ever. Not any of it.'

'No, I didn't. No reason to. And I can see you're gob-smacked, I don't blame you. The possibility of being a human being didn't arise before now, I was too busy being Master of the Universe.'

I blushed.

'Yes, I knew,' he said wryly. 'I'm not stupid, lass, or deaf!'

How was I supposed to react to all of this? It appears that I had been recruited to his corner so was I now to behave as though the affair had never happened? For the moment, I chose to be practical. 'Jerry, what about money? How would we live?'

'We'd live. Maybe we wouldn't be able to eat caviar every day, but we don't eat it now anyway and, as your dad would say, it was far from it we were both reared. The mortgage is paid off and my own kids will be off my hands in less than two years so there won't be any more payments there.'

He sat forward again, toying with one of his rashers, pushing it around. 'You may think I'm being cavalier about this. I'm not. While I can't claim I had made an actual plan, now that the idea has been forefronted, as it were, I've discovered, my indiscretion notwithstanding, that downscaling my life is an option that has been simmering quietly in my brain for a long time. And, of course, money is a part of it. But the golden handshake, retirement gratuity, whatever you want to call it – lump sum anyway – would be substantial, Tess. Very substantial. I've a good contract, it's watertight. There'll be to-ing and fro-ing of course but, in essence, they'll have to buy it out.'

He was watching for my reaction. It may seem strange but I had never enquired as to the exact details of Jerry's remuneration. My attitude had not been logical: while enjoying the fruits of my husband's huge salary, perks and so on, the pleasure had been marred by lower-middle-class guilt about living in luxury while the poor, the starving, the homeless, had to struggle. And so I had salved my conscience, or tried to, by supporting lots of charities. (Even now, I hated pushing this conversation, but, in the context of our joint future, it was vitally important.) 'Substantial? How substantial?'

'A seven-figure sum, details to be worked out, but at least one and a half million. Sterling. That's a good deal more than two in euros. And I have shares in the company – which have bucked the trend and are worth quite a lot – plus my share options. I can cash them in now or leave them and wait until the optimum time. Even without them the total right now, contract and shares, would be three and a half million plus. Don't forget, I'll have a very good pension. Fifty per cent of my salary. My solicitor will see to that. And I've taken a keen interest in the way our pension fund has performed. Believe me, it's secure and, although it's lost a small bit, we're doing better than most.'

I could not take this in. Not all in one go. All that money – I would have to add more charities to the list.

As I continued to gape, he mistook my astonishment for something else, perhaps disappointment. 'It's a lot of money, Tess,' his tone was wry. 'We won't starve.'

He sat back in his chair again and became still. 'You may not believe this, Tess, but in the last couple of days, your father's illness has had a profound effect on me. I keep thinking about that legal counsel and what his life might have been like had he been given a leotard and tights instead of being stuffed into a suit that was too tight for him and being strangled on a tie and small-talk. His mouth talked a blue streak, Tess, but his eyes were always looking somewhere out of the room. I thought it was arrogance, or shyness. It was desperation.

'And then, when I looked at your dad the other evening, all that work, all those hours he stood behind that damned counter, and for what? The most he knew of the world, the most he'll ever know now, is the railway line between Ballina and Dublin.'

That hurt, a lot. 'Daddy had a good life in his own estimation, and he has made friends, which is more than you have, might I point out? He is someone who will be missed by his community.'

'Yes. He will. But how did he feel when he was fifty and he saw the rest of his life mapped out on a prairie with no horizon? Did anyone ever ask him?'

Too much. Too close. 'I can't react to all of this off the top of my head. You'll have to give me time.'

'Time is not something I have to play around with. I'm sorry to say this but your reaction, I'm afraid, is your own affair. I wouldn't blame you if you threw me out after what I've done, and I'll have to deal with it. If the situation were reversed, I'd probably throw you out.'

'I see.'

I did not see. My tired brain was wrestling with itself. In the ten years we had known one another, I had never known Jerry Brennan to make long speeches. Within the past couple of days and nights, he had pronounced more than in all our lives together. And what speeches! Had I lost sight of my husband entirely? Had I ever seen him in the first place?

He was watching. 'Spit it out, love. Is your instinct to get rid of me? Don't be afraid. I'll understand. Better say it straight and get it over with.'

The corporate table across the room again rocked with male mirth. Jerry spun angrily to glare at them. When he turned back his eyes were blazing. 'That illustrates perfectly why I want out. I hate this phoney socialising and what it represents. I just hate it.'

I looked at my barely touched meal and then at my watch. 'I have to keep an eye on the clock. I'm worried that I haven't heard from Frederick.'

'So that's it, is it?' His gaze was steady. 'That's the end of the conversation? You're sloughing me off as usual for one of your children?'

'That's not fair. You know it's not. You have an affair, I'm reeling from discovering that, then you get sued and then suspended and now you hit me with this. It's not fair to rush me.'

'You're right.' He pushed away his own plate. He had done better than I, but there was still a considerable amount of food left. 'I'm sorry. I just got angry there for a second. Forgive me?'

'Yes.'

'I'll just add one more thing to the mix, shall I, and then I'll leave you to think about things? But don't hang about, OK? We've talked about money, and now you know where we stand. I know how much the house means to you. Probably means more to you than me.'

He cut off my protest. 'Don't. We all have passions and you're in love with Arkady. My mam was big into the saying that there's nowt so queer as folk.' He smiled. 'All I want to say is that, whatever you decide, whether to throw me out or not, the house will be yours and I'll not be a niggard. But I'm leaving the rat race as soon as I can make a deal. That's decided.'

'I'm not even to be consulted about this?'

'I'm consulting you now. As I told you, your way of life won't change. I'm changing only mine.' He looked at me from under his eyebrows. 'He talked to me, do you know that? I asked him once why he didn't ease off in that shop, why he didn't spend some of the money he was so obviously making. He told me that he had to work so hard because his parents left nothing to him and he wanted to have something to leave to you.'

'I have to go across to the Aer Lingus information desk,' I said gruffly. The image of my father carefully stashing money in the bank for me was too painful to consider.

'Why don't I come with you?'

'If you want to.'

The girl at the information desk was helpful. My name and address had been registered as the contact for picking up Tom, and his flight was due in twenty minutes. But why hadn't Frederick called me? I looked at the face of my mobile. On, battery full.

'Given what we've just been talking about, in case you're worrying about the money being there to care for your Dad—'

'Don't, Jerry.' It was too close to the bone.

'I just want you to know that of course—'

'Don't.'

'All right.'

We were now waiting behind the roped-off area, both faced front with eyes raised to watch the electronic arrivals board. Beside us, all the other greeters were similarly occupied, as though the board was a UFO or Holy Writ.

'Do you really want to join a circus?'

'Of course not.' He laughed. 'It was a figure of speech. But,' he continued quietly, 'if you do decide to keep me around the place, there is one thing I'd like as a matter of urgency. I'd like for my own kids to get to know me again. Do you think I could ask them over to stay? They mightn't come, but I could work on it.'

I looked sideways at him although he had not lowered his gaze from the board. He had never before asked this, and any time I had suggested it, he had brushed it aside, telling me that their mother would not hear of such a thing.

A series of echoing announcements blasted over the public-address system. While I was waiting for them to be finished, I remembered those conversations I had had with Rita in Collioure just a few short weeks previously. How juvenile my own feelings of discontent and alienation now seemed in light of the real events that had roared up to knock me over like a skittle.

The announcements finished and I resumed watching the board. 'Your children will be welcome in Arkady.'

CHAPTER FORTY-ONE

All the way home, Tom was as composed as he always was. I had decided not to interrogate him immediately, even though, with Jerry driving his own car, I would have had ample opportunity to do so since it took me almost two hours to stop-start my way to Howth through the evening traffic.

When I finally drove in to Arkady, Jerry's car was parked in its usual spot. 'I'll take in your bag,' I said to Tom. 'Would you like to go over to Colin's house for a while?'

'I want to see Norma,' he said.

'All right. But Jerry and I have to talk with each other in private for a little while. Maybe I could drive you over to his house after supper?'

'No, thank you.' He looked fully at me with frighteningly adult eyes. 'But don't worry, Mum, Norma and me will stay out of your way.'

I sensed something odd. 'Why don't you want to go and play with Colin? I thought you were great friends. Whatever row or misunderstanding you had that night—'

'His mother said I wasn't to come any more,' he said matter-of-factly.

'But why?'

'I dunno!' he shrugged. Then, 'Did Norma get any bigger?' He jumped out of the car before I could ask anything more.

Mrs Byrne was leaving as I went into the house and, between chatting to her and organising supper, I did not get a chance to do anything about this strange situation until about seven o'clock that evening. Jack was out as usual, and Jerry had gone up to his study, to organise his accounts, he said.

Tom was ensconced with Norma in front of the television. I
had thought carefully about how, without frightening him, I could
suss out the reason for his premature return and had decided I
should not pursue him this evening; rather, I would try to
question him subtly over the next few days any time I spotted a
natural opening.

For the present, everything in Arkady was under control. I
picked up the telephone. First, I called the London land line
Frederick had given me to tell him and his friends that Tom had
arrived safely and also to apologise to them for what had
happened. I was still puzzled as to why he hadn't contacted me as
arranged, but reasoned that perhaps he had tried; the mobile
networks can be extremely busy in the afternoons.

The number rang into an answering-machine: 'Hi there,
we're not at home, please leave a message, and thank you for
calling.' The voice was the Australian's. I left my message for
Frederick.

I called Daddy next but his line was engaged. That was a good
sign. He was talking to someone. My image now was of him alone
in bed. Maybe in pain. No lights on in the house to save money.
More money for me.

Next on the list was Colin's mother. Tom had so few friends
that each one had to be preserved and cultivated, and I owed it to
him to try to fix whatever had gone wrong. She answered after
four rings: 'Hello-oo?' in a sing-song voice.

'Hello, Sybil,' I said, equally lightly, as though this were purely a
social call. 'This is Tess Brennan. Tom's mother?'

'Oh,' her tone changed. 'Yes?'

Something was definitely wrong. 'I'm sorry to ring out of the
blue like this,' I said quickly, 'and Tom doesn't know I am doing
this – he'd kill me actually, you know how they are.' I laughed
in an attempt to forge a mothers' conspiracy but the laugh fell
into stony silence. 'Can you tell me what happened?' I blurted
then.

'I think you'd better ask Tom that,' she said, after a pause.

'I have. He says he doesn't know.'

There was silence again at the other end of the line. I could hear
cheerful pop music and two children arguing in the background.

'Look,' I said desperately, 'if he's done something wrong, I really need to know about it.'

She hesitated. Then, sounding marginally more friendly: 'Have you time for a cup of tea or a drink or something? Walls have ears around here.'

'Certainly. Right now, if you like.'

'Fine, I think I can get away. Give me fifteen minutes and I'll meet you in the bar of the Marine.' She hung up.

I, too, hung up, but a lot more slowly, then stuck my head in through the door of the television room to tell Tom I was going out for a while.

'Where are you going?'

Could I have seen a small flicker of fear? I decided that my imagination, already overwrought, was playing yet more tricks. 'Just down to the village, I won't be long,' I said, 'and if Jerry comes downstairs and is looking for me, tell him I've gone to Superquinn. Mrs Byrne needs a few cleaning supplies. OK?'

'OK.' He hoisted Norma, who had strayed off his lap on to the sofa, back into captivity and returned to watching TV.

The Royal Marine in Sutton stands at a busy road junction and when I swung into the crowded car park, I saw that Sybil's car, a four-wheel-drive monster, distinguished by its turquoise paint-work, was already there. Colin's family lives quite close to the hotel.

She was sitting in the lobby with her back to the plate-glass window so her face was in shadow and I had no advance opportunity to figure out how bad this was going to be. She is a striking woman, statuesque, with luxuriant, Titian hair framing strong features. On the few occasions we had met, I had found her quite intimidating. She is lady captain of a golf club and a single-handed yachtswoman and, I sensed, brooked no nonsense from anyone.

After the usual pleasantries, ordering drinks and so on, I came straight to the point. 'Please, Sybil, please tell me what's happened. My son says you don't want him to play with yours any more. It's important that we try to sort this out. Tom is not just an ordinary kid, he, well, he's different. He hasn't many friends. And if it's just a matter of a simple row between the two of them, I'm hoping that if we intervene, maybe it could be put right. Maybe it was just a misunderstanding.'

'Tom's different, all right,' she said slowly, 'but I don't think anyone misunderstood . . .' She glanced sidelong at me. 'I can see you're in the dark about this and maybe I should have told you at the time. But to be frank about it, I didn't know quite how to approach you. Maybe I hoped that by cutting Tom out, the incident might just go away. Even on the way down here my instinct was just to turn back and go home.'

This was startling stuff, but I held myself under rigid control as she took a sip from her glass of Guinness. 'I'm sorry, Tess, there's no other way to say this. Tom showed Colin some pictures that night.'

'Pictures? What do you mean, "pictures"?' Then it dawned on me. 'Do you mean pornography?'

She nodded. 'You could certainly call it that.'

'But—' I grasped at a straw '—could your son have been lying?'

'We don't bring up our children to lie,' she said stiffly. 'I saw them for myself. He came downstairs and I could see he was upset so I quizzed him, got it out of him, and before he could warn Tom, ran up to his bedroom where the two of them were to sleep. The pictures were in a magazine.'

My blood surged with disbelief. 'Was it *Playboy* or something like that? All kids do it, Sybil, it's part of growing up.'

She took another drink. 'I hate this, I really do, and I can see how upset you are. In the context of the dreadful things you read about in the newspapers, it wasn't that serious, I suppose, because as far as I've been able to find out, nothing of a physical nature actually went on that night. But this wasn't *Playboy*. It was the real thing, graphical homosexual sex, cartoons *and real photographs*, between young boys and also between grown men and boys. Your son told my son that this was natural, that people did it all the time in ancient Greece but the Victorians had made it illegal because they disapproved of all the pleasures of the flesh, something like that. Those words may not be totally accurate but the sense is. Ancient Greece and the Victorians came into it, I'm sure about that.

'The whole incident upset Colin terribly. I think he got the impression that Tom wanted him to try something like they had seen in those pictures, so I'm sure you understand why I had to put a stop to the friendship between them.'

'Of course I understand, of course . . .' My poor heart had received so many shocks lately it should have been numbed. But this took me off the scale. 'I just don't know how that could have happened. I'm so sorry.'

And then, instantly, I did realise how it had happened. Frederick.

Frederick, the expert on ancient Greece, with whom I had sent my son to London, at his suggestion.

How could you have done that? You are his mother. You colluded. How could you not have seen?

You didn't see because you were caught up in a sexual fantasy. There are no words for your dereliction, for your selfishness, your stupidity . . .

Oh, God, Tom. Tom, I'm so sorry.

She was watching my reaction. 'I'm sorry,' she said, 'I can see how shocked you are. Have you any idea where he might have picked up that – that *thing*? Probably at school, is my guess, but it is not as simple as one publication.' Her disgust was almost palpable. 'My problem, and yours now, is that I got the impression from Colin that your Tom was buying into that stuff.'

'I know exactly where he got it,' I said grimly. 'And I'll deal with it. Please apologise to your son on behalf of my family. For myself, I don't know what to say. I'm as appalled as you are.'

'Good.' She left it at that.

There seemed no more to be said and, by tacit agreement, we left the rest of our drinks and went to the door. 'I was furious, naturally,' she said, just before we parted, 'and in a sense I suppose I blamed you for lax discipline, or something like that. I'm sorry, I can see I was wrong. Maybe this incident was a blessing in disguise for you. At least you know now.'

'Yes – maybe. I don't know about the blessing part. It should not have happened in the first place. I am at fault there, for not noticing. Thank you.'

'Good luck.' We shook hands.

Barely noticing where I was going, I drove up Carrickbrack Road, my brain so overpowered it had slowed to idling speed, repeating on a loop within itself the phrase I had heard from Mrs

Byrne so often: *Look what's after happening now!* It was only when I became aware of impatient honking behind me that I saw I was going at about ten miles per hour. I glanced in the rear-view mirror and saw I was being tailgated by a huge Land Rover; I pulled in to let it and the rest of the cars in the tailback pass.

My brain refused to cope with what it had to handle. I had to get back to Tom, and quickly, but how was I going to deal with this? I had to warn, confront, divert him, but if I handled it badly, would I elevate what might have been just a once-off aberration, albeit a dangerous one, towards an adolescent obsession? I had had little experience of such things, I had never in my life even glimpsed a piece of hard-core pornography and had certainly never expected to be confronted with it.

And what had happened in London?

I panicked in the stifling car and, on an impulse, cut the engine, got out and crossed the road towards St Fintan's cemetery where, now and then, I had taken walks among the dead, always envying them their perpetual peace, and their eternal view towards a sliver of sea and the city under its stratum of thin smog. Just five minutes, I thought. I'll be better able to tackle the situation if I can calm down in five minutes' worth of fresh air. I pulled at the gates. Locked.

'Good evening.'

I started. A woman with two large dogs was passing behind me and I realised how I must seem to her: a madwoman demanding entrance to a locked graveyard. I loosed my grip on the gates. 'Good evening.'

I watched the woman and her dogs for a few seconds, then left the dead to their own tasks and crossed back to my car.

I fired the engine and guided the car uphill towards Arkady but, horror, like a swarm of coal-black bees, blocked the sky ahead. *Think positive, Tess. Find something positive.* To keep going, I forced myself to draw up a mental inventory: I was healthy, more healthy than I deserved to be. I was solvent beyond my ambition, with good friends and a decent family, my father's imminent death was in the natural order, the sexual harassment case, on the surface, had nothing to do with me, even my husband's adultery was commonplace and, please God, not fatal to our marriage or our home.

But what had emphatically to do with me was what I had done to Tom. I had no absolute confirmation, not yet, but my list dissipated as every nerve in my body screamed accusations. Blinded by ignorance and lust, I had offered my son to the plate of a sex offender.

Even if Frederick turned out to be purer than pure, and this was a false alarm, the fact that it had never occurred to me to question my son's safety in the care of a stranger was unforgivable and I should, would, pay for it.

I would have to face this alone. Jerry had to be told, of course, and maybe Jack, but no one else. If I spread my load by involving Maddy and Rita I would not be paying my penalties and tolls.

Arkady came into view, its roofs gleaming after a recent shower. *Dear God*, I prayed, *let me do the right thing for Tom*.

I had read enough in the newspapers to know that the right thing to do was to telephone the police.

CHAPTER FORTY-TWO

The dinner-table in San Lorenzo was even more chaotic than usual that day. Because of the atrocious summer we were having, the big stores in town had brought forward their end-of-season sales, so my girls and their platoons of friends were getting ready to blast off into town. I couldn't even tell you how many there were, too many to sit at the table anyway, so they were sprawled in every nook and cranny of the kitchen.

Betty was doing only mornings for me for a week or so because her mother had been taken to hospital the day before for a routine operation, but at least she had been there to help me for this dinner. We had done the old Irish thing of putting heaps of spuds and plates of meat all along the middle of the table, giving everyone a bare plate and telling them all to dig in. Which they did, in spades. The place sounded like a hen run when the fox got in. Ricky was OK with it, but I could see Maddy's eyes were out on stalks.

'I don't know how you do it, Rita.' After they had all gone off to get the two o'clock bus, she was helping me stack the industrial-sized dishwasher in the scullery. 'You're a marvel, you really are.'

'Yup,' I said back to her, 'I am, amn't I?' Things had seriously got better with her, I could see that.

'It's been great, Rita,' she said now, 'but I really will have to go home.'

'Ah, stay another day. Sure what's your rush?' But to tell you the truth I was just as glad. I have the stamina of a Tibetan yak, thank God, but after the events of the previous few days, I felt I could now do with a little bit of peace for myself. 'I'll do these later.' I piled the saucepans and the roaster into the Belfast sink, then switched on the dishwasher. 'Come on into the conservatory. It's warmer in there.'

Ricky came in to join us for a quick one. 'That was a bit of a scrum, wha'? Any tea left in that pot, girls?'

'Plenty.' I shook the teapot. 'Get yourself a cup.'

The three of us settled in for a natter. I love our conservatory, which runs along the entire back of the house, even though it's furnished like somebody's holiday caravan, with past-their-best and impulse buys that turned out not to match anything else we own. 'I see Fergus is in the news these days.' Ricky was adding milk to his tea and didn't see the frantic signals I was trying to send him.

'Oh?' Maddy sat up and I could see that, despite all the good progress she had made, she was tensing up. Tact had never been Ricky Sleator's middle name.

I had seen the photograph in the newspaper but had hidden it: I didn't want to get Maddy all riled up again. Now he'd gone and ruined it on me. 'You didn't see it?' He stirred his tea as if he was trying to bore a hole from here to Australia through the bottom of the cup. 'They're having a sit-in out there, him and the other actors. Picture of them all outside the studios, waving placards. Personally, I don't think picketing'll do them any good. When those suits out there in that place slash something, it stays slashed.'

'Have you got that paper handy, Ricky?' Maddy's voice was pretend-casual.

'It's in the shop.' He still hadn't twigged. He stuck out his two little legs in front of him. 'I'll bring it home at tea-time.'

'Ah, no, I'll be gone by then.' She took a mouthful of her own tea. 'I'll get a copy on the way home.'

'Will we put on *Liveline*?' I asked loudly. 'See who's giving out about what these days?'

'Sure.' *Then*, wouldn't you know, he looked at us. When it was too late. I could have murdered him, the eejit.

Liveline let me down: they were taking an ad break when I switched it on. 'Funny,' I said quickly, because it was all I could think of to change the subject, 'we haven't heard from Tess at all in the last couple of days.'

'Bloody men!' Maddy took another swig of her tea. 'Saving your presence, of course, Ricky.'

'Oh, God,' he groaned, 'open season on blokes again. I'm off to where it's safe. See yiz!' He jumped up and scuttled through the door.

'Of course I didn't mean him.' Maddy turned to me. 'Sorry, Rita.'

'Ah, let him go,' I said comfortably, although I did think his reaction had been a bit over the top. After all, she was our guest. 'He doesn't mind, really. It's all an act. Before you go, how would you like a walk or something? The forecast is good, we could drive to the beach at Gormanston or even Laytown. Get a bit of fresh air.'

'Yes, that might be nice,' she said. Then, 'Let's ring Tess. Maybe she could do with an outing too. Even if she isn't contacting us, I wouldn't like her to think we didn't care. Like, she's always full of concern for any of our problems, certainly for mine. You know, when I thought about it, I wasn't all that surprised about Jerry. I never thought that relationship was brilliant. He makes no effort at all with Jack and Tom.'

Then, after all I've said about Jerry down through the years, I found myself defending the bugger. 'I don't totally blame him for that – he could make more effort, yes, but I think with his own kids on his conscience, it's hard for him to play Superdad to Tess's. And that young Tommy would try anyone's patience. Ooh, listen! A row!' I turned up the radio, where the ad break was over and two women were at it hammer and tongs. Something to do with a sex shop in some country town.

Although I didn't say it to Maddy, I believe Jerry's attitude to the two boys is not only because of guilt concerning his own kids, it has a lot to do with territory. It's very primitive, you see. If you watch carefully enough, you'll see males of all species, even youngsters, protecting their own patches. But, then, it's easy for me to say these things, isn't it? I see it from the outside, like looking in at a zoo. I don't have to put up with it in my own house where Ricky is undisputed cock-of-the-walk. Tess has three of them. 'Have you told your mam and dad yet, Maddy?' I felt she was holding out on telling them as a sort of charm: if she spilled the beans to her family, the separation would be a fact, while as long as she didn't tell them, his absence wasn't a done deal. I do that sort of bargaining process myself.

'No,' she wouldn't look at me, 'but I rang them last night to say I'd go down this weekend. I need to see Colm too, bring him home. There's a lot we have to talk about.'

'Great!' So I had been wrong. 'Don't drive, be good to yourself. The train is great and that road to Cork is a nightmare. So here's the plan. I'll pick you up, drop you to the station, just say the word. In the meantime you book yourself CityGold, have breakfast served up to you, read the papers, bring your mobile with you and make calls. Relax, Maddy, you deserve it.'

She went to her room to pack and I took advantage of the temporary breather and went upstairs to what we grandly call the computer room – a bedroom with a PC in it – to see if any of the family had sent me any e-mails. They're usually jokes, but at least it shows they're thinking about me.

In bed that night with Ricky, I ate the face off of him for his lack of cop. 'Try to stay off the subject of Fergus when she's around, willya? And Tess and Jerry.' I gave him an affectionate wallop with my pillow. 'And men in general.'

'Sorry.' He was wounded. 'I was only making conversation, Reet. It's hard to know what to say to her. I thought she'd be interested.'

'Yeah, well, think in future!'

I fixed my pillows and pulled the duvet up around my ears. It was great that Maddy seemed to be coming to terms with things, I thought, but she wasn't out of danger yet. She probably needed a good shrink, especially since it was not going to be easy for her to stay off the bottle. Thinking she'd stay for a few days, I had laid in a stock of Amé and Aqua Libra and a few alcohol-free Beck's beers for her, arguing with Ricky, whose opinion was that it would be better to behave normally. 'Otherwise she'll feel like a right freak. Anyway, she knows we usually have a jar at night when we're watching the telly. This is real life, this is Ireland, there's drink all around her. All she has to do is get into her car and go to the nearest pub or off-licence or even the corner Spar and she can get as much as she wants.'

Yes. But my opinion, which was the one that counted with *my* friends, was that Maddy was fragile and needed all the support she could get.

On the other hand, maybe she was stronger than I gave her credit for. As a person, she had certainly come a long way from the frightened, tearful mess I had driven to the hospital.

I yawned, stretching my arms and legs. 'I'm going to turn out.'

'I want to finish this, mind if I keep the light on?' Ricky liked to do his long tots, as he called them – his daily accounts – last thing at night.

'No problem.' I turned my back to him and settled into the groove on my side of the bed. 'Nighty-night!'

I was on that delicious doorstep of sleep where every bone in your body has found its own niche in the mattress when I felt him tap my shoulder. 'Reet?'

'Mmm . . .'

'Listen, there's something I have to get off me chest.'

'Can't it wait?'

'Not really.' His voice was really miserable. Not my Rick at all. I snapped to and sat up pronto. 'What?'

It came out, all in a rush. 'Honest to God, Rita, I don't know how it happened. I just don't. We were all delirious over there, it was hot and the drink was very strong, you don't know how strong that Saki stuff is, it's rocket fuel.'

I felt freezing all of a sudden. 'Get to the point.'

He shuffled around it and hummed and hawed and said that he was very, very sorry. 'I can't understand it, but it wasn't that bad, really.'

'Get to the *point*, Rick!' I was determined to make him say the actual words.

He lowered his head until his chin was nearly invisible against his Yogi Bear pyjamas. 'I – I had a one-night stand with a Swedish woman,' he whispered.

I tried to take this in. I couldn't freak. Not right away. 'I see,' I said. 'A Swedish woman. Was this Japan or Korea?'

'Japan.' He looked sideways at me and I could almost read what he was thinking. *She's not freaking out. This mightn't be too bad.* It was written in big white lights over his bloody head. I didn't move.

Instead I fixed on the mirror on the wardrobe against the end wall of the bedroom. In it, I could see the two of us sitting side by side in the bed. Darby and Joan. All we needed were the nightcaps. Some frigging Darby and Joan now . . .

Through this mirror I could see him shooting little looks at me. 'They were playing in Korea, but she was in the pub where we were. And they won, you see.' He looked at me again to clock how I was taking it. I was damned if I'd show him. 'As I said, Reet,' he yammered on, 'I don't know what came over me, it was after their game with the Brits and we were all in this huge pub, the place was electric and afterwards there was karaoke and everyone was langered. We were singing "The Fields of Athenry" and they were singing Abba songs and the Brits were singing "Rule Britannia" and the Japs were singing, well, whatever it is the Japs sing. Everyone was falling all over everyone else and the next thing I knew this blonde one was all over me.'

He stopped then. 'I'm awful sorry, Rita,' he said, in this real small voice. 'Will you forgive me? It's never happened before and it never will again, I promise on my sacred word of honour. I don't know what came over me.'

'That's the third time you've said that by my count.' I had thought that I was feeling nothing, but I wasn't. I was raging.

There was I, confiding everything in this little shagger about my two friends whose husbands had done the dirty on them, blow by bloody blow nearly, and there he was sympathising! 'Get out,' I said. 'Get out and don't ever let me see your fat little face again.'

He was shocked. Genuinely poleaxed. I can't think what he could have been expecting. A big hug, maybe? 'Come on, Reet,' he begged, 'don't be like this. Can you not forgive me? I was feeling awful about it, you knew I was feeling awful, you kept going on at me about being quiet, remember? It was just the one time, I was drunk – I'm really very sorry.'

He was playing the guilty little boy now, looking for sympathy, and I couldn't stand it. 'Did you not hear me? Is there silage between those ears of yours? Get out. Get out of this bed this minute and take your bag and baggage and get out of my sight.'

He didn't move. Just kept looking at me like a dead herring. So

I gave him this big shove and he toppled out of the bed on to the floor. '*Out*, I said!'

He sat there stupidly on the floor, with his long tots all around him while I pulled up his side of the duvet, taking care to make it smooth and perfect. I lay back then, on my back, real stiff, on my side of the bed.

He scrambled to his feet. 'But where'll I go?'

'Try the Swedish Embassy.'

He tried it on then, puffing himself up a bit. 'Feckit, this is my house too.'

'It won't be your house by the time I'm finished with you.' I was addressing the ceiling. 'And, by the way, you can explain to the girls why you're gone. I certainly won't lower myself. I'll be out of the house between two and four tomorrow afternoon. You can come then to give them the great news, and collect whatever you want to take with you while you're at it.'

'This is ridiculous. I didn't even have to tell you.'

That was the first time I felt little midgets of upset mixed in with the rage. He was right. I never would have found out, or even suspected. But then I realised that this didn't help: it made things even worse. I sat up so quickly I got dizzy. 'Why, for fuck's sake, did you have to tell me, then?'

'It was on me conscience. Will you not let bygones be bygones, Reet? Please. I'll make it up to you, I promise.'

'You must be joking!' But for a moment or two I did get a bit iffy. After all, it was just the one time. I did believe him about that.

But as I stared at him, pathetic in his pyjamas, I got this vision of the two of them. Of this Swedish Amazon type, massaging him, and wrapping her long gorgeous legs around him and whipping him with twigs, or whatever they do up there, and his flesh wobbling and him screaming for more, more . . . more . . .

Stuff that he's never asked me to do for him, never.

'Fuck off, Ricky,' I said. 'Just fuck off, will you?'

I turned round into my place in the bed so my back was to him and lay down again. And when I heard him pooching around, picking up his fecking long tots, getting dressed, opening the wardrobe door and so on, I didn't even cry. I was completely determined not to cry.

CHAPTER FORTY-THREE

The two detectives, Nugent and Marsh, know their business: as Jerry watches them dully, they begin dismantling his computer set-up with quiet, careful efficiency, detaching the server from the rest of the equipment.

I hate seeing my husband the way he is at present: it takes the floor from under my own feet. In spite of all the personal traumas we've been through – are still going through – I am still not used to seeing him at sixes and sevens, and this latest development, on top of everything else, has knocked him severely. Apart altogether from what might or might not have happened to Tom, and despite my attempts to reassure him, Jerry remains convinced the police will suspect him of being somehow in collusion with Frederick. 'I'm the step-father. They're always the prime suspects.'

Neither we nor the Gárdaí, nor the London Metropolitan police have managed to contact Frederick: the phone numbers he gave me are on continuous divert.

Whatever shred of self-deceiving hope I had entertained disappeared when I got back from the Royal Marine that night and talked to Tom, although, predictably, our chat had revealed very little. The most important detail I extracted from him was that Frederick and his grown-up friend, whose name was Charles, had taken him and the other boy swimming and that he hadn't liked what had happened at the swimming-pool. 'But my daddy was there and he told me to come home.'

'Your daddy?'

'He's a lifeguard.'

'But that was in France. He was a lifeguard in France, Tom. You told me he was wearing goggles.'

'Well, he wasn't wearing his goggles this time,' he shrugged, 'but he was at the swimming-pool in London too. He probably followed me there.'

'What did he look like?'

'Like my daddy.' Wearily.

'Well, what did he say to you, then?'

'He told me to come home. He said I should tell Frederick straight away that I needed to go home. I didn't tell him straight away, though, I waited until we got back to the flat.'

'What was happening to you that Daddy saw?'

His expression closed over.

'You're not in any trouble, Tom, all I want to know is that you're safe. Why won't you tell me?'

I could see him withdrawing further, curling into his safety zone and knew it would be useless to push any harder. I did, however, have something concrete with which to tax him. 'You remember when you came home early from Colin's house,' I said quickly, 'and his mum told you not to visit there any more?'

'Yes?' He was wary now.

We were in his bedroom, he was in bed and, rather than make him feel trapped, I got up from the chair in which I had been sitting and put a little distance between us, pretending to adjust my hair in a mirror, while watching his reflection. 'That was to do with pictures in a magazine, wasn't it?'

'Maybe.' Clever and composed as he was, I could see he did not quite know where this was going to lead. I turned round.

'I was talking to Colin's mother. And I know that Frederick gave you that magazine.' I held my breath.

'Only a few people are allowed to see it, Mum,' he said slowly, 'people who are very fit, like me and Frederick. It's sort of a club that the ancient Greeks had, like the first Olympics. I showed Colin because he was my friend and I thought he might like to be in the club too. He's a good footballer.'

He had unwittingly confirmed where he got the pornography. I was appalled, but did my best not to show it. 'Is this sort of a secret society?' I asked, as casually as I could.

He shrugged again. 'I dunno. But it's only for very special people. People who are not ordinary.'

'Well, you didn't like what happened at the pool.'

'That was different.'

'How?'

'I'm not supposed to tell anyone. Bad things will happen to me if I do. Bad people are always trying to find out about our club so they can destroy us.'

'Us?'

'The people in the club. Once you're in it you'll never be able to leave it, Mum. It's for ever. Like being a priest.'

'So what are the rules? Every club has rules, darling.'

'I can't tell you that.'

'Did Frederick break one of the rules? Is that why you came home?'

He hesitated and I could see I was losing him again. I rushed on to a different track: 'Do you think I'm a bad person, Tom? Bad so I can't know about the club? Is that why you won't tell me?'

'You're not a boy. It's only for boys.' He closed his eyes. 'I want to go to sleep, Mum. I'm tired.'

'Would you tell Jack? He's a boy. Or Jerry?'

'I'm tired now, Mum.' And that was that. But before I left his room, I walked deliberately to the side of his bed. His eyes were closed and I wanted him to hear me approach. 'That took a lot of courage, Tom, to tell Frederick and his friend that you wanted to come home. But whatever you think now, or what Frederick has told you, those pictures you showed your friend are not all right. You have to trust me on this. I'm your mum, Tom, and I'm not just being pernickety about it. Club or not, those pictures are wrong. Very wrong. You need to know that. We'll have to talk about them again. Where are they now?'

'Colin's mother put them in their bin.' He did not open his eyes.

'All right. But if anyone, *anyone*, Tom, wants to do something to you, or you to do something to them, something that you've seen in those pictures, you don't have to just because they tell you you can't be in a club unless you do.' I put a hand on his cool forehead. 'Do you understand?'

His nod was barely perceptible.

I had done my best. The Gárdaí, being trained and experienced, would have to do their best too. I leaned down and kissed his cheek. 'Goodnight, sweetheart, you're a really terrific boy. I think you're great and I love you.'

Nugent and Ms Marsh have almost finished disassembling the computer. My prayer now is that these specialists, while having Tom's best interests at heart, will not channel those best interests towards psychiatric care. I am weary of defending my son from that and want to be true to the decision I made on the beach in Collioure not to pursue – or allow – it any more. I know I may have no choice but I truly believe that Tom has been given extraordinary internal resources, and if I can redouble my efforts with him and continue to provide security, understanding and love, I'm convinced he will be OK.

When I telephoned the police, one of the first things I had been asked was if our visitor had at any stage taken photographs or videos of Tom. 'Of course not.' I was scandalised.

The officer had persisted: was I sure? Had I been with the two of them at all times?

I had not, of course. For instance, the two of them had gone swimming a lot together.

Then, I remembered the snaps I had thought so beautiful: Tom in his swimsuit by the pool in Collioure. With hindsight, I could see how carefully the young body had been framed and lit. Why could I not have seen it at the time?

I did not because of an adolescent crush on the photographer. I would never forgive myself for that – and it was no consolation to know that Daddy had not seen anything amiss in them either . . .

What is going on right now in Jerry's study is as a result of my confirming that I had given Frederick access to a computer while he was staying here. They're taking it away to check whether or not it has been used to upload images.

Of Tom.

When I was told they were going to do this, I cracked. It was nearly the worst, and after putting down the telephone, I immediately got on to poor Rita, pouring it all into her capacious ear. She never even hinted at an 'I-told-you-so'.

Despite her best efforts to keep Maddy at San Lorenzo, she had apparently gone home by the time I called. 'Can I pass on the news?' For some reason, Rita sounded chastened, a rare disposition for her. 'She'll want to know. God, poor little Tommy! Poor you. And poor Jerry too, Jesus!'

She hesitated, then: 'Listen, Tess, I don't know whether I should tell you this at this point or not, but—'

'Tell me. For God's sake, tell me. Nothing would surprise me at this point.'

She hesitated again. Rita is a voluble person and these gaps were puzzling.

'Are you OK, Rita?'

'Great! Never better. It's just that I met Mrs Vitelli, would you believe?'

It took a few moments for me to make the connection. Tom's situation had knocked even Susan Vitelli Moore to the back of the queue. 'What did she say?'

'She's a mother, Tess. What do you think she'd say? The only reason I'm mentioning it is that I don't think they're going to take it lying down – ah, sugar, you've enough on your plate. Forget I opened my mouth. Lookit, you'll all survive this. I know you will. I'll be praying for you tomorrow when the police come. Ring me when it's over.'

'I will.' I had no desire to delve into what Mrs Vitelli had told her but presumed it had to do with sexual harassment. 'Love to Maddy.'

'Maddy's going to be all right too, I'd bet on it. We're all going to be fine. Chin up! Hang in there!'

'I will. Thanks for listening.'

'De nada.'

'This is all we need to take, sir,' says Nugent, hefting the server in both arms. 'I'll put it in the car, shall I?'

The woman Gárda, Marsh, glances at Jerry. She has not opened her mouth since we came into the study. 'Don't worry, Mr Brennan,' she says now, 'we'll have this back to you as soon as possible, but it will take some time.'

Jerry nods and we all stand around for a moment or two, as though waiting for someone to make the first move. I can hear the sound of Norma's claws as, yipping, she races around on the hall tiles below. I had installed a child gate at the foot of the stairs, lacing it with chicken wire because she was so small and could squeeze through the bars. She hates it when she is not at the centre of the action. And although Tom is watching television on the ground floor, she obviously knows that, at present, the action is upstairs.

'Excuse me.' I pass Nugent in the doorway, then precede him down the stairs to open the child gate for him. Wriggling ecstatically, Norma rushes up to greet us.

'How old is she?' The female detective hunkers down to tickle her ears, sending her into a frenzy of licking and finger-nipping.

'We're not sure.' I am finding this exchange surreal in present circumstances. 'The vet says maybe eight weeks now.'

'She's a little dote.' The woman stands up. 'You'll have your hands full with that one. Collies are the most intelligent, you know, and they like to be busy. We have one at home and she's the head of the family, runs the house. You'll have to find duties for her or she'll make them for herself.'

'Thank you, I'll remember that.' I pick up the pup and, with her under one arm, while Marsh waits politely, open the front door for Nugent and his burden. Behind me, Jerry is carefully relatching the child gate.

'What happens next?' I ask, when Nugent returns.

'We'll need to have a chat with yourself and your husband,' he replies. Beside me, I feel Jerry's body tauten. If the detective notices anything he does not show it. 'I do gather, though, from last night's report that you weren't able to get much out of the child.'

'No. Sorry.'

'I'm not surprised at that. There is normally a threat of some kind to keep them in line. But you also said he didn't seem all that upset?'

I glance at Jerry. 'He's an unusual child. Self-contained. You'll see for yourself when you talk to him. Tom runs his own agenda. Jerry and I are far more disturbed than he is, I think, but maybe that's just on the surface.'

The woman's shrewd eyes flicker towards Jerry, and I realise that Nugent is also watching him carefully. So my husband has grounds for his belief that they might indeed suspect him. This murky, horrid swamp is going to drown us all.

I stand straighter. 'I'm not saying you are, but in case you are thinking what I *think* you're thinking about my husband in this context, Naomi – that's your name, isn't it?'

'Yes.'

'Well, if you are you can put it right out of your mind – you too, Mr Nugent. Jerry's relationship with both my sons has been less than ideal over the years and, as a result, I don't think he has ever been alone with either of them. Ever.' I turn to him. 'Is that right, Jerry?'

'Now that I think about it, it probably is.' He looks shocked.

'No football matches, fishing, even baby-sitting, right?' This is to benefit Jerry in these people's eyes, of course, but it is for me too. I am making a point for me and Tom and Jack. And I can see he gets it. So do the two Gárdaí.

'But you were in the house, Mr Brennan,' Nugent says, after an awkward pause. 'You must understand that at this stage we have to keep all our options open.'

'So I am a suspect? You think I'm in league with this – this . . .' Words fail Jerry.

'Unfortunately we have learned that we cannot rule anything out.' Nugent's tone is carefully smooth. 'That's why we're here. To disentangle fact and myth from actuality. And our primary consideration, of course, is the child.' In spite of the pompous words his expression, hardly comforting, is not hostile either. 'We've done an initial cross-check with other forces and the FBI but this man's name has not brought up anything so far.' *And neither had the name 'Jeremiah Brennan'* is the implication as he gazes at Jerry. 'So far, we have to keep everything under the microscope. I'm sure you understand.'

'We understand,' I say, as forcefully as I can.

We are all standing around in the hall, the two of us ill at ease, the two of them completely comfortable, it seems. 'Can we at least sit down for this?'

'Of course.'

Over the next forty-five minutes in the drawing room, the interview they conduct, almost exclusively with me – to Jerry's obvious relief – is thorough, professional, and intimidating only in

so far as the subject matter is so horrific. I fill them in on the little
Tom has told me and the woman does most of the questioning,
with Nugent taking notes and contributing occasionally. 'Why do
you think he approached you in that restaurant, Mrs Brennan? Was
your son sitting with you at the table?'

'I don't think so, I think he may have been at a slot machine or
something like that. Near us.'

'So it wasn't obvious that he was with you at the time?'

'No. Well – yes. Maybe.' I try to think back to that day in Pals
(what an ironic name *that* has turned out to be!) but can
remember only Frederick himself, Rita's obvious disapproval and a
torrent of chat about archaeology. And my fatal invitation to him,
of course. 'I really can't be accurate about this. He certainly knew
Tom was with us pretty early on but whether he approached us
because of Tom or because ours was the only table with seats I
can't really say.'

'No matter,' says Nugent, 'but these guys hunt, you know. He
probably did suss you out.'

'So he is definitely a paedophile?' My heart is hammering.
'From what we've told you, you can say that?'

'The jury is still out, of course, and everyone is innocent
until . . . et cetera . . .' He waves his free hand dismissively in the
air, 'but I do think we're beginning to build a picture here.
There's one thing we need to be careful about and it's not just
words. Paedophilia is a condition, Mrs Brennan, different from
other forms of child sexual abuse. I don't mean to be pedantic,
but there is a serious distinction and the courts take it seriously,
unlike the media, unfortunately, who bandy this word around as
a catch-all for every pervert and scumbag going. If this guy is a
true paedophile, he will be genuinely shocked if confronted
with the accusation that he is doing harm to children. In his
mind he is not, he is loving them and they are loving him.
Giving and taking love. What we come up against much more
commonly, and what is confused with paedophilia in the public
mind and in the media, are what we now call "adults with a
sexual interest in pre-pubescent children". It's a mouthful, I
know that, but it's self-explanatory. Our Mr Yarso may well be a
paedophile, but statistically he is more likely to be what I've just

described. We won't know until we get him.'

He stands up and walks to the window, looks out for a minute, then turns back to face us. 'Bear with me, because I want you to be clear about this from the start. It will affect what charges might be pressed, what defence, even what sentence. And from your point of view, of course, the difference is academic.' He sighs, then comes back to rejoin us. 'From what you've told me so far, there seems to be little doubt that this guy was, at the very least, grooming your son. They do it in progressive stages. Swimming together would be ideal from their point of view. Then reassurances that it is all right to be in the same toilet together, that kind of thing. Then maybe showering together, playing games. Along the way they create mystery, exclude the family, draw the victims into a sort of clubbiness.'

. . . the club. Once you're in it you'll never be able to leave it, Mum. It's forever. Like being a priest . . .'Why us?' I cried. I was in agony. 'Why not some other child?'

His gaze is compassionate now. 'I can see how upsetting this is for you. But we won't ever know for sure why, Mrs Brennan. We never know. It's to do with their own preferences, what age group they prefer, whether they like blond kids or dark kids, girls or boys or both, even kids that remind them of something that happened to them in their childhood. We're learning more every day so we can try to keep ahead of them, but it's not easy. The probability is, though, that if you had not had the kind of child who fitted, he would have moved on to someone else.'

I remember Frederick's reported 'luck' in finding the English couple who gave him a lift for the entire length of France. They too had a little boy.

'Are you all right, Mrs Brennan?' Naomi Marsh, who is sitting on the same sofa as me, touches my arm. 'Would you like us to take a break?'

'No,' I choke, 'it's all right. I've just remembered something else.'

'However trivial it is, we'd like to know.'

'It's not trivial.'

When I tell them, they exchange glances. 'That's really excellent,' says Nugent. 'We might be able to trace his entry into the

UK. Do you have the approximate date?'

Twenty minutes later they say they want to talk to Tom. Nugent stands up. 'Naomi will do it initially. Could you take her to him to introduce her?'

'Will I be able to stay with him while they're talking?'

'Naomi is an expert in this, Mrs Brennan,' he says, gently enough. 'Tom will tell her more than he would ever tell you.'

Another kick to my shattered sense of motherhood.

CHAPTER FORTY-FOUR

It is lunchtime, the day after the police visit, and I am alone except for Mrs Byrne, who is driving me crazy. Usually so self-sufficient in the house, she is obviously desperate to make out what is going on, and all morning has followed me from room to room.

Jack is on his way out to Kitty's, and Norma, on a makeshift lead, has gone for her first walk on the pier with Tom. It was Jerry's idea to try this, and to drive them down to the village. He volunteered it at breakfast-time. (With everything else going on, I have not yet taken in the novelty, if that is what you would call it, of him being around to have breakfast with us.) I have not fully forgiven – and certainly not forgotten – but in my mind SVM, as an issue in herself, has been overtaken, virtually swamped, by others more pressing. And Jerry is doing his best to be supportive and accommodating.

About fifteen minutes ago, in dire need of some privacy, I told Mrs Byrne, truthfully, that I had a bad headache and fled from her covert scrutiny to the safety of our bedroom. Now, sitting at my dressing-table with the door of the room firmly shut, I am waiting for the paracetamol I have taken to do something about the pain.

I am also staring at the list I have just compiled:

Tom
Daddy
Jerry
Rita and Ricky
Mad and Fergus

And now Jack and Kitty.

Jack has dumped Kitty. There is no other way to put it.

Included in such a catalogue of personal disasters, a blighted teenage romance seems trivial, but it is far from trivial to him. And not to her: he says she is devastated. 'Do you think she'd feel a bit better about it, Mum, if I said I still wanted us to be friends?' This was last night, just after he came in. The house was mostly in darkness, but for me sleep was elusive and I had been padding around in my dressing-gown.

Having done the deed, as it were, I could see he was now frantic at having caused such hurt, so upset that he blurted out his news immediately on encountering me in the hallway. 'Come on into the kitchen, Jack, have a cup of tea with me. I was just about to make myself one.'

He slumped miserably at one of the counters while I plugged in the kettle. In adolescence he had never opened up on anything personal, and I forced all other considerations into the background. 'Everyone reacts differently, Jack,' I was treading carefully, 'but sometimes, when you have been together as boyfriend and girlfriend, it is hard to revert back to ordinary friendship. A sort of bitterness sets in. But if you really want my opinion, I think that, yes, you should ask her if she would like to stay friends. Since you're the one who's breaking it off, you do owe it to her at least to let her make the choice. She'll probably reject the offer – I know I would. She will probably even lash out at you, and you'll have to take that. But she would certainly respect you for offering. It's hard, but the right thing to do. Her memory of your relationship, and of how you behaved, will be important in the future.'

He did not respond but I saw he was considering it.

The kettle pinged and I turned away to deal with it. 'After all, you never know what might happen in the future between you two.'

'I don't think so, Mum.' His tone was flat. 'But maybe you're right. I'll go out tomorrow.'

'You'll be glad in the long-term.' I gave him time, concentrating on the tea. When it was ready, I turned round and gave him his. 'Here you go – careful, it's hot! So what happened? Do you want to talk about it?'

He shook his head. 'We just weren't ready. At least I don't think I was.' Then, obviously feeling he had gone too far, he eased himself off his stool and, cup in hand, slouched off towards the door. 'I'll take this upstairs. Night, Mum, thanks.'

I cannot in conscience say that this was a breakthrough between us, but it was unusual enough to merit a mention. And now, here he is on his way out to San Lorenzo in an effort to do the right thing. I am proud of him.

So maybe he and Kitty do not need to be on my list after all: I scratch off their names and stare now at my handwriting, only half seeing it: are the remaining items in the right order? Have I the correct number one?

With Maddy's alcoholism, should she and Fergus not be placed above Rita and Ricky? I write out a new, clean list. Nero fiddling while Rome burns.

Oh dear! I must not be flippant; I have found myself becoming facetious now and then during the past couple of days, it is as if the area of my brain designated for 'trouble' is full.

Yesterday is a blur, of Gárdaí, of people ringing, people telling me things, of faces in varying degrees of pain and distress (Jerry's and Jack's) of avid curiosity (Mrs Byrne's) of bland composure (Tom's).

I am sure my disbelieving response was difficult for Rita to take when she telephoned to tell me this morning she had kicked Ricky out and why. He is such an unlikely Lothario, an innocent one at that. Almost endearingly so, because she would never have guessed if he had not felt the need to confess.

I did my best to console her, but found myself, incredibly for someone in my own position, defending adultery. 'I know you're upset now, Rita, but think about it. Think how happy you have been and are, deep down. It was an indiscretion, a once-off, and I could well believe he was not the only one over there who strayed, what with geishas and tea-houses and . . .' but I could not remember anything else I had read about the morals and culture of Japan.

She refused to be mollified, no matter what I said. This was a new aspect of Rita's character. I would have been adamant that, of the three of us, she was the one to take such an event in her stride. She would be upset, yes, who would not? But she would have laid into him, they would have had a volcanic row, and then she and Ricky would have put it behind them.

I could not have been more mistaken. Big, warm Rita, earth mother to us all, was adamant she was not taking him back. 'He can live in the shop. He can go live in Tokyo as far as I'm concerned. No, no, no! *Sayonara*, Ricky!'

'But what about the girls, Rita? What are you going to tell them?' I wondered if Kitty had told her about Jack.

Obviously not, because she continued vitriolically about Ricky, almost yelling: 'The truth, what else? What else does he deserve? But he needn't think that I'm going to do his dirty work for him, I've told the little shit that it's his job to tell them. And if he doesn't, I certainly will. In spades. He won't like what I say about him.' Hardly believing this was Rita, I let her rant on, then she stopped dead. 'I'm so sorry, Tess. I shouldn't be going on like this. This is nothing compared to what you're going through. Tell me about the police and all.'

I gave her a précis of what had happened and eventually we parted with a promise to stay in touch. I tried once more to make her see sense: 'It's the age we're all at, Rita. These things happen. We survive it.'

But she would not give the suggestion the tiniest hearing. 'No, no, *no!*' She finished up, however, with an offer to help me in any way she could. She has such a good heart. She will change her mind, she will have to. There is no better matched couple than Rita and Ricky; it is inconceivable that they would split up.

At present there seems to be no constant in my life any more. Except Arkady, of course.

The paracetamol is kicking in and I feel marginally better. Only physically, of course, because, like a plague of leeches, the ramifications of what has happened to Tom are bleeding my heart dry.

The outcome of his interview with the police was upsetting on the one hand, reassuring on the other, and Naomi Marsh was smiling ruefully when she emerged from the television room. 'I see what you mean about him being unusual,' she said to Jerry and me, when she rejoined us in the drawing room. 'I'm not a psychiatrist – and we will put him in for a bit of counselling – but

I would be inclined to stick my neck out at this point and reassure you that the damage is fairly minimal.'

'Did he tell you what happened?' I was almost afraid to hear.

'All I can tell you is what he told me. But it does fit a pattern.' She glanced at her colleague. Then, 'I think we mentioned grooming to you before. He was certainly being groomed. Desensitising him would be part of it, things like getting him to look at that pornographic magazine you mentioned and discussing it with him as though there was nothing wrong with it.

'And I would suspect that those pictures of him in his swimming togs would have already been put into circulation. We won't know until we check your computer, various websites and the computer of this mysterious London "friend", but what usually happens is that these pictures are a prelude to something more graphic, a teaser if you like.'

' "More graphic"?' I was almost afraid to hear the answer.

Slowly, choosing her words, she said, 'An offer to trade. With more explicit pictures, possibly nude, or even in sexually compromising positions.'

I could not speak.

'But, please, Mrs Brennan, let's not jump to too many conclusions. At this stage, I don't think this has happened in Tom's case. Yes, the offer to trade may well have occurred but as far as I can find out, your son wasn't asked to pose for a camera or to participate in any sexual act. Not up to the time he went to that swimming-pool, anyway.'

She told us then what she believed happened to frighten Tom into coming home.

He and the other boy had been taken by the two men, Frederick and this friend, Charles, not to a public swimming-baths but to a private leisure club, which was virtually empty at that time of day, so that they were the only people in the dressing room where they were getting ready to go into the pool. There was a lot of horseplay among the four of them, apparently, chasing each other around the confined place, smacking with towels and so on, and then the other boy, Evan, had climbed, naked, on to Frederick's lap for a tickling session. Charles had then chased Tom around the dressing room, yelling playfully at him that he was next.

When Tom resisted, Frederick, over Evan's screams and giggles, had threatened, half-joking-whole-in-earnest, to pull down my son's pants, and put him across his knee to give him a good spanking because he was not doing what he was told. It was at that point that Tom had decided enough was enough.

'Some of it is me filling in the gaps,' the Gárda was watching for my reaction, 'but I'd be fairly sure that's an accurate picture of what happened. Your son is a remarkable boy.' She hesitated. 'He did say something about his father intervening to tell him to ring you.'

'It's not the first time. He has created an image of his father for himself that seems to be very real for him.' I was more concerned with the scene in that leisure centre. 'Should that other boy's mother not have stopped all this? Surely she should have known.'

'Did you?' The detective looked keenly at me.

Touché.

Jerry, who had taken almost no part in any of this, intervened: 'What would be the logical next step for that creep if Tom . . .' he paused, searching for words '. . . if Tom wasn't the kind of person he is? If he was more vulnerable, for instance?'

'Well, Tom is Tom, luckily for us all. And this case is quite unusual, in that he was taken to London so soon into his grooming, and with consent all round, but one scenario might be that he would have been returned home, as per arrangements and if you didn't notice anything amiss, which you probably wouldn't at this stage, you could soon have expected another visit from Mr Yarso.'

'How would he explain that?' Jerry frowned.

'He's resourceful and plausible,' the Gárda was again rueful, 'as you've discovered.'

'Should we talk to young Tom some more about it? Should we let him know that we're aware now what happened?'

'I'd leave the initiative to him at this point.' Nugent took up the running. 'He'll tell you when he feels he wants to do so. But he will need to see someone in the meantime. This is part of the process and we'll make the appointments for you.'

'There may be things he is holding back,' this was Naomi Marsh again, 'and he may be so practised in keeping his feelings to himself that there could be something going on there that I've missed. I spoke to him for less than an hour, after all.'

Privately, I doubted that Tom would ever talk to me or anyone else about what happened that day. And although I was extremely reluctant to let him re-enter the all-consuming maw of counselling, I needed to think calmly about my strategy in this regard. I was hardly in a position to demur.

One other thing: no more than I was proud of Jack, I was also very, very proud of my second son, of such a resourceful, brave person.

The Gárdaí left shortly afterwards, with further reassurances and promises to keep us in regular touch with their progress. 'We'll find him, Mrs Brennan,' said Nugent. 'These people are watchful and clever, but we're getting cleverer.'

The paracetamol has now done its work and the pain in my head is easing. But with relief comes the sense of disorientation I always feel when I take any drug, however mild.

Tom is safe for the present on the pier. That's grand.

Daddy.

I have spoken to Daddy twice since he got home, of course not breathing a word about what has been going on in Arkady. I lift the telephone now with no expectation of any change but there is a gap between the receiver being lifted and his 'hello', which is very weak.

'Daddy, are you all right?'

'Oh, hello, Teresa. Sorry, I can't talk now, the doctor is here. Nothing to be alarmed about.'

'Could I have a word with him, please, Daddy?'

I wait while the phone is being passed.

What the doctor tells me is that he will ring me later. 'I am in the middle of examining him, Teresa, but as he says, nothing to worry about at present.'

As I hang up, I am convinced the sentiment is phoney.

When the doctor does ring me, about twenty minutes later, it is from his car. 'I think we'll send him into the hospital for a few days, Teresa.' Although the tone is still reassuring, I am not fooled.

'Why? What's happening?'

'I don't like the sound of his chest. He has developed a bit of an infection. His resistance would be pretty low at this point and I'd be worried that it could turn into pneumonia.'

I remember the moment on Howth pier when I felt the baton of responsibility being passed to me. 'I can't leave here for family reasons at the moment. But if he is to go into hospital, I want it to be in Dublin. I'll talk to him myself and tell him.'

'He wouldn't be able for the journey, Teresa.'

'Yes, he would, by private ambulance. Please arrange it – I suppose his charts and so on will have to come up with him?'

'It's his call, Teresa.' But I can hear a note of deference, even respect, creeping in.

'Yes it is, ultimately,' I say crisply, 'but I think he will do as I say this time. He should not have gone home at all.' What I really mean is I should not have let him. It was the final test and I failed it – I would not fail again. 'I'll telephone him straight away and tell him. Will you arrange a place for him somewhere. The Blackrock Clinic or the Mater Private, anywhere where he will be looked after properly. The cost is not a problem, although I believe he has the highest level of cover in the VHI.'

'He has indeed. Right. I'll call you back when I've sorted it. He'll need to come today. And he'll have to have a nurse go with him.'

'Fine.' I hang up.

When I was small, our shop was no better than a huckster's where every penny was scrutinised; in my first marriage, money was never in any sort of supply and we had to scrimp.

Since coming to live in Arkady, I have felt quite guilty about achieving middle class when we hear and read, day and night, about the plight of huge numbers in Irish society. Right at this moment, however, if it means buying a few weeks of extra life in decent surroundings for my dad, I have no qualms whatsoever about being in the top ten per cent or whatever class category we fall into.

I take two deep breaths and dial Daddy's number again. 'Hello?' I can hear the wheeze, now that I am listening for it.

'Daddy, it's me. I don't want any objections to this. You're apparently going into hospital for a few days.'

'That's right.'

'Well, I've spoken to Dr Williams now and what we're going to do is get you the best care available in this country. We're getting you a private ambulance and you're coming to Dublin.'

'Teresa—'

'Daddy, I said I want no arguments about this. You deserve it and I deserve it too. I can't leave here right now and I want to be near you. I need to have you up here near me, Daddy.'

There is a brief silence. Then, 'All right. What hospital am I going to?'

'We don't know yet. It depends where we can find a bed for you.' After days of feeling as though I were being tossed around by outside forces, it feels really good to be taking charge of something. 'You leave that to us. And I'll be there to meet the ambulance. All right? Have you anyone to help you pack?'

'Mrs Moran is here.'

'Good.' Mrs Moran is our nearest neighbour. 'Tell her to pack your best pyjamas, Daddy, you're going to be mixing with high society!'

He chuckles at this, but the chuckle catches him in a coughing spasm. I wait until it finished. 'I'm only kidding. We can buy whatever you need when you get here. And, Daddy?'

'Yes?'

'I'm really glad.'

'We'll see.'

As the receiver is replaced, I remember a line from Hugh Leonard's play *Da*: 'Love turned upside down is love for all that.'

CHAPTER FORTY-FIVE

L ove . . . upside down . . .
    Love . . . for all that . . .
As I dashed between Arkady and the hospital during the
following week, I could not shake Hugh Leonard's phrases, or
variations of them, out of my brain, even as I remained mired in
the woes of everyone else on my wretched list.

So far Tom has not received any counselling, although his first
appointment, in a facility called, horribly, a 'unit', is looming.

You might think my attitude ill advised in this matter, but
having been through the mill with him, I believe that I am in a
better position to know what is best for my son than some
stranger who has a vested interest in finding damage. If that sounds
arrogant, I am sorry. I have no time at present for any niceties. I
feel pared, or peeled, reduced to Essence of Teresa. There is
neither time nor space for fluff or padding. Or even for Tess.

One thing I think I might do is go back to seek advice again
from the nun whom I had thought so wise. But not until
afterwards.

Afterwards: the euphemism for bereavement, loneliness, for all
the business of practical and emotional cleaning up after the rituals
of death. I say it frequently now, never having to spell out what I
mean. We say, 'Yes, afterwards,' or 'Not till afterwards,' and there is
no need to say any more. Everyone understands.

He had seemed to rally a little in the days after his ambulance
arrival from Ballina, and although in the end it did not prove
possible, we even talked of him coming out to stay with us for a
few days. I was desperate for him to come, just one more time; it
was as if I was trying to stoke all the love and emotion I had never

been able to express in the previous half-century into one last-night bonfire. I tried to convince him, assuring him he would be no bother because we would engage the home-care team from the hospice and, in addition, hire round-the-clock private nursing care.

He was horrified at the latter suggestion. 'Do you have any idea how much that would cost, Teresa?'

Then one day, when I went in, he was unconscious. Pneumonia.

At ten o'clock that evening, the registrar, a tiny man, Indian or Pakistani, finally came to see me. 'He is very ill, Mrs Brennan, very, very ill now.'

'I know he is.'

'Very ill. The pneumonia.' He gazed at me from under his eyebrows. 'Is there anyone you would like us to telephone?'

He was signalling.

'You mean he is about to die?'

'That is my judgement.' Softly. 'Yes.'

'My husband. Could you telephone my husband, please? The number is at the nurse's station.' (I had asked Jerry to stay at home with Tom, who had been showing no signs of trauma, but I was taking no risks.) 'May I go in to see him?'

'Of course. He may not know you. But be assured he will hear you.'

Daddy's room was lit only with the night-light in the ceiling. As I sat by his bed, I longed to take his hand but was unable to cross the lifelong physical barrier we had created together to the extent that even our hello and goodbye hugs, sanctioned because they were conventional, had always felt awkward and unbecoming.

'Kiss your mammy, now,' he had said, when I was with him, in circumstances similar to this, forty years ago. 'Tell her you'll be good.'

As I think I told you, I now find it difficult to separate the true images I have retained from the short life-span I had with my mother from those manufactured by longing and memory. But I do remember that one accurately. I was standing at almost eye-level with this skeletal creature lying on a hard hospital bed. My hair was streeling from a badly tied bow and kept getting in my eyes. Her eyes were small red slits in a wizened face, which had shrunk so much it was triangular, like a squirrel's. I was terrified of it.

Notwithstanding this, I knew that within this creature was my real mammy. 'I'll be good, Mammy,' I told her obediently, and looked up at Daddy.

'Now kiss her.'

I hesitated, then closed my eyes. Quickly, I pressed my lips to the papery cheek.

'Good girl,' Daddy said, when I stood up and opened my eyes again.

Then a dreadful thing happened. My mammy, who I had been warned couldn't talk to me or answer any of my questions, was crying. Not out loud, like I did, but with a sound like the squeak from the chain of my bicycle. The tears, only small ones, like drizzle, were coming out of those red slits. 'Run along, now, Teresa. Here, buy yourself a Honeybee.' Daddy, whose face had gone all funny, like an old man's, pressed a penny into my hand.

I escaped. But for years afterwards, even still, the memory of those last few moments of my mother's conscious life, at least those I was allowed to see, can crease me with grief.

I became aware of a small movement and turned towards the bed. My eyes had adjusted to the extent that I could see that Daddy's, alert but opaque above his oxygen mask, were looking straight at me. 'Daddy?' I laid my hand, millimetres away from his, on the counterpane. His eyes did not waver. Although I could see only the lower half of the irises, they quivered with intensity.

Beside my hand, his twitched. It was clear he desperately wanted to say something. I bent my ear to his mouth but could hear nothing except the sustained hiss of the oxygen.

'I know you wanted to – to stay at home,' my tongue refused to employ the word 'die', 'but I am so glad you came up here. Please, if you can, stay a little bit longer for me, Daddy.'

His hand twitched again. Then, slowly, he brought it up to the mask and lifted it slightly while his lips moved in a faint 'OK, Teresa.'

But he was almost gone. I could see it, felt it in every line of my own body.

I did not want to distress him. 'You rest now, Daddy. I'll be back in a minute, but I need to go powder my nose.' He attempted to smile but the oxygen mask slipped a little.

I adjusted it for him, carefully repositioning the white elastic behind his paper-thin ears. My daddy always had sticky-out ears.

I made it to the door of the room at a normal pace, but once in the corridor, I fled to the bathroom and wept until my stomach hurt. By the time I had pulled myself together sufficiently to go back, he was again unconscious.

He did not die that night, or the next, or the next again. Although I grieved worse when I was away from his bedside, a sort of resignation set in, and while I was with him I was able to carry on as if I was coping well. Since I could not contribute much to his care, I simply sat by him, day after day. Waiting.

There is an inevitability about these ultimate rituals. During my mother's prolonged dying, I had been too young to take part in the rubrics, which in her case took place in a public ward in full view of fifteen other women, but the words and details came rushing back as I became part of Daddy's.

We're going to try another antibiotic, Mrs Brennan.

Nurse – hello? Excuse me – sorry, could you come in, please? The drip is empty.

His eyes opened for a few seconds, I wonder can he hear us?

His fingers seem to be colder – Nurse? Is that significant?

Is he in pain, do you think, Doctor?

All concealing the real and only question: *when?*

As the days dragged on, a routine was established. I spent the daytime hours at the hospital while Jerry, Jack (sometimes with Tom) and Rita took turns in the evenings. Maddy, who was in Ballineen with her parents and Colm, had offered to come back to be part of this unofficial roster but I thanked her for the offer and told her I would call on her if we absolutely needed her help.

The three hours before the final crisis, were, paradoxically, the most peaceful for me since I had accepted that my dad was going to die. He was very calm, breathing shallowly, but regularly, although the interval between the breaths was lengthening. His heart was strong, the nurses said, adding in low tones that it might actually be another couple of days. Instinct told me they were wrong.

Rita, having extracted from me a promise to telephone her immediately if there were any developments, went home to the girls. She had remained immovable in her decision to cut Ricky out of her life permanently and not even the broken hearts of her daughters, who refused to accept that their father was gone for good, could sway her. I marvelled at her strength.

On that last day, I sent Jack and Tom home in a taxi at about four o'clock. Having been in the hospital since ten that morning, I could see they had had enough. They had loved their grand-father, but only casually, not their fault but his and mine. And after so many days, the portentous newness of being present at a death-bed was becoming mundane.

Jerry, having stayed all night and slept during the day, came back to the hospital at around eight o'clock. At about five minutes to nine, the medics asked us to leave for a few minutes. This was a regular occurrence, so I was not alarmed. 'Could we go outside for a breath of fresh air?' I asked Jerry. Again I had a violent headache. Except for sporadic catnaps, I had not slept for many days; neither had I eaten anything more substantial than a Mars bar.

'Sure.' He held the door for me. 'I could do with clearing my own head.'

We sat on a low wall fronting the ambulance bay on Eccles Street. Traffic was light and the stone of the Georgian terrace opposite was bronzed by the setting sun. 'Puts things in perspec-tive, doesn't it?' I watched a taxi pull up in the ambulance bay.

Instead of answering, Jerry reached into his inside pocket. 'Do you mind if I have a cigarette?'

'Time you quit again, before it gets too much of a hold on you.'

'I don't like it. I hate it, actually. But it's something that just happened. So far it's fewer than ten a day. I hope I can keep it at that.' He shook a cigarette out of the packet and lit it with a cheap disposable lighter.

During those long days and nights of watching, Jerry and I talked as we had not talked for many years. In consideration of my concerns, he was not harping on about his own, but it was not hard to see how upset he was: despite a high ambition, walking away from his job was proving not quite so simple as when he had spoken about it and he was having to treat his severance negotiations as determinedly as if he were conducting a deal on behalf of the company.

In this he had found a bridge between workaholism and retirement and, somewhat like the busy collie dog described by Naomi Marsh, he was creating jobs for himself, filling his days with study of financial plans, or going into town to consult personally with people about issues that might have taken two or three minutes on the telephone.

And, I have to say, he had taken to heart what I had said about his lack of involvement with Tom and Jack. It was early to make predictions, but we might yet become a family.

'Tess, once again, I can't tell you how sorry I am.' He blew smoke gently through his nose. 'This is positively the last time I'll say it, but if I could turn the clock back, I would. And not only about recent events. I've been a rotten husband. I still wouldn't blame you if you gave me my marching orders but it was only when I thought I'd lose you that I saw how much you mean to me. How much we have built together, thanks largely to you.'

'Don't. It's of no consequence. Not now.'

'Lovely evening.' The driver of the taxi that had pulled up in front of us heaved himself out of his vehicle. He smiled at us as he ambled past into the hospital and I doubt if I have ever envied anyone more.

I dreaded all that still lay in wait for me, all that picking over those unanswered questions . . .

'At least we managed to keep it from your father.' Jerry's voice was as tired as I felt but his expression was that of a boy. He wanted reassurance. I could not give it. Not yet. 'I hope we did.'

An ambulance pulled up, not rushing. The back doors opened and an old lady, swathed in blankets as though she were a new-born infant, was carried towards the glass doors. As she passed us, she smiled, so unexpectedly that I found myself smiling in return. I glanced at Jerry, but he was not looking in her direction.

I touched his arm so as not to startle him. 'We should get back in there again, I suppose.'

'Sure.' He stubbed out his cigarette.

I stood up, dizzy from lack of sleep, and stretched my arms above my head, which served only to increase the lightheadedness.

'I'll sleep for three solid days afterwards.'

When we stepped out of the lift on to Daddy's corridor, there was activity around his door. A staff nurse spotted us, rushed towards us. 'Where were you? We were looking everywhere for you.'

I knew immediately. I leaned against the wall, my chest hollow. 'He's gone?'

She took my hand and put her free arm round me, empathising as only an Irish nurse can. 'I'm sorry, I'm really sorry. We did all we could but he slipped away on us when none of us was looking.'

Daddy died in his private room at the Mater Hospital in Dublin at twenty past nine on a beautiful Friday evening. At twenty minutes to ten we went in to see him; they had removed all the needles and masks and drains, had fixed him straight under his too-smooth coverlet, and placed a small rolled towel under his jaw to keep it shut. The translucent sky outside his window was filled with crows. A loose, lazy gather prior to roosting.

I had not been there for him.

Love turned upside down.

And all his life Daddy had hated crows.

CHAPTER FORTY-SIX

He would have loved his funeral. He excelled at going to funerals, as many people from rural Ireland do (although the townspeople of Ballina would not like to hear themselves so described).

I doubt, however, that he would have foreseen the splendour of clerical representation we see now on the altar of St Muiredeach's where his Mass is being concelebrated by an auxiliary bishop and five priests from the diocese; nor, being modest above all else, would he have contemplated such a huge turnout of neighbours and friends.

His solicitor gave precise instructions and, as a result, the arrangements had proven surprisingly easy – and, being Daddy, very frugal: no music, no flowers. No waste. No humbug.

So what would he have made, then, of the ranks of local dignitaries crowding the front pews? Two TDs, from the constituency, three county councillors, three bank managers (two retired, one current) and, resplendent in their chains of office, a tintinnabulation of bigwigs from the Chambers of Commerce of three towns, the local Lions Club and even the golf club, although Daddy did not play golf. He would have been much more at home, I think, with his fellow shopkeepers, the postman, the local minibus driver and the nuns from Gortnor Abbey, where I went to school.

As for the readings, he had asked in his instructions that Jack and Tom read the Prayers of the Faithful, which they do with great aplomb and that Jerry, a non-practising member of the Church of England, do one of the other readings. Of course, Jerry has been to Catholic funerals before this one but this is his first time to mount an altar of Rome. I can see, however, that he has no fear: he is used to speaking in public.

The reading Daddy had chosen specifically for Jerry is a simple one and very traditional:

> Absolve, O Lord, the souls of all the faithful departed from every bond of sin. And by the help of Thy grace, may they be enabled to escape the judgement of vengeance. And enjoy the blessedness of light eternal.

'Amen,' says the congregation, loudly. But before he comes off the altar, after his voice dies away in the reverberating PA, Jerry takes a moment and looks down at me.

Or had I imagined this? Daddy could not have known. Those instructions had been given to the solicitor long before he came to Dublin . . .

I remain dry-eyed during that entire Mass, the trek to the cemetery after it, the committal, and all the way through the soup-and-sandwiches reception in the Downhill Hotel where I make sure everyone has drinks, shake hands, smile, introduce Jerry, the boys, Maddy, Colm, Rita and her girls, and am introduced in turn by those I know to those I do not.

At one point I find myself alone beside the buffet table. Maddy and Colm are nearby, half hidden by a palm tree in a huge Oriental pot. They don't know I am within earshot and I don't want to tell them, because what they are saying is clearly private. 'Are you sure?' This is Maddy. 'I want you to be sure. I wouldn't make any fuss. I'd understand, it's whatever is best for you, darling.'

'I told you,' Colm's voice is passionate, not a characteristic I would have associated with him, 'I want to stay with you, Mum. I *want* to live with you, it's *not a favour*! I keep telling you. All that was necessary was for you to act like a human *being* towards me and Dad and stop downing him all the time. He's not a monster.'

'I'm sorry. I didn't realise.'

I can see one of the chain-wearers bearing down on me and move to intercept him, my hand outstretched. Good timing. That conversation is truly none of my business. But I am very, very glad.

I try to include Ricky, who had arrived alone and is lurking mournfully on the fringes of the crowd. Having sympathised with me, he is polite but uncharacteristically aloof, despite my urgings that he should come over to join Jerry and me and our family. His attitude seems to be that if Rita will not have him he does not want anyone else, so he stays, staring cow-eyed at his wife who is in full black regalia, while his agitated daughters shuttle in small convoys between him and their mother. At one point I see him take out his roll of notes and peel off a few for a triumphant Alice.

And now I see that Kitty and Jack, having started the day by giving each other a wide berth, are actually talking together in a corner of the room. It is a start, I think, as I try to interpret the body language, but before I can zero in properly, I am interrupted.

Actually, I surprise myself with how much I am noticing, how well I am getting through this – Teresa the nodding doll, moving through the day like an automaton. I had started my grieving, I think, on that day Daddy and I took our walk on the pier in Howth. I will continue with it, no doubt, during other days in the future.

The done thing after a funeral in Ballina is that close family and friends repair to the house of the deceased for another tranche of drink and sandwiches, but I am physically and mentally wrung dry and cannot face it.

Tom's appointment at his 'unit' is at four o'clock the following afternoon, and although I could have cancelled it in the circumstances, I use it now as an excuse – fibbing that I have to have him in 'the consultant's rooms' at eleven in the morning. We have to get home, I tell all and sundry, because this appointment has been hard won. Everyone understands. Waiting lists for consultants are the stuff of legend. And on such a day, providentially, no one asks me what type of consultant it is.

With no further destination, people are drifting away and I have a few words with Daddy's neighbour, Mrs Moran, who holds a key to the house. 'I'll come down again, probably next week, to make a stab at fixing things up. In the meantime, would you keep an eye, please, Mrs Moran? He always spoke so highly of you. I want to thank you very, very much for all you did for him.' I am aware that she is 'remembered' in his will, although it is not appropriate at present to tell her so.

'Sure I did nothing at all. It was a pleasure to talk to him. He was a gentleman, Teresa, a proper gentleman, Lord rest his soul. I'll miss him, we all will. What's going to happen to the house? That's a fine warm house.'

'I don't know, actually. That's something we'll have to think about a bit. It's too soon.'

'Of course it is, of course it is.' The question is standard at every funeral. The prospect of property on the market twitches the ears of the Irish mourner.

I am dreading the prospect of going back to that house, whenever it happens. This is when mourning will properly escalate and not only for Daddy: my mother's things have never been cleared out. Although I had offered to do so many times, he would never let me touch anything of hers and could not bear to dispose of them himself.

Their bedroom reeks of mothballs and decaying leather, and during my last visit, I noticed he had put fresh lavender sachets in the bottom of her wardrobe where her few dresses are still draped over heavy wooden hangers alongside her woollen coat, her shop pinafore, a few blouses and skirts and a matted cardigan. Mammy's purse is still in her handbag on the floor of the wardrobe. In it is a crumpled ten-shilling note, five old pennies, green with age, a cheap Miraculous Medal, a raffle ticket for a Christmas ham and a Fox's glacier mint still transparent in its Cellophane wrapper.

The goodbyes are protracted: everyone, from priest to postman, wants to shake my hand and say a few words about my father, so by the time we leave the hotel I am hoarse and my legs ache as badly as if they had been injured.

As we drive along the banks of the surging Moy towards the Dublin road I know I will be back in Ballina again, but never again as a right. From now on, although people will be welcoming and will accord me the status of being native born, I will in reality be a visitor. Just another tourist. More knowledgeable and with deeper memories, but a tourist just the same. It is too soon to know what this will mean.

The boys, almost as tired as I am, are already asleep in the back seat and I know I will soon be with them. But I am thirsty and open the glove compartment to retrieve my bottle of Evian.

There is it, the envelope he had given me. I had forgotten it, but I can now hear his voice, frail but authoritative, calling after me from the grave: 'Tsk! Tsk! I *told* you to put that away, Teresa.'

'What's that? Money?' Jerry looks at it.

'Daddy gave it to me.'

'Looks like there's a fair bit of it.'

I open the envelope. Not for myself, but for Daddy. The numbers are rounded. One hundred one hundreds. Ten thousand euros. Even. Mathematically satisfying: I can almost see him checking the bank-teller's work. 'It's ten thousand. What will I do with it?'

'It's yours, Tess. What do you want to do with it?'

I cannot think of a single thing I want in the material sense. I have no hobbies except tennis and my racquet is perfect.

I think. Daddy had definitely wanted me to have something of my own from him. 'Maybe a cello?' I look uncertainly at the money, but although I like the idea in principle, my heart is not really in it. All I can see is Daddy's work-roughened hands counting and counting and counting. Doing without, being a have-not so his daughter can have. More than she has already. Guilty again about 'money following money', another saying of Daddy's, I put the envelope back in the glove compartment. 'Or maybe I'll give it to Concern or Goal or Oxfam or some outfit like that. I can't think at the moment.'

Jerry is driving my car – the Sentinel Group was no slouch in requesting the return of the one supplied to him. He picks up speed as the road widens. 'Well, it's a good dilemma to have. Go to sleep, if you can.' The suggestion is redundant, I could not have stayed awake if I tried.

The journey takes just over three and a half hours and I wake just as we are turning on to Carrickbrack Road. I switch on my mobile, which immediately beeps. Seven messages.

Six are from people sympathising and apologising for not being able to travel to Ballina for the funeral. The seventh is from Naomi Marsh. I press her call-back number, a mobile. She answers right away. 'Can you talk, Mrs Brennan? Is this a bad time? I can call you back, if you wish.' I glance behind me. Both Tom and Jack are dead to the world. 'Go ahead.'

She has some news for us.

Frederick's last name is not Yarso, his real name is John Frederick Young. He is not a university lecturer, he is not from Oshkosh and, possibly most wounding of all, he is not an archaeologist.

His identity had been found quite easily as a result of the description we had given and when added to the name and address we had given for his London friend. He is, or was, a freelance reporter working mostly in Chicago and other Illinois towns and cities, and although he has no criminal record, he is wanted for questioning by police in his home state on foot of a complaint made by a young boy whom he befriended at a swimming-pool.

Frederick's – or John's – friend, Charles, is a known sex offender. The two men have now disappeared, along with Charles's partner and her ten-year-old son. 'This child may or may not be this man's son, we don't know yet,' says Naomi Marsh, in her soft, precise voice.

There is more. The Gárdaí have been trying for some time to find evidence linking a known sex-offenders' ring in the UK with one in Ireland but had so far been unable to latch on to anything concrete. 'It's early days, very early days, and it will take months and months, but we think we've found something on your husband's computer which might establish that this man got an introduction to the guy in London through contacts here.'

'Contacts here? But his meeting us was pure chance. We were in France – no, Spain.'

'He has contacts here,' she insists. 'There was a large element of chance in your meeting, but my guess is he heard your Irish accent in that restaurant and once he had established you had a son, he—'

'That Charles person wasn't a friend at all? But I thought—' I am beginning to shake.

'We believe they made contact via your husband's computer.'

I am overwhelmed. She senses this. 'I know you're upset about what you see as your responsibility in this, Mrs Brennan,' she says quietly, 'but believe me, you don't know what you're dealing with here. You couldn't have. If he hadn't had the opportunity to take Tom to London, he would have found some other outlet here. So don't blame yourself, and remember Tom seems to be remarkably unscathed. And from our point of view, this could be the breakthrough we've been looking for.' I can hear a sort of excitement breaking through.

At this moment, I do not give two hoots for the Gárdaí and their projects and their possible breakthroughs. My son's bravery might have cracked open a ring? Two rings? All I can see is the abyss into which I had cast Tom. I cannot hear any more. 'Thank you, Naomi. We'll talk again.' I am shaking so much my fingers cannot find the button on the phone to cut her off.

'Are you all right?' Jerry slows the car.

'I'm fine. I'll tell you later.' My teeth are chattering. 'I just want to get home, please. As quickly as possible. I think I might be car sick.' The words *known sex offender* and *rings* are rolling like thunder in the sky above Howth head. Up to this moment, even though I had thought I had fully taken in the situation, clearly I had not even begun.

And, of course, I cannot alarm Tom by letting him see in any way what I am feeling, although what I want to do is hug him to me so hard he may be in danger of suffering broken bones.

It is some hours later, and I have calmed down considerably, by the time Jerry and I get the opportunity to talk privately. In the meantime I have had to deal with neighbours, many of whom are virtually strangers, who drop by to express condolences in a steady stream from the time they see the car return. Their kindness and concern are wonderful but I am dropping on my feet with exhaustion.

Eventually we are alone in the kitchen. I have hardly finished telling him about Naomi Marsh's call when Jerry, whose posture has become progressively stiffer, smashes his fist on the granite. 'What I want to do is find that bastard and garrotte him. If I was still CEO of Sentinel, I'd use every resource of every newspaper and every poxy little radio station and, I tell you, we'd get the bollocks – this is the first time since I left that I've regretted resigning.'

I stand up and throw the dregs of my coffee into the sink. I do not want him to see my face. 'Why don't you get angry with *me*? It would make me feel better, in a way. Everyone is so understanding about my role in this, except me.'

'I'm hardly in a position to get angry with you, am I?'

'I wish someone would!' I turn round, blazing. 'Tom, you, the police, anyone! Daddy would have. He would have been appalled at what I did.'

The image of my father's tight thin lips on the day I left him at the railway station for the last time, his last attempt to tell me that he loved me, rose before my eyes and the storm, long threatened, erupted. Jerry was beside me immediately but I backed away from him, lashing out, 'Go away. I don't want you to hold me. I don't want your sympathy either. Go and get Susan to hold you!'

'Mum? Jerry?' Neither of us has noticed Jack come in. His face is white. 'What's going on?'

'Your mother's upset, Jack.' Jerry moves to take charge.

'I can see that for myself, I'm not stupid.' Jack's fright, and the customary antipathy between the two of them, makes him shout louder than he perhaps intended.

His appearance has acted on me like a shower of ice and I am again in control. Swiftly, I move between Jerry and him. A row between them now would be the last straw. 'I'm fine. But everything just crowded in on top of me, Jack. I'm sorry you had to see me like this. It's been a rough day.'

He teeters on the balls of his feet, looking from one to the other of us as though trying to decide what to do next.

Then an extraordinary thing happens. Jerry holds out his hand. 'It is probably not the time or the place, son, but I want to apologise for being nasty to you in the past. Will you forgive me?'

Jack's eyes widen with shock. 'What?'

'Can we shake on it? Start again? If you're willing, I am. I don't think we'll be going fishing straight away, or rollerblading, but we could take the first step. Maybe begin to get to know each other.'

Poor Jack has no idea how to take this. 'All right,' he mutters.

Jerry's hand is still outstretched. He stretches it further. Jack takes it but will not meet his eyes.

It is a breakthrough of sorts, but Jack cannot wait now to get out of the kitchen. He breaks into a sort of shambling trot between the island unit and the door. As for me, I feel I've gone forty rounds with the heavyweight champion of the world, and I have not won the bout. 'What brought that on?' I blow my nose on a tissue as a thunderous rock beat explodes from the top of the stairs. Jack has turned his stereo on. Full, by the sound of it.

Jerry closes the door. 'I think you know what brought it on. You're not the only one who has been shocked in the last couple of weeks, Tess. I've been doing a lot of thinking too.'

'There's no quick fix.'

'Of course there isn't. But quick fixes are usually temporary. I'm interested in something much more permanent. If you'll have me. And if it's not too late for us to start again too. Remember music? We used to enjoy that together.'

'We did.' For a moment, I think he is going to try to take me in his arms and am glad when he turns away, picks up his cup and carries it to the sink to rinse it out. An embrace would have been too much. Far too much at this stage and on this awful day.

CHAPTER FORTY-SEVEN

I do not wake up next morning until a quarter past eleven. There must have been a conspiracy to keep me asleep because the house is silent. I cannot even hear Mrs Byrne: big as the house is she can usually be traced by decibel.

For the first few moments, I wallow in the snug comfort of the bed but then my brain, refreshed, ticks over and I remember that Rita and Maddy are coming to Arkady at one o'clock for lunch, just the three of us.

It comes to me then what has happened to us all in the last few weeks.

No, Tess. No more whingeing and feeling sorry for yourself. Deal with the world! I stumble out of the bed and, in the bathroom, turn the shower to its fullest, most needle-sharp power.

A few minutes later when I am drying my hair, Tom comes into the room. He is carrying a large piece of art paper.

I switch off the dryer. 'Good morning, sweetheart, I'm sorry I wasn't there to give you breakfast. Everything OK downstairs?'

'I drew a picture of Norma for you, Mum.'

From the hall downstairs, I can hear said pup giving out socks at not being allowed to follow her master up the stairs. In fact, I can hear her indulging in her favourite entertainment: no matter what toys we give her, what turns her on is to swing out of the tassels on the curtain tiebacks. 'Thanks a million, what a treat – can I see it?'

Who was it – Shakespeare? – who said something about having tears and preparing to shed them now? Looking at Tom's artwork draws tears from me, all right. In it, a small black and white dog glows against an orange and magenta sun, so bright it is luminous and so huge it fills the entire background. Norma, with one paw raised cheekily, is smiling, showing a shocking pink tongue. He had painted her eyes, in reality a deep brown, with the colour we used to call Virgin-Mary-blue when I was in school.

'And is this Granddad?' I point to a jaunty man sitting in the very heart of the sun. The figure is returning the dog's salute by tipping his flat cap with some object. Jimmy O'Dea as Darby O'Gill. Barry Fitzgerald as himself.

'Yes, that's him.'

'What has he got in his hand?'

'That's his pipe.' The fact that my father never smoked a pipe in his life is irrelevant. This figure is astonishing in the sophistication of its line, and although overall it is a child's painting, pulsing with a child's delight, it has been executed with an adult's eye for colour, composition and immediacy. 'I did it for you, Mum, because I know you're sad. That's normal. But I wanted to show you that Granddad's happy.'

'Have you any more like this?'

'No,' he shakes his head, 'I don't paint much. Only when I feel like it.'

'Well, I'm so glad you felt like it this morning – thank you so much, and do paint some more. You're a really good artist.' I hug him to me, dizzy with love and relief. His oddness had saved him. I am now sure of it because no traumatised child could paint a picture of such dazzling colour and childlike joy. I will allow the counsellors their time with him because I had been given to understand that I had little choice but to do so but, starting this afternoon at four o'clock, I will monitor the process, as they call it, very carefully. He will have to unlearn certain things he has apparently been groomed – horrible term – to find acceptable. That is obvious. But I will not allow his individuality to be leached.

Anyway, look at this! I pick up his painting again as he trots off. Those counsellors, with their training and manuals and clipboards, and their soft voices modulated to the pitch they have found most effective for reaching pain, will not have a chance against this boy. He will dazzle them like he has dazzled me.

When I get down to the kitchen, Mrs Byrne is polishing the

'good' silver cutlery using a thickly folded towel on the worktop as a sound baffle. She puts down the cake slice on which she has been working. 'Ah, Mrs B! You're up! Mr B said not to disturb you this morning, not after the days you've had recently, you crathur, you! It'll take a bit of time,' she adds, in her most doom-laden voice, 'but he had a good life. Would you like a cup of tea and a little egg?'

Without waiting for my reply, she bustles across to the egg-holder and pops one into a saucepan. 'Go on into the drawing room. I'll call you when it's ready.'

'I think I'll just sit here, Mrs B. I've probably slept too long. I'm feeling quite woozy as a matter of fact.'

'Go on into the drawing room. I insist! Go on, go on!' She flapped her hands at me. Her keenness to get me out from under her feet was puzzling because she usually loves to chat. Rather than make an issue out of it, however, I turn round and head for the drawing room as ordered.

Then I see why she was so insistent. A bulky, *very* bulky, package is on the floor just inside the door. Wrapped in thick brown paper, it is in the shape of a cello case and pinned to it is an envelope addressed to me in Jerry's scrawl. I open it and find a note:

Gone until about four thirty. I had a look up in the attic and your cello is fit only for the dump. This is leased for six months, with an option to buy if you like it. If you don't, there's always the tin whistle! No, no, don't thank me! I expect you to become a virtuoso and to keep me – and Arkady – in the style to which we have become accustomed.

P.S. This is the last time I'm saying sorry. I'm boring even myself. But I really mean it. J.

I hear a noise behind me. Mrs Byrne has not been able to resist following me. 'Isn't he a great husband, Mrs B? Not like some I could mention – I know you like your egg hard, I'll call you!' And she goes back to her domain.

The cello, when I unwrap it, is a gem with the superb patina of age. I lift the bow out of the baize-lined case and resin it with my new, pristine lump. Then, reverently, I take out the instrument itself and carry it, with its bow, to the hall chair beside the front door, which is the nearest suitable seat. With its little steel foot adjusted to the right height for me, it is exactly the right fit: it slips into position between my knees as if carved for them.

I experiment for a minute or two with the pegs and long, legato bowing on the A string, thrilling to the way the rich deep sound reverberates outwards and upwards from the hall throughout the house. At a corporate function once, I was marooned beside a bored string quartet with one of Jerry's guests. We were both desperately searching for something to say to each other. 'Isn't that music wonderful?' he said finally. 'Balm for the soul.' Quite a cliché, yet it is possible to see its truthfulness while merely tuning up this cello, from which the notes drawn are as mellow as a rope of thick honey.

Then I am called to the kitchen to eat my egg. While eating it, to the bonging of the Angelus bell on RTE radio, I tell myself that a cello is not going to fix my life or make the hurt go away, but maybe Jerry and I do have a chance now.

Maddy and Rita arrive together shortly after one o'clock. As I open the door to them I can see by their lugubrious expressions that they have come armed with sympathy, in the expectation of having to prop me up. 'What's happened?' Rita, still outside and as always the most direct of us, sees immediately that they could lighten up a little. 'What's happened?'

'Come in, nothing's happened.'

I take their coats as she hands me a brown-paper bag in which there are several shrink-wrapped deli sandwiches. That had been the deal. No hassle for me. They'd bring the food, I'd supply the coffee.

'We've all had a shocking time since we went to that bloody villa,' she announces now. 'I'm sick of feeling bad. I'm taking a short, one-hour holiday, Tess, if it's not too crass to say such a thing on the day after your poor daddy's been buried. I don't mean to belittle your loss, though—'

'I agree,' I say swiftly. 'We can all afford to take an hour off. Happiness is a decision after all. I think that was what it said in the "Happiness Is" cartoon in the *Evening Herald*.'

'Tra-la! Get her!' This is Maddy, who, now that I see her, looks markedly less fraught than she has looked in weeks, even months.

'I'm starving,' Rita announces, as I close the door. 'Can we eat straight away?'

A sort of schoolgirl madness takes us over. After all the trauma, we seem to have kicked the pendulum and pushed it high in the opposite direction. 'Mrs Byrne is enthroned,' I said. 'Come on into the drawing room. That's where I've put the coffee.'

'What's that?' Rita spotted the cello case, leaning against the end of the stairs.

'What does it look like? Come on in and I'll tell you.'

While neither is remotely interested in music, certainly not to the degree that I am, both immediately understand the symbolism of the gift. 'But wait until I show you this.' I produce Tom's painting, knowing he is safely out of hearing. I might face a long haul on all scores, but for the first time in weeks, I am beginning to feel a little lighter. Maybe the cartoon was right. Maybe happiness is a decision.

'It's your daddy's gift to you. They both are, the cello and the painting.' This was Maddy.

'I thought you were an atheist, Maddy.'

'I am. It doesn't mean that I don't believe in souls and the afterlife.'

'Oh, come on, let's not get bogged down in this kind of stuff.' Rita plonks on to one of my sofas. 'Do you know what I got to thinking about at your da's funeral, Tess? No disrespect now, but I got to thinking back to Seomra a Seacht. We were queens then and we didn't know it. And do you remember when we thought rich people had no problems? When we hadn't a tosser between us?'

'But we're not rich, Rita. We're all right, but I wouldn't say we're rich.' Maddy is perplexed.

'Are we not?' Rita unwraps one of the sandwiches and takes a savage bite. 'Well, I tell you what, girls, I'd prefer to be back there with me sanity and me pride!' She stops. 'So what else is new? Good new only. Bad new can wait.'

'I have a bit of news,' Maddy says uncertainly, looking at Rita as though she might blow up.

'Well, come on, spit it out!' Rita is getting angrier by the minute. Her bonhomie had not lasted all that long.

'Whether it's good or bad I don't know yet. But it's positive at any rate.' Mad blushes, then takes a dainty bite from her own tuna-salad-on-rye.

'Hooray! That's the spirit! Good old Maddy!'

'Rita! Give her a chance!' I can see Rita's anger is at boiling speed. 'What is it, Mad?'

'Well, as I said, it might come to nothing.'

'Don't tease.' Rita pucked her in the upper arm.

'All right. Wait for it! I've written a synopsis of a novel and the first chapter. I didn't tell you before now because I couldn't bear the thought of another public failure. But when I got back from the funeral yesterday, the letter was there from the publisher. Oh, girls, they want me to write three more chapters. They didn't just reject me!' When she is excited Maddy's Cork accent deepens. It had been a long time since we had heard it happen.

'That's tremendous, Maddy. Well done!' I'm excited for her. 'What's this novel about?'

'Well, I always wanted to write a play, as you know, and over the years I've been cobbling together bits and pieces of scenes, dialogue, that sort of thing. But I never actually got them together into a play. But when I did—'

'What's it about?' Rita cuts in.

'You'll make fun of me.'

'Cross my heart!' Rita draws a little cross on her breast with her index finger.

'Well,' Mad, scanning for ridicule, continues shyly, 'it's actually about a fifty-year-old woman whose husband leaves her for a bimbo and who has to check herself into a rehab clinic.' Her blush deepens. 'I've set most of the novel in the clinic. In the synopsis anyway. But that may change. Maybe you think that's too close to the bone?'

I daren't look at Rita and feel I have to say something quickly before she does, but Rita's loyalty overcomes her temper. 'Good for you. All the very best books are written from experience.'

'Are you sure you're not making fun of me now?'

'Of course we aren't,' I say. 'I think it's a marvellous idea. Oh, Mad, I'm so happy for you! I'm only sorry I don't have a bottle of champagne . . .' I trailed off. 'Sorry – I didn't mean . . .'

Her chin comes up. 'You don't have to apologise,' she says, gazing steadily from me to Rita and back again. 'It's something I'm going to have to get used to. And although it's not getting any easier, there are compensations.'

'Like?' I am curious.

She hesitates. 'Like, no hangovers, for a start. And beginning to enjoy my food. Also . . .' She falters again, then smiles wryly. 'You probably won't believe this, but me and Fergus are being civilised with each other. We can talk without fighting immediately. I think I can even detect a bit of respect for me now.'

'That's great,' Rita thumps her affectionately. 'But don't get carried away, love, it'll be hard until the day you die. Ricky says . . .' Her expression hardens. 'Sorry. Lost my drift there for a second.'

'Oh, for God's sake, Rita, why don't you let him come home?' Maddy puts down her cup with a distinct bang. 'I can't listen to this any more. He's been punished enough, he was abject at the funeral, *abject*! Why don't you look at the way Tess has handled things? She's had a lot more provocation yet she can forgive Jerry.'

I decide not to say anything. Have I forgiven Jerry?

'You're a great one to talk.' But then Rita becomes wary. 'All right, I take that back. You *are* a great one to talk. I can see that.'

'No. I'm not that great. I'll never come to terms with it, but I do accept that he's gone. At least, I think I do. I think I'm going to live at any rate.' She smiles. 'You're both great. I don't know what I'd do without ye.'

'Attagirl.' Rita pats her back, but she is tense and uneasy, so unlike the Rita we know. I do not dare confront her, however. 'More coffee?'

The doorbell rings. I hear Mrs Byrne click-clacking across the tiles to answer it and they both look more interested in who it might be than I am. 'It's probably another Mass card. I don't know how I'm going to get to reply to them all. There are hundreds and hundreds of them – oh!'

Ricky Sleator, red-faced and shuffling, is standing in the doorway of our drawing room. 'How'r' yiz, girls.' His face is beetroot now, 'I was just passing and I saw all the cars . . .'

'Oh, passing, were you?' Rita's red is redder than her husband's. 'In a bleedin' cul-de-sac?' She gets up, seeming quite controlled, but I have never seen so much rage and indignation so tightly contained in one quivering skin. 'Have you been following me, Ricky Sleator?'

'Reet, come on . . .' He puts out his hands in supplication. 'I'm not following you. No way. But I came all the way out here.'

She has walked over to him. In heels, she towers over him. 'You're nothing but a corner boy, Ricky Sleator,' she hisses, her face inches from his and her Dublin accent grown so ripe you could bottle it. 'If your ma could see you now, if she knew what you'd done, she'd turn in her grave.' Then she draws back and, before he has time to react, punches him with her right fist, slam in the middle of his face, hard, so hard he goes down on my drawing room floor like a sackful of cabbage. She has not finished. 'And if you ever, ever do anything like that again,' she bends over him, spitting each word, 'I'll swing for you. Do you hear me? Now, get up out of that and let this be an end to it. We all have enough trouble. Real trouble, without you and your feckin' Japanese andramartins!'

'You biffed me, Reet!' Ricky, blood spouting from his nose, stays where he is. His expression is rapturous. 'You biffed me.'

'It's nothing to what you'll get from me if I ever hear the word "Japan" again! Now get up out of that – and go back to the shop. I'll see you at tea time.'

She sails back to the sofa.

Maddy and I are transfixed as he scrambles to his feet. I have no idea what to say or do as Ricky, still bleeding, apologising profusely, but beaming with happiness, leaves us.

Rita, on the other hand, is unruffled. With that one punch, her anger seems to have evaporated; she even looks physically to have shrunk a little. 'Sorry about that, Tess, Maddy,' she says. 'Something had to be done.' She sighs. 'It must be something in the water.'

'What?' Maddy and I, startled, say the word in unison.

'I mean, look at us, girls,' she sighs again, 'what are we like? All three of us in the same boat.'

'Give over, Rita.' Maddy chuckles. That killer punch has

released tension in more than Rita. 'It's not as if the three of them woke up all together one morning and said, "Hey! Wouldn't it be a great idea if we all went out and cheated on our wives?" And it's not as if they all did the same thing or in the same way. It's our age, Rita. That's all it is. Something has to give, doesn't it?'

While Rita and I both stare at her in amazement, she laughs again, a little uneasily this time. 'Was that me who said that? But it isn't a conspiracy against us, it couldn't be.'

'It's something anyway.' Rita looks at me. 'How is the Master of the Universe, by the way?'

I find I do not want to discuss Jerry with them. Not now anyway. 'He's fine,' I say quickly, 'I think we might be able to work things out. Not overnight, of course.'

'I blame that bleedin' villa!' Rita takes the hint. 'Where'll we go next year?'

'Let's think about that.' This is me again. 'Maybe we could scale it down a bit. Remember, Rita, your idea about just the three of us going off together?' I'm thinking of Maddy, but also of myself. If I could leave Jerry to his own devices, with all that that implies, what a declaration of trust it would be. And if he, no longer running the world, could fulfil the role of sole guardian of Tom and Jack while I was away . . .

I should not presume. But we had a year to work on it.

It could not have happened without Susan Vitelli Moore, I think then. How odd.

'Could we stick each other for a whole month?' Rita looks from one to the other of us. 'Let's not get carried away.'

I feel a grin coming on.

'God,' Maddy looks into the bottom of her cup, 'did we ever think—'

'No, we didn't. And thank God we couldn't!' Rita stands up decisively. 'Now, I've got to get back. I'm sure they're running amok over there. And I want to sort out the tea. That little shyster probably hasn't been eating properly.' She brushes crumbs off her skirt, then comes over to me. 'Thanks, Tess, for everything. And chin up, you know all you have to do is lift the phone, day or night.'

'I know that, Rita. And listen – I'm glad things have worked out.'

'You and me both. Sure I was lost without the little shite!'

Maddy, too, is standing. I turn to her and throw my arms round her. 'The very best of luck with those chapters, Mad – I have a real feeling the tide is turning for you.' In my heart, I believe it is because she no longer has Fergus Griggs undermining her and pulling her down, but of course I do not say this.

She is shaky, but brave. 'Yeah. It's a whole new world, isn't it?'

I hug her tighter. 'You'll be famous. Don't forget Rita and me when you're having tea in the Ritz with your agent, sure you won't?'

'Please, don't. I shouldn't have told you. If it doesn't work out—'

'If it doesn't what's the difference?' This is Rita. 'What's the bloody difference? You gave it a go, that's the main thing. We're all going to give it a go, aren't we?'

As I close the door behind them and Arkady's soft warm cloak falls round my shoulders, I know that, no matter what happens now, the road ahead could not under any circumstances be as rocky as the one I have been on during the past two months. But that is the best I can say for it. There are no magic wands available here.

I feel strong, though, and quiet, perhaps because I have had a night's sleep, perhaps because I have seen what can be effected by one simple, quick punch.

Perhaps because I am actually stronger than I was at the beginning of all this.

Mrs Byrne is humming along to a song on the radio. She lets something fall to the kitchen floor. Something breakable. And now, adding to the pop song, comes the comforting domestic sound of crockery being scraped into a dustpan.

Through the window beside the front door, I can see Tom on the driveway, patiently trying to teach Norma to fetch. She is not an easy pupil.

And Jack? Where is Jack? I have no idea, but wherever he is, he is going to be all right.

The crockery clear-up has finished in the kitchen. I walk over and touch the cello case, symbol of far more than just a desire to renew a hobby. Will Jerry and I survive as a couple? Time will tell, although if I were to put a bet on it, I believe we have more than an even chance. Hardly a romantic notion, but at our age and stage, bedrock, foundation, whatever you want to call it, is what counts. You could even call it love.

Whatever happens next, I will always have Arkady to fall back on – but what price a mere house? Maybe that's what I have been forced to learn here. Arkady or my family? No choice, really.

The television-room door is open. I can visualise my dad sitting on the couch in there, his *Irish Independent* carefully folded under his arm. He will not allow me to fall, he liked and respected Jerry. He loved me.

My father loved me. As do my sons and husband still, I suspect. I love and am loved.